Readers love the
Kildevil Cove Murder Mysteries
by J.S. COOK

Dark Water

"…Cook fills every page with the sounds and sights of Kildevil Cove, the diverse crew of characters, and the increasingly disturbing secrets that begin to surface with the washed-up-bones of a long dead teenager."

—Paranormal Romance Guild

"…the murder/mystery was engaging, there is plenty of character building, the backdrop was fascinating to me, and the slow romantic development matched the mood of the book perfectly."

—Rainbow Book Reviews

Dark Mire

"Cook outdid herself with the second installment in Kildevil Cove Murder Mysteries series. Psychological, twisted, dark, emotional, suspenseful, and at times just plain scary!"

—QueeRomance Ink

By J.S. COOK

Because You Despise Me

KILDEVIL COVE MURDER MYSTERIES
Dark Water
Dark Mire
Dark Tide
Dark Souls

Published by DSP PUBLICATIONS
www.dsppublications.com

DARK SOULS

J.S. COOK

DSP PUBLICATIONS

Published by

DSP PUBLICATIONS

5032 Capital Circle SW, Suite 2, PMB# 279, Tallahassee, FL 32305-7886 USA
www.dsppublications.com

Dark Souls
© 2022 J.S. Cook

Cover Art
© 2022 L.C. Chase
http://www.lcchase.com
Cover content is for illustrative purposes only and any person depicted on the cover is a model.

Trade Paperback ISBN: 978-1-64108-367-6
Digital ISBN: 978-1-64108-366-9
Trade Paperback published May 2022
v. 1.0

Printed in the United States of America
ⓒ

This paper meets the requirements of
ANSI/NISO Z39.48-1992 (Permanence of Paper).

For Paul, as always.

DARK SOULS

J.S. COOK

PROLOGUE

IT WAS ten-thirty on a Monday morning in January and full daylight somewhere above the clouds, but here, at sea level, it was nearly as dark as night. The few streetlights evident in the village tried valiantly to pierce the veil of blowing snow, but with little effect. Visibility was about one metre and closing fast. Anyone with any sense at all was safe at home, tucked up in their beds. It had been snowing for two days, with an ambient temperature of -25C, not including the wind that was freezing cold, straight out of the northeast, a sustained fury of 100 kilometres per hour, blown across the Labrador Sea from Greenland like a floating pall of ice.

A small open boat drifted on the waves, just inside the harbour of Kildevil Cove, a Newfoundland fishing village located halfway up the island's Avalon Peninsula. The boat rose and fell, rocking violently, unmoored and going nowhere. But it wasn't empty.

Its hapless occupant was swallowed in gloom, nearly forgotten, a frozen monument. She was a long way from home and close to death, deep in the final throes of hypothermia, her body too weak to shiver. Her jaw ached where one of her molars had been savagely torn out, but the flesh no longer bled, the wound stanched by the searing cold. It felt like she had been here forever.

THERE HAD been a party the night before, a belated New Year's celebration at the home of some friends. She wanted to make an occasion of it, so she wore the new silver cocktail dress ordered special from the States, and a pink faux-fur jacket and silver heels. She looked amazing. Afterwards, in the small hours of the morning, she'd said her lingering goodbyes and gone outside to wait for the cab she'd called when her expected ride fell through. Miracle it was that someone answered the call this hour of the morning, and she was some glad. Saved her from accepting a ride from Roy Fitzpatrick, who was a friggin' old perv. While she waited, she smoked a cigarette. She wasn't supposed to smoke, not in her condition, and God help her if Mam or Dad found out.

The night was clear and very cold, and she walked briskly back and forth while she smoked, the sharp toes of her inadequate shoes kicking up small plumes of snow. It should have taken no more than five minutes, but three cigarettes later there was still no taxi, and she was on the verge of going back inside when she saw the headlights piercing the darkness over Buckler's Hill.

"About time," she said when it appeared, a white passenger van with a red stripe and the taxi company's seagull logo painted on the door. "What took ye so long? Lord Christ, I'm froze, sure." All she could see was the back of the driver's head with its stringy dark hair. The rear-view mirror was tilted away from him, obscuring his face. "Burke's Lane, down past the shop. Big white house with the post office in front." He said nothing, put the car in gear, and pulled out onto the road.

She settled back in the seat and scrolled through some text messages on her phone. It had been a decent party, and everybody said she looked like a million in her new dress. All done up like a stick of chewing gum she was, so. Some fella working on the rig asked for her phone number and sent a picture he'd taken, the two of them together. He was tall and blond, blue-eyed, a Norwegian, the kind of fella you took home for the night and kept if you had any luck at all.

She glanced out the side window. "Hey! You're after missing the turn-off, bhoy. Pull your head out of your arse."

This was met with silence. The driver didn't even turn to look at her.

"Do ye hear me? 'Tis no good taking me the long way around, thinking you're going to get more money outta me, because you're not." What should have been a relatively brief cab ride was turning into something else. "Stop the car. I'm getting out." Again there was no reply. She slid across the seat and tried the door handle. It was locked. "I s'pose you thinks this is funny." The car was picking up speed, the driver taking the curves at a dangerous velocity. "Let me out!"

They crested Buckler's Hill and plunged down the other side, and the taxi slid dangerously on the icy road, skating across the double yellow line and bouncing off the guardrail. She had a momentary glimpse of a long embankment sloping down to the sea before the car righted itself, skidding onto the rumble strip before regaining the right-hand lane. Whatever game this man was playing, it wasn't funny. It was entirely possible that he meant her harm. She fumbled for her phone, swiped through to the keypad, cursed when she realised there was no mobile reception whatsoever. *Of course*, she thought, *the hills*.

The hills rose to the right, towering above her, dark, massed shapes, glistening with ice. Deadly. A boy she'd been at school with had fallen to his death clambering down the face of them, trying one summer's day to gain the patch of wild blueberries that lay some metres below. No mobile reception because the hills blocked radio signals, not only because of their size and position. No, there was something else. Iron. There was iron in the rock.

The taxi slowed, turned off the main road and onto a narrow lane that sloped down towards the sea.

"This is not where I wanted to be," she said. The loudness of her own voice shocked her, resonating like a shout in the profound silence. "This is the wrong place." He pulled the vehicle to the side and stopped.

I'll get out now. I will. She heard a click as the door locks disengaged, and then she lunged for the handle, forcing the door out and away from her. But she miscalculated the distance to the ground and tripped, falling to her knees in the snow. The shock of the cold took her breath away.

"Jesus." It came out as a whisper or a prayer. "Jesus."

She couldn't see his face as he came around the back end of the vehicle and grabbed her under the arms to haul her to her feet. A dark woollen scarf obscured his features, and he'd pulled a hood up over his head, leaving nothing bare except a pale space just under the eyes.

"Let me go." She struggled briefly, and he backhanded her savagely across the mouth, knocking her to the ground. "Please." It was hard to pull her body up into a sitting position; the cold had numbed her muscles and a queer lassitude tugged at her. Too much wine at the party, that was it. She liked a drink. Liked it too much. That was the trouble. "Please," she said again, and "Jesus." A sharp pain lanced the side of her neck, and she gasped. "No." Shaking it off was too much trouble. "No. Jesus."

The world went away.

SHE CAME to in a boat, and she was very cold, barely alive, shivering violently under a fall of snow as thick as shaken feathers. She managed with great effort to pull herself into a sitting position so she could peer over the gunwales. There was nothing around her but open sea. She had been set adrift and left in an open boat that was rapidly filling up with snow. Her muscles contracted, cramping violently, and her mouth opened to allow a small cry to escape, a tiny whimper no larger than the mew of a newborn kitten.

"Mam." How did she get here? "Ma—"

It was hard to breathe, and she needed to urinate so bad that it hurt. She opened her thighs and let it run from her, a welcome spill of warmth that swiftly vanished, leaving her colder than before. Her heart thumped in her chest, a slow and ponderous drumbeat.

Someone called her name; she raised her head. "Rose?" Her older sister. She was here. "Rose." So difficult to speak through split, abraded lips made raw by the cold. *Tell Mam*, she thought. *Tell Mam I'm here.* Christmas Eve, decorating the tree with Rose and Dad and Mam, waiting for Joey to come home from the offshore.

No—that was incorrect. Joey wasn't coming. The helicopter... something had happened to the helicopter. There was a monument put up, out by the war memorial, a metal plaque inscribed with all the names of those who'd died. Go back, remember it again: Christmas Eve, decorating the tree with Rose and Dad and Mam. *Some people like to pick the flowers.* She liked to pick the flowers too, but only in the summertime. Only in the summer.

"Mam."

It was better now to rest for a while. Just a little while. Just rest.

WHEN THE storm subsided, as it would eventually, the boat would drift ashore, coming to rest under an outcropping of rock inside the harbour mouth. In this stationary position, it would fill with snow until the slight figure lying in it was nearly obscured, as staid and motionless as one of the ancient dead.

CHAPTER ONE

FORMER ROYAL Newfoundland Constabulary Inspector Deiniol "Danny" Quirke stood at the window of the converted fishing room on a cliff overlooking the harbour at Kildevil Cove, watching the storm through binoculars and thinking of nothing in particular. It had been snowing quite literally for days. Several hours ago he had wrapped himself in his warmest clothes and ventured out, squinting his way through the blizzard to the shed for another yaffle of firewood to feed the Jøtul wood stove, which cheerfully ate everything he gave it and demanded more. At least it kept the room tolerably warm, or as warm as Danny liked it, which was about fourteen degrees Celsius, no more than that. There was space on top for a kettle full of water, kept perennially near boiling so that a cup of tea was ready in a moment's time, and the frying pan he used to cook thick fillets of halibut or white puddings bought from Heaney's shop out on the Point, and the occasional fried egg cooked in pork fat, about as bad for his fifty-three-year-old arteries as anything you could eat. It wasn't something he cared too much about these days. He seemed to live on foods he could cook quickly: fish and potatoes, ham and eggs, the odd bowl of homemade soup dropped off by some elderly lady in the village who worried about his health.

Shocking what was after happening to him, they said. After letting himself go, he is, so, God love him. Good thing his poor sainted mother isn't alive to see it, although she's probably spinning in her grave, God rest her soul. He knew what they thought of him, saw it in the pitying glances that followed him in the shops, or on one of his rare trips to Strange Brew to get a coffee. To them he was a figure of considerable attraction, a tragic soul now relegated to the arse end of what had been a promising police career. Funny what happened when your former supervisor was into human trafficking and you got caught in the backdraft. Guilt by association, even though he'd always done his best to keep his hands clean.

Something was moving out there on the water, a slice of dark material moving on the swells, lifting and lowering at the behest of the wind. He took the binoculars away, adjusted the sights, then looked through them again. Yes, there it was, a small wooden boat, unmoored and drifting near the harbour mouth, the oarlocks empty. Who in their right mind would be out in a boat on a day like this? Was anyone in it? Or had it simply broken loose from the wharf? He stared at it until his eyes began to ache, straining to peer through the heavy veil of January snow, then put the binoculars away. No point in trying to see something that simply wasn't there. When the storm subsided, someone from the town would go out and retrieve the boat, haul it back ashore to safety. It was only an empty boat, nothing to concern himself with. Let some other fool take care of it.

He went back to the desk in front of the window and shuffled aside a pile of file folders, flicking through them until he found the one he wanted. The kettle whistled, briefly coming to a temporary boil, then fell silent. The wind baffled down the chimney, spat gusts of snow-flavoured cold into the woodstove, and the windows rattled. He was as alone as he had ever been.

He opened the file, paging through a stack of photographs he'd already seen a dozen times, looking for something new, some clue that probably didn't exist. It was a very old cold case—these being his only assignment at present—the murder of twelve-year-old Vanessa Tulk thirty years previous. The young girl disappeared one hot August day while hitch-hiking alone between Carbonear and Heart's Content; her body turned up two days later in a bog and was found by some berry pickers who had gone in there looking for cloudberries. The case was ruled a suicide and shelved, but the pathologist who did the autopsy reported the cause of death as a fractured skull. Danny wondered how she could have fractured her own skull, and did she do that before or after she turned up in the berry bog?

Without thinking he reached for the phone to call Tadhg, then remembered. Old habits and all that. Tadhg wasn't here anymore; he had shoved off for Ireland on a fool's errand, leaving only harsh words behind. Tadhg wasn't his anymore. The pain of it stuck into him, a jagged splinter, but he was used to it by now, and he allowed the sting of it to penetrate. It was time he was moving on, but moving on was difficult when you had nothing to move on to, when there was nowhere else to go.

He fetched down a cup from the shelf, dropped a teabag into it, and filled it from the kettle. How many cups was that today? At least a dozen. No wonder his heart was beating a mile a minute, fluttering underneath his breastbone like a netted bird. He poured milk into the cup from the carton he kept cold between two panes of the window and went to sit down at the desk again. Vanessa Tulk was still dead. She'd been that way for a very long time.

The jangling of his mobile phone startled him, loud as an air raid siren in the tiny flat. He picked it up from where it lay face down on the desk and turned it over. Maybe it was Tadhg. Maybe he....

No such luck. The caller was RNC Chief Adrian Molloy, his new boss, a transplant from Northern Ireland and Moira Fraser's substitute. "Hello?"

"Is that you, Danny?" Molloy's voice was slightly nasal and deceptively soft. Danny knew from recent experience it could cut like steel. "What is it you're at today?"

"The Tulk case, sir." He touched the corner of one of the autopsy photos with his fingertips. "I've been combing back through the original evidence, but I don't think we're going to get anywhere."

"Yes, well, put that aside for now," Molloy said. "There's been a report of a body found in a small open boat just inside the harbour. You need to take a look."

"Sir, with respect, I can't do that. I'm no longer in charge here. You'd best get hold of Cillian Riley at the station." Danny's suspected involvement with Moira Fraser's sex trafficking ring had seen him removed from his official position of inspector with the Kildevil Cove RNC substation while the whole mess was under investigation. The accusation that he'd been involved was a load of shite, but it was the kind of shite that stuck.

"I don't want Riley. I want you. Do you want to do this?"

Danny glanced out the window. "Dirty weather out there the day."

"Aw, but you're a hearty Newfoundlander, Danny." Molloy's voice was steeped in sarcasm. "Surely to God you don't mind a bit of snow?"

"I'll dress warm, sir." If Molloy wanted him looking at a body in a blizzard, he'd go—but privately Danny thought the chief inspector was out of his goddamn mind. He ended the call, then went to pull on heavy wool underwear and wool socks, a bulky pullover layered under thick wool trousers, and all of it topped off with a down-filled parka. He shoved his feet into a pair of Sorel boots, laced them tightly, and added a dark watch cap of Icelandic wool and a pair of "trigger mitts" his grandmother had knit for him many years before.

Is it cold in Newfoundland? Someone had asked him this at a police conference in Aberdeen back in the early 2000s. *Is the weather always bad?* He tried to remember how he'd answered them. *There are days in July when the light is long and the wind is warm and it's every bit as good as Heaven... and then there's days during the dead of winter when it's early dark and cold as hell and you wish you were anywhere else on earth.* That about summed it up.

He went outside, praying that the ancient Land Rover he was driving nowadays would start. With his demotion had come a pay cut, and he'd had to sell the Audi Quattro, was lucky enough to find the Rover for sale online at a price he could afford. The ad had stated only "it runs," but that was enough for Danny. As it was, the purchase cleaned him out, leaving little to live on for the foreseeable future, but his expenses these days were minimal. It went with not having a life anymore. The Rover was rusted all to hell, and the driver's side door had been warped in an accident and didn't meet flush with the frame so that rain and snow got inside the cab during inclement weather. It was a standard shift, which Danny hated driving, with a dicky clutch that sometimes stuck and sometimes did as it was told with no warning whatsoever. But today it started when he turned the key, and he was grateful. The rest he'd deal with later on.

He stopped by the station first, where Cillian Riley had been acting as supervisor and chief investigator in his absence. It was still snowing hard, and the wind was bitingly cold, shaking his flimsy vehicle, and he was glad to get into the warm. He stamped the snow off his boots inside the front door, took off his cap and gloves and stuffed them into the pockets of his parka. There was no one at the reception desk, so he rang the bell, feeling a little surge of gladness when Constable—no, he was a sergeant now—Kevin Carbage came to let him in.

"It's some good to see you, sir." Carbage didn't seem to know what to do with his hands. He leaned forward like he wanted to embrace Danny, then thought better of it, dropping his arms to his sides. Danny had already stepped into the anticipated hug, and Kevin's sudden capitulation left him hanging, his posture suggesting a lunge rather than an embrace. It wasn't Kevin's fault. No one knew what to make of him these days. He couldn't blame them for being awkward in his presence.

"Where's Riley?" Danny asked. He couldn't bring himself to say "Inspector Riley," even though that was the former sergeant's rank now. "Chief Inspector Molloy called. There's a body in a dory just offshore. He wants us to check it out."

"He's...." Kevin looked distinctly uncomfortable. He glanced away, wetting his lips. "He moved into your old office, sir."

"Good for him. Okay if I just go down?" Danny gestured towards the end of the hall.

"I'll have to let you in, sir." Kevin produced a white key card and motioned for Danny to follow him. "It's procedure." A bright red spot appeared on each cheekbone, and he ducked his head. *Christ*, Danny thought, *they're walking on eggshells around me*. He didn't like the feeling.

Inspector Cillian Riley was sitting behind Danny's desk, reading the contents of a file folder, when Danny appeared. He'd changed the office around, moved the filing cabinet to one side from its former position next to the bookcase and added some scenic posters of the local area. A stack of law books sat on the floor in front of the desk. Danny had heard Riley was planning to apply to law school in the fall.

"Well, Inspector Riley," Danny said with forced cheer, "you've done well for yourself."

"Oh." Riley dropped the file and stood up. "Sir. I didn't know you were coming." He glanced around. "We figured it was best if I moved in here... for the time being. Just until you're back." He came out from around the desk and grasped Danny's hand. "Are you back?"

"No, Cillian." Danny turned away for a moment, pretending interest in one of the posters. "I like what you've done with the place. It's nice."

"Sir—Danny—I can have this moved out in—"

"Cillian... it's fine." Danny reached out to squeeze his shoulder. "This is your office now. No, I'm here because Chief Inspector Molloy called me. There's a body in an open boat just offshore, and he asked me to check it out." He tried to smile, but his face felt frozen. Damn Molloy for tossing him into this! The entire situation was awkward as hell. "Thought I'd come by and see if you're up for it." He glanced pointedly at the coat rack set to one side of the desk. "Have you got any proper winter gear, or what?"

"Give me a minute," Riley said. "Got a heavy parka hung up in the break room."

THEY TOOK one of the patrol cars down to the harbour. It had been fitted with heavy winter tires, but even then the vehicle skidded and slipped. Riley, unused to driving in snow, was tight-lipped, his ungloved hands white-knuckled on the steering wheel. Danny pitied him. In order to drive in Newfoundland winter weather, you really needed to be born to it, and Riley, coming from Newcastle, had probably never seen a winter like this in his entire life.

"Just pull to the side," Danny directed, pointing at an abandoned fishing room a few feet up from the water. "We'll need the ambulance, so it's best to keep out of the way."

Riley stepped on the brakes, but the car continued on for some distance before finally coming to a stop. He shoved it up into park and sat quiet for a moment, hands trembling. "You can drive back" was all he said.

A second car pulled up behind them, and Danny was shocked to see Adrian Molloy climb out. He went to meet him. "Surprised to see you here, sir."

"I'm surprised to see anybody in this fucking weather," Molloy said. "What is it you fellas say around here? ''Tis not fit for chick nor child.'" He jerked his chin at the boat bobbing just offshore. "I believe in being hands-on, Constable. More than that bloody Fraser woman, at any rate. Come on. Let's go see what we've got."

Danny followed him down to the water's edge, squinting through the wind-driven snow at the small dory. There was definitely somebody in it, but the boat had filled with so much snow that it was impossible to tell anything much about its occupant.

"That's a nasty way to die," Molloy said. "Do you suppose he's frozen solid?"

"Wouldn't surprise me, sir." Danny yanked his watch cap on, pulling it down firmly over his ears, and tugged the hood of his parka over his head. "Think of me fondly," he murmured and waded into the icy North Atlantic. Somewhere behind him he heard someone cry out, "Lord Christ, man, what the hell are you doing?" Molloy, he thought. Had to be.

The first shock of cold made him gasp aloud, but it soon passed. He knew he had mere seconds to reach the boat before the icy water stole the feeling from his feet. Already he could feel the chill of it, crawling up his legs, as far now as his upper thighs. For the first few steps, the bottom was sandy and relatively level, and he strode forward, confident that what he was treading on would hold him. But just before he reached the small craft, the underwater landscape dropped off suddenly and he stepped forward into empty sea. It closed over his head and rushed into the open places of his body, filling his mouth and eyes, his ears. His heavy woollen clothes were quickly soaked, immeasurably heavy now, dragging him under, and he kicked against the tide, clawed and freezing fingers reaching for the gunwale of the boat. He was so close he could see it. He slapped at the water, reached again, lungs straining with the effort of holding his breath. His vision was going, everything around him turning red, and then his right hand caught hold of something solid and he was pulling the boat towards him, rolling over the side, and falling into the relative safety of the little dory.

"...of God!" Molloy exclaimed. "For the love of Jesus, are you all right?" He'd waded out up to his waist.

"Yeah," Danny managed to say, coughing and spitting out water as Molloy retreated back to shore. "Fine." He'd lost his gloves somewhere underwater, but it didn't matter now. He leaned over the frozen figure and scraped the snow away from the face, wondering what he'd see and hoping it was no one he knew.

A young woman, perhaps twenty-five years old, lying on her back with her head turned to the side as if she were seeing something over her shoulder. Long strands of her blond hair were frozen to her neck in complicated whorls, and her face was bone white, as if her body had been drained of blood. She lay with her hands clasped to her bosom, fingers tightly curled.

"Female," Danny called out. He touched her cheek and her lower lip, where a drop of blood clung, as perfect as a polished ruby. "She's not dressed for the weather, that's for sure." He ran a hand down the front of her body, brushing away the snow. The silver cocktail sheath and soaking-wet faux-fur jacket were no protection against the freezing temperature or the quickly falling snow. "Ah, ye poor young maid," he murmured. "You're cold enough to be prayed for, you are, so."

Her eyes opened.

"She's still alive!" It seemed impossible, but he'd heard of such things before—people frozen who revived, as if the extreme cold preserved them somehow. He leaned over her, touched her cheek. She gave no indication she was even aware of him, but reassurance was a habit. "You're safe. I'm a police officer. We're going to get you to hospital."

Riley and Molloy were already wading into the water, each grabbing the gunwale on either side of the small craft and guiding it ashore. When the keel was on solid ground, Molloy moved to take the girl from Danny.

"Dear God," he murmured, "she's frozen near solid." He carried her to his car while Riley called an ambulance.

"They're on the way from Old Perlican," Riley said when the call ended. "Gonna take a while, with this weather." He was hunched into himself, his clothes streaming with cold seawater. "Guess I don't need a bath now." His habitual good-natured grin was shot through with violent shudders. "Fuck, that's cold."

"You should go home and change," Danny told him. "Get a hot cup of tea down you, warm yourself up."

Riley nodded. "What about you? You're soaked as well."

"I'll wait in the car with Molloy until the ambulance comes."

"How do you think she ended up out there?" Riley gestured at the sea with his chin.

"No idea," Danny replied.

"She raped?" It was a crude but necessary question.

"No. Doesn't look like it, but Regan will find out for sure." Danny hated cases like this: a pointless and brutal assault with no apparent motive and no reason why a young woman should be set adrift to die of cold.

"But she survived." Riley burrowed into his soaking parka. "I'll see you back at the station."

"Yeah." Danny only half heard him. "Okay." He went to Molloy's vehicle to check on the girl. She was lying on the back seat, wrapped in blankets, apparently unconscious. Molloy had the heat up on bust and was sitting with her head in his lap, smoothing back her long blond hair.

"Has she said anything?" Danny asked.

"Not a peep," Molloy replied, not taking his eyes off the girl. "Did you see the bruising on her face?" He pointed at her left cheek. "Somebody hit her pretty hard."

He shook his head. "Let's hope the ambulance gets here soon."

"You should get in yourself," Molloy said. "You're soaked to the skin, Danny. You'll catch your death."

He climbed into the front seat and warmed his hands in front of the heating vents while the wind raged outside, shaking the vehicle. "I need to get pictures of the boat," Danny said after a moment, "before I send forensics out." Bobbi Lambert, the forensics chief, wouldn't thank him for it, and that was too bad, but it had to be done. He ought to have taken photos of the girl in situ, but now that she was no longer a corpse….

A wash of red light slid across his vision as the ambulance pulled up close to where Molloy had parked. "Not before time," Molloy commented, sliding out of the back seat. "The quicker they can get this wee girl properly warmed up, the better."

"Flowers," she murmured as two EMTs, both clad in heavy boots and winter parkas, lifted her onto a stretcher. "Pick the flowers."

"What did she say?" Danny pushed the nearest paramedic aside and leaned over the girl. "Tell me," he said.

"He said he had to pick the flowers." Her gaze slid over him, eyes wide open but unfocused. "Pick all the flowers."

"Who did?" The cold forgotten now, he bent close to her. "Who said it?"

"The man without a face."

Chapter Two

THE WEATHER had begun to clear, the sky an almost painful blue, when Danny arrived home. He'd lingered after the ambulance had gone to get some photos of the dory, but the rest would have to wait. The wool trousers and sweater had kept him warm even though they were wet, but the down-filled parka was soaked with seawater and beginning to freeze. He needed to get in the warm and get changed into dry things.

The air was very cold, and his ungloved fingers stuck to the metal doorknob of his rented cottage when he turned it. He went in, pleased to see that the fire he'd laid in the woodstove earlier that morning hadn't gone out and the flat was pleasantly warm. He dropped his wet parka in a heap by the door and kicked off his boots before moving across the room to shove two thick birch junks into the Jøtul's sturdy cast-iron mouth and winch the door closed. The kettle was still hot when he hovered a hand near it. A cup of tea, then. Barry's, it was. Maybe he'd really go for it and make a full pot.

"Hello, Danny." The woman rose from where she'd been sitting by the window. "I daresay you're surprised to see me."

He startled, nearly falling, put out a hand to steady himself, and caught the searing side of the kettle with his palm.

"Jesus!" He yanked his arm back, but it was too late, and the stink of burned flesh in his nostrils confirmed he'd left part of his hand on the kettle. "Oh Christ! Where did ye come from? What are ye doing here?" The kitchen faucet jerked and sputtered when he turned it on, coughing out an incomplete stream of cold water, but it was enough. He held his burned hand under it, almost sobbing with the pain.

She rushed to his side, ran a hand over his bent back. "Let me see it. Is it bad?"

"Don't touch." The pain settled into a nauseating throb, the damaged nerves sparking like the cut ends of an electric wire and sending a queer thrill up his arm. "It's fine."

"It's not fine." She leaned over to look, and her long red hair brushed against his face, releasing a hint of perfume. She at least was still comely as ever, for all that they were the same age, or close enough. "You need a doctor to look at this."

"Leave it." He shut the water off, wrapped a clean tea towel around his damaged hand. "I'll put something on it later."

"It's a second-degree burn. It needs looking after." She was beautifully dressed, well turned out in a green wool coat and matching tam, black leather boots. "I'll make some tea. Go and sit down."

"Don't order me around in my own fucking house," he growled but did as he was told, collapsing down onto an old tan sofa that he'd salvaged from the side of the road.

"Sure ye don't call this a house, do ye?" She shrugged out of her coat, left it draped over the back of a chair, then took down the box of Barry's teabags from the cupboard. "Got a teapot?"

"Under the sink." He watched her moving about the kitchen like she'd spent every day of her life in it. "You look good. How's the boyfriend?"

"I didn't come here to talk about Malcolm." She splashed some boiling water into the bone china teapot that had belonged to their grandmother and dumped it down the sink, then tossed in three teabags. "I haven't heard from you in six months. Last we spoke, ye were doing great, flying high, and then you vanish off the radar." She lifted the kettle again, decanting a stream of water on top of the teabags and fitting the lid on the pot. The warm scent of strong Irish tea rose into the air like a pleasant childhood memory. "What happened?"

"You know what happened." He stared at her, still not entirely sure he wasn't hallucinating. "You tore the guts out of my fucking life, Sandra. That's what happened." Worse, she'd done it slowly and systematically, revealing the truth a little at a time, only giving him what she, in her stubborn belief that she knew best, thought he could handle until the entire secret was out. "Why are you here?" He didn't feel like being polite to the woman he'd once thought of as his sister. "Because I have work to do."

"I heard from Tadhg," she said. She tossed it off casually, like she was reporting some fact of the weather or something. "He emailed me. I figured you should know."

"You couldn't call me?" The pain in his burned hand was bringing involuntary tears to his eyes, which annoyed him. She probably thought it was her.

"I've been trying. You don't answer. Where's the bathroom?"

"First door on your right."

She left the tea steeping in the pot, came back with a roll of gauze and some antiseptic ointment. "Let me see that hand."

"Jesus, Mary, and Joseph, will ye go away from my fucking hand already!" He yanked his arm back, but that didn't deter Sandra. She was like a thorn, working its way into his flesh whether he willed it or no.

"Let me see." She unwrapped the tea towel and let it fall. There was a bright red streak across his palm where the skin had split, seeping clear fluid, and several smaller burns of similar magnitude, all badly blistered. "Does it hurt?"

Danny glared at her. "Like a bastard." Then, realising what he'd said, "Yes, Sandra, it hurts like me."

"Don't say that." She crouched next to him on the couch and squeezed ointment out of the tube onto his burns. "It sounds like ye're blaming me, and it's not my fault." She wrapped his hand in clean white gauze, working quickly, tucking the cut ends of the fabric into a bow. "There. You're all set." She sat back on her heels. "Tadhg asked about you."

He tried to stem the bitterness before he spoke, but he needn't have bothered. It spilled out of him like bile. "Did he, now? That's a first."

Sandra rose to her feet, went to tend the teapot, lifting the lid and peering in at the hot brew. "Don't you want to know about him?"

"I know plenty. Leave it bide, Sandra. It's nothing to do with you." Danny knew exactly what Tadhg was up to. He'd made it his business to know. But he would let Sandra go on with it for the satisfaction of keeping his cards close to his chest. Two could play at that game.

"Oh," she said. She sounded disappointed. "Do you not have a fridge?" She glanced round the small space he'd set aside for his kitchen.

"If ye're looking for milk, it's in between the windowpanes over there." He pointed with his chin. "Haven't gotten around to getting a fridge yet. Didn't think I'd be here long."

She retrieved the milk, poured a generous measure into each of the cups, then decanted the hot tea in on top of it. "Here." She handed a cup across to him. "Get that down ye. Ye looks like the living dead, ye do so."

"Thanks."

There was only one other chair in the whole place, a relic from the 1960s, dark green with skinny wooden legs and a padded seat and arms. She hauled it over to where he was and sank into it, her cup cradled between her palms. They were silent together for a while, him and her, as the wind howled around the eaves of the structure and battered at the whisper-thin windowpanes. "Are ye punishing yourself?" she asked, lifting the cup to her lips. "Is that what this is?"

He deliberately ignored the question, knowing full well that he looked like absolute shite. The pain of his burned hand hissed and sizzled along his nerves, and part of him—a fairly large part, truth be told—wanted to drop his head and cry like a child. What would she do, he wondered, if he gave in to it, let himself weep and howl like a lost soul in Purgatory? Would she offer up a prayer for him? No, fuck it. They'd never been particularly pious, him and her.

"I haven't seen him in… well, I haven't seen him since the two of you—" She bit off the end of the sentence and swallowed it whole. "Anyway, I logged on to my email one morning late last week. Friday, it was. There was a message from him."

"And?"

Sandra shook her head, her long red hair swirling about her face. "He's not good, Danny. Malcolm has been looking for him. So have I. He's gone to ground right and proper this time."

"Is that right?" Danny said sourly. "Go on, I'm listening." He'd let her think whatever she bloody well wanted to think about Tadhg, his whereabouts, and the situation between them.

She sighed. "When he first contacted Malcolm about the rebuilding project on Grandar's land, it seemed like a great idea." She turned the cup, gazing down into its liquid depths. "Malcolm was all for it. I mean, this thing had been planned to the finest degree. It was as damn near perfect as you could wish."

Of course it was. Danny and Tadhg had sat together in front of the fire in Danny's rented house out on the Point, poring over the blueprints together, looking at concept drawings, dreaming.

"But then little things started going wrong," Sandra continued. "One of the subcontractors was crooked. He started cutting corners, substituting cheap materials, and a lot of the installations weren't up to proper code. He insisted on being paid, and Malcolm agreed to pay him up front, as long as he received his investment back in kind once the place was open for business. Only the subcontractor fucked off and took the money with him. The work he'd done wasn't worth shite." She sipped her tea. "They—Tadhg and Malcolm—lost a lot of money."

"What did the email say?" he asked. *Tell me something I don't know.*

"He apologised. It was no more than we'd expect, but Danny… I'm worried. He said he blamed himself for Malcolm losing his investment, and he'd see it put right." She paused and rubbed her forehead. "You know I know things, Danny. I can see things. I'm like Nan that way." She laid her cool fingers on his uninjured wrist. "I think he might harm himself. He made sure to get his daughter out of the way before he disappeared, sent her to live with her mother. He provided for her safety."

"You say Malcolm is looking for him now?" He didn't know Sandra's man that well, but it was the sort of thing he'd do, especially with Sandra pushing at him. She could be a proper pain in the arse, that one.

"Yes."

"Had any luck, has he?"

Sandra looked uncomfortable. "Well, no, not really."

"Well, that's that, isn't it?" He stood up, went and dumped the tea down the sink. Bitterness surged through him like a tsunami, a wash of emotion burning like acid. "Anyway, I've got work to do." He turned and she was standing in front of him, arms wrapped around her torso like she was cold. "We found a young woman floating in a boat, nearly dead of hypothermia, and my new boss wants me to look into it. It's not every day the North Atlantic brings you a nice fresh one, is it?"

"You're not even going to bother?"

"No, Sandra, I'm not even going to bother. I don't give a fuck where he is, to be perfectly honest." It was a lie, and a mean one at that, but the pain in his hand and his heart wouldn't let him give in. "And until you decided to get on your high horse and ride into town, I'd been doing a good job of forgetting him entirely."

Her forehead creased, and her pretty mouth turned down at the corners. In a moment she would be crying, and then all of his resolve would dissolve like sugar in a rainstorm. "You don't mean that."

"Oh, for God's sake!" He still had the empty teacup in his hand, and he flung it away from him. It sailed past her and bounced off, landing somewhere on the other side of the room. "Don't I? What the hell d'ye think this is, Sandra?" He gestured at the space around them. "Does it look to you like I'm having any fun? Living in this shithole with everything I ever cared about gone?"

She drew a sharp inbreath that sounded like a sob. "You're my brother."

"No, I'm not, and I never was, Sandra." He pointed to where she'd left her things. "Now take your coat and go."

"You don't mean that," she repeated. She moved to touch him, but he flinched away.

"I do." He turned his back on her, pretending interest in the scene outside the kitchen window, holding his breath tight inside the resounding hollow of his chest until she'd gone and he was alone again. He realised he was still standing there in his wet clothes, so he went into the portion of the repurposed fishing shed where his bed was to fetch clean things. The room had no bedroom as such, but he'd partitioned off a section at the rear of the building with a blanket hung on a string.

He's in trouble.

Well, that was a safe assumption, wasn't it? He unzipped his sodden trousers and let them fall, then drew off his woollen long johns and undershirt and tossed them onto the floor. His socks and underwear went next, and he spent an uncomfortable few seconds shivering while he rummaged through the chest of drawers.

I think he might harm himself.

No, Danny didn't think Tadhg would do that. Whatever else he was, he was a father who loved his daughter. But put himself in harm's way? That he would do.

Danny grimaced as he pulled on a clean pair of jeans and zipped them up. And she had her nerve, that bloody Sandra, coming here being all solicitous after what she'd put him through.

His mobile phone buzzed from where he'd tossed it on the bed, interrupting his black mood, and he reached for it automatically. It was Adrian Molloy.

"Danny, bad news. She didn't make it, that wee girl."

"What?"

"I've just heard from the hospital at Carbonear. She's dead."

CHAPTER THREE

"IT'S CALLED rewarming shock." Doctor Regan Lampe, dressed in her habitual green scrubs and wearing a face shield, moved around to the opposite side of the table. She had called early on this cold Tuesday and invited Danny to observe the autopsy in the hopes it might provide some useful information on the girl's death. "External rewarming is sometimes to blame. The body goes into shock, and there's a sudden drop in blood pressure." She plucked a plastic apron off a nearby shelf and tied it around her slender waist. "If they'd introduced warm fluids into the peritoneal cavity, it might have saved her." She shrugged. "Or it might not."

"Is that your professional opinion?" Danny asked. He shivered. The morgue at Carbonear General Hospital was warm enough, but the place always made him acutely uncomfortable. Maybe it was the room itself, low-ceilinged, dimly lit and oppressive, or perhaps it was being surrounded by corpses that reminded him too much of his own mortality. He wasn't getting any younger.

"Everything is my professional opinion," she snapped.

The body of the young woman they'd found in the dory lay naked on the steel autopsy table, her head elevated on a plastic block. Under the wan fluorescent lights, she appeared even paler, as if the cold had leached the blood from her.

"I thought she was dead," Danny said, "when I saw her." He'd waded into the freezing North Atlantic with hardly a thought for his own safety, but it wasn't heroism or anything like it. His innate curiosity demanded to know who or what was in the boat. It would probably get him killed one of these days. Tadhg had always said—

He quashed the thought.

"Well, she's dead now." Regan picked up a scalpel. "She wouldn't have survived to begin with if it had been *less* frigid out. I've seen it before. You lot didn't do her any favours trying to warm her up yourselves before the ambulance came. Step back, unless you want to get splashed."

He watched as she drew the sharp blade up the body, from the girl's pubis to the hollow of her throat, before extending the incision out towards each shoulder in the traditional Y-cut. "Did the ER staff give you her personal effects?" Regan asked.

"They did." Danny had collected a plastic bag from an apologetic male nurse who'd met him in the ER after he arrived. He'd seemed to feel her death was his fault, and he told Danny over and over that they'd done everything they could for her. "There was a wallet amongst her things. Name's Gail Russell. She was twenty-four, unmarried." He wasn't sure why he was telling Regan this. More than likely she didn't care. Whoever ended up on her autopsy table was nothing more than meat to her.

Regan grunted, a small sound that might have meant anything or nothing at all. She spread open the flesh of the chest, moving the scalpel in a flaying motion, cutting through the thin layer of fat and exposing the bones of the ribs and the intercostal muscles. The sound the knife made unnerved Danny, a rough tearing noise like someone ripping into a piece of fabric. His gorge rose, and he fought to swallow back the rising nausea. He ought to be used to this by now; in his career he'd seen so many autopsies that he'd lost count. Why was this particular one bothering him?

She was alive when you found her. She spoke to you.

Maybe that was it.

"Not much subcutaneous fat, although the muscles are flabby." Her knife sliced through the pectoral muscles, pushing the tissue aside. "Hardly any muscle tone." She glanced up at Danny. "He took one of her molars, did you know? The cold would have stopped most of the bleeding."

"What?" That would account for the dot of blood he'd found on her lower lip. "Really?"

Regan nodded towards the head. "Open her mouth and take a look."

His stomach recoiled at the thought, and he regretted bitterly the breakfast he'd eaten. "I'll take your word for it."

She scoffed. "Oh for God's sake." Dropping the scalpel back onto the tray, she moved towards the head of the table. "Come here." With an index finger hooked into the side of the woman's mouth, she pulled the cheek away from the oral cavity. "One of the big ones in the back. Must have pulled it out with pliers. Bet that hurt like a bitch. No anaesthetic, not even lidocaine in the gums?" She shook her head. "Nasty."

Danny remembered his conversation with Riley at the scene. "When you did your preliminary examination of the body, did you notice… anything?"

Regan glanced up at him sharply. "Like what?"

"Any external or internal assault."

She picked up the scalpel and went back to the girl's chest. "She wasn't raped," she told him flatly. "Apart from the bruising on her cheek and the missing tooth, I found no other evidence of assault. Whoever did this, he handled her with kid gloves, in a manner of speaking."

"Okay." The tooth was doubtless a souvenir, but why had he set the girl adrift in a dory while she was still alive? He watched wordlessly as Regan sheared through the ribs on each side of the thoracic cavity, lifting the chest plate back out of the way. She snipped through the pericardium, the sac surrounding the heart. "Fuck," she muttered, "that's too big."

"What is it?"

Regan lifted the heart in one hand and cut it free. She laid the displaced organ on a second table under the light and cut into it with her scalpel, slicing it into a neat cross section. "Look. The right ventricle is seriously enlarged." She dug into the central portion of it with a gloved finger. "Septal defect. Yep. Stenosis of the pulmonary valve... and the aorta's not right."

Danny blinked. "In English?"

"Tetralogy of Fallot," Regan told him. "How the hell did she even survive into adulthood?"

"So she had a bad heart."

"This is a very bad heart. She was born with it. This girl should be blue—cyanotic—from lack of oxygen." She turned and dropped the two pieces of the organ into a kidney-shaped pan behind her. "It's the sort of condition where, if it's not operated on early in the child's life, they usually don't survive. The ones who do live severely shortened lives." She moved back to the table and picked up one of the hands. "See? Look at these clubbed finger ends. That's characteristic. She was a very sick girl. At this point I can't say for sure what killed her, the cold or her heart." Regan laid the hand back down. "I'll draw blood and order a tox screen. That'll tell us more." She paused, glancing up at him. "Does she have any family?"

"I don't know yet. I came as soon as Molloy told me she'd died." He gazed down at her dead face, remembering the blot of blood resting in the centre of her lower lip. She'd survived into adulthood only to die from hypothermia after some sadistic bastard had brutalised her. "Okay if I get her prints?"

"Fine," Regan replied, "but stay out of my way."

He fetched the portable print kit he'd brought and went round to the opposite side of the table to pick up the same hand Regan had held. It was a matter of moments to roll each of the dead girl's fingertips onto the ink pad and then onto the appropriate space on a blank ten-card. It remained to be seen if the database would return any hits on the prints, and he'd learned not to hope for too much.

"I have to go." He reached to tear off the paper apron he was wearing. "Thanks for…." It wasn't really what he wanted to say. "Thanks."

"Bye." Regan said. She didn't even look up as he left, letting the door swing shut behind him.

DANNY DIDN'T expect to receive Regan's post-mortem report until a day or two later, so he was surprised when he got back to the station to find it waiting in his email. He scanned it quickly and made notes about the details of her injuries as well as the cause of death: hypothermia, coupled with a massive dose of ketamine her assailant had probably injected. Danny texted Regan his thanks and received no reply, which was what he'd expected. He was just preparing notes for the team briefing when Cillian Riley showed up, carrying two coffees from Strange Brew. "Tell me one of those is for me," Danny said.

Riley grinned. "Of course." He handed the cardboard container over. "Cold enough to kill you out there today." The temperature had risen perhaps a degree or two from the previous day, and the sun was shining with a pale, wan light. The remnants of the blizzard had blown out to sea, leaving behind vast drifts taller than a man. The ploughs had been out, pushing back what had fallen on the roads, leaving behind a thin skin of hard-packed snow that was treacherous to vehicles and pedestrians alike despite the generous coating of grit the highways department had applied.

"You'll eventually get used to the winters around here," Danny commented. He peeled back the plastic lid of his coffee and inhaled gratefully. "Flat white. Thanks, Cillian. You're a godsend, you are, so."

"No, I won't get used to them," Riley retorted and shivered. He took a couple of sips of coffee. "Listen, you remember what you said the other day about the office?"

"Yes. You should stay, move your desk in here. There's plenty of room for two, and I could use the company. Besides—" Danny shifted uncomfortably. "—you're still in charge of the station, at least until the inquiry is over. I'm only here to manage this one case." He nodded towards the doorway. "Get Dougie and Kevin to help, but not yet." He plucked a laptop off his desk. "Briefing room? Let's get everyone together."

The Kildevil Cove police station had previously been a Loyal Orange Lodge building, dating to the early twentieth century. When Danny's former boss, Moira Fraser, had elected to set up a Royal Newfoundland Constabulary detachment in the Cove, she'd hired Tadhg to convert the old building into something more fit for purpose. What he'd come up with was brilliant, a remastered heritage building with an altered layout housing everything a police station needed, including a forensics lab. The briefing room had originally been the old lodge's grand hall, complete with a mural of William of Orange astride a prancing stallion. In truth, the steed resembled a Great Dane more than a horse, but this was a minor detail. Danny had contemplated having it painted over, but the station personnel liked it, so he'd left it alone.

Word had already gotten out about the girl in the boat, and the team, including Kevin and June Carbage, Dougie Hughes, and Sarah Avery, were already waiting in the briefing room, some of them still wearing their heavy parkas. Riley had mentioned that the furnace was on the blink—something else for Danny to put on his "to do" list. He greeted everyone as he came in, then set up his laptop on the table at the front of the room. "Dougie, can you get the lights?"

"'Course, sir." Hughes was still limping from a bad leg injury the previous summer that had put him on desk duty for several months. He flipped the wall switch so that the room went dark, and the quiet murmur of conversation died away.

"Gail Russell." Danny paged through to the first photo, an image of the girl in situ. "By now you have heard about the young woman we found floating in a dory just inside the harbour yesterday morning. When we found her, she was near death from severe hypothermia, and one of her molars had been forcibly removed. The cold stopped the bleeding." He showed them the close-up of the wound. "She succumbed to hypothermia in hospital. Doctor Lampe's autopsy revealed a congenital heart condition that probably hastened this woman's death, but blood tests reveal she had been injected with an overdose of ketamine." The next photo was of Gail Russell's face. "She was slapped or punched, as you can see by the bruising over the cheekbone, but apart from that and the missing tooth, her assailant inflicted no further damage." He waited while the assembled group scribbled notes. "This is a murder case, make no mistake. Whoever put her in that boat did so because he intended to cause her death."

Hughes stuck his hand up. "Maybe it was a prank, sir? A joke that went wrong, like."

Danny shook his head. "Putting someone adrift in an open boat at the height of a blizzard and in minus twenty-five temperatures isn't a joke," he said. "This was done with malicious intent." He paused to sip his coffee. "When she was being loaded into the ambulance, she said something about a man with no face. Whether this refers to her attacker, we have no way of knowing."

"He could have had his face covered," Riley said. "It was pretty cold out last night, so he'd probably been wearing a scarf."

"True," Danny agreed. "Or perhaps he suffered an injury that damaged his face, making his features unrecognisable. Sadly, we'll never know what Gail Russell meant by it."

"What do we know about her, sir?" Kevin Carbage asked. He was sitting next to his twin sister, June, both of them holding mugs of tea.

"Personnel at Carbonear General passed on her personal effects, such as they are. We have her wallet, containing a driver's licence and various bank and credit cards, as well as a small amount of cash. Her mobile phone, if she had one, is missing. We know her name is Gail Russell, as I said, and she is from the local area, but right now that's about it." He retrieved the fingerprints he'd taken at the autopsy and handed them to Kevin. "Run these through the system and see if there's a match, and check the database for any previous arrests or convictions, the usual."

"I know this girl," June said suddenly. "She's Rose Davies's younger sister."

"Davies?" Danny forced himself to say the name. "No, Gail's surname is Russell."

"Davies is her married name," June replied. "She married a man from Wales. It's a Welsh name."

A flush of heat rose prickling into Danny's face and his throat closed over. *You've been lied to all your life.* That was how she'd told the truth to him, Sandra, in an email message late at night, when he was alone and vulnerable. *You're not a Quirke, Danny. You never were. Your mother's name was Angharad Davies.* It had all made sense then—his sense of never really belonging to his family, of feeling forever the outsider. And the other thing, his rare Rh-null blood type that no one else had but him.

"Davies," he said again. The hollow ringing in his ears subsided a little. "And does she live locally?"

"No, she moved away when they married, but I believe their parents are still alive." June was looking at him queerly, obviously aware that he wasn't feeling like himself. Her gaze lingered on his bandaged hand. Knowing June, she probably wanted to ask if he was all right but wouldn't do it in front of the others.

"They'll have to be informed," he said. "It's impossible to pinpoint how long Gail Russell was in the boat, but it was long enough for hypothermia to set in. At this time of year and with the high winds and the temperature as low as it is, that's a matter of minutes, not hours, which means whoever put her in the boat did so after ten in the morning." He projected a photo of the boat he'd taken after the girl had been removed to the ambulance. "The boat was launched from somewhere close by and ended up inside the harbour, either by accident or by design. Constable Hughes, I need you to come up with a list of possible places, coves or beaches in close proximity, where this might have occurred."

Hughes's hand shot up again. "No, I cannot define 'close,'" Danny said before Hughes had a chance to ask. "All we know is the girl was in the boat for about half an hour. The rest you'll have to figure out on your own." He paused and looked over the assembled group. "Ask around—as discreetly as you can—and see if anyone in the local area is missing a dory. Say that we've had a report of a stolen boat and we're checking on it."

"What if they ask questions?" Riley. "Maybe somebody else saw the girl in the boat. It's bound to be all around town by now."

"I can't do anything about local gossip, but I want to remind you that confidentiality is important here. It is vital—I can't stress this enough—that nothing about this case gets out. You do not talk about this to anybody. Not your family, not your spouse or partner, not even the parish priest. Is that clear?"

There were murmurs of "Yes, sir" and "Clear, sir" and several nodding heads. It hadn't escaped Danny's attention that his team, some of whom now outranked him, had fallen back into the old habit of deferring to him as if he were still their chief. He supposed that ought to seem strange, but it would make the investigation go easier. Molloy *had* put him in charge of the case. *Leave it be, Danny.*

"Gail Russell was a vulnerable person suffering from a chronic illness. She was abducted, injected with drugs, and set adrift in an open boat to die. Your duty is to her. I want you to find out everything you can about her. Someone wanted this young woman dead. We need to find out why."

June approached him as he was gathering his things. "Sir, I'd like to go with you to notify Gail's parents. I knew them quite well when I was younger." She gazed pointedly at his bandaged hand.

"Good idea," Danny said. He ignored the implied question. "Best do it now and get it over with."

GAIL RUSSELL'S parents lived in a white house just off the main road in Old Perlican, a two-storey clapboard dwelling with a mansard roof. Because of the recent blizzard, there was nowhere to park, so Danny pulled the patrol car as close as possible to the shoulder and put the emergency flashers on.

"They should be home," June said, reaching to unfasten her seat belt. "Her mother's never been strong—she's got a real bad heart—and her father keeps to himself." A black pickup truck sat in the drive, buried up to its windshield in snow, and there were no fresh footprints leading either to or from the front door.

Danny zipped up his parka and drew his gloves on. "Just so you know, I hate these visits."

June's gaze was sympathetic. "Me too, sir."

The front walk hadn't been shoveled, and they were forced to wade through knee-deep drifts in order to reach it. The air was intensely cold, and drawing breath felt like being stabbed in the sinuses; their exhalations formed tiny ice crystals that hung in mid-air. Danny took off his glove and rapped on the door—there was no doorbell—then waited. "Maybe they aren't home." He secretly hoped this could be put off until later, which was nonsense. Either way, he'd have to face them sometime.

"There's smoke coming out of the chimney," June said. "They're home."

He knocked again, and again they waited, until there was a shuffling sound on the other side of the door. The lock clicked open, and the door swung back a scant six inches to reveal a woman's face. She looked about Danny's own age, but time had not been nearly as kind to her. Her complexion was the dull grey of cigarette ash, and her eyes watered.

"Mrs. Russell?" June stepped forward to speak to her. "It's June Carbage. Do you remember me?"

The woman's tired gaze travelled to the police car parked in front of the house. "It's not good news, is it." It was a statement, not a question.

"Inspector Deiniol Quirke, RNC." Danny had decided to use his former title for simple convenience while on this case. He was reasonably certain his team would not object. While he'd been given a formal ID as Constable Quirke, Molloy had not, for whatever reason, asked him to turn over his Inspector's ID. Danny took that as a hopeful sign.

"May we come in?"

"Yes, come in." She held the door open and stood back for them to enter. The interior of the house was very warm, but Mrs. Russell was wearing a knitted cardigan over a heavy wool sweater. Danny imagined her condition made the cold especially hard to bear. "Eliol is upstairs taking a spell," she said. "I'll have to go up and get 'un."

"That's too hard on ye, sure," June said. "I'll sing out for him, will I?"

"Yes, sing out."

The three of them waited while Eliol Russell was summoned from upstairs. He appeared on the top landing, wearing a heavy sweater and a pair of thick fleece jogging pants. "What's after happening?" He came down the stairs at a fast clip, his large feet hardly making a sound. He was an absolute giant of a man, easily two metres tall and skeletally thin, with the unusually long limbs typical of Marfan syndrome. He walked with a stoop, his shoulders curved forward and his handsome leonine head held at an angle. "Ye crowd is from the police, is ye?"

"I'm Inspector Deiniol Quirke," Danny said, "and this is Sergeant June Carbage. We need to speak to you and your wife, Mr. Russell."

"Come into the front room," Mrs. Russell said. "I'll put the kettle on."

"That won't be necessary." News of a sudden death usually shocked the next of kin, and Danny had seen all sorts of reactions over the years. Some people went completely silent, withdrawing into themselves, while others raged and shouted. He himself had been shoved, punched, slapped, and vomited on, and one grieving father had driven him from the house at the end of a hunting rifle. He didn't want to be holding a scalding cup of tea when any of that happened. "Perhaps we can just talk."

"It's awful cold out, though," Mrs. Russell persisted.

"Elsie, they don't want any tea," her husband said. He put an arm round her waist and steered her gently into the sitting room, Danny and June following.

The interior of the house was decorated with the usual mementos and souvenirs local people seemed to favour: family photos; a graduation picture of Gail in cap and gown, holding a bouquet of roses; a statue of Saint Andrew, the patron saint of fishermen, holding his cross; a coloured print of the Sacred Heart, and a photograph of a fluffy white cat lying on a cushion. A chair sat next to the fireplace, and Mr. Russell helped his wife into it. He drew a throw blanket over her legs.

"Now you bide there," he said, patting her lap affectionately before moving to take a seat on the sofa nearby. The love between them was apparent in the tenderness Eliol Russell showed his wife, and now Danny was going to shatter their world with a handful of carefully chosen words.

"We have some very bad news to tell you," Danny began, watching their faces cautiously. He'd learned to always leave a space between that sentence and the rest of what he had to tell them. That minor caesura gave them time to prepare for the inevitable shock that was coming. "Your daughter Gail was found yesterday morning in an advanced state of hypothermia. She received medical attention at Carbonear General Hospital, but they were unable to save her. I'm afraid—" His voice caught hard in his throat and he swallowed, forced himself to go on. "—she died."

Elsie Russell half rose out of her chair, then fell back and began to sob—dry, heaving sobs that shook her frail body like epileptic convulsions. Her husband went to her, wrapped his arms around her, murmuring something Danny couldn't make out. He exchanged a glance with June, who said, "I'll get you some water," and disappeared into the hallway. For a moment or two Danny stood there in the middle of the room, feeling utterly useless, a spare part.

"What happened to her?" Eliol asked.

"She was found drifting in an open dory in the harbour. The clothes she was wearing were inadequate. I'm so sorry."

"It was a new dress," Elsie said, her voice barely a whisper. "We give it to her for Christmas. I asked her what she wanted and she said that dress, so we sent down the States for it."

"Yes," Danny replied. "She was wearing a party dress when she was found."

"Why would someone put her in a boat?" Eliol again. He'd risen from his wife's side and stood wringing his long pale hands together. "What was she doing in a boat?"

"We don't know yet. The investigation is ongoing." Danny glanced back at the hallway just as June appeared with a glass of water. She offered it to Mrs. Russell, but the woman waved it away. "When did you last see your daughter?" He flipped open his notebook. Now probably wasn't the right time to ask such questions, and of course he'd make a follow-up visit, but they needed information to go on.

"Sunday night," Eliol answered. "About eight o'clock, I suppose. She was going to a party, down to Sheila and Roy Fitzpatrick's house. That's why she was all dressed up. 'Twas a Sunday night, mind, and we don't normally like her to be out on the Sabbath, but you knows the Fitzpatricks, now, they haves the youngsters over to theirs all the time. Queer bunch, they are. Never pays no heed to what day it is." He fell silent, seeming to lapse into thought. "She's a good girl, our Gail. Never done nothing wrong to nobody. I wasn't going to begrudge her a night out, especially to a New Year's party."

Danny had to swallow the lump in his throat from the poignancy of Eliol's answer.

"Did she go with anyone," June asked, "or by herself?"

"I don't… let me think." Eliol rubbed a hand across his forehead. "Didn't that one Doris pick her up?" he asked his wife. "Don Coombs's young maid."

"I believe she did." Elsie nodded slowly. "My, it's some cold in here," she said. What little colour she possessed had completely drained from her gaunt face.

"Mr. Russell, your wife may be in shock," June told him. "Can you find another blanket? I'll make her a hot cup of tea."

A cup of tea, Danny thought, was the remedy for whatever ailed you, the one thing almost everyone had available in times of crisis. He closed his notebook and went to Mrs. Russell, crouching beside her chair. "Hold on to my hand," he told her quietly. She grasped his fingers, squeezing with an unexpected strength.

"You're adopted too," she said, "like our Gail." The unusual utterance struck him; it was an odd thing to say under the circumstances. *Does everyone in the village know what I didn't for most of my life?*

Mrs. Russell's eyes were a curious pale grey, almost silver. "My mother was friends with yours. She was a nurse down to the hospital." She gazed at him intently, as if memorising his features. "Ye favours your mother," she said, "ye do, so. She had lovely red hair, blue eyes like yours. Sin what happened to her."

"What happened to her?" But he never got to hear her answer because June was back with a cup of tea, Eliol Russell came downstairs with a heavy blanket to wrap around Elsie's shoulders, and the moment passed. Danny wasn't about to press her further, not now when she had just learned of her daughter's death. He stood and moved away.

"That's nice and strong," June said of the tea, "and I put extra sugar in it."

"She said she was going to that party with Doris Coombs," Eliol told them. He'd pulled a straight-backed chair close to his wife's and sat holding her free hand. "We got a phone call from her later on in the evening. Said Doris had to go home early, but she was going to call a taxi. That's the last we heard of her."

Danny fumbled for his notebook. "What time was this?"

"Must have been around midnight, I suppose. The wife goes to bed early, but I likes to stay up and watch the late news. I was just after putting another junk of wood in the fire when the phone rang."

"She was calling you from the Fitzpatricks' house?"

"Yes, it were," he said. "Nice people. Decent people. They always was right good to Gail, knowing she was sick." What rotten odds, Danny wondered, had saddled this family with a mother and a daughter both dying of heart disease? Had the Russells known Gail was ill when they adopted her?

"Do you know this Roy Fitzpatrick?" Danny asked June, who nodded. "Gail told you this was a New Year's party?" He looked to Eliol, who nodded.

"Gail said they were having a few people over for a meal." It must have been some dinner party, Danny thought, to warrant a silk cocktail dress and stiletto heels. "They used to do that every so often, just a bit of fun. Gail wasn't feeling all that well, but she knew they thought a lot of her, so."

Elsie Russell shuddered as though a cold draught had passed by, even though the sitting room was warm enough. The wail she uttered was like the dying cry of a wild animal and raised the hair on Danny's arms. "Oh my God," she gasped. "Oh my God."

"Is there anyone we can call for you?" June asked, clearly alarmed. "A member of the clergy?"

"No, no, just go, the two of ye!" Elsie's face was twisted with uncommon rage, and she raised her fists, brandishing them in June's direction. "Ye brought a curse into this house." She sagged back in her chair. "A curse. Oh my God."

Eliol Russell saw them to the door. Danny apologised for being the bearer of such devastating news.

"When will we be able to bury her?"

"I'll request—" Danny nearly said "the body" but stopped himself just in time. "I'll request that Gail be released to the funeral home as soon as possible. Someone will be in touch." He handed Russell one of his cards. "If there is anything you need, please let me know. Again, I'm very sorry for your loss."

Danny stepped out into the frigid winter landscape and closed his eyes against the sudden chill.

CHAPTER FOUR

HE WAS careful to leave no trace and to remain unseen, even when appearing in broad daylight and in plain sight. Before the Bad Thing, he'd held himself back, not wanting to appear too forward, too needy, too demanding of the love that he had no right to. It was better to escape the common gaze. It was Mam who taught him that, in a thousand little ways, with her eyes and her hands and voice. Seen and not heard, that's what she always wanted. *Not one peep am I to be hearing out of you. Not one. Now go in there. Go in.* Into the hall closet, the one with the wide door and plenty of room to sit on the stacks of clean bed linen. He'd take the clock in with him, the special one with the numbers that lit up, and so he always knew what time it was, daylight or dark. He could trace the minutes around its reassuring bland face, and it would keep him company.

He arrived home early the next morning, when the sky was still black and the stars shone like particles of ice. The garage doors were unlocked, and so he just had to get out and open the doors, drive all the way in and turn the engine off. Always turn the engine off. Don't ever sit in a closed garage with the engine running. That was the wrong thing to do, even in the cold. Especially in the cold. A body could linger much too long. The clock on the car's dashboard read 4:30 a.m., as did the watch strapped to his right wrist and the other one on his left. The snow crunched under his feet when he got out, and the sound of the car door closing seemed unnaturally loud. He closed and locked the double doors behind him and went along the pathway to where the house perched, halfway up the side of a cliff, a weathered biscuit box with long, narrow windows gazing at the sea. Originally it had stood on a larger spit of land, a miniature peninsula jutting out into the North Atlantic, but over time the sea had eroded it so that now the house teetered dangerously, barely clinging to its foundation. In a year or ten, the land beneath it would disappear, and then it would fall into the water, be reduced to wreckage, carried out to sea like flotsam.

No lights showed when he pushed the door open and went inside, but the fire he'd laid in the woodstove hadn't entirely gone out. He stirred the embers with a poker and put a piece of driftwood on top of the reddened coals. When that was done he took his coat off, hanging it carefully on the hook beside the kitchen door and smoothing the wrinkles out of it, dusting down the dark wool with the flat of his hand. The wall of clocks was undisturbed, but he made sure to touch each one, making minute adjustments on one or two, moving the hour hand a millimetre back, slowing a pendulum. He whispered as he did it, to them and to himself, calling each by name because names were the most important thing of all, and each one needed to hear its name spoken aloud. Time was finite, but he was infinite, a field of energy stretching out in all directions, crackling like electricity. He'd never told anybody that, not even Mam. He could imagine what she'd say: *Go 'way with ye, ye bloody idiot. Sure ye're cracked, you are, so.* Mam liked to act as if she knew everything, but that wasn't true. No one knew everything, not even God if you believed in him.

When he'd finished with the clocks, he went through to a back bedroom, a dark rectangle of space set so close against the cliff that the single window looked out onto a vertical wall of stone. He pulled the cord hanging from the ceiling and a lightbulb came on, bathing the room in harsh white light, painful to the eyes. There was minimal furniture in the space, only a wooden kitchen chair and an old-fashioned iron bed complete with a sagging mattress covered in a dirty chenille bedspread. He bent and felt under the mattress, grimacing when his hand caught on the bare metal springs. It was here. It had to be here. There was nowhere else for it to be, and objects didn't vanish and spontaneously reappear in another location. Newton's first rule: *an object remains at rest.* His fingers closed on a small metal tin, and he smiled, pulled it out. It was approximately the size of an Altoids container, flat with rounded corners, enamelled black, with pretty blossoms and the word "Flowers" printed on it. When he shook it, something inside rattled. It made a little shiver down inside him, and he liked it. He wanted to exercise discipline, however, and not handle the artifacts too much. If you handled something too much, if you looked at it too often, it lost its shine, became too commonplace to have value. So just one, for now, like taking a candy from a dish. You only chose one, not a whole handful, and if he ever tried to take more, Mam would smack his hands. *One, not ten. Greedy guts.*

He reached in and plucked one out, holding it gently between his fingertips. It was perfect: three long and curving roots, five gentle bumps on the surface, and not a trace of anything to mar the precious ivory. The molar was as flawless as a pearl. He hid it in the palm of his other hand and held it, warming it with his body's heat until it almost became a part of him.

Almost.

So far he had collected three, but he needed more. Insatiable, he was, where his prizes were concerned. He pressed the tooth against the middle of his lower lip, the tip of his tongue flicking out to touch it before retracting. No, it was too much. This pleasure was too keen for him. It wasn't time, not yet.

He put the molar with the rest and slid the tin back underneath the mattress.

DANNY HAD trouble tracking down Doris Coombs, the woman who had given Gail Russell a ride to the New Year's party. She wasn't listed in the telephone directory, and the police database returned no hits, so she had no criminal record, or at least no charges. He wasn't prepared to go back to the Russells with further questions, not just now when their grief was so raw, but it was important to reconstruct what Gail did in the time leading up to her death.

He was sitting in his office when Dougie Hughes tapped on the door. "Still looking for Doris Coombs, sir?" he asked. Danny indicated that he was. "Might have something for you." Dougie handed across a slip of paper with a phone number written on it. "Asked the wife if she knew anybody by that name. Turns out this Doris does volunteer work with the United Church, sorting out clothes and dishes and stuff for the jumble sales. My missus is always down to the church hall looking for bargains." He grinned. "It's shocking expensive with a young one. Anyway, that's her number."

"Thanks, Constable. This is very helpful."

He rang the number, but there was no answer. He left a brief message on her voicemail, asking her to call him back immediately, and got on to tracking down the couple who'd hosted the party, Sheila and Roy Fitzpatrick. Unlike Kevin and June, who'd lived here all their lives, Danny had been away until fifteen months or so previous. The people he'd known as a boy in Kildevil Cove had grown up and moved on to lives of their own and, like many of their parents, had left the island to seek work on the mainland after the collapse of the cod fishery in the 1990s. Their grandparents, if any survived, were up in years, and many of them were no longer in their right minds, having fallen prey to dementia or other ills that robbed them of their memories and, in some cases, their reason. The Fitzpatricks weren't listed in the phone directory either, which meant they probably didn't have a landline. He got up from his desk and went to look for June, found her in the break room chatting with Cillian Riley, who had just poured himself a cup of tea.

"I heard it was rough at the Russells' house," Riley said. He gazed pointedly at Danny's bandaged hand but didn't ask what had happened.

"You heard right," Danny replied, "That sort of thing's never easy." He nodded at the still-steaming kettle. "Enough hot water in that for me?"

"Let me get you one," June said, reaching into the cupboard for a clean mug. "Sorry, sir. I guess I'm not thinking. I should have asked if you wanted one when we got back."

"You're not my secretary." Danny smiled at her. "I don't expect to be waited on hand and foot. It's not your job. I daresay you know that by now."

"Of course, sir. It's Tadhg's job—" She saw her error too late and backpedalled furiously. "What I mean, sir…." Her cheeks flushed a deep crimson. "Sorry."

The mention of Tadhg's name was like a sucker punch to the gut, and he turned away to hide his emotional reaction from them. Barely three months had passed, not nearly enough time to erase the pain. He still woke in the night from unsettling dreams of Tadhg in peril, exiled at the end of the world somewhere and needing him or stranded on the far side of some alien shore. He recognised the dreams as his subconscious trying to sort things out, but he wished it would shut the hell up.

"It's fine, Sergeant." He struggled to keep his voice light. "Any milk left, or are we all out?"

"Right here." Riley opened the fridge and handed out a carton.

"Um, June," Danny started, eager to turn the conversation to a different topic, "I'm looking for a Sheila and Roy Fitzpatrick. You indicated you knew of them when the Russells said that's where Gail went to the New Year's party."

"Oh yes, of course." She tapped her mug with her fingernails. "They live up the harbour. You know where Wanda Slade's house is? Halfway out to the fish plant, across from the old elementary school."

Danny gazed at her, as confused as if she'd just given him directions to the moon. "Where?" He glanced at Riley, who saw it and hid his grin in the rim of his cup.

"I can take you there," June said. "They're a bit out of the way. The Fitzpatricks live off the grid. Homesteaders, I think you call it. It's pretty amazing what they've done with their place. They source all their own electricity and everything."

"Well, come on, then." Danny laid aside his tea. "Let me grab my coat from my office. I'll meet you at the front door."

He jogged down the corridor and plucked his parka off the coat tree just inside his office door. Something on the desk caught his eye, and he reached for it, a small white envelope with his name written on the front in block letters: Danny. Not Inspector Quirke or Constable Quirke or even Mr. Quirke, but Danny. The envelope was unsealed, and there was nothing inside except a photograph of two boys sitting on a rough rail fence in front of a wood frame house. Danny recognised himself in the blond boy wearing blue jeans and a short-sleeved shirt. The other boy, also wearing jeans but with a Mickey Mouse T-shirt, was Tadhg. The date stamped on the bottom of the photo was 1979. He and Tadhg were twelve.

He staggered back a pace, turned the picture over. There was nothing written on the back, no indication of where it had come from or who had sent it. He remembered that day so clearly. Late June, with warm sun and a light westerly wind. He and Tadhg were pestering Mrs. Heaney to let them go in swimming at Single's Brook, where all the Cove children swam. Danny had worn swimming trunks underneath his jeans, he remembered, and had left the house earlier that morning with a towel slung over the crossbar of his bike. It was a good memory.

Who sent me this? Why?

"Sir?" June appeared at his door. "Everything all right?"

"Yes, of course." He shoved the envelope into the back pocket of his jeans. "Sorry, Sergeant. Yes, let's... we should go to see those people." He shrugged into his parka and zipped it up. *Sandra.* Sandra must have sent the photograph, or dropped it off more likely. "June, did you see my sister come in here?"

"Sandra?" She shook her head and started down the corridor. "No, sir. I thought she was in Portugal."

Danny drew level with her so they were walking side by side. "She is. I mean, she was. She showed up at my flat out of the blue."

June nodded at his bandaged hand. "Is that how that happened?"

"It's part of it." He silently begged her not to ask anything further. This wasn't a conversation he wanted to have with a colleague, even one he considered a friend.

JUNE WAS right when she said the Fitzpatricks lived on the outskirts of Kildevil Cove. Their homestead was several kilometres off the main road and located deep in the woods next to a pond. Danny wasn't sure what he'd expected of modern homesteaders who chose to live off-grid, but it wasn't this. A huge Nordic-style house rose out of the snow, its exterior walls clad in narrow boards stained dark grey, inset with large windows to let the light in. At one end, a glassed-in conservatory was lush with greenery, a profusion of houseplants growing out of pots and hanging baskets, and the roof of the house was sod. A man was busy clearing snow away from the front door. He looked up when they arrived and waved.

"Friendly bunch, are they?" Danny asked.

"Modern hippies," June replied.

"Oh." He fervently hoped nobody would try to hug him.

"Roy!" June called out to him as she and Danny got out of the patrol car. "How's it going?"

He abandoned his shovel in a nearby snowbank and came to meet them. "Not too bad, June. How's yourself? Amy doing all right?"

"Best kind," June replied. "She's on sabbatical right now, doing a course in the States."

"Oh my. Left you on your own, eh?"

June took this opportunity to introduce him. "This is my boss, Inspector Danny Quirke. We'd like to ask you some questions about the New Year's party."

"How's ye?" Roy shook Danny's hand. His grip was gentle, but there was an undercurrent of strength, and something in his forthright gaze indicated he was not a man to be trifled with. "The New Year's party? Why? What's after happening?"

June glanced at Danny. "One of the young women who attended your party has come to harm."

Fitzpatrick reared back a pace. "What?" He looked from June to Danny and back again. "Surely to God you don't think—"

"At this stage we are just asking some questions," Danny interjected. "You'd be doing us a favour if you could help."

"Oh." He drew a slow breath. "Well, Sheila's in the house. Why don't ye go on in, and I'll be in now the once."

"We'd prefer to speak with both you and your wife at the same time." He'd be damned if he'd let Fitzpatrick wriggle out of it. "Take a break from your shovelling. It's freezing cold out here."

Fitzpatrick's expression said he'd rather be anywhere else, but he consented, leading Danny and June into the house. Like the exterior, the inside was a predominantly Scandinavian design, with cool tones of grey and white and large windows to let in as much natural light as possible—a rare commodity at this latitude in winter. Sheila Fitzpatrick was a pretty woman in her mid-thirties, the type often called "pleasantly plump," with a girlish face and curly blond hair. She was dressed simply in jeans and a man's flannel shirt with the sleeves rolled up, her hands plunged elbow-deep into a pan of bread dough. She was pink-cheeked and sweating—and visibly pregnant.

"I'm sorry to arrive unannounced," Danny said. "But as I told your husband—"

"Oh, Roy's not my husband." Her smile plumped her cheeks into round pink mounds. "He's my brother."

"I see." Why had Roy not bothered to correct Danny's original assumption that Sheila was his wife? "As I told your brother, we're investigating the death of a young woman who attended your New Year's party, and we'd like to ask you some questions. I'm sorry this couldn't wait for a more opportune time"—Danny was nothing of the sort; he actually didn't give a damn what the Fitzpatricks were doing, but pretending politeness sometimes smoothed the way in police work—"but it's vital we find out where Gail Russell was and what she was doing in the days leading up to her death."

"It wasn't us!" Sheila, alarmed, lifted her hands out of the bread dough. "How could you even think such a thing?" She advanced towards Danny, and he saw that she walked with a slight limp. "You're not from here, are you?" To June she said, "Why would you bring this man to our house?"

"Sheila, please." June grabbed a tea towel from a nearby hook and handed it to her. "You're dripping dough all over the place." She waited while the woman cleaned her hands. "Inspector Quirke is from the Cove. He's been away for a while and only came back last year."

"Is there somewhere we could sit and talk?" Danny glanced around the kitchen. "Here, if you like." He indicated the blond wood table. "May I sit down?"

"Yes, of course." Sheila went to the sink and rinsed her hands under the water. "Forgive me, Inspector. We're not used to being accused." As she reached for a clean towel, the underside of her right arm was towards him, clearly visible below the rolled-up sleeve of her shirt. A dark bruise the approximate width of a man's palm darkened the pale skin. It was the kind of bruise you got when someone grabbed you hard and held on.

"No one is accusing you of anything," June said. She pulled out a chair and sat, and Danny did the same, unzipping his heavy parka. It was warm in the house, courtesy of the old-fashioned Enterprise wood-and-oil stove in the corner of the kitchen, which Sheila had no doubt been heating up to bake bread. Danny remembered his own grandmother baking bread that way.

Except she's not your grandmother, not really. And she never was. The thought came out of nowhere, but he welcomed it. It was good to remind himself of who he really was, and also who he wasn't. The family he'd assumed was his own were no blood kin at all, and the truth of how he'd come to live in their house was too appalling to contemplate for any length of time, unless he had a fair amount of whiskey in him.

How was it she was never charged? He'd asked Sandra this, soon after the truth came out. *How could she do that and get away with it?* She gave him some platitudes about it being different back in those days and people not asking too many questions, and it being for the best. Nothing she said answered the question he'd asked, and eventually he gave up asking.

"So what happened to Gail?" Roy asked. He'd come in behind them, took his boots off in the porch that adjoined the kitchen. He padded across the wooden floor, feet soundless in his wool socks, and went to warm his hands at the stove, rubbing them together. There was a curious wound at the base of his right thumb, a livid red semicircle with an indented edge, approximately crescent shaped. Danny shifted his gaze to June, saw that she'd noticed it as well.

"She died," June said. "We're not prepared to say more than that until our investigation is completed." She already had her notebook out, her pen poised over it. "How many people attended the New Year's party," she asked, "approximately?"

Roy turned from where he stood. "Must have been fifty or sixty," he said.

"That's a lot," Danny observed. "But you certainly have the room for it."

"We have something for the young people once a month," Sheila said, bringing a huge copper kettle from the stove and using it to fill a teapot. "Games night, pizza and movie night, trivia night. They love it."

"So you host a youth club here in your home?" June jotted something in her notebook.

"More or less," Sheila told her. "There's not a lot for them to be doing around here. Oh, the Lions Club has a pool room and dartboards and such, but that's about it. If they're out beating the roads, they're more likely to get into trouble. Drinking and whatnot." She went to the cupboard to gather mugs for the tea, then took a jug of milk from the fridge. "That's our own milk," she told them. "From our cow."

"Can you provide a list of who was at your New Year's party?" It would help, Danny thought, if they could speak to each of the young people who were there that night.

"Not really," Roy said. "We don't take attendance. It's more like a come-all-ye. Whoever wants to show up, shows up." He held out the mug Sheila had given him, and she filled it from the pot. "Anyone who wants to come, 'long as they behaves theirselves."

"So it's an open house."

"Yes," Sheila confirmed. It wasn't the answer he was hoping for. She filled a mug with tea and pushed it towards him.

"But you do know some of the people who attended," June said. "And can give us a list of the ones you remember?"

"I suppose, bhoy." Sheila looked put out at this question and turned to glance at her abandoned bread dough on the counter behind her. "There was Darcy Tucker. That's Bob Tucker's girl. She came with her boyfriend, Ryan Fiander. Roy, who else was it?"

"I don't know." Roy shook his head. "I'd have to think about it."

This was getting them nowhere. Danny decided to try a different tack. "If you could write up a list and forward it to the police station, that would be great," he said. Either the Fitzpatricks were deliberately keeping the details of the party from him, or they were more feeble-minded than he'd initially thought. Maybe their own parents had been brother and sister, he thought sourly. "Do you remember what time Gail Russell left the party?"

"Yes," Sheila said. "Just after midnight." She looked to Roy for confirmation.

"That's right," he told them. "Just after twelve o'clock. Everything was finished then. We cleaned up the kitchen and went on to bed."

June tapped her pen against the edge of the table. "So Gail was the last person to leave the party?"

"That's right," Roy repeated. It seemed to be his stock answer.

"And she left in a taxi?" June asked.

"Yes, Shore Taxi," Sheila said. "'Tis the only one around here."

Danny made a note of this. "Did you see her get into the cab?"

"No." Roy shook his head. "I never seen her."

"I did." Sheila looked at Danny. "I watched through the window to make sure she got in okay. She insisted on going outside to smoke a cigarette while she waited, but she called just before she left. It seemed to take a long time for the cab to come. She was out there for close to half an hour."

"Just outside your front gate, I take it?"

Sheila nodded.

"And you say she smoked while she waited."

"Yes. That's why she wanted to wait outside, so she could smoke. She was out there at least half an hour before the cab came."

"Did she smoke the whole time she was waiting?" Danny asked.

She thought for a moment. "I think so. I left the window once to get a glass of water from the tap, but yes, I think so. She liked a smoke, Gail did. She shouldn't have. I suppose you knows she had a bad heart."

He jotted "heavy smoker" in his notebook. "Sheila, you said you saw her get into the cab. Can you describe it?"

"I can do better than that." She got up and went to a small shelf in the corner, a "whatnot," his grandmother would have called it, and retrieved something from one of the cubbyholes. She came back and passed it to Danny. "That's their card."

It was a plain white business card with a photo of a taxicab on the front. The cab was painted white, with a red stripe down the side and a logo of a seagull on the driver's side door. "Do all their cabs look the same?"

"Yes. They're all the same kind of car. Four doors. I don't know what you call it."

"A sedan?" June put in.

"Yes, that's it. A sedan." Sheila's face clouded, and she frowned. "That's the queer thing about it, though. It wasn't a sedan that came for Gail. It was a van."

June shot him a look. "A van?"

"One of those passenger vans, the big ones. Like a church bus," Sheila replied. "But it had to be one of their cabs. It looked the same, white with a red stripe and the seagull on the door."

"And you saw her get in." He wanted to be very sure on this point.

"Yes. She waved to me from the back seat. Then they drove away." Sheila picked up her cup and took a sip. She was apparently trying to appear calm, but her hands shook, and Danny wondered why.

"Did you get a look at the driver?" June again.

"No. I just saw the back of his head. I couldn't see much because it was too dark." She got up from the table abruptly and went to the window. "I should have made her stay the night. If she stayed the night, she'd be alive now."

June went to where the distraught woman was and laid a hand on her shoulder. "You don't know that, Sheila. You had no way of knowing anything was going to happen to her."

Roy was curiously silent during all of this, gazing into his teacup. The merest hint of a smile began to play about his thin lips, but disappeared quickly when he realised Danny was watching him. "No way of knowing," he murmured.

Danny stood up, leaving his tea untouched, and motioned to June. "Thank you both," he said. He passed Roy one of his business cards. "If you think of anything else that might be useful, please give myself or Sergeant Carbage here a call. We'll see ourselves out."

"And we didn't even get to try the milk," June said, once they were outside, "from their cow."

"They claim to have a cow, but I don't see a stable anywhere." Danny turned in a slow circle so he could take in all of the property. "Do you?"

"Perhaps we should do a little walkabout, sir." She pulled up the hood of her parka as a fresh gust of wind-driven snow swirled about them. The sun was shining, but there was no heat in it, and the wind, straight out of the northeast, was bitterly cold.

"Good idea," Danny said. "Let's walk fast so my blood doesn't freeze." The level rays of the low winter sun reflected off the snow and made his eyes water. He turned his back to it. "Did you see that mark at the base of his thumb?" he asked June.

"I did."

"What did that look like to you?" They paused in front of a root cellar and peered into the open door. Wooden vegetable bins had been built into the walls, but there was precious little left in each. He hoped the Fitzpatricks had some other means of supply.

June raised her eyebrows. "It looked like a bite mark, sir."

"That's what I thought too." Sheila was pregnant, but there had been no talk of a husband or boyfriend, so who was the baby's father? Or had she chosen, as some women did, to keep that knowledge to herself? Maybe she'd decided to become a single mother on purpose and felt that the details of the baby's conception were nobody else's business. "It's in a very specific area." He laid his gloved hand across his own mouth and closed his teeth together. "It's where you'd bite somebody who had their hand over your mouth, trying to keep you quiet." He stopped walking and turned to look at June. "Isn't it?"

She nodded. "It is, sir."

The freezing air stung his nostrils as he drew in a deep breath. "Yes, I thought so as well. So who's he trying to keep quiet, and why?" He pulled a face. "Don't suppose you want to go back and ask."

June scoffed. "It wouldn't be my first choice. The Fitzpatricks are friendly enough on the surface, but their secrets are their own. They wouldn't thank me for pushing in."

They had completed an entire circuit of the land at the front of the property and were just about to go behind the house when the door opened and Roy Fitzpatrick came running towards them.

"Don't ye go back there!" he shouted. He was wild-eyed, coatless, waving his arms like a madman. "Ye can't go back there! Don't go there. Stay where you're to."

Danny stopped, reaching out a hand to halt June in her tracks. "Is there something wrong, Mr. Fitzpatrick?"

He came to where they were. "We don't allow nobody there."

"And why is that?" Danny asked. "We just want to see your cow."

Fitzpatrick glanced back at the house. Sheila stood in one of the large windows, watching them, her arms crossed on her chest. "We don't allow it." He drew himself up to his full height. "You wants to go over there, you come back with a warrant."

"We're just leaving," Danny said. He raised his hands to shoulder height to show he didn't intend any further interference. "Thanks for all your help."

When he and June reached the car, he went past it, continuing on down the long driveway to where it met the main road. "Sir?" June called. "I haven't got a key."

He had little hope of finding footprints at this stage, seeing how it had been snowing since Gail Russell left the Fitzpatrick party, but Danny wasn't looking for footprints. He stopped a bit past the front gate and bent to look more closely at the ground. A bright, clean layer of fresh powder had been laid down overnight, each individual snowflake a perfect little crystal. He took off his gloves to sift through them.

"What are you looking for?" June appeared beside him.

"Sheila said Gail was smoking that night while she waited for the cab," Danny said.

"Okay."

"Just making sure."

"Sir, is it that important?"

"Maybe not." He glanced up at her. He stood up and presented the single cigarette butt on the palm of his hand. "There's only the one. Sheila said she thought Gail was smoking the whole time."

June uttered an odd noise halfway between a sigh and a groan. "Sir, with respect, that doesn't prove anything."

"No, but it tells me either Sheila Fitzpatrick wasn't paying as much attention to a guest standing out in the cold waiting as she said she was or she wasn't telling the whole truth. Unreliable witness, or being deliberately misleading?"

"Why would she lie about something like that?"

Danny wrapped the cigarette butt in a clean tissue and put it in his pocket. "I don't know. I don't know that she did. But there's something off about those two. We'll know more when we talk to the others who were at the party."

CHAPTER FIVE

IT WAS already half-past nine when Tadhg Heaney arrived for his shift at Kenneally's Bar on Thomas Street in Dublin. Tonight was a Monday evening, so he was working a short shift, but by the time he cleaned up, wiped the bar and tables, and closed out the till, it would be at least two in the morning. It was no odds to him either way. He had nothing and no one to go home to—if the word "home" could even be applied to the shitty one-bedroom flat he occupied in a building near the Guinness Storehouse.

The job he was lucky to have, landing on his feet after a hastily arranged five-hour flight from Newfoundland with Lily in tow, sobbing most of the way because they'd had to leave her dog, Easter, behind. They'd found a good home for her with June Carbage and her partner, Amy, but still and all, Lily cried to break her heart, as if the dog had died or something. As soon as they touched down, Lily was shunted off to live with her mother, Gwen, who had divorced Tom Farrage, her arsehole husband, and now made a decent enough salary working as an estate agent in Dalkey. He would have preferred to keep Lily with him, but it wasn't possible. Where he was going, she couldn't follow, and it wasn't a fit place for a young girl anyway.

"I still don't know why we had to leave," she'd lamented when the taxi dropped her at the front door of Gwen's handsome red-brick cottage at the end of Coliemore Road in Dalkey, close to the sea.

"Lily, please don't make this any harder than it already is." He wrapped an arm around her shoulders, but she twisted away from him to ring the doorbell. "I promise you will love your new school, and I'll come visit as soon as I can."

"I want to go back to our house," she said.

"We don't own Eigus anymore." It hurt like hell to even say it, but the sooner she accepted the truth, the better. "It's all gone—the house, the boat, the island. Now, you know this."

"I miss Easter." Her voice trembled on the edge of weeping. "Why did we have to give her away?"

"Because it would cost too much to fly her across the ocean. Anyway, she'd probably have to stay in quarantine for a while, and you still wouldn't get to see her. At least this way you can FaceTime with her." June had promised to stay in regular contact with Lily, who was afraid the dog would forget her. "Dogs never forget the people who love them," Tadhg had told her the day they brought Easter to June's place and handed her over. "She'll know you when you come back." But Lily wouldn't be consoled, and Tadhg hated himself. He'd shed tears over the dog too. He loved her. She was a dear little creature.

But all that was in the past now.

He went behind the bar, nodding hello to a couple of the regulars who sat propped up over their pints like they'd been there for donkey's years. They appeared late most afternoons and stayed for the bulk of the evening, drinking morosely and saying little. At first Tadhg had assumed the two old men were pals or even related, since they always sat on adjacent bar stools, but they shared no conversation and mostly ignored each other.

"Sure 'tis a fine night," Tadhg offered. He expected no reply, so he went to the till and counted up the float that Frank Mooney, the other bartender, would have left for him, and had a quick scan of the day's receipts. Kenneally's wasn't the kind of local pub where people went to socialise or catch up on the news of the day. Those who frequented the place sat in tight little knots of two and three, muttering to each other over their drinks and casting suspicious looks around the room from the corners of their eyes. Tadhg had never set much store by stereotypes, but every single person he'd ever seen in Kenneally's could have come from a Ken Bruen novel.

"Hello, Tadhg, how's yourself?" Mooney appeared from the back room, pulling on his coat. And before Tadhg could reply, "Donal said to make sure you close on time tonight. A few of Rory Taight's boys were in here earlier, making shapes. I think they got a notion to mix it up with Kenny Cooke's crowd."

"I'm to be breaking up fights now?" Tadhg asked, incredulous. "Is that how it is?"

Mooney raised his hands to shoulder height. "I'm just tellin' ye."

"Fine." That was all he needed, Taight's bunch in here kicking the shite out of Kenny Cooke. He'd pull the fire alarm if he thought he'd get away with it. "You off now?"

"Fucking right I am," Mooney said. The bar was strictly non-smoking, but he'd already fired up a Marlboro red and was sucking like it had a nipple on it. "See ya." The front door swung open, letting in a blast of cold rain, and he was gone.

Tadhg busied himself checking that there were enough clean pint glasses and shot glasses, and he made a note of the liquid levels in each of the spirit optics, just in case Donal, the owner, accused him of helping himself. Tadhg didn't drink at work, and he bloody well wouldn't touch Donal's overpriced, watered-down booze. He saved his drinking for when he was alone, with the door of his flat closed and locked against the outside world. No one he worked with was interested enough to ask where he came from or why he was in Dublin. Most people accepted his accent at face value and assumed he was from Waterford or Wexford, or even Cork. He never bothered to correct them. The reason he'd ended up in Dublin was because it was familiar, close enough in language and culture to home, and also because he was known to no one. It was also where the man who'd ruined him had fled to, and Tadhg intended to find him, supposing it was the last thing he did.

His mobile phone rang as he was mixing a vodka and orange for an older woman with a small dog and a string bag full of shopping. He handed it off, took her money, and thanked her, then checked the screen to see who'd called. It wasn't Danny, of course. It would never again be Danny, no matter how much he wanted it. The caller was a man named Stephen Power, someone Tadhg knew as well as he knew anyone in Dublin. "Well?"

Power laughed long and uproariously at this. "Have patience," he soothed. "Rome wasn't built in a day."

"I don't give a flying fuck about Rome." He gritted his teeth until his jaw ached. "Did you find him?"

"I never did," Power responded, "but I will."

"You've been saying that for three weeks. Hurry up. I'm not made of money." He and Lily had been in Dublin for several months now, and what he'd managed to raise on the sale of Eigus was dwindling fast. Lily's school fees had proved to be more exorbitant than expected, and she needed uniforms and books and all the rest of it. Then there was the rent on his flat, and public transportation, clothes, food. There was no end to the expense, and Dublin wasn't a cheap city to live in.

"I did come across some information that I hope will be useful," Power told him. "But it's got to be allowed to mature."

"How long?"

"Two, three days at the most."

"I want details," Tadhg said. An elderly man came wobbling up to the bar and laid his empty pint glass down, the sides still streaked with foam. "Mother of God, Tomas," Tadhg said to him, "ye must have inhaled that. Another one?"

Power huffed impatiently on the other end. "Are you listening?"

"Yes. Hold on." He switched out the pint glass for a clean one and placed it under the tap, then set about pulling another. His first day at Kenneally's, he'd tossed out several pints that were nothing but foam. His form had improved since then, and he could pull a perfect Guinness almost every time, stopping in the middle to let the bubbles rise, then finishing it off with a gorgeous creamy head on it. He laid it on the bar, told the elderly punter to wait, but knew from experience he was wasting his breath. The old fella snatched it up, tossed some coins on the bar, and went away, bearing his beer in front of him like the Holy Grail. "What kind of information?"

"Let's just say I've been tracking your man, and I think I've got a line on him." Power chuckled. "That's all you need to know."

"Yes, but—" Power had already hung up. Tadhg cursed quietly under his breath and went to stack some dirty glasses in the dishwasher. When he returned to the bar, the old man was back with his empty glass.

"One more and then you're cut off," Tadhg told him. "Last thing I want is you passed out on the floor." He pulled the third and final pint and put his hand out for the money. The old man spit in it instead. Tadhg snatched back the pint and put it under the bar. "Get out," he said. "You're fucking barred." He ran his hand under hot water, scrubbing vigorously with soap while his insides crawled with disgust. Dirty old fucker.

The rest of the night was quiet, and he relaxed a little. Around midnight Abi, one of the barmaids, asked if he wanted anything from the chippy next door, but he declined. The pub had mostly emptied out by then, the cold wind and driving rain keeping everyone at home. If it continued quiet like this, he'd probably close up early. No point in burning the electric, and Donal would give him shit for it anyway. Abi came back with chips, and he took one when she offered, then told her she could go home if she fancied an early night.

"Nobody here, is there?" she asked. "Just as well. You take care, Tadhg." She patted his cheek on her way out. He followed her to the door and locked it behind her, then went to sweep up and wipe down the tables before removing the night's take and putting it into an envelope. He would drop it into the bank's night deposit on his way home.

"Tadhg Heaney."

The voice seemed to come from nowhere, and he startled, turning around. A tall man about his own age was standing in front of the bar. He was wearing a rumpled green parka—the same type Tadhg and his brother Declan used to wear to school in the winter when they were boys—and faded jeans. He had the kind of weathered face that indicated a life lived hard, and there was a thin white scar running from the left corner of his mouth towards his chin. His blue eyes were hard as flint, his gaze pitiless, and Tadhg wondered if he'd come to kill him, or worse—to beat him until he wished he were dead.

"How'd you get in here? The door was locked. I should tell you that you're being filmed. All this is being filmed." He nodded at the camera mounted near the ceiling behind the bar.

"That?" The stranger grinned, revealing perfect white teeth. "That doesn't work. Never has. In all the years I've known him, Donal's been too fucking cheap to pay for anything like that." He took his hand out of his pocket and held it out towards Tadhg. "Kai McNamara." He gestured with the other hand at the spirit optics. "How about you pour us a couple Jameson and we'll talk." It wasn't a question. "I'll wait." McNamara moved to a nearby booth and settled himself into it, shrugging out of his parka. He produced a pack of Marlboros and eased one out, lit it. There were No Smoking signs prominently displayed everywhere. Tadhg didn't bother saying anything. He sensed there was little point.

"How do you know Donal?" he asked, laying down McNamara's Jameson.

"I know everybody in these parts. There's not much gets by me." He winked at Tadhg and took a long draught of the whiskey.

"Sounds like a line from a film," Tadhg said. "John Wayne or Gary Cooper. That's the one. *High Noon*. Are you the sheriff or the renegade?"

McNamara laughed. "You're funny." He pointed at Tadhg with his cigarette. "But funny won't save you now. That wee shite you were talking to, Stevie Power? He's little better than useless."

"How do you know who I was talking to?" Tadhg slid into the seat opposite. "I was told he's the man."

"You were told wrong." McNamara's pitiless blue gaze dissected him, like a cat pulling apart a mouse. He wasn't the kind of man Tadhg would enjoy running afoul of, or meeting in a dark lane some night. "Stevie boy is a lying little shite. He's been stringing you along." A bus thundered past, rattling the windowpanes. "See, Stephen has gotten himself involved with some very bad people. He's after pissing them off. He'll be dead before daylight." He grinned and drew on his cigarette. "Not much good to you then, is he?"

"And why should I trust you?" He took a slug of the whiskey, let it roll around on his tongue awhile. It warmed the inside of his mouth like a lover's kiss.

"Word's gotten round about you." McNamara drained the whiskey and put the glass down with a thump. "Dublin's a city, sure enough, but there's parts of it that are like a small town. People talk about some fella with an accent they can't quite place. You're not quite Dublin, but you're not Cork either, and there's a touch of Waterford or even Galway in the mix." He leaned his elbows on the table and gazed at Tadhg. "Who are you, Tadhg Heaney, and where do you come from? Not Ireland. That's for bloody well sure."

A sudden banging on the outside door made Tadhg jump in his seat. He craned his neck to see who was there. Three young women, scantily clad in miniskirts and high-heeled shoes, peered in at him. "We're shut!" he called. At the sight of him they leaned against the glass, made kissing noises, posturing and begging to be let in. "We're shut," he repeated. "Go on home out of it." One of the three pressed her open mouth against the window, a fleshy wet orifice, and rotated her tongue in slow circles. She was no older than Lily. Tadhg ignored her, turning back to McNamara. "I don't know who you are," Tadhg said, "and I've no reason to trust you. Now, if you've finished your whiskey, I suggest you go on your way." He made to stand up but was abruptly restrained by McNamara's hand on his sleeve.

"Your little buddy, the one who ripped you off back home? He's been a busy boy. Made enemies all over. There are impatient people who want to talk to him, but they can't do a proper job of it while you're in the way." McNamara stood up and pulled on his parka. "If you're smart, you'll go home. Get out of Dublin. Forget what you came for." He reached into a pocket, and Tadhg tensed, thinking the Irishman was going to pull a gun. Instead he pressed a small card into Tadhg's hand. "That number gets me night or day. Call me if you like, but either way I'll be in touch."

Tadhg looked at the card. It was a standard business card, simpler than most he'd seen. Kai McNamara: Fixer. That was all it said. "What's a fixer?"

McNamara zipped up his parka. "Tell your man Donal to get that lock repaired."

CILLIAN RILEY had gone with Kevin Carbage to check where the boat that held Gail Russell might have been launched from, while June was tracking down every bit of information she could find on the Fitzpatricks, so Danny went to question Doris Coombs on his own. She lived in a rented house next to the United Church, a pleasant biscuit-box with white clapboard and a turquoise door. He knocked twice and waited but heard nothing from inside. He'd finally made contact with her the previous evening, informing her that he wanted to talk and trying to pin her down on when might be a good time to do so. She was helping out with a clothing drive for the local women's shelter, she'd said, but would be home later that afternoon. It was now half-past four, and Danny worried that he might have come on a fool's errand. He stepped back and looked to the upper-storey windows, both of which were showing lights. Either she was home or she was one of those people who liked to leave the place appearing somewhat inhabited when she went out. Danny did the same. There was nothing worse than coming home in the dark to a cold, empty space that fairly rang with its own silence.

"Miss Coombs?" he called and knocked again. "It's Danny Quirke. I wonder if I might have a word."

Still no reply. He drew a deep breath, the cold air stinging his nostrils. His hands inside the woollen trigger mitts were freezing, and he had to stamp his feet to keep the blood flowing. He could have sent one of the constables to do this, but he'd wanted to get out of the office, and he always preferred to do the interviews himself rather than get the information second-hand from someone else. "Miss Coombs?"

He was about to turn and leave when the door suddenly swung open, releasing a waft of cinnamon. A young woman reached out, caught hold of his sleeve, and pulled him into the front porch. "Sh," she said, speaking in a near whisper. She put a finger to his lips. "I can't abide noise." She nodded at his feet. "Take your boots off and come into the warm. I just took buns out of the oven."

He did as she asked, then followed her towards the back of the house and into the kitchen. A wealth of home-baked goods sat cooling on the table: bread, raisin buns, cinnamon rolls, several pies, and two pound cakes, only recently tipped out of their pans.

"Have a chair," she said, sliding one out from the table. "I'll make tea."

Danny sank into the chair gratefully and allowed himself to inhale the delicious aromas. He couldn't remember the last time he'd had anything baked, and even the delicacies on offer at Strange Brew, the Cove's one and only coffee shop, didn't hold a candle to this. "You've been busy."

"Yes." She moved to fill an electric kettle at the sink. "Cold outside."

"It is, so." He watched her carefully, intrigued by the fluidity of her movements and the way her entire body seemed to flow from one place to another. Despite the cold outside, she was barefoot, and she walked with her weight shifted forward on the balls of her feet. It reminded him of how his grandmother and some of the older women in the village danced at weddings and parties, up on their toes and moving as lightly as thistledown. "I wanted to talk to you about Gail Russell."

"Of course." She leaned down and gazed into his face. "You're not long up out of a sickbed."

"No, I haven't been ill."

"You are." One hand hovered near his cheek, and he wasn't sure if she was going to caress him or strike him. Her voice never rose above a whisper as she laid the pads of her fingers lightly on his skin. "It won't be easily remedied either. Oh, you poor man. You poor man." Her eyes were blue, flecked with gold, the pupils wide and tranquil as pools of dark water. She stepped back, letting her hand drop to her side. "Tea's ready." The kettle shrilled, and she moved to switch it off, the spell suddenly broken. She deftly filled two cups, letting the tea steep while she fetched sugar and milk and brought out two plates, placing one before him. "Have a raisin bun," she said. "Those ones are your favourite."

He took one from the stack in front of him, still warm from the oven's heat, and broke it open, spread butter on it. The tea was hot and fragrant, dosed with just the right amount of milk.

"Miss Coombs, you were a good friend to Gail." He fetched his notebook out of his parka pocket and flipped it open to a clean page. "I wonder if you can recount for me what happened the night of the New Year's party at the Fitzpatricks'."

"I picked her up around half-past eight at her place," she whispered. "We were going to drive to the party together. There was a load of people there."

"I'm sorry," Danny interjected, "could you speak up?"

She stared at him. "No," she said, "I can't. My vocal cords were damaged in an accident when I was seventeen."

"Oh." He felt like two cents. "I'm so sorry. Please forgive me. I—"

"Go ahead. Ask your questions."

He tried to get it over with as quick as possible, painfully aware of his faux pas and wanting to bolt out of there. Had she left the party with Gail? No. Gail had called a taxi. Which taxi company? There was only one, Shore Taxi. Did Doris see the driver who picked her up? No. She was still inside the Fitzpatrick home. Had anyone else at the party seen Gail leave? No, not to her knowledge. "Sheila Fitzpatrick said Gail left around midnight. Is that correct?"

"No." She gazed at the pattern on her teacup. "No, it was a lot later than that. Must have been around two o'clock, two thirty."

So the Fitzpatricks had lied. Gail had actually been there much later than midnight.

"Who else was there?"

"Let me think." She got up and went to the kitchen counter, came back with a notebook and a pen. "Not as many as usual. Maybe a dozen or so, no more." Yet the Fitzpatricks had claimed there were fifty or sixty guests. "Gary Reardon. Glenn Mitchell. Anita Ryall," she said, jotting the names down. "Michelle Thomas, Alicia Jones, Pauline Thorne. How's many is that? Six. Myself and Gail, that's eight. Lisa Cluney, her brother Randy, and Doreen Snook." She finished writing and handed him the list. "That's who was there."

Danny took the slip of paper from her and examined it. "You're sure?"

She shrugged. "I got a pretty good memory."

"How long did the party go on?" he asked. "Were any of the others still there when Gail left?"

"Just me and Sheila and Roy," Doris told him. "I stuck around till about three, after Gail left, then walked home. Roy offered to drive me, but...." She trailed off.

"But you didn't want to accept a ride from him."

"No," she said, "I wouldn't get into a car with him."

"Why not?" It was too early in the game to make any suppositions, but maybe Gail's abductor was Roy Fitzpatrick. Danny hadn't forgotten the weird bite mark on the man's hand. "Were you afraid of him?"

"Not afraid of him as such." She moved her shoulders up and down like someone feeling a draught. "He's a bit strange."

"In what way?" There was a whirring noise from another room, the sound of a pendulum clock gathering itself to strike the hour. Danny held his breath, waiting for it, but it never came.

"He'd never do nothing to you," Doris said. "Nothing bad. But he got a queer sense of humour."

"Can you give me an example?" He drank some of his tea to give her time to think.

"Well, last Christmas or the Christmas before... I can't remember which one it was, not really." She glanced at him, then away. "I asked for a ride home. He wouldn't let me out of the car."

Danny's pen hovered over the page of his notebook. "Wouldn't let you out of the car."

"He drove past my front door twice. Just driving, like. Going around in circles, he was. I told him I wanted to get out, but he just laughed. He said he'd take me home when he was ready."

Jesus. "And he thought this was funny?"

"He was laughing his head off."

"And this was at night." Queer sense of humour indeed.

"Yes, it was about half-past twelve. I had to get mad with him before he'd let me out of the car." She clasped her hands around her cup as if warming them.

"Did he let you out?"

"He went around once more, then let me out."

"That sounds pretty creepy." He couldn't imagine being a vulnerable young woman and trusting someone she thought was a friend to drive her home, only to find herself held captive in a moving automobile with a lunatic. "Has he ever done that to anyone else that you know of?"

"I don't know." She turned her cup in a circle.

"Doris, do you know if Gail ever reported being watched or followed?" It wasn't the sort of question he wanted to ask the Russells. If she was like most younger people, Gail probably wouldn't have confided in her parents anyway. It was more likely she'd talk to a friend. "Any strange phone calls, online harassment that you can remember?"

A chime sounded from the oven, and she got up. "My fruitcake is done," she said. "I have to take it out." She busied herself for several long moments, keeping her back to him. It was almost like she was avoiding the question.

"Doris?" Danny prompted gently. "Did Gail ever say anything about someone watching her or following her?"

She dumped the cake onto a wire rack and put the empty pan into the sink. "She got a boyfriend," she said at last. "Had a boyfriend, I mean." Her fingers tightened on the edge of the countertop. "Roland Evans. They broke up before Christmas."

"Was Roland at the party?" Danny asked and, when she shook her head, "Was he bothering her?"

Doris turned around to look at him, one hand loosely clasping her throat. "He used to follow her home. If she went out somewhere, it was like he always knew where she went and when she was leaving, and he'd follow her. She didn't like it."

It sounded to Danny like he'd been stalking her. "Thank you, Doris. You've been very helpful." He stood up and pulled his parka on. "And thank you for the tea."

"You're welcome." She walked to the front porch with him, hovering nearby as he pulled his boots on. "I had a dream about her," she said as he was leaving. "She was lying on a bed of snow. That's a queer sort of dream. Lying on a bed of snow."

CHAPTER SIX

DANNY STOPPED back at the station after leaving Doris Coombs and handed over the list of party attendees to Dougie Hughes. "Get in touch with each of these people. Ask them what time Gail Russell left the party and if anybody went with her." He'd asked the Fitzpatricks for the names of the partygoers but wasn't holding his breath that it would arrive anytime soon. They had lied about the number of guests to begin with, perhaps because they didn't want the police talking to the actual attendees. In any case, the list Doris Coombs had given him was just as good. "If you can find out as soon as, that'd be great."

Danny continued to mull over Roy and Sheila Fitzpatrick on his way home. The information Doris Coombs had given him, along with his uneasiness about them at the first interview, had aroused his suspicions that the Fitzpatricks weren't as innocent as they claimed. Roy Fitzpatrick's behaviour at the house pretty much proved that: What was he hiding in the stable that he didn't want the police to see? Granted, Danny could go back with a warrant, but the delay would certainly give Roy plenty of time to move whatever he was hiding to another location. The bite mark on Roy's thumb was recent, and had most likely been incurred during a struggle of some kind; the dark bruise on his sister Sheila's arm suggested they'd had a physical confrontation. Did Roy abuse her? Was he in the habit of beating her when she didn't do what he wanted? And what was it he wanted, anyway? He hadn't bothered to correct Danny when he referred to Sheila as "your wife." Were they in an incestuous relationship?

It was after six, black dark and very cold, when Danny arrived back at his flat. He put his key into the lock and pushed the door open, kicked off his snowy boots and shrugged out of the heavy parka. His knees, which had always given him trouble, were aching like the devil, his burned hand hurt, and he felt about a hundred years old. He wanted to fold himself down onto something comfortable and stay there.

"You're home." Sandra came to greet him. "About time. I figured the fairies were after getting ye. By the way, ye should lock your door, though if ye had I couldn't have got in." Despite her years in Portugal, she had retained her island accent, the lilting mixture of Waterford Irish and West Country English that so intrigued and captivated people.

"You're still here." He'd hoped she'd have gone by now, though she'd told him the night before that she'd found lodging at a B and B in the village, the only one that stayed open during the winter. "Why are you still here?"

"Don't be an arsehole." She caught him by the wrist. "Come in, and let's get a look at that hand."

He followed her into the kitchen, feeling like an intruder in his own home. She had rearranged everything, moving the kettle to the other side of the small worktop and placing the table and chairs close to the window.

"You don't have to look after me." He yanked his arm back.

"Clearly someone needs to," she retorted. She was dressed simply today, in jeans and an Icelandic sweater, woolly socks on her feet. "Because ye looks like something no one owns."

He sat down at the table. The window overlooked the road, and he could see all the way to the elementary school. It had begun to snow, large flakes that drifted down like feathers, utterly silent, and there was no wind. To the left and just past the United Church, he could see the broad expanse of Meade Gardens, the old potato patch where local people still put in seed every spring, and the hills rising behind it, their tops dusted with silver. It was beautiful.

He heard Sandra rattling around in the bathroom, washing her hands and rummaging in the medicine cabinet. Then she sat down opposite him and cut through the old bandage with a pair of medical scissors. "That still looks nasty," she said, "but better than it did." The blister on his hand had broken, and fluid had seeped into the bandage. He winced when she touched it with cool fingers. "Not infected, and that's good." She applied antibiotic ointment and redressed the wound, taping the bandage down around his wrist. "Bit tidier than last time." Her smile came and went. "You're still pissed at me."

Danny drew his hand back. "No. I don't know." He sighed. "Sandra...." Maybe now wasn't the best time to pose the question that he'd been obsessing over for months. "I talked to a woman today who worked with my... with Angharad Davies at the hospital in Old Perlican. Your mother worked there too, you told me." Ever since finding out the truth of his parentage, he made sure to phrase it thus: "your mother," not wanting to lay claim to something that wasn't his.

"Yes?"

"So your mother just... what? Stole me?"

Affection and compassion mingled in Sandra's gaze. "Danny, you don't have to dig around in it if you don't want to. That isn't why I told you the truth."

"Did she steal me? Just answer the question."

Sandra toyed with the discarded bandage, rolling it into a ball. "The way Mam told it, Angharad found herself pregnant for one of the doctors on the ward, some fella from away."

"Pregnant with me."

"Yes. Back then it was different. There was no such thing as being a single mother and raising the child yourself. From what Mam said, he refused to...." Her gaze flicked to him, then abruptly away. "He wouldn't acknowledge the child."

"I see." The idea that he was unwanted—a mistake—made him feel cold and sick inside, but it was no more than he'd expected ever since Sandra told him the truth about his origins.

"Angharad asked Mam to take you. She was going to sign papers and everything." Sandra reached out and laid a hand on his wrist. Her fingers were cool. "What happened was no one's fault. Angharad wasn't in her right mind. A lot of women have serious post-partum depression."

A stab of fear lanced through him. "What are you trying to say? What happened?"

"She killed herself," Sandra said quietly. "She took an overdose of narcotics from the hospital's drug supply. Mam found her." Her hand tightened around his wrist, but Danny pulled away. So that was the answer Elsie Russell hadn't had a chance to give him. Angharad Davies was a suicide.

"I'm really tired," Danny said. He couldn't look at Sandra.

"Go and lie down for a bit," she said. She rose to put away the first aid kit. "I'm making chili for supper. It's been simmering all day. When you get up, we can have a bite to eat and talk."

"I don't want to talk." Danny rose from the table. "Not about Tadhg and not about Angharad." He headed towards the bed in its curtained-off alcove at the other end of the space and fell onto it.

"Supper in half an hour," Sandra called.

"Fine." He closed his eyes and tried to relax, but his body was so taut with stress that even his eyelids twitched. Tadhg. Angharad. He didn't want to talk about either of them, didn't want to think about any of it. He was a Welsh woman's bastard son, the unwanted child of a suicide. Lord Christ, Sandra would have done better to leave him in ignorance. And Tadhg, then. They'd promised their lives to each other, and Tadhg up and vanished, over the sea to Ireland on a moment's whim, leaving him alone. Playing him for the fool. Holding him up to ridicule and pity, everyone in Kildevil Cove knowing what happened to him—Tadhg and Moira Fraser's mess, people trafficking and Martin Belshawe....

"DANNY." SANDRA shook him awake. "Supper's on the table. Come and eat."

He came to full consciousness slowly, blinking, trying to remember where he was. He sat up, groaning with the effort, and scrubbed both hands through his hair. "Sandra."

"Come and eat," she repeated.

He shuffled into the bathroom and ran the cold water, splashing some on his face to wake himself up. The smells from the kitchen were enticing, and he realised it had been hours since he'd last eaten. When he sat down at the table, he saw that Sandra had lit candles and arranged each of their place settings to look like they were dining in a restaurant.

"This is nice," he said, although privately he wondered what the point was. If he'd been alone, he'd have probably made cheese on toast and eaten it standing over the sink.

"I hope you're hungry," Sandra said. She ladled a generous portion of chili into a bowl and put it in front of him. "I made enough for the whole town."

Fresh-baked rolls with butter, sour cream for the chili, and an apple pie for dessert rounded out the repast. Danny wasn't sure of his own appetite and felt distinctly queasy after what Sandra had disclosed, but the food was hot and tasty, and he more than did justice to the meal.

"That was really good. Thank you." The heat from the wood stove was making him drowsy, and he yawned. His pre-supper nap had done little to refresh him, only made him groggy, but it was far too early to go to bed.

"Ye need looking after, Dan. Ye looks like death warmed up, ye do, so." She stirred milk into her tea and took a sip.

"So, is this the talk you were intending to give me?" He was too full to drink the tea, so he laid it aside. "Or are you just warming up?" He knew her well, this woman he'd thought was his sister, and she knew him. "You don't owe me any familial charity, Sandra. We're not family. We never were."

She ignored the dig. "You took off the ring he gave you."

Anger flared in his gut, sudden as a struck match. "That's over with."

"Danny, he didn't leave you and run away. That's not what—"

"Well, what the hell is it, then?" He pushed back the chair and got up from the table. "We were all set to make a life together, and I wake up one morning to an empty bed and he's gone. No explanation, Sandra. Just gone." As before, he wasn't being entirely truthful. He knew exactly why Tadhg had fled.

"If you'd just listen!"

Danny began collecting their empty bowls and plates from the table and stacked them in the sink. "There's nothing to listen to. He had no reason to do what he did." He ran the hot water, squirted in some dish liquid.

"He had every reason." She picked a clean dish towel off the hook and came to where he was. "You don't know the whole story."

"I know more than you think. Sandra—"

His mobile phone shrilled, cutting him off. Cillian Riley was calling. "What is it?"

"We've found another one."

"TWO BOYS were drilling a hole," Riley said. "For ice fishing. The auger went through her forehead." He shivered. "It's not pretty."

He and Danny were crouched over a hole in the ice of Purchase Pond, just off the main road leading into the Cove. A portion of the pond and surrounding shoreline had been cordoned off and a tent erected over the site where the girl's body was located. A second tent housed members of Bobbi Lambert's forensics team.

"I wonder how long she's been in there," Danny murmured.

"It's been cold like this for a month," Riley responded. "I'd say for a good long while."

Danny turned to look at him. "Think it's related to Gail Russell?"

Riley shrugged. "Damned if I know."

They both straightened as Kevin Carbage approached. The sergeant was dressed warmly in a thick parka and ski pants with heavy boots, but the powerful lights around the crime scene illuminated the redness in his cheeks and nose.

"God, it's cold," he said. He nodded at Danny and Riley. "No signs of any other footprints, just the two lads. If anybody else has been in or out of here, I can't tell. This snow has everything covered." He stuck his hands into his armpits.

"Where are the two boys who found her?"

"I took their statements and sent them home," Kevin replied. "I'm satisfied they're nothing to do with it, but we can always contact them later if need be."

"That white house just on the road there," Danny asked, "who owns it?"

"Uhh...." Kevin was visibly shivering. "Frank and Tassie Belbin. They've been there for donkey's years."

"Okay. So they might have seen her in the area." It was the longest of long shots, Danny knew, but it was worthwhile knocking on their door to find out. "Thanks, Kevin. Look, there's a heater in the other tent, and hot coffee. Go on in and get warmed up. We might be here a while." He patted Kevin on the back, sending him on his way. "We're going to need a flatbed truck," he told Riley, "with a crane, to get this out of here." Partial exhumation would take place by first melting the ice around the body with warm water, then sawing down into the frozen pond, leaving a wide margin so as not to damage the corpse. Danny had been present at a similar case some years before, when a young boy had fallen into the aptly named Deadman's Pond on Signal Hill in St. John's. A sudden cold snap froze the body where it fell, and it took more than seven hours to extricate the corpse, still sealed in a block of ice.

"Heaney's has got a flatbed," Riley said. "The fish factory. They use it for transport, but I saw it parked day before yesterday." He reached into his parka and pulled out his mobile. "I'll ring them and see if it's available."

Danny would have preferred to borrow a truck from anyone else, but the fish plant, being close, was the logical choice. "All right," he said. "The quicker we get this done, the better. If you can supervise, I'm going to have a word with Frank and Tassie Belbin, see if they noticed anyone on the road. She might have been taking a walk and fell in."

Riley nodded. "I'll stick around here, then." He grinned. "For however long it takes."

Ultimately the entire process took several hours, and it was the middle of the night before the driver from Heaney's was able to secure straps around the enormous block of ice and lift it onto the flatbed for transport. The pond had frozen nearly to the bottom, and it had taken several men with chainsaws to work down deep enough to extricate the girl's body. It would be taken to a makeshift mortuary set up in a local boatshed, where the ice would be allowed to melt, freeing the corpse completely. Danny had contacted Regan Lampe earlier in the evening to let her know a second body was on its way, then went to find Frank and Tassie Belbin. He'd managed to catch them at home, watching TV.

Mrs. Belbin was about seventy, plump and self-satisfied, with her silver hair professionally styled and gold rings in her ears. She greeted him warmly enough at the door but didn't invite him in, even when he showed his badge. No, she told him, she hadn't seen anyone on the road going to the pond, not since the summer berry pickers, and she wouldn't have noticed anyway because she kept herself to herself and didn't have time to be, as she put it, "gawking out the window at all hours like some."

"Would your husband have seen anyone?" Danny peered past her, into the interior of the house, but could see no one else and heard nothing besides the overloud boom of the television. "Perhaps I could speak to him."

"He's in the toilet." She looked him up and down, her gaze dismissive. "He never seen nothing, either."

"Are you sure? I'd rather speak with him if I c—"

The door closed in his face.

He stopped at home long enough to shower, change, and eat a little something before returning to the police station to write a preliminary report. He'd expected to be tired after a night with no sleep, but the discovery of the second body left him curiously stimulated and unable to stay still. What little fatigue he felt he dosed with coffee until his hands and eyelids twitched and his pulse thundered in his ears. He pondered whether to take Kevin or Riley and pay a return visit to the Fitzpatricks, but the issue of what time Gail Russell had left the party was minor and could wait till later. Instead, he called the dispatcher at Shore Taxi to find out which of their drivers might have picked Gail up the night before she was set adrift in Kildevil Cove. Their bare-bones website advertised it as a "full-service taxi and limousine company," but there were only four cars in the entire fleet. A middle-aged man answered the phone and told Danny they didn't disclose that sort of information but relented when threatened with a warrant. Danny waited, listening to the shuffling of paper and the man's sotto voce complaints until he came back on the line.

"Wasn't one of ours."

"What? Are you sure?"

"Yes, I'm sure." The man coughed, a long, tubercular rattle. "Nobody was working that night. Business always dries up after the holidays is over, so they was all home. Dispatcher too."

Danny couldn't believe what he was hearing. "So you're telling me that your cabs weren't running on the night in question."

"That's what I just said."

"And your dispatcher wasn't there either? What's his name? Do you have a phone number for him?"

"Calls himself Dosh. That's not his real name, though. He's a queer hand. He don't got a phone."

"How does he know when to come to work?"

"Works the night. He just shows up. Sometimes he don't."

Danny sighed. It sounded like this Dosh, whoever he was, came and went at his own pleasure and probably got paid in cash. A lot of local people did it: piecework or temporary employment for cash on the barrelhead and no questions asked. "Do you know where he lives?"

"He won't tell me. Not here in the Cove, I don't think." It sounded as if the man couldn't care less where the dispatcher lived or what he did when he wasn't actually at work. "But he'd be the one answering the phone by nights, that fella."

"Do you have a record of the calls to your office from that night?" Danny asked.

"What night?" The man's tone hovered dangerously close to belligerent.

"Monday, January fifteenth." He'd already told him this.

"Don't keep no records if the office is closed. Try the phone company," the man said and hung up.

If the only taxi service in the area wasn't running, then who had picked Gail Russell up after the Fitzpatricks' party? Doris Coombs said Gail had taken a taxi, that neither she nor Gail would have accepted a ride from Roy Fitzpatrick on account of his strangeness. Yet Gail had called a cab, and that cab had picked her up in front of the Fitzpatrick house and taken her away, and the next time she was seen, she was near death in an open boat, floating in the harbour. In the ambulance she'd said something about a man with "no face" and picking flowers. Likely this was just the inane babble of a mind disconnected from reality, but he didn't want to simply let it go. What if the man with no face had been the one driving the cab—the supposed cab—that had picked her up from the party? The sort of person who preyed upon vulnerable young women was likely to invent some sort of camouflage to keep from being recognised.

Danny tapped the intercom to call Kevin Carbage. "Sergeant, can you convene everybody in the briefing room in five minutes? Something new has come to light with the Gail Russell case."

"Will do, sir."

He gathered his notes on the information he'd been able to amass so far and went down to the briefing room. Materials pertinent to the Gail Russell case had been arranged on one wall, including photographs of the boat, as well as those of the scene and its surroundings. The clothes she had been wearing when Danny retrieved her from the dory were with Bobbi Lambert, being tested for trace evidence, but she'd made proper forensic photographs of each item separately; these were posted as well. The silky evening dress, the high-heeled shoes, and the pink faux-fur coat had been pitifully inadequate against the frigid cold of a Newfoundland winter.

"Right, so this won't take long." He glanced around at the assembled faces: June and Kevin Carbage, Cillian Riley, constables Dougie Hughes and Sarah Avery. "Doris Coombs said that Gail Russell took a taxi home from the Fitzpatricks' party and that she left around half-past two in the morning. Not midnight, as the Fitzpatricks told Sergeant Carbage and myself." He'd located the Shore Taxi website and printed off a photo of one of their cars. "The only taxi service in the area is Shore Taxi. Now, I called them, and the dispatcher said none of their drivers were working the night Gail Russell supposedly caught a cab home." He handed the photo of the cab to Cillian Riley, who glanced at it and passed it to Kevin. "Their cars are very distinctive, as you can see from the photo: white, with a red stripe and a logo of a seagull on the driver's side door. You see this car and you know it's a cab, so you trust that it's safe to get into. So whoever picked Gail up was using a car made to look like a Shore Taxi cab, quite possibly to entice her to get in."

Dougie Hughes glanced at the picture of the cab. "But she called the dispatcher, didn't she? So it would have rung through to the taxi office. Mightn't they have a record of who called?"

"Not according to them," Danny said. "Hughes, I want you to get on to the phone company. Get a record of every number that called Shore Taxi on Monday, January fifteenth, between the hours of 10:00 p.m. and 5:00 a.m. the next morning and find out who those numbers belong to."

"Will do, sir."

"How are you coming along with the list of party attendees?"

"Haven't been able to contact anybody except for the first two on the list, and they both said Gail didn't leave until at least two thirty in the morning."

"Okay, keep at it." He glanced to where Kevin Carbage was sitting. "Kevin, what's the story with the boat? Have you made any headway with figuring out where it was launched?"

"I pulled up satellite photos of the area," Kevin said. This meant he'd gone on Google Earth, more than likely. "And myself and Inspector Riley hiked around the coast to have a look. Given the time period and the tidal streams on that date, it would have most likely been launched around Big Brook, probably down behind the old powerhouse."

Danny nodded. He knew the area well. When he and Tadhg were boys, they'd often gone swimming in the ocean near there. It was supposed to be off-limits, on account of the electrical generating station, but there was little real danger, as the plant was entirely enclosed and they'd had sense enough to stay away from the substation. Besides, most locals knew that the really dangerous area was located just behind the dam on Purchase Pond, where the water intake was. Get caught in that and you'd be pulled into the flumes and ground into mincemeat at the other end.

"Did you notice anything suspicious in the area?"

"There's a derelict house north of Big Brook," Riley said. "It's been there a while."

"Habitable?"

Riley shrugged. "I wouldn't live there. Kev and I had a look inside, but I don't think anyone's been there for awhile. Mind you, there were cold ashes in the woodstove and the walls were heavily graffitied with the usual—Fuck the Police, that sort of business. If anyone's actually living there, they're being bloody quiet about it, and they've no taste for the creature comforts."

"Think we should send forensics in?" Danny asked. Any clue at all, however small, would give them an advantage.

"Wouldn't hurt." Riley glanced at Kevin. "There's one other thing too. We noticed tire tracks leading into and out of the area, but no vehicle. I dunno, could be kids. I took photos of the tracks. Don't know if Bobbi will be able to make anything out of them or not."

"What about the house itself?"

"Took snaps of that and all," Riley told him. "I've sent them over to Bobbi to have a look."

Danny nodded. "Okay, why don't we have a look around some of the other derelict properties in the area. He may not have taken Gail to this particular house. He may have taken her somewhere else. It would be somewhere out of the way and therefore unlikely to attract attention. Most of you are familiar enough with the local area, so have a look inside any abandoned properties you know of. If we find anything suggestive, we'll get Bobbi's team in to have a look."

He turned to the large whiteboard that occupied his end of the room and drew a rough outline of Purchase Pond, including the dam and the water intake for the powerhouse. "As you all know, the body of a second woman has been found, roughly about here." He indicated the spot with an X. "We don't know yet if her death is anything to do with Gail Russell, so we're best off not making any assumptions. She may be a suicide. She may have fallen into the pond and drowned by accident. There's only one house in the area where she was found, and that belongs to the Belbins." He flicked through his notebook until he came to the correct page. "I spoke with Mrs. Tassie Belbin. She and her husband Frank live in the house right on the road that leads to the pond. She claims to have seen nothing since the summer. Wouldn't let me speak to the husband."

"Let me guess," June piped up, "he was in the toilet."

"Oh, so you know them," Danny said.

"Put it this way," she said, grinning, "they're a couple of real tight-arses. You're lucky you got that much out of her. When we were youngsters, we used to go there on Halloween, looking for candies. She never gave us the time of day."

"That was my impression too." He turned back to the whiteboard. "The location where the body was found is close to the water intake for the powerhouse. Now, that part of the pond almost never freezes completely, and the pull from the intake would have dragged her body downstream, towards the dam—*unless* the body was weighted down with something extremely heavy, which means this wasn't suicide."

"Couldn't she have put rocks in her pockets?" Sarah Avery asked.

"She could," Danny allowed, "but the amount of weight required to fix a body in place against the pull of the water intake was probably more than she could have carried herself. I think someone put her in the pond and weighed her body down so it wouldn't move." He glanced round the room. "We'll know more once Dr. Lampe is able to perform a proper post-mortem. June, you get on to the weather office and find out when that pond first froze and if there's been a thaw between then and now. That should give us some idea of when she went in there."

"Will do, sir."

"Cillian, can you and Kevin forward me a copy of the photos you took of the house and surroundings, including the tire tracks? Same ones you sent to Bobbi. I'd like to take a look for myself."

"Of course."

"Bear in mind we are still looking for Gail Russell. The discovery of this second body adds an additional victim. They may or may not be related, so treat them as separate cases until we know more."

He stopped by the break room on his way to his office and made another cup of coffee. The caffeine rush from earlier in the morning had worn off by now, and he needed to stay awake and alert until at least early afternoon. He had some overtime left from before the whole Moira Fraser debacle, so if necessary he could knock off a couple of hours early. As soon as he got back to his desk, he rang Adrian Molloy to advise him about the girl in the pond. Molloy was in a meeting, so Danny left the message with the constable who answered the phone. Then he pulled up the photographs Kevin and Riley had taken at Big Brook.

The tire tracks were clear and deeply imprinted, and there were two sets: one where the vehicle drove into the site and the other where it reversed out. The tires were the type with treads that had to be aligned a certain way—in this case, with the apex of the tread pattern pointing towards the front of the vehicle—so it was easy to see the direction in which the vehicle had travelled. The tires weren't new, as there was evidence of wear, and the front right tire had at some point picked up a nail or screw. The impression of the screw head was clearly visible in the photographs. Judging by the width, they were heavy-duty winter tires of a standard type available just about anywhere. He pulled up the forensic database of tire impressions and checked through it. According to that, these were Coldmax Arctic tires, readily available anywhere on the island, of comparable price and quality as most other general-purpose snow tires.

Danny did a quick Google search for garages and automotive supply shops within a fifty-kilometre radius of the Cove. There was Canadian Tire, located in Harbour Grace, and Mike's Garage in Winterton; a glance at both websites revealed they each sold Coldmax Arctic tires. He rang Mike's Garage, and a young woman confirmed that yes, they had sold and installed the winter tires for the entire Shore Taxi fleet. Had anyone else in the area purchased Coldmax tires? Danny sighed aloud when she confirmed that most people in the Cove and surrounding area used Coldmax, because they were relatively inexpensive as well as long-wearing and puncture resistant. So that particular tire could have belonged to anyone at all. He needed to get a look at all the taxicabs in the Shore Taxi fleet to see if one of them had a screw embedded in the tire.

In addition to the tire tracks, there was a single footprint made with the right foot, as if the driver of the vehicle had opened the door, placed one foot on the ground, then changed his mind. The sole of the boot or shoe had numerous small metal or rubber spikes, something Danny had seen before but couldn't remember where. Crampons? Was the driver into winter hiking or ice climbing? Surely he wouldn't wear metal spikes while driving. There was uneven wear on the outer side of the sole, as if the wearer's feet tended to roll outwards.

Danny sat back in his chair and rubbed his eyes. His head felt like it was full of bees, and apart from the brief nap he'd had before supper the night before, he couldn't remember the last time he'd really slept. But he had work to do, so sleep would have to wait. He called Shore Taxi. The phone was answered by the same man he'd spoken to before.

"Inspector Deiniol Quirke, RNC. Are any of your cabs out at the moment? No? I'm coming over. I need to have a look at your tires."

CHAPTER SEVEN

TADHG WOKE with the distinct feeling of being watched. He blinked repeatedly, trying to make sense of the pale oval hovering above him. Eventually it resolved into Kai McNamara's sardonic stubbled face. "Morning, beautiful," McNamara said. "Or should I say, evening."

Tadhg sat up, somehow not surprised to find McNamara in his flat. "How did you get in here? And how the hell did you know where I live?"

"'Bout bloody time you woke up," McNamara said. "I've been waiting for ages."

Tadhg had a vague recollection of coming home from Kenneally's and crawling inside a bottle of whiskey, getting shit-faced drunk, and roaming around the flat pulling pictures off the walls. Around daylight he'd collapsed into bed, then woke up a couple hours later, stumbling to the toilet to vomit copiously before passing out on the tiles. He had no idea how he'd gotten from there to his bed, but obviously he'd managed under his own steam, unless... "How long have you been here?"

"Long enough to keep you from choking on your own vomit," McNamara said. "About six thirty this morning. You should put a pillow and a blanket in there for next time."

"Oh, fuck off," Tadhg moaned. "What the hell would you know about it, anyway?"

The Irishman gazed at him steadily. "Plenty. I'd know plenty." He glanced around the flat. "Been redecorating, I see. Can't say I blame you. You want to tear down those girlie pictures and put up some shots of your dear old island." Tadhg must have looked shocked, for McNamara continued, "I've been asking around. You're a long way from home, boyo, and quite out of your depth as well."

Tadhg threw back the covers and put his feet to the floor. "I don't know what you're talking about. Listen, I need to get a shower and something to eat, then—"

McNamara's expression hardened. "We're going on a date, me and you. I've come to pick you up. So shut your gob and get your fucking glad rags on. I've not got all night. And by the way, there's something you need to know."

"What?" Tadhg stood up gingerly, wincing at the soreness in his abdominal muscles. He felt like he'd vomited his insides out.

"Your little pal Stevie Power is dead," McNamara said grimly. "The Guards hauled him out of the Liffey as he was floating past O'Connell Bridge."

"Dead."

"As a fucking doornail."

Tadhg stood up and looked out the window. The sun was going down, casting a pall of stained orange light over the city and bathing the far side of the street in shadow. In the near distance, he could just make out the spire of John's Lane Church.

"So I'm well and truly fucked," he muttered. He flinched as a pile of cloth struck him in the back. He bent and picked up the jeans and sweater.

"Get dressed," McNamara said. "It's time you met some people."

Ten minutes later they were standing in the street, the wind blowing a bitterly cold rain into their faces. Tadhg shivered, still feeling light-headed and weak from the excesses of the previous night and with little sense of time or place. The entire scene felt unreal, like he was watching everything through the wrong end of a telescope or wading through a troublesome dream. He gazed blearily at McNamara as the Irishman paused to light a Marlboro, the flame of his antique Zippo fluttering in the cold. There was a screech of tires in the near distance and the sound of a vehicle accelerating; a black sedan pulled up and all the doors flew open at once.

"Get in the fookin' car, will yez!" Hard hands caught hold of his arm and yanked him forwards, nearly pulling him off his feet. He was shoved into the back seat, and a hood was thrown over his head. He heard three distinct thuds as the car's doors closed, and then, "Lord fuck," McNamara said wearily. "We're in it now."

KAI MCNAMARA didn't seem to be nearly as bothered as Tadhg was about their increasingly weird circumstances, given that he was leaning against the wall smoking yet another Marlboro. The man who'd pulled the hood over Tadhg's head had guided him up over a set of stairs in the dark and into a room before removing the hood roughly and shoving him towards a chair. "Sit down," he barked. Tadhg didn't bother to argue.

The room was shabby, the windows covered over with old newspapers, and someone had spray painted female breasts and male genitalia on the walls in red, along with pentagrams and anarchy symbols. The remnants of a sofa rested against one end of the room, the cushions long destroyed and the stuffing pulled out so all that remained were the naked springs. Maybe they used it for torture, he thought, and fervently hoped they wouldn't use it on him.

He couldn't figure out if McNamara was in on this or not, and he cursed himself for so willingly going with the Irishman. Maybe this whole business was so they could rob him, in which case they'd be horribly disappointed, because Tadhg's wallet contained nothing but a five-euro note and a dry-cleaning ticket. Or maybe they were going to beat the shite out of him and dump his body somewhere for the cops to find.

"How about a drink?" McNamara asked the room in general. "Got anything decent about the premises?"

"Give 'im both a drink, Gerry," a second voice said. Tadhg swivelled his head and saw a dark-haired man about his own age, dressed in jeans and a tracksuit jacket, with a lot of gold chains around his neck. He sat arse-foremost on a straight-backed chair, his folded arms resting along the back, a gun in one hand. "Next thing they'll be asking for dancin' girls." He pronounced it "gairls," in a Liverpool accent.

"None o' that shite ye gave me last time," McNamara said comfortably. "Just about burned a hole in my stomach." He looked around as the first man handed out red plastic cups, filling them from a bottle of Jameson. "That's the stuff." McNamara lifted his drink. "*Slàinte Mhath*," he said in Irish and downed it.

Tadhg was given a cup. He looked into it. "Not poison, is it?"

The man on the chair sniggered. "You're the laughing boy, aren't ye?" He pointed the gun in Tadhg's direction. "Laughing boy goes boom!" He mimed pulling the trigger.

"Jonjo, give that up," the one called Gerry said. He filled a cup for himself and drank it off. "A little drink and then a bit of business."

Tadhg sipped at the liquid. It tasted of whiskey and nothing else, so he necked it. It made a nice warm pool in the pit of his stomach, which would no doubt comfort him when Gerry and the lunatic named Jonjo killed him stone dead.

"Now then." Gerry brought a wooden chair from somewhere else in the flat, placed it in front of Tadhg, and sat in it. "I wonder if you understand just what you're dealing with, you."

"I understand Stevie Power is dead," Tadhg replied, wondering why he wasn't nervous. Perhaps the whiskey had done its work already, or perhaps it was the years he'd spent in little rooms not unlike this one, hammering out business deals with men just as crude and venal as Gerry. "And I understand you might know something about that."

"What are you doing over here anyway?" Gerry asked. Jonjo sniggered behind him. "You don't belong here. I'll tell you what you should do." He leaned forward, his beefy forearms resting on his thighs. "You should get the next plane back to where you came from. That'd do you the world of good."

"I'm not going anywhere until I find out what happened to my money," Tadhg replied. He gazed into Gerry's eyes, saw an emotional flatness and the same lack of intelligence he'd encountered in any number of cheap thugs over the years. "And I'm pretty sure you don't know, so bring me to the fucker who stole from me, or send me away, or shoot me."

"Better listen to him, Gerry," McNamara said. The Irishman's blue eyes twinkled with laughter. "He wants information, and I told him we could help him out." He tilted his head to the side. "You'd help him out, wouldn't you, Gerry? After everything I've done for you."

Jonjo racked the slide on his Glock and sighted along the barrel.

"Stevie Power led you down the garden path," Gerry said with a glance at McNamara. "Now he's after taking your money. Listen, I'll tell you something, boyo, and if you've got any brains at all, you'd best pay attention. The man who stole from you is called Donny Phelan. He's small fry, nothing for you to worry about."

"Yeah, Donny Phelan," Tadhg said. "I employed him as a construction labourer." And somewhere between the start of his employment and the end of it, he'd persuaded Tadhg to hire a new accountant, a man who came highly recommended, with a wall full of diplomas and degrees from all the best universities. Between the two of them, they'd embezzled the bulk of Tadhg's operating capital and put him out of business. "He ripped me off, and I fucking want him." He wondered what he'd do when he actually got hold of Donny Phelan. Probably not anything Danny would be proud of, but that hardly mattered anymore.

"Ah, but see, that's the trouble." Jonjo rose from the chair and tucked the Glock down the back of his jeans. He came to where Tadhg was sitting and regarded him idly, hands in his pockets. "Phelan took your money and used it to set himself up in business. Only the business he's in? Happens to be the same business other folk are in, and these other folk don't care for Donny, not at all." He grinned. "They want him out of the picture by any means poss. They're looking for him."

"Donny's as hot as fuck now," Gerry continued, "and where he's gone, nobody knows. He's keeping a low profile. He figured to buy himself a few nice juicy girls with your money and farm them out, like you do."

Tadhg was confused. "Farm them…?" Then it struck him. "Oh."

"So you see"—Jonjo leaned in and touched each button on Tadhg's shirt with his forefinger, counting them off in time with his words—"being involved with Donny right now is bad for your health." He flicked the point of Tadhg's chin with his finger and thumb.

"There's only room for so much traffic on this street," Gerry said. "So I'm sorry Donny took your cash, but you'd best clear off. Take yourself back home." He gazed at Tadhg expectantly.

"No," Tadhg said.

"Are you fucking mental?" Jonjo screamed, then whipped the gun out and shoved it in Tadhg's face. "I could kill you right now. I could fucking kill you."

"Jonjo!" McNamara laid a hand on his shoulder. "I think that's enough." He caught hold of Jonjo's wrist and lowered his arm for him. "No point in losing our heads, is there?"

Jonjo stared at Tadhg, his features suffused with blood. Gerry bit at a hangnail on the side of his thumb and spit it out. Somewhere outside, a truck rumbled by, its rubber tires loud on the cobblestones.

"Right?" McNamara prompted. The easy-going manner had disappeared; his lean frame was as taut as piano wire.

"I intend to get my money back," Tadhg said, "so I need to find Donny Phelan."

"It won't be easy," Gerry said. "He's gone deep."

"Then so will I."

"He's already spent the money." Gerry again. "No chance getting it off him now."

"I'll let him tell me that."

"Do you want to end up like Stevie Power?" Jonjo, coherent again, asked. Tadhg sensed this was a rhetorical question, so he didn't reply. "Because you're going the right way for it. We want Donny Phelan ourselves, but we can't get him if you're fucking about."

"Then find him," Tadhg said through gritted teeth, "instead of pissing about."

Jonjo slid from stillness into motion, and the barrel of the Glock was pressed against Tadhg's forehead. Tadhg swiveled his gaze to look up at him.

There's a gun against your head, he thought, *so say something constructive, you stupid bastard, or Lily loses her father right here and now.*

"I can help you," he said finally. Jonjo blinked and took the gun away. Tadhg could still feel the impress of it against his skull.

"How?" Gerry wanted to know.

"I've done business all over the world. I know people. Some of them owe me favours," Tadhg told him. "I have no problem calling those favours in."

Gerry looked at McNamara. "Is he serious?"

McNamara shrugged. "Sounds like it."

"So what's in it for us?"

"I get my money back," Tadhg said, "and you get Donny Phelan."

"What if he hasn't got your money? And why couldn't these friends of yours find Donny on their own? Why involve us?"

"Then you still get Donny Phelan." The whiskey's warmth had long since fled, and now the room seemed bitterly cold, a chill that spread along Tadhg's veins, down into his legs and feet. "And I'm involving you because I'm not interested in treading on anybody's toes."

"Do you fucking believe this fella?" Gerry nodded at McNamara. "Is he soft in the head or something?" He turned to look at Jonjo, the two of them seeming to communicate silently. "Tell you what," he said after a moment, "we'll think about it, won't we, Jonjo?" He gestured towards the door. "The two of yez go on now. I'll be in touch."

"SO TELL me something," McNamara said, turning his pint glass in circles on the tabletop, "are you suicidal or insane?"

"Maybe." Tadhg grinned. They were seated across from each other in a pub a couple of streets away, drinking to take the chill off. He still felt cold and curiously disembodied, like he was watching himself from a small distance away. "You can't let fellas like that get under your skin."

"Why do I get the feeling not much gets under your skin?" McNamara lit a Marlboro with a flourish and shook out the match.

"I'm a businessman," Tadhg replied. "If I went around jumping at every shadow, I wouldn't get much done. And I wouldn't make any money. I like money. Making it, spending it."

McNamara drained the last of his pint and signalled the barmaid for another. "What are you really doing over here anyway?"

"I told you. Looking for Donny Phelan." He glanced up as the girl appeared with two pints of Smithwick's. "God love ye," he said and put some banknotes on her tray. "Keep it, love." Tadhg applied himself to his pint, sighed deeply. "And what are you doing?" he asked McNamara. "Apart from the vague job description on your business card."

The Irishman smiled wistfully. "That would take far too long to tell." He raised his pint glass. "Slàinte Mhath."

"That all you're going to tell me?"

"For now." McNamara indicated the pints on the table. "Drink up," he said. "It's getting late. I'll walk you home."

"Going to kiss me goodnight?" Tadhg asked, laughing.

"Shut your gob," McNamara growled, mock-serious now. "I'm not that kind of girl." He peered at Tadhg through narrowed eyes. "How exactly are you going to find Phelan?"

"I haven't figured that out yet," Tadhg confessed and was surprised when McNamara burst into noisy laughter.

"That," he said, when the fit had subsided, "is the kind of shite that'll get you killed in this town."

"I'm serious," Tadhg replied, feeling a little hurt that McNamara found him ridiculous. "I know a lot of people. If I ask the right questions, get some wheels turning, I can find Donny Phelan." He took a long drink of the Smithwick's and wiped his mouth with the back of his hand.

"And what are you going to do with him when you find him?"

He thought about it for a moment. "I'm going to wipe the fucking floor with him," he said. McNamara didn't laugh this time.

"You're serious," he said. He glanced Tadhg up and down. "What are you going to hit him with?"

"My fists." The idea gave him a thrill of excitement that wasn't entirely alien to his nature. He'd never confess such a thing to Danny, who would no doubt be appalled at Tadhg's propensity for violence. "This man stole from me." He leaned over the table. "He drove me into bankruptcy and destroyed my business. My daughter lost her home." His fists clenched as he remembered Lily sitting beside him on the flight across the Atlantic, sobbing into her hands. It wasn't something he found easy to forget or to forgive. No doubt Danny would tell him to leave the matter to the police, but that option didn't appeal to Tadhg. Some problems you had to solve on your own.

McNamara shook his head. "I don't think you know what you're getting yourself into." He drained the rest of his pint and stood up. "These aren't the kind of men you're used to dealing with. They don't give two fucks about doing things the decent way. They'll blow your brains out."

Tadhg swallowed what was left in the glass and got to his feet, reaching for his coat. "I can handle myself." He remembered the cold barrel of Jonjo's gun against his forehead and wished he felt as confident as he sounded. They went out into the night, McNamara holding the door for him. The rain had stopped, and the wet streets and pavements gleamed under the reflected light of nearby pubs and shops. He and McNamara walked in silence for a while, each sunk in his own thoughts.

"Will you help me?" Tadhg asked finally.

McNamara turned to gaze at him, his expression grave, and Tadhg wondered what the Irishman was thinking about to turn him so darkly sombre. "Probably," he said, then, "more than likely."

They had reached Tadhg's building by now, and he paused in front of his door. "What are you getting out of this?"

"Maybe I like the company." McNamara tilted his head, waved, and walked away, his lanky frame readily swallowed up by the night.

DANNY WAS dreaming he was sitting at a card table in a shabby flat somewhere, playing cards with a group of men he'd never seen before. There was a pile of money in the middle of the table, bills of various denominations from different countries in the world: euros and American dollars and Swiss francs and British pounds. He glanced down at the cards in his hand: an ace of hearts, an ace of spades, an eight of clubs, a four of hearts, and a two of diamonds. Nothing.

The bald man across the table from him was huge, his bulky muscles straining at the seams of his blue shirt. He nodded at Danny and said, in a Russian accent, "You're all done, boy." Someone grabbed him from behind, clamping a hand over his mouth, and then he was being dragged backwards through a series of corridors that got progressively smaller and narrower, until he could go no farther. There was laughing, and he heard the Russian saying, over and over, *You got nothing, boy.*

He woke with a gasp and sat up. No one's hand was over his mouth. There was no Russian. He was alone in his flat. He drew several deep breaths to calm the anxious hammering of his heart and looked around. The clock on the nightstand read 6:00 p.m. He'd slept for most of the day. Obviously, he'd left the radio on somewhere because he could hear music. There was a radio in the kitchen, but he didn't remember leaving it on. The only time he listened to it was when he was eating breakfast. Had he turned it on when he came home? Probably not. So where was the music coming from?

He picked up his mobile phone off the nightstand and turned it over. No missed calls, no voicemails, no texts, and the phone wasn't playing music. Perhaps he'd dreamt it? But his dream had been so vivid that he could still see images from it now, in his mind's eye: the enormous Russian, his muscles straining at the seams of his shirt; the cards in his own hand; the pile of money on the table. He threw off the duvet and looked down at himself, remembering that he'd gone to sleep fully dressed. The music continued, a lilting old-fashioned melody that seemed oddly familiar. As he got up and moved towards the kitchen, the tune grew louder, and he could hear its other elements now, a strange hissing crackle, like someone crumpling cellophane between their hands. The woman's voice was a high soprano, clear and agile despite the uneven quality of the recording, and now he was close enough to hear the words: "'Tis the last rose of summer left blooming alone/all her lovely companions are faded and gone."

There was an object on the kitchen table, an old tape recorder of the type his grandfather had owned, with a slot for a cassette tape and a flexible plastic carrying handle. Danny had never seen it before in his life. Certainly he had no use for such an item and couldn't imagine where it had come from. He leaned over it, listening, watching in fascination as the tape spooled from one reel to the other. "No flower of her kindred, no rosebud is nigh/to reflect back her blushes and give sigh for sigh."

The front door of his flat yawned wide to the cold evening air. He'd left it unlocked again—nothing worth stealing, but he hadn't thought about the possibility of anyone leaving him something. Someone had been here and left the tape recorder. Why? Possibly it was a message, but what sort of message? The song had no personal significance to him. He knew it, had learned it in music class at school, and now and then some folk band somewhere saw fit to resurrect it, put their own personal spin on it. It was beautiful, yes, but undeniably morbid, the tale of someone who destroys a single rose out of kindness, rather than allow it to suffer its continued loneliness. His late wife, Alison, had always loved the song, but Danny thought it depressing. Picking a flower to kill it and thus save it from suffering....

Pick the flowers.

The song came to an end, and the tape player clicked off. He stared at it, his entire body suddenly hot despite the cold air pouring through the opened door. Pick the flowers. Pick the rose and kill it so it doesn't suffer. Death as a cure. The last rose of summer, left all alone, so pick it, kill it, put it out of its misery.

He fumbled for his mobile and punched in Cillian Riley's number, started speaking as soon as Riley picked up. "Cillian. Someone came in and left me a tape. A song. There's a song on it. 'The Last Rose of Summer.' Get Bobbi and forensics over here right now. Fingerprints."

"Sir?" Kevin Carbage's confused voice reached his ear as from a long distance. "Sorry, I picked up Cillian's phone."

"What?"

"I'm at his house. We just finished supper. Hang on, let me get him for you."

There was a shuffle on the other end, and he heard Riley murmur something. "Danny? What's wrong?"

He repeated what he'd said to Kevin, added, "Someone's been in my flat. I woke up and the song was playing. It's definitely a message."

"I'm on my way," Riley said and rang off.

He and Kevin Carbage showed up at Danny's door five minutes later, heavy parkas thrown over their civilian clothes. Danny had already gone outside and examined the ground around his front door for footprints, but it had been snowing for a while, and whatever impressions the intruder's feet might have made were long since obscured.

Bobbi's team bagged the tape recorder and the tape to carry away for trace evidence. "They must have copied it from an old wax-cylinder recording," she told Danny, "or something of similar vintage, judging by the sound quality. I didn't think there were any surviving recordings of her."

"Who?"

"Georgina Stirling," she told him. "From Twillingate. Newfoundland's first opera prima donna. Went as Marie Toulinguet. Don't you even know your own history?"

He dimly remembered the name from a Newfoundland culture course they'd had to take in grade ten. "Marie Toulinguet, yes." Why would someone leave him a recording of her singing an old Irish song? It made zero sense. "From Twillingate, you said." There had been something in the news recently about that town, something significant, but he couldn't remember what it was. Unlikely it had anything to do with this, though, and he wasn't about to jump to any conclusions.

"Yeah," Bobbi replied. "Oh, she was the real deal. Sang all over the world for kings and even the pope." She handed the bagged tape recorder to a forensics tech, who carried it outside to the police van. "Are you all right?"

"I'm fine."

"You don't look fine." Bobbi raked a hand through her short red hair. "By the by, that clothing from the girl in the boat. Something interesting came back, but I wasn't sure about it."

"What was it?"

"Carpet fibres. Automotive carpet. Queer thing is, they don't match any fibres in our database, so either it's a foreign car or it's an older model, maybe refurbished, some kind of vehicle no longer in regular circulation."

A brief spark of excitement fizzed along his nerves. "Really?"

"Yup. I sent it to the RCMP lab. They're better equipped than we are. Hopefully they'll turn up something." She glanced around. "That's everything I can do here for now. Do you need me to stay?"

"No, go on home to Stan and the kids." Eighteen months ago Bobbi had given birth to twin boys, whom she doted on. It wasn't fair to keep her from her family. "You'll be just in time to tuck the boys in."

"*Pffft.*" She laughed. "Tucking them in isn't the hard part. It's getting the little friggers to go to sleep." A quick glance around to ascertain she'd left nothing behind and she was gone, leaving Cillian Riley, Kevin Carbage, and Danny.

"We can stay if you want," Kevin said. He hovered close to Riley, a hand on the other man's back.

"We've no big plans," Riley said, "so if you want us to hang about for a bit?"

"No, you two go on." Danny waved them towards the front door. "I'm fine. There's nothing dangerous happening here. It's just… weird." He forced himself to smile at them. "Weird is something I can handle." He refrained from commenting on their apparent relationship. They'd been dancing around each other for a while, but whatever was between them now was their business, not his. He wished them luck with it. "I'll be all right. If I need saving, I'll call you."

They took themselves off then, Riley reminding Danny to lock the door and check to make sure the windows were secure. This last made him smile. The flat was a rough conversion of a former fishing shed. He was lucky it even had windows. But he made a circuit of the place anyway, checking the big picture window overlooking the road and the smaller ones at the back of the building. Whoever had left the tape recorder hadn't come in that way. They'd used the front door and left it gaping wide on purpose so Danny would know they'd been there. It was intended to make him unsettled, and it had succeeded. From now on he wouldn't be able to move around the place without feeling as if he were being watched, his every move scrutinised.

That the song was a message he had no doubt, but who had sent it, and what were they trying to tell him? Did it have to do with Gail Russell's final words to him as they put her in the ambulance? He had no way of knowing, and any conclusions he might draw at this early juncture were likely to be unwarranted.

He shoved another birch log into the Jøtul and took the kettle to the sink to fill it with water. The carton of milk he kept between the panes of the kitchen window was still good, and a cup of tea would help calm his mind. That was the beauty of tea. It was helpful in just about any situation. He gazed out at the falling snow while waiting for the kettle to boil. There was no foot traffic passing along the road outside, no vehicles of any kind, just emptiness and the silent drift of snowflakes tumbling to earth.

Tadhg loved it when it snowed, was forever on at Danny to get dressed up warm and go for a walk with him. He never regretted it, being with Tadhg in that white silence, in no hurry to go anywhere, content to simply be in the moment. If he wanted to go for a walk in the snow now, he'd be going by himself, and it wasn't the same. It wasn't the same at all. It never would be again.

The kettle's shrill whistle snapped him out of his self-pitying reverie. He plucked it off the stove and poured hot water over the teabag in his favourite china mug. A quick survey of the cupboards revealed there wasn't much in the house for eating except Sandra's leftover chili, stored in neatly labelled containers on a shelf by the window. The one place that sold takeout food was closed by now, the woman who owned it likely gone home to her family like Bobbi Lambert was, and Kevin, and Cillian Riley. They all had someone waiting for them, wondering when they'd be back, worrying for their safety, bothering about them….

His mobile buzzed in his back pocket, and he pulled it out: a text message from an unknown number. Maybe this would be a follow-up to the tape recorder. He swiped the green circle to accept and open the message, which consisted of a single line of text: "When true hearts lie withered and fond ones are flown/Oh who would inhabit this bleak world alone?"

The sender had included a photograph of a man standing in front of a large white building that Danny recognised as his late grandfather's old stable. The man was dressed in work wear—jeans and a toolbelt, a grubby T-shirt, steel-toed boots, and a white hard hat.

Tadhg.

CHAPTER EIGHT

SANDRA'S REACTION to the text was about what Danny had expected. "Lord Christ, Dan. This is a threat. He's clearly in danger from whoever sent you this."

"Don't you think I've considered that possibility?" He glanced up from the coffee he hadn't touched. "I've been awake all night trying to figure out who might have sent this and what they want." He raised the cup to his lips, stopped short of actually taking a sip. "I've got Dougie Hughes working on unblocking the number it came from, and I've been in touch with someone in Dublin to keep an eye on him." He glanced around Strange Brew, his gaze resting on Jennice, the owner of the café, behind the counter up front. It was ten thirty on a cold January Thursday, and he'd agreed to meet his sister for coffee somewhere besides the police station.

"Tadhg is in Dublin?" she asked. "You know that for sure?"

"Yes," Danny admitted. "I have for some time."

"Ye could have told me that," Sandra said.

"I know. I'm sorry."

"Somehow I doubt that." She didn't sound angry, though. Sandra took a sip of her flat white and set the cup down, swiping milk foam from her top lip with an index finger. "Who do you know in Dublin? A cop?"

"No, not a cop. Not exactly." He wasn't doing justice to Strange Brew's great coffee. He forced himself to take a sip and then another. His stomach felt like a bag of live eels this morning. "Someone I used to know. I trust him. He's a good man."

"That doesn't reassure me, Danny." Sandra's gaze bored into him. She swiped a long tendril of her light red hair back behind her ear. "And it shouldn't reassure you."

"I'm not reassured," he snapped. "I know the people he's involved with over there, and I know the kind of danger he's in. If he had—" *If he had any brains at all he'd cut his losses and get the hell out of there.* This was what he wanted to say, but he didn't dare utter it out loud. It was a testament to Tadhg's innate stubbornness that he'd gone after the man who'd stolen from him. He could never let things go, was never content to let the police or some other official agency handle it. Oh no, not Tadhg. He had to wade in up to his hips and, like as not, get into more trouble than he was prepared to handle. "He should have let the police handle it."

Sandra gave him a sardonic look. "You know what he's like. He's got nothing left to lose now."

"Except his life." Saying it aloud made it real, and he shuddered as a sudden cold wave passed over him. He pushed the coffee away. "I should go over there."

"Maybe you should." She raised an eyebrow. "Or maybe ye'll get yourself into the same pickle. I'm worried for Tadhg, sure. But you're still my only brother, Danny, whether you want it or not."

He was saved from responding by his mobile phone's insistent buzz. He picked it up: Regan Lampe. "Regan." There was no point in offering her a greeting or other nicety. Regan had no use for social conventions. "What's on the go?"

"The girl is finally thawed out," she said. "Enough for them to move the body to a hearse. We're taking her to Carbonear General this morning." The body had been set to thaw in a temporary mortuary in a boat shed.

"So you'll do the autopsy today?" He fumbled in his pocket for some cash and laid a handful of coins on the table, then stood, reaching for his parka with his free hand.

"I'll do the autopsy when I have time to do it," she said sharply, "so don't get ahead of yourself. Anyway, that's not why I called. Once the ice melted, they were able to lift the body out. The girl had a backpack with her. I figured you'd want to see it."

"I do." A backpack. Hopefully it would provide the means to identify her. "I'm on my way."

"Hurry up, then. I haven't got all day. As soon as the hearse gets here, we're gone."

Danny closed out the connection. He hoped he had time to get to Regan and the corpse before the hearse arrived, but he needed to move. "That was Regan Lampe. I have to go. Are you okay here on your own?"

Sandra rolled her eyes. "I guess I'll have to be."

"It's work. I'm sorry." He bent and kissed the top of her head. "Maybe we can have supper tonight?" He zipped up his parka and pulled on his woollen hat. The temperature outside was a chilly -18 Celsius, with a stiff wind from the northeast. He had no desire to expose any more flesh than was strictly necessary. "I'll try and get back at a reasonable hour." Without waiting for her response, and with a wave to Jennice, he left the warm café and went out into the cold.

"WE HAVEN'T moved her. She's still over here." Regan met Danny at the door of the boat shed. The huge block of ice in which she'd been encased had dissolved, freeing the corpse, as well as a collection of sticks, pebbles, and silt from the bottom of the pond. "The backpack was lying beneath the body."

"So she was wearing it when she went in." Danny crouched as far as his painful knees would allow and looked into the dead girl's face. The cold water temperature had preserved her features and had even fixed in place her final facial expression. She looked placid, resigned, not like someone who had struggled and fought to breathe in her last moments. "Can you help me take it off?" She'd worn the pack with the straps pulled over both shoulders, so Regan sat the corpse somewhat upright while he pulled the bag free.

"Aren't you afraid of disturbing evidence?" Regan asked.

"I'll get Bobbi's crew to collect whatever debris remains after you remove her to the morgue, and we won't handle the backpack any more than is strictly necessary," he replied. "I'm hoping there's something in here that will identify her."

They both glanced up at the sound of a vehicle outside. "That'll be the hearse," Regan said. Two of the Green brothers from Winterton appeared, wheeling a mortuary cot between them. They greeted Danny and Regan quietly, then lifted the girl's body with all the gravitas their profession demanded, zipped her into a body bag, and laid her on the cot. Danny waited while Regan gave them instructions, and once they left, he called Bobbi Lambert to send two forensics technicians to the site to collect whatever evidence remained.

"You okay for now?" Regan asked, once this was done.

"Yep. Thanks, Regan. I'll be in touch." He turned to go, then stopped and turned back. "When you do the post-mortem, can you take a look inside her mouth?"

"I usually do," she said. "Why?"

"Let me know if there are any teeth missing." *Pick the flowers.*

"Same as the last girl?"

"Same as the last girl."

AS SOON as Danny returned to the station, he took the backpack to Bobbi's lab and they opened it together. It was loaded down with rocks, each the size of a softball or larger, of the type found along the path leading to the pond. He wondered if there were additional stones in her pockets, which would fit with the pattern of drowning suicides. Even someone who wanted to die would find it extremely difficult to sink down into the water and remain submerged long enough for their lungs to fill with water. The primitive breathing reflex would drive them to the surface, which was why people intent on drowning themselves usually added extra weight.

"We've had a look at the tape recorder," Bobbi said as she deftly turned the now empty bag inside out. "No joy there, I'm afraid. He must have worn gloves, because we couldn't find even a single fingerprint."

"I expected as much," Danny replied. He watched as Bobbi examined the interior seams of the knapsack carefully before reaching for a long pair of tweezers. She plucked something from the lining and held it up. "Well, look at that."

Danny squinted. "I don't see anything," he said.

Bobbi passed him a magnifying glass. "Look again."

When he peered through the glass, he could see what looked like a tiny tuft of wool, no more than a millimetre or two across. It was dark blue, almost black. "What is it?"

"Carpet fibre."

"So her killer left a trace behind," Danny said.

Bobbi smirked. "They always do. Let's see what else is here."

Despite what he had hoped, the pack contained nothing that could identify the girl, only a scrap of waterlogged paper, folded and stuck together. Bobbi promised she would try to prise it open and examine it as soon as it dried. Besides that, there was a faded photograph of a young woman in 1970s clothing, standing in front of a Christmas tree. He made a copy of the photograph and took it with him to the briefing room, where the others had been gathered. The recent spate of frigid weather hadn't done people any favours. Cillian Riley was stuffed up with a miserable head cold, and Dougie Hughes had a cough that made him sound like a Victorian-era consumptive.

"I'm still working on it, sir," he said, when Danny asked about the text he'd received from a blocked phone number. "It's encrypted from arse to altitude, but I think I know how to get around it. I might have something later on this afternoon." He had also gotten in contact with the phone company and was able to furnish Danny with a list of numbers that had called Shore Taxi on the night Gail Russell was assaulted. "Followed up on them, but there's nothing too surprising. There were six in all. Five were local people who said they forgot the taxis weren't running, and the last was Gail Russell's mobile phone."

"So she did phone the taxi stand," Danny mused. "And got an answer from somebody, even though it was closed. Maybe the number forwards to the dispatcher's mobile when the office is closed?"

"Something about that, sir," Hughes continued. "I talked to a buddy of mine who works for the phone company. He said it's possible to hack into somebody's phone and reroute calls using the call-forwarding feature."

"So Gail could have been calling the taxi company but her call actually went elsewhere?" If so, it meant her attacker was technologically sophisticated and knew his way around complex modern telephone systems and computers.

"Exactly, sir. I also called the taxi company and spoke to the owner, and he said their calls don't get forwarded after hours," Hughes told him. "If the taxi stand is shut, there's no cars on the road anyway."

"Still and all, Gail spoke to somebody. She called the taxi stand and a taxi came and got her. Whether he knows it or not, that call was answered on the night that Gail Russell died—and it's highly likely whoever answered it is the same person who abducted her and put her in that boat." Danny didn't put too much store in anything the taxi company owner said, and he wasn't about to take the man's word for it that no taxis had gone out from the stand that night. "Get on to the phone company again, Hughes. That call went somewhere. We need to know where it went and who answered it."

"Yes, sir. Oh, and those names you gave me." Hughes brandished his notebook. "The people at the party? I've been in touch with most of them. Gail didn't leave the party any earlier than two thirty or three in the morning. She was outside waiting for a cab for about half an hour."

"Okay, thanks." Waiting half an hour for a cab that wasn't running, from a cab stand that was closed and that arguably forwarded the calls to either an answering service or a second number. Whose? "So someone picked Gail Russell up very early in the morning and took her away in a vehicle that was either a legitimate taxicab from Shore Taxi or looked enough like one for her to get into it." He paged through his own notes on the case. "Further to the forensic photos of the tire tracks, the prints were made by Coldmax Arctic snow tires, a readily available brand you can get anywhere around here. Shore Taxi uses them. I had a look at all their tires, but none of them picked up a screw, and none of them had been in to have the tires switched over. We're probably looking at a fake, a separate vehicle done up to look like a Shore Taxi." The owner hadn't been exactly cordial when Danny showed up, asking to see all four cars in their fleet, complaining about "police harassment" and how his civil rights were being violated. "A lot of local people use these same tires, but it's a waste of time asking if anybody's car has a recent puncture. Besides, I don't want this detail getting out, not yet. Let whoever drove that vehicle think he's in the clear." He turned a page. "Kevin, any sign of a boat yet?"

Carbage shook his head. "Not so far, but we're still looking. Myself and June have been going door to door, but nobody's had anything stolen. I think it's just too cold for people to be out very much." He glanced over at his sister. "We might need to go a bit farther afield."

"Let's wait until you've covered everybody in the Cove first before we go up and down the shore," Danny said. "More than likely, somebody knows something, so we want to make sure we don't scare them off."

Sarah Avery lifted her hand. "Sir, Constable Hughes and I have been looking into derelict properties like you asked." She glanced across at Hughes, who nodded at her. "There are three within Kildevil Cove itself and one on the outskirts, a seasonal cabin located on the shore of First Pond."

"That's pretty far in the backcountry, isn't it?"

She nodded. "It is, sir, so I'm thinking we can probably rule that one out. Our killer needed somewhere close to the sea so he could set Gail Russell adrift in a dory. This wouldn't be practical to his purposes."

"What about the others?"

"A fishing stage located on Offer Island—it's not really an island—and an abandoned house off the main highway, right down by the water. It used to belong to the Landry family years ago. The third one was a hangout back in the 1980s, on the road between the Cove and New Melbourne. It's been closed since the 1990s and boarded up."

"Bobbi?" He located her in the assembled group. "Can we get forensics into the old Landry house and the other two, to swab for DNA and trace?"

The forensics chief huffed out an audible sigh. "I'm up to me arse, but I'll see what I can do."

"Thanks, Bobbi. I really appreciate it." This wasn't mere lip service; he understood how difficult it was for a small police detachment to operate with limited funding and even more limited personnel. His team so often went above and beyond, and it hadn't escaped his notice.

"Okay, the girl we found in Purchase Pond," he continued. He put the photograph up on the whiteboard. "Dr. Lampe has taken possession of the body. There was a backpack found with her, and we've opened it, but so far there's nothing to indicate who she was. We will broadcast her photo and hope that someone comes forward who might know her. In the meantime, we found this picture—" He projected the image of the young woman in 1970s clothing so they could all see it. "—in the bag, along with what might be a letter. Right now it's being dried out, but Bobbi is hopeful we'll be able to get some idea of what's written there.

And you all know about the tape recorder that was left in my flat. The song that was playing is an old Irish traditional tune that might possibly reference the first victim. When Gail was being loaded into the ambulance, she said something to me about picking flowers. The song makes direct reference to that. In addition, the recording is of opera singer Georgina Stirling, stage name Marie Toulinguet, from Twillingate. This could possibly be another connection. Either way, the tape recorder is definitely a message meant for me. What that is, I have no idea." He smiled and offered a shrug. "Sorry. Not much good, I know."

"Sir, I got hold of Gary Lockwood at the weather office," June piped up from the back of the room. "According to their records, Purchase Pond froze in late December, just before Christmas, and we haven't had a thaw since then. So it looks as if the second victim has been in there for at least a month." This tallied with Riley's estimated time of death at the scene.

"Good. Dr. Lampe will be able to narrow down the time frame a bit more, I hope." He didn't know if this would be possible but felt compelled to give them something. Trying to determine time of death from a corpse that had been in water was a tricky process, even for someone as skilled and astute as Regan, and this one had not only been in water, but had frozen there. About the only thing she had to go on was stomach contents, and that was only useful if the victim had eaten two to three hours before she died.

"Sir?" Sarah Avery. "Would it be useful to try and determine where the tape recorder was purchased? If someone bought it recently—" She stopped herself there, probably realising that finding a store that even sold such an archaic model was futile.

"It was more likely the tape recorder belonged to someone the attacker knew," Danny replied gently. "Maybe an elderly relative."

"Of course, sir." She blushed. "Sorry, sir."

"One more thing. Constable Hughes may have mentioned that I received an anonymous text message from someone possibly related to these two cases. We don't know who sent the message or what the reason was." He wasn't about to tell them he'd received a photo of Tadhg and an implied threat that Tadhg's life was in danger. His personal life was off-limits. "I'm leaving that aside until we know more. For now, keep digging into Gail Russell's disappearance. I'm going to track down her boyfriend, Roland Evans. I want to speak to him as soon as possible. Everybody keep me informed, especially if you find something significant, and even if you don't."

He approached Bobbi as the meeting broke up. "Would if help if I recruit a few bodies to help you with the workload?"

"How are you going to do that?"

"The university's currently running a forensic-science program. Maybe I can pull a few of their students to come and give us a hand." Field work of that sort would likely be worth transferrable credits. "What do you think? They wouldn't get in your way—just do the technical stuff, collecting trace and swabbing for DNA."

Bobbi smiled like a thousand-kilo weight had just rolled off her. "That would be fantastic. Thank you, sir."

He left her at the door to the lab and went to phone Dr. Leyden, a forensic anthropologist who'd taught Danny at university. "Winter break is coming up," Leyden said after they'd exchanged greetings, "and some of them would love a chance to do fieldwork. How many do you want?"

"How many have you got?" In the end, Leyden promised to send four senior students who would agree to work for room and board. Danny would find them lodging with local families, and their presence would help take some of the workload.

"They'll be on the next bus from town," Leyden said and rang off.

DANNY HAD been back to visit the Russells since the first time, and Gail's father confirmed that Roland Evans worked part-time as a truck driver for the Heaneys. Since there wasn't much currently on the go at the fish plant, it was likely he'd find Roland at home. He lived in a rented house on a narrow rural lane in a part of the Cove called the Meades. The house was a standard single-storey cottage, badly maintained, with peeling paint and a fence that looked to be held together by rubber bands and prayer. There was no vehicle in the drive and no evidence that anything besides the council snowplough had been there. Danny parked on the road outside and went to the kitchen door. The kitchen was the traditional place for Newfoundland families to gather, even in more modern homes. The front entrance was seldom if ever in use and in many cases was blocked off inside by furniture. He knocked on the door and waited, but there was no response. When his second appeal for entry went unanswered, he turned the door handle. It was unlocked, and he went inside. "Mr. Evans? It's Inspector Quirke from the RNC. I'd like to have a word with you."

The house's interior gave the lie to its external appearance. The porch and kitchen were spotlessly clean, the tiled floor gleaming, and everything was in its place. The room had been painted beige, but not recently. Paler rectangles on a couple of the walls indicated that pictures or other decorations had hung there until very recently. He crossed to the stove and felt the kettle—cold. No smell of recent cooking, nor any other clue, suggested human activity. A small sitting room was situated off the kitchen, with an old-fashioned sofa set of the type that was popular in the late 1960s: upholstered in scratchy green polyester and featuring several round throw pillows with knitted covers. The wallpaper showed brighter patches where pictures must also have hung. Was Evans preparing to move? Was that why he'd taken them down? Or had he merely gotten tired of looking at the same images and planned to change them for something else?

"Mr. Evans? Are you at home?" A narrow hallway led to a trio of small bedrooms at the back of the house. Like the kitchen and sitting room, the first two were empty, both beds made with a chenille bedspread, pulled tight. The curtains were drawn, presumably to block out the glare from the fresh snow outside. Or maybe not. Some people liked more privacy than others. At the end of the hall was a bathroom containing a bathtub, toilet, and pedestal sink with a small vanity counter, on which had been arranged an electric razor, plugged in and charging, a comb, and a blue toothbrush standing upright in a water glass. He opened the medicine cabinet but found nothing more exciting than dental floss and a bottle of aspirin.

That left the third bedroom. Unlike the first two, the door of this room was closed. Danny withdrew a pair of nitrile gloves from his coat pocket and put them on. He laid his palm against the lintel and leaned in, listening.

"Mr. Evans? I'm going to open the door."

Situations like this made him nervous, not knowing what he would find. Some people ran to hide, while others might bolt out a window or make their escape through the basement. Several times he'd been surprised by a suspect suddenly bursting out of a closet or wardrobe or sliding from under a bed. A desperate, panicked person might do anything to get away, and all too often they were armed.

He pushed the door open slowly, keeping it between himself and whoever might be inside. "Roland? Are you in here?"

His mobile phone buzzed, and he cursed aloud, snatching it out of his pocket. "Yes?"

"It's Riley." He sounded apologetic. "Haven't managed to track down Roland Evans yet."

"I'm in his house," Danny replied. "I think—" He stopped talking as the still figure on the bed claimed the whole of his attention.

Whatever else Roland Evans might have been, he was no longer a threat to Danny or anyone else. He lay on the bed fully clothed, his arms and legs flung wide, eyes open and staring. He had been impaled through the throat by a long screwdriver and was as dead as it was possible to be.

"I've found him."

CHAPTER NINE

THE CLOCKS needed winding, but they always did. It was important. It was one of his responsibilities, now that *she* was gone. Wind the clocks and take his insulin. Wind the clocks and put the needle in the soft flesh of his lower belly, even though it hurt. Always wind the clocks first thing in the morning, and that wasn't as easy as people might think. Some of them had complicated keys, which he always kept in the little compartment at the back. That meant taking the clocks down. They had to be cleaned as well. Some of them were fast while others were slow, and it was difficult to get them all to run on time. Things had to be done correctly. She taught him that, and if ever he wasn't paying attention, if he wasn't listening and looking, she'd up hand and clout him a good one, or take him by the scruff and haul him into the bedroom and smack him. She never used her hand for that. She had a leather belt the old fella left behind, and she'd strip him naked and make him put his back to her, and she'd whip and whip until her arm got tired. She told him stories while she did it, stories about him. *You are an ugly fucking cunt, my son, and you will ever be that way. There is no salvation for you, not in this world or the next. You turns my guts, you do so. You makes me want to vomit.*

It wasn't always like this. Years ago when they lived over on the other shore, he could go to school. He was still like everybody else then, before the Bad Thing. She always said if it wasn't for the Bad Thing.... No. He refused to remember. Besides, he had a new one to add to his tin, a fresh flower plucked that same morning and another innocent put out of his misery. This was important; he was doing God's work. Be gentle, be gentle. Sometimes they fought, and it wasn't easy, but he had to do it. It had to be done. The world was too harsh for them, and they were so alone, as lonely as he was, empty inside. He heard it when he listened late at night, when they called out for someone to help them. They were calling for him. Roland Evans called for him, just like the Russell girl, and like the others. None of them knew there was an end to their suffering until he came. The man without a face, without a name. Someone nobody knew.

He plucked the tooth out of the tin and held it in the hollow of his palm. There was a smear of blood on it, and part of the flesh had come away as well, but it didn't matter. He'd clean it later and purify it. When he had enough, he'd make a picture of them, perhaps on a piece of dark velvet so it would look like stars, like stars in the sky, like night. It was night when the Bad Thing happened. He understood, because she explained it to him, that the Bad Thing was punishment for what the old fella did. The punishment would be visited upon the children and the children's children, until ten or even twenty generations, because what the old fella did was so bad.

There would never be anything he could do that was as bad as that.

He'd used his time wisely these past few days. The Russell girl, her pretty eyes now closed forever, and Roland Evans, a spectacularly weak vessel holding nothing. He was a God-fearing one, religious, and that was part of the clean-up there as well. *Leave no trace*. Roland had a Bible in every room, and holy pictures on the walls in the kitchen and the sitting room, a crucifix hanging over his bed, a grotesque thing with a naked suffering Jesus writhing under his crown of thorns. He'd taken them all down, hiding them in the bag he carried with him, to be disposed of later. He always wore white during these excursions, when it was time, when his hour had at last come round and he could hear them singing. Every single person alive on the planet had a song. That's what she had always told him. Every living thing possessed its own song, and she would know. She had been a music teacher, and she wore white, the colour of purity.

He had been conceived in sin. He knew this. She never failed to remind him of it. *You are nothing but dirt, and to dirt you shall return*. What the sin was, he never knew, and he understood not to press her on the matter in case she flew into another of her rages. What the old fella did, she told him, was the greatest sin there was, a disgusting sin, and he must never speak of it. The little he could piece together from newspapers and gossip was a jumble of confusing images: a woman with her skirts pulled up and a building on fire; a lady singing at the front of a church while the light from the stained-glass windows threw multicoloured jewels upon her; some vast disappointment of his grandmother that no one ever spoke about. *It was the drink that did it. He was a divil for the drink, and she was just as bad, just as bad as him. Dirty old bugger.*

The sins, visited upon the sons and daughters. He had to make sure it didn't happen.

BOBBI LAMBERT stuck her index finger into Roland Evans's dead mouth and felt around. "Ha!" she exclaimed. She straightened up. "He's missing a molar. Couldn't tell you which one it is. You'd have to ask a dentist. But it's gone all right, and recently taken. The empty socket is still soft."

"Time of death?" Danny asked.

"Lord Jesus, bhoy, gimme a minute." She dug into her case and came out with a thermometer, which she plunged into the dead man's abdomen. She waited a moment, then pulled it out. "Let's see… ambient room temperature is twenty-two Celsius. Alive, he'd be about thirty-seven. Right now he's thirty-five. I'd say about… hmm… four or five hours."

It was just past eleven at present, which meant Evans had been killed around 6:00 a.m. At this time of year, it was still completely dark at six in the morning, so whoever did this to Evans did so presumably without being observed. There were no CCTV cameras in Kildevil Cove—the very idea seemed ridiculous—so Danny would get no help there. He'd have to send constables door to door in order to determine if anyone had seen anything. With luck—Danny didn't believe in luck—some neighbourhood curtain twitcher would have been looking out the window and saw whoever it was. Could they give an accurate description? Possibly, although eyewitness accounts were notoriously unreliable. He'd already set up a secure cordon around Evans's house, and by now the flashing lights of the police vehicles had attracted a small coterie of the curious. Kevin Carbage and Dougie Hughes had arrived along with Bobbi and were now stationed outside. It might be useful to speak to some of the onlookers.

Carbage was sitting inside a police cruiser parked at the top of the lane; Hughes was standing at the other end, speaking to a trio of small boys. They became suddenly shy as Danny approached.

"No, it's all right." He beckoned them closer. They were about eight or nine years old. "I just wanted to say hello. My name's Danny."

"Have you got a gun?" One boy, gangly and loose-limbed, edged away from the group and moved towards him.

"No," Danny replied, "I don't carry a gun."

"Sure, cops always got guns!" a second boy said scornfully. He was wearing a heavy winter parka, snow pants, and a hockey-themed cap. His pale face was spangled with freckles, and there was a scrape on his chin, likely the result of some boyish misadventure.

"We don't carry guns in the Cove," Danny said. "What's your name?"

"Seamus. Seamus Ryan."

The other two gasped. "G'wan, bhoy!" one of them said. "Sure ye can't be telling them your name. They'll arrest ye!"

"I only arrest people who have done something wrong." Danny smiled. "Have you done anything wrong?"

The middle boy called out, "Sure, one time in school he—" This resulted in a temporary scuffle as the other two jumped on him.

Danny waited while the childish fracas died away, then asked, "Do you know who lives in this house?"

"Das Roly's house, sure," the smallest of the three said. His bright green scarf, decorated with cartoon ninja turtles, covered his mouth and chin. "Roly drives the truck. He's after giving us a lift loads of times, and he lets me blow the horn." He glanced at the others, then back to Danny. "Can I see your badge?"

Danny showed it to him. "Have you boys seen anyone around here who shouldn't be? Maybe someone went into Roly's house."

They conferred amongst themselves briefly; then the freckled boy said, "I seen the ghost."

Something about this affected the boys; they all fell silent.

"The ghost?" Danny looked at Hughes, who shrugged.

"There's a ghost in the Cove, sure." The boy with the turtle scarf kicked at a snowdrift. "We seen 'un, me and Harry and Seamus."

"You saw a ghost? And you weren't scared?"

"I was scared," Seamus said. "Me mother says that's the Divil."

"What did the ghost do?"

The smaller boy spoke up. "He come out of the woods over there by the swings and went up behind, and then he went over by Roly's house."

"The playground," Hughes supplied, "is just behind us, over there."

"Oh." There hadn't been a playground when Danny was a boy. This must have been built in recent years. "And he came out of the woods and went behind Roly's house?"

"He went *in* Roly's house!" the freckled boy, Seamus, said.

"When was this?" Danny took out his notebook and flipped through to a blank page. "Can you tell me all about the ghost?"

The ghost came out of the woods, the boys told him, but only in the dark. Sometimes they were out after supper for a little while if they had no homework, and one time they saw him hiding in the trees. Last year he was hanging around the school in the evenings, and some of the children reported seeing him on the Point, near Heaney's fish plant. Several days ago, they had seen him going into Roland Evans's house and coming out again. "Was Roly home when he visited?"

"No," Seamus said.

Harry, the middle boy, disagreed. "Yes, he was!"

Danny put his notebook away. Whether or not this "ghost" was real, he had no way to tell, and sometimes children's imaginations ran away with them. Still and all, there might be something to it. "You've been very helpful. Thank you."

"Is Roly dead?" Seamus asked.

"Go on home now," Hughes told them. "This isn't a good place to play. Go on." When they'd moved reluctantly down the road, he turned to Danny. "Do you think there's anything to it, sir? This ghost?"

"I think we should have a look around the playground and the woods." Danny glanced at the assembled crowd. "Call for an ambulance, and then you and Kevin disperse these people. When you've done that, meet me at the playground."

He jogged the short distance down the road and into the narrow lane leading off it. There was a house on the left-hand side, belonging to local fisherman Harvey Blake, and across from it was Soldiers Pond, where he and Tadhg and the others had skated and played shinny when they were children. Blake's youngest son, Mike, pestered his father to repair an old snowmobile that had been rusting in the shed, and they spent many a winter afternoon buzzing up and down the frozen surface of the pond on it. Unlike the old-fashioned playground equipment popular in the 1970s, everything here was made of indestructible plastic, die-cast pieces in bright primary colours. There was a swing set, the swings now removed and stored away for winter, and a merry-go-round up to its axle in snow, and a slide. Danny put one foot on the merry-go-round and pushed it, but it had frozen in place and refused to move.

The bright sunlight glancing off the snow threw glare into his face, making his eyes water, and he wished fervently for a pair of sunglasses. There were no footprints save his own near the merry-go-round nor any of the other playground equipment, so he veered to the right, where the small patch of ground allotted for the swings gave onto a stand of trees.

"Anything, sir?" Kevin appeared, red-cheeked and red-nosed.

"Nothing so far," Danny replied. He nodded at Hughes as the constable joined them. "Hughes, you start at that end." He pointed to the entrance to the playground. "Kevin will start over here." The top, near the slide. "I want you to move in straight lines from right to left, continuing until you are facing each other. Pick up anything you find, no matter how inconsequential it might seem." Gesturing at the trees, he said, "I'm going in there, see if I can find a path. I might pick up something this ghost left behind him."

"If he exists," Kevin said.

Danny nodded. "If he exists."

He set off into the trees, walking slowly with his eyes on the ground. It was easier to see in here, out of the direct and painful glare of the sun. It didn't take long for him to find the path, which was well-trodden and obviously a common thoroughfare for people living in the area. It had other uses too, judging by the number of empty beer bottles and used condoms he found tossed away. He pulled off his heavy winter mitts, replacing them with a pair of nitrile gloves from his pocket. It was slow going in the snow, but he combed the area methodically, turning over rocks and sticks, putting his hands into drifts and pulling out everything from discarded construction nails to a red plastic button that had probably fallen from someone's winter coat to a small silver coffee spoon. His hope of finding fresh, unadulterated footprints was dashed, as a great many people had traversed this path in recent days, leaving behind so many different prints there was no distinguishing one from another.

The path terminated just behind Evans's house, at the fence. He climbed over, dropped into the soft snow, and ploughed through the drifts until he reached the road.

His mobile rang; the call was from Regan Lampe. "What have you got?" he asked.

"The girl in the pond? Her pockets were full of rocks, big ones," Regan said, "so your victim might be a suicide after all. She's not missing any teeth either."

Fuck. "So no link to Gail Russell."

"I didn't say that," she retorted, "and don't go putting words in my mouth."

Danny clenched his teeth until his jaw ached. "Anything else?"

"You'll get my report." She disconnected.

He walked a short distance away and forced himself to take several long, deep breaths. Her apparent snappishness was just Regan being Regan. She didn't mean anything by it, and she was like this with everyone, not just him. So the girl in the pond didn't appear to be connected to Gail Russell, but Roland Evans was. Which meant the girl in the pond was, what? Incidental? Genuinely a suicide? Maybe the letter he and Bobbi had found in her backpack would shed some light on how she'd ended up frozen in a pond.

Kevin Carbage came jogging up to him. "Sir, I've just been talking to the Greens. There's no hearse available at the moment, so I called Carbonear and asked them for an ambulance."

"Good job," Danny replied. At this juncture, an ambulance was better than a hearse. Onlookers who saw a hearse knew someone had died. An ambulance, on the other hand, merely meant someone was ill or injured. It wouldn't do to have Cove residents thinking a serial killer was at work. The last thing Danny needed was general hysteria. "Find anything in the playground?"

"No, sir. Dougie didn't get anything either."

Danny went back inside the house, but Bobbi Lambert's forensics technicians were busy in the various rooms, and he concluded he'd just be in the way. Carbage and Hughes would ensure Roland Evans's remains were safely conveyed to Carbonear General Hospital, so there was nothing more for him to do here. He might as well return to the station and get forensics started on the things he'd found along the path.

He dropped into Bobbi's lab as soon as he got back and handed the spoon over to one of her technicians. "This might be absolutely nothing," Danny said, "but if you could look it over and find out where it came from, maybe?"

The technician, a young man with a bun and wire-rimmed glasses, stared at him. "It's a spoon, sir."

"I know it's a bloody spoon. It looks old." He was beginning to feel like an idiot. "If you could swab it for trace."

"Of course, sir." He turned it over. "There's a group of hallmarks on the back."

Danny leaned closer, peering at it. He recognised a thistle, a three-towered castle, some sort of small bird, and a series of letters and numbers. "So each of these means something."

"Oh yes. My grandmother collects antique silver."

"Pity your grandmother doesn't work here," Danny replied and regretted it. "Can you look into that for me and let me know what you find?"

"Right away, sir."

Danny left him pondering it and went to find Constable Avery. He'd assigned her to keep a record of calls and emails from the public in response to the photo they'd broadcast of the girl found in Purchase Pond. He caught up with her in the break room.

"Just getting myself a cup of tea, sir, and then I'll be right back at it," she said.

Danny laughed. "You're entitled to a break, Constable—and I wouldn't begrudge anybody a cup of tea on a cold morning like this. Any calls in response to our unknown lady of the lake?" He checked the level of water in the kettle, refilled it from the sink, and flicked it back on.

"Not much, sir. I had a call from someone in St. John's who claims to have seen her at university before the Christmas break. They gave some identifying details. An email from a man in Heart's Content who thinks she might be his niece, a girl named Lizzie Stride. I think we might be on to something with him." She opened the fridge and took out a carton of milk. "He said she was staying with him and her grandmother for the Christmas holidays, but left a few days before the twenty-fifth to stay with a girlfriend in Old Perlican. She was hitch-hiking, he said."

When would young people ever learn that hitch-hiking was as dangerous now as it had ever been? In a sparsely populated rural area, with large distances between the towns and villages, anyone could come by and entice a vulnerable person into their car. "I'm assuming she never arrived."

"She was supposed to call him when she got there," Sarah replied, "but he never heard from her. From what he says, they had an argument before she left, so it's possible she didn't call because she was pissed off with him." She handed the milk across to him.

"Did he call the girlfriend's house?" Danny wondered aloud. "They'd be able to tell him if the niece arrived or not."

"Yes, sir, I asked him that, and he said he did but there was no answer. According to him, they're a flighty bunch, liable to go off for the day and not tell anyone where they're going."

"All right." The kettle came to a boil and flicked itself off. "Good work, Constable. Can you follow up with him, get some more identifying details if he has them? The usual: hair colour, eye colour, any distinguishing marks or tattoos."

"Of course, sir. I'll let you know when I'm on to something." She took her tea and left the break room, and Danny returned to the office he now shared with Cillian Riley. The Englishman had demurred several times, insisting that Danny needed his own space, but the office really was too large for one person, and Cillian, now of higher rank than Danny, shouldn't be seated with the constables. It wasn't right. He and Danny had moved Danny's desk and filing cabinet in, repatriated his houseplants to the windowsill, and hung up his posters again. It made a nice change from the almost institutional aesthetic the office had previously featured, and Danny was glad of the company.

"Didn't know you were here," Danny said, setting his cup of tea down, "or I'd have brought you one."

"Just finished one myself." Riley held up the empty mug. "Pondering another, though. Perishing cold out there this morning. How the hell do you people stand it?"

Danny pretended to think about this for a moment. "We drink large amounts of alcohol until spring," he said, laughing, "which happens around the end of June. By the way, have you seen our icebergs?"

"Now that is a sight to behold," Riley replied. "Big buggers, aren't they? And Greenland sends you some every year?"

"Yes, although with the climate changing as fast as it is, that might not last." Danny sat down and took a sip of his tea. "Global warming and all that."

"Doesn't bloody well feel like it's warming up around here. What's it out there this morning? Minus fifteen?" He turned his gaze to his computer monitor and clicked on something. "Got a minute?"

"Sure." Danny got up and went to stand by Riley's desk. He'd opened a folder containing photos Bobbi Lambert's forensics technicians had taken of the derelict house. Danny intuited where this might be going and said, "But nobody lives there, you said."

"We didn't think so. But there's something about this that doesn't sit right with me." Riley clicked on a photo of the house's sitting room and enlarged it. He pointed at a graffito on the wall: Fuck the Police.

Danny shrugged. "Pretty standard, as far as I know."

Riley turned in his chair to look at him. "In a place as small as this? Sure, I can see it in a big city. But think about graffiti you've seen around here."

"I haven't seen any graffiti around here."

"Exactly. And when there is some—say, on cliffs next to the road—it's always people's initials or Karen Loves Jo, that sort of thing. Right?"

To his shame, he hadn't thought of it, but Riley might be on to something. "Yes. Love hearts and initials."

"When have you ever seen Fuck the Police? Maybe in St. John's, but there's a hundred thousand people there. You've got to expect that criminal element, don't you?"

"Are you saying we haven't got a criminal element here?"

Riley gave him a withering look. "I grew up in Liverpool. What's criminal here? Taking one codfish too many during the recreational fishery?"

Danny grudgingly admitted he was right. "So what are you saying?"

"I think someone's gone to a certain amount of trouble to make this house *look* like it's uninhabited." Riley switched the view to another part of the same room. "There's rubbish in the corners, just the right amount. A broken mirror standing against the wall. Mouldy cardboard boxes, empty tins, crisp bags, cigarette ends… it's all there. He's done everything but piss in the corners."

"How do you know he didn't piss in the corners?"

"He might have done." Riley navigated to a portion of the photo showing a wood-and-oil stove next to a kitchen table. "Have a look at that." Danny looked, but didn't see anything that caught his attention. "The table's clean. There's rubbish piled on part of it, but the empty part is clean, like someone's recently used it." He clicked through to another photograph, this one of a bedroom. It showed three beds side by side. The bed in the middle was made up, complete with coverlet and pillow, while the beds on either side were not. "What about this?"

"One of the beds has blankets and a pillow," Danny said. "So you think he is living there?"

"I do." Riley took a healthy slug of his tea. "We haven't got the forensics back yet, but I'm betting Bobbi's team will find evidence of recent human habitation, despite appearances. It's like you said earlier, maybe he's moving around from one derelict property to another, so my thinking is, he's never staying in one place for any length of time."

"Okay, so he's coming and going from these empty buildings, but no one has ever seen him. What do you suggest?"

"Motion detection camera," Riley said. "A camera trap."

"Because we have money in the budget for that."

Riley rolled his eyes. "Don't be sarky."

"I'll ask Molloy," Danny said, "but don't expect too much. We're a small substation in a tiny village where, officially, nothing much ever happens. Maybe RNC headquarters has something we can borrow. I'll see what I can do." He returned to his own desk, opened his email program, and fired off a quick request to Molloy, sweetened with the promise of a full report on the body found in Purchase Pond as soon as the autopsy results were available. He'd already notified Molloy about Roland Evans's death during a quick phone call earlier in the morning, and hoped that would hold his supervisor until he could brief him properly.

He went back to the lab, looking for Bobbi Lambert, and found her sitting at a table surrounded by plastic evidence bags and wearing a harassed expression. Across the room a forensics technician was peering down the eyepiece of a microscope.

"Don't be asking me for nothing," Bobbi said, waving a warning finger at him. "Like I said to ye before, I'm up to me arse, I am, so. When this is done, there's all the Roland Evans stuff."

"I've got good news on that front," Danny said, and told her about the forensic anthro students on their way from the university.

"Thanks be to Jesus," she said wryly. "Maybe now I'll get out from under some of it." She shifted a plastic evidence bag full of clothing to one side of her worktop and replaced it with another containing a pair of shoes.

"Is all this from Gail Russell?" He recognised the cocktail sheath she'd been wearing, and her shoes.

"This, and the laboratory samples." She nodded at the tech across the room. "That's what Brodie is working on now."

Danny moved over to where Brodie was. "Anything interesting?"

The man looked up from the microscope. "Fibres from the taxicab upholstery as well as carpet fibres from the trunk." He blinked. "Sir."

"The trunk?"

"Yes, sir. At some point during the time she was with him, she travelled in the trunk."

Nothing on the body had indicated that Gail Russell had been restrained, and he seriously doubted anyone would consent to ride in the trunk of a taxicab. Danny was claustrophobic, and the notion gave him the willies. He wasn't all that comfortable riding in a spacious modern elevator. "We know he administered ketamine at some point. Maybe he used the trunk to transport her to wherever the boat was launched."

"Sir?"

"Nothing, Brodie. Thinking out loud." If he used the trunk of the car to transport her, then the boat launch site might not be as close as they'd anticipated. No, she was alive when they found her, and he well knew how swiftly hypothermia could set in under blizzard conditions and in those temperatures. Transportation of the victim in the trunk of the car didn't necessarily mean the launch site was farther from the town. She was likely injected with the ketamine before or when she was placed in the dory and the boat shoved into the sea from a convenient beach or slipway. The sequence of events wasn't that hard to reconstruct; in milder conditions and better weather he might have tried a live re-enactment using station personnel, but he doubted anyone would consent to being set adrift in a small boat this time of the year. Whoever the killer was, he had a certain amount of forethought and cunning, which indicated a person of organised habits. This was no sloppy misfit with a grudge against the world.

"Inspector." The man he'd left the spoon with appeared in Danny's field of view. "I don't know if this is meaningful, but the bird, right here." He indicated the spot with a gloved pinky finger. "It's a nightingale."

"A nightingale."

"Not sure if that's worth anything." He shrugged. "Thought I'd let you know."

"Well, thank you." Danny made a mental note to look up silver hallmarks on the internet. Maybe the nightingale was significant.

A young man was waiting for him when he returned to his office. He wore heavy winter clothing, and his boots left damp patches on the floor. He was wearing a parka emblazoned with the logo of a resort in Cavendish, a few miles up the shore. "Are you Inspector Quirke?"

"I am." Danny indicated his open office door. "Will you come in and have a seat?"

"I can't stay. I just came to bring you this." He handed across a plastic bag. "Sorry it took me so long to get it back to you. We got really busy in the fall, and then during Christmas it was nonstop."

The bag contained a wristwatch. Specifically, it contained a man's Omega eighteen karat yellow-gold wristwatch on a leather strap. Tadhg's watch.

"The cleaning staff found that in the room you and Mr. Heaney rented Thanksgiving weekend."

He'd surprised Tadhg with the reservation at the last minute, showing up at the construction site with bags already packed and Lily and Easter dispatched to a school friend's house for the weekend. It was one of the most romantic things he'd ever done, and he was terrified Tadhg would refuse, so he'd taken the initiative and made all the arrangements beforehand, including champagne in the room and reservations for dinner out at The Doctor's House, a nearby inn and spa.

"Yes," Danny managed to say, aware the young man was staring at him. "Thank you for coming all this way with it."

"It's a beautiful timepiece. I didn't want to trust it to the postal service."

Danny reached for his wallet. "Let me give you something for your trouble."

"Oh no, sir, that's not necessary." He grinned. "Just make sure you come back again soon, you and Mr. Heaney." He zipped up his parka and turned to go. "That'd suit us better than anything. Bye now."

As soon as he'd gone, Danny took the package into his office and sat down at his desk. He opened the bag and took out the watch. It was so typical of Tadhg to leave behind a watch that cost in excess of $3500. Danny often teased him about his habit of leaving valuable things lying about. *You're so careless with your toys.*

It had been a wonderful weekend. They'd slept late and then drove to Bay Roberts to hike the Mad Rocks trail in the warm early October sunshine, stopping at noon to picnic on a cliff overlooking the sea before making their way back to the resort to close themselves into their room and hang a Do Not Disturb sign on the door.

Danny put the watch to his nose; a faint trace of Tadhg's cologne remained, and he breathed it in. As scent so often did, it reminded him of times past and of the happiness they'd once had, him and Tadhg.

He should have known it wouldn't last.

His mobile buzzed. He hurriedly shoved the watch into his desk drawer and picked up the phone. The caller was Adrian Molloy.

"Danny, what in the name of God is going on over there? There's a third victim?"

Obviously Molloy had read the email he'd sent earlier. "Yes, sir. We think it might be related to Gail Russell, although we won't be sure until the autopsy results come back."

"Your report says he was impaled through the throat with a screwdriver. That's not usual, is it?"

"No, sir. I don't think there's ever been anything like that around here, not in recent memory." The Deborah Harris case of a year or so previous was the closest instance he could think of. A young mother who had recently given birth was discovered dead in a bog, one of her eyes gouged out.

"What are your thoughts?" Molloy asked. "You said this Roland Evans had a tooth missing and recently extracted, just like the Russell girl. Do you think they're related?"

Danny was hesitant to subscribe to the idea that a serial killer was loose in Kildevil Cove, even though it seemed like his supervisor was asking just that. "Sir, you know as well as I do that serial killings are extremely rare, despite what TV shows would have us think. So far, the resemblance between the Roland Evans and Gail Russell murders is superficial at best. For all we know, he might have pulled out his own tooth."

"Mother of God! Do people do that around there?"

Danny rolled his eyes, grateful Molloy couldn't see him. "No, sir. We have modern dentistry, believe it or not."

"Is that cheek I'm hearing? Don't you be giving me any cheek, now."

"Sorry, sir." He wasn't. "I'll get a full report to you as soon as I have all the details."

"See that you do." He ended the call before Danny could say anything else.

"Got something for you." Bobbi Lambert was standing in the doorway, a file folder under her arm. "Brodie's been looking at some skin cells we recovered from the derelict house."

Danny felt the quickening of hope and hastily pushed it aside. "And?"

"They're alive. Shed skin lives for thirty days, give or take."

"Jesus God, Bobbi, spit it out."

"There's been someone in that house at some time during the last thirty days." She winked at him. "Someone living. Now what's a living person doing in a derelict house?"

"Your expression tells me there's more than that."

"Loads more." She whipped out the file folder and laid it down on his desk. "We swabbed the bed for trace and found it. Semen—quite a lot of it. Whoever's been staying there likes spanking the monkey."

Danny squeezed his eyes shut. "Yuck."

"That's not all. Your man's got a very low sperm count. Chances are he's diabetic or suffering from some congenital disorder that's affecting testosterone levels." Danny started to ask for clarification, but she backed away, palms up. "I'm not a doctor. I'm just telling you what we found. Someone's been flitting in and out of there like a ghost."

A ghost. So Seamus Ryan and the other boys were right. There was indeed a ghost in Kildevil Cove. One with an affinity for antique silver spoons and compulsive masturbation.

CHAPTER TEN

DANNY GOT to the station early the next morning, hoping for a quiet Friday and an even quieter weekend. Another blizzard was forecast for late Friday night, heavy snow with winds gusting to 150 kilometres per hour, and no let-up for at least twenty-four hours. That ought to keep any would-be criminals at home. The weather this morning was bitterly cold, -30 Celsius with ice fog hanging in the air. His ancient Land Rover had been parked on the road all night, and it took him nearly twenty minutes of alternately swearing and praying to get it to start. He had just poured his first cup of tea and was taking it back to his office when his mobile rang.

"Your man Evans was dying." Regan Lampe's voice sounded crisp and well-rested. "Emery-Dreifuss muscular dystrophy. He probably used braces sometimes to walk."

Thus kindly I scatter.... "He was?"

"The enlarged heart tipped me off. That particular version of MD almost always presents with cardiomyopathy. And the tooth was pulled out perimortem. The cavity in the jawbone was pretty big. I'd say they used pliers or vise grips, something like that. There'd be tool marks on the tooth."

"I haven't got the tooth," Danny reminded her. "Cause of death?"

She scoffed. "Oh, come on!"

"The screwdriver through the throat," he said.

"Yes. It was a reverse of the old 'icepick to the back of the neck' killings you read about in detective novels."

Regan Lampe read detective novels? "I see."

"Transected the spinal cord from the front," she replied. "Tore a nice big hole in the trachea too." She sounded almost cheerful. "And I found a large amount of ketamine in his blood."

"Like Gail Russell?"

"Yes."

"All right. Thanks, Regan." He rang off and sat for a moment gazing out the window of his office. A light breeze had sprung up and was dancing gently along the snow, sending spindrift into the air. The weak winter sunlight seemed hazy, a harbinger of the storm to come. So the cases were connected. Whoever had set Gail Russell adrift in an open dory had killed Roland

Evans with a screwdriver. He didn't lack for imagination, whoever he was. Danny sighed, wishing he had access to a decent criminal profiler about now, someone who could theorise about the killer's potential motive and where he was likely to strike next. Evans and Gail were both vulnerable by virtue of their illnesses, so was that the common ground? If there were others in the Cove with chronic conditions, would they turn up on the list of victims? Or was the killer selecting those who were most at risk? Roland Evans lived alone, but Gail Russell lived with her parents, both of whom seemed to dote on her. So it probably wasn't isolation. It didn't add up.

Danny remembered something a professor in his forensic psychology class had told them when he was at university. *Identify with your victim, but not to the point that you lose your objectivity.* That was easier said than done. Danny had never suffered from a chronic disease or disability, unless you counted his rare RH null blood type as a disability, and didn't to his knowledge have any illness that would cut short his lifespan. He'd managed to make it to fifty-three without most of the ailments others his age suffered— the exception being his increasingly stiff and painful knees. What was it like to live as Gail Russell did, an adult in the care of her ageing parents? How much control had they exercised over her? Certainly, she was permitted to attend parties at the Fitzpatricks' house, but did she go anywhere else? Doris Coombs had indicated that Roland Evans had been in a relationship with Gail, that he followed her around. Where had she gone that he followed her? Had she been doing something he disliked or his religion disapproved of?

The front door of the station banged shut, and a gust of cold air wafted down the corridor towards him. He heard someone kicking snow off their boots; then Cillian Riley appeared, wearing a parka and wrapped in scarves. "Motive," Danny said, by way of greeting.

Riley raised an eyebrow as soon as one was free. "Good morning to you too."

"Regan just called. Roland Evans was missing a tooth."

"Same as Gail Russell." He shrugged out of his parka and hung it on the coat tree. "So they're connected."

"It looks that way," Danny replied. "What I'm trying to figure out is motive. Why would someone decide to take out the sick and the weak? Is he on a mission or something? Culling the herd?" At Riley's quizzical look, he added, "Roland Evans had muscular dystrophy."

The Englishman seemed taken aback at this. "Oh."

"I ran him through the database—Roland. He doesn't have so much as a parking ticket. He attends the local Apostolic church and teaches Sunday School."

"Squeaky clean, then."

"Is anyone?" Danny clicked on the link for the police database and brought up the search page. "Look." Riley came round the desk. "Nothing. Renews his driving licence dead on time, every five years. No tickets, no cautions, spotless record. Both parents dead. According to Dougie Hughes, he's a quiet sort. Doesn't socialise with anyone except that church he goes to."

"Then we should definitely talk to them," Riley said. "They're the crowd that knew him best."

"But he seems too good to be true. I can't see anybody being that perfect, can you? Everybody makes mistakes. Surely to God he's done something wrong at some point."

Riley moved to sit down, turning on his computer. "You think the killer is punishing them for their sins? What about Gail Russell?"

"I don't know." He picked up a pencil and tapped it against the edge of the desk. "Maybe we should speak to her parents again."

"I wouldn't. In my experience, parents aren't reliable. They always tend to see their kids in black and white, either all good, Mummy and Daddy's perfect little angel, or all bad. It's not helpful." Riley's computer beeped and whirred itself to life. "What about social media—Facebook, Twitter, that sort of thing? See who she friended online, talk to them."

Danny was briefly ashamed he hadn't thought of this. It was practically procedure nowadays, in addition to tracking a victim's closest contacts. "I'll get one of the constables to do it, see if anybody jumps out at them. It's a good idea to get everybody together. Now that we know Evans's death is linked to Gail's, we can combine both investigations."

Half an hour later, having briefed everyone on recent developments, Danny was on his way to speak to Pastor Greg Jesso, head of the Apostolic church in Kildevil Cove, having called to make sure Jesso would be at home. He needed more information about Evans's relationship with Gail Russell, but he doubted Pastor Jesso would see fit to divulge any details of Evans's private life. Later, he'd contact Evans's brother Bruce in Alberta to break the news of Roland's death, as soon as the disparity in time zones allowed. Maybe the brother knew something about Roland and Gail's relationship.

Jesso lived in a modest white bungalow on the Cove's main road, right next to the church. In keeping with their faith, the church was of plain construction, unadorned with stained-glass windows and having only a modest steeple topped with a cross. He greeted Danny warmly at the door and invited him in.

"Cold day today," he said. He was about sixty, with grey hair that had receded from an already-high forehead, giving him the look of an intellectual or an aesthete. His dark eyes and broad cheekbones indicated his Aboriginal heritage. "Won't you come into the kitchen? Mrs. Jesso has just made a pot of tea."

Danny toed off his boots. "So you aren't averse to the use of stimulants?"

"Tea isn't a stimulant, Inspector. It's a gift from the Almighty." He indicated that Danny should precede him into the kitchen, where the table had been prepared for his arrival. He was touched that the Jessos had set out a tray of fancy home-baked cookies and cake, knowing they could ill afford it. The Cove's congregation was small, and most people who attended Jesso's church were not well off.

"Thank you, Pastor Jesso. This looks wonderful." He'd already eaten a hearty breakfast earlier that morning, but he wasn't about to offend Mrs. Jesso's hospitality. She appeared at the periphery of his vision, flitting in and out of the bedrooms, her arms laden with clean linen. "I'm afraid I have some bad news about a member of your congregation."

"Oh?" Jesso had just filled Danny's teacup and was now filling his own.

"I believe Roland Evans attended church here?" He wasn't sure how close Jesso was to his parishioners, and he didn't know the man well enough to predict how he'd react to news of Evans's violent death.

"Yes." Jesso offered the plate of cookies. "I know Roland."

"I regret to tell you that he died, we think in the early hours of this morning, around six, at his home." From the corner of his eye he could see Mrs. Jesso lingering near the kitchen door. "He was murdered."

There was a resonating shriek that fractured into violent sobbing, as Mrs. Jesso flung herself to the floor, arms flailing and beating at the air. "No, no, he's not. No, he's not, he's not, he's not, he's not!"

Jesso rose from his chair and went to lift her up, and Danny saw her clearly for the first time. She was at least thirty years younger than Jesso, and pretty, with dark hair partly confined by a kerchief and vivid blue eyes. Her oval face was distorted by the violence of her sobs.

"Irene, my dear, this isn't doing you any good," Jesso soothed.

Danny abandoned his tea and stood up. "Mrs. Jesso, I'm very sorry."

She tore the kerchief from her hair and flung it in his direction. "You're lying. He can't be dead, he can't be."

"Irene, don't be carrying on like this." Jesso got an arm around her waist and moved her into the hallway. "You must pray," Danny heard him saying from the bedroom, "you must plead the Lord's blood and his protection."

When Jesso returned to the kitchen he was gravely apologetic. "Inspector, I'm afraid now isn't a good time. I must apologise for my wife. She's unwell."

Danny had seen "unwell." This wasn't it. "Is there someone I can call? To sit with you both? Perhaps a doctor?"

"That won't be necessary," Jesso replied. "With rest and an abundance of prayer, Irene will soon be herself again."

"I would like to speak to the members of your congregation about Roland Evans," Danny said. "I wonder if you might furnish me with a list of their names and contact information."

Jesso glanced around him, as if he expected this to appear from thin air. Clearly his wife's reaction to the news of Evans's death had unsettled him. "Of course. I have a list in my office. If you'll wait here…."

Danny went out to the porch and put his boots back on, zipped up his parka. He took out his mobile phone and sent a brief text message to Cillian Riley: *Strange reaction to Evans's death. Mrs. Jesso.* He looked up to see Jesso approach with a typed sheet of paper in his hand.

"Here you are," he said, handing it over. "I hope this will suffice."

Danny glanced at it, noting the names. "There are no more than fifty people here."

Jesso spread his hands in an attitude of surrender. "I regret to say many have fallen by the wayside."

"Thank you for this," Danny said, tucking it into his pocket. "I'll be in touch if I have any more questions." He looked past Jesso's shoulder towards the bedroom, where a low moaning sound was emanating, like an animal in pain. "I hope your wife feels better very soon."

CILLIAN RILEY stopped in at Strange Brew to pick up a sandwich and a cup of coffee for himself at noon. After Danny had scanned the list of parishioners and texted it to him, Riley had split it between himself and Kevin Carbage, and they were aiming to make contact with as many people on the list as possible before the blizzard started. Several of Jesso's congregation came from some of the outlying areas, and Kevin, having lost the coin toss, was on his way across the Heart's Content barrens to interview those members living in Victoria and Carbonear. Riley was going to cover the rest of them, most of whom lived in Kildevil Cove and its environs.

"Chicken salad sandwich?" Jennice asked. Her pregnancy had progressed to the point where she was almost as wide as she was tall, but it hadn't dimmed her good nature. "And a large coffee, right? See, I'm not too far gone. I remember some things."

"Oh no, I wanted a ham and cheese," Riley teased, "and builder's tea. Can't you pregnant ladies get anything right?" He handed her some money. "Not long now, is it?"

She patted her bulging belly. "Any second now," she replied, passing him back some coins. "I wish she'd hurry up. I'm wore out." She plucked a sandwich out from the cooler and deftly poured a coffee from a fresh pot, added cream and sugar in the right amounts, and packed everything into a paper bag for him. "Where's your other half today?"

"What?" Riley's face felt suddenly hot.

"Sergeant Carbage." She grinned at him. "Oh, don't think I haven't noticed. I'm pregnant, not stupid."

"On his way to Carbonear," Riley said.

"Hope he gets back before the blizzard hits." She nodded at the windows of the café. "It's supposed to be nasty." She fell silent, the tip of her tongue working the ring in her bottom lip. He'd noticed her doing it before and wondered if the repetitive gesture was meant to soothe her.

"Dave working today?" Jennice's husband was a finish carpenter who built and installed custom cabinets. His skills were in demand, and he often worked away from the Cove for weeks at a time.

"Yeah. He's over in Shearstown," she said, her gaze faraway.

"He's sensible," Riley said, reaching out to pat her hand. "He'll be home well before the weather." He searched for something more reassuring to say than this, but couldn't come up with anything. "I'll see you later, right?"

"Of course. Yes." She drew herself up. "Be careful out there."

He went out and got into the cruiser, unable to shake a persistent feeling of unease. Riley's experience with blizzards was limited to the two and a half years he'd lived on the island, first in St. John's and now here. A native of Newcastle, he'd never seen snow in the amounts that normally fell during a Newfoundland winter, nor had he ever experienced wind of such sustained speed and destructive power. It wasn't uncommon for tractor-trailers to be pushed sideways off the road in certain parts of the island, and in the old days of the railway, even trains were toppled. If bad weather was forecast, you hunkered down and stayed inside until the threat had passed.

His first winter in Kildevil Cove, he'd learned the hard way that nature was not to be trifled with. A storm had been forecast to begin later that night, and Riley had gone out for a run around four in the afternoon, thinking that the few snowflakes that drifted down so beautifully were no real threat. Within twenty minutes, the postcard-pretty scene had shifted into something of apocalyptic terror, as the snow thickened and the wind, straight out of the northeast, ramped up to 100 kilometres per hour. Visibility was non-existent, and in the growing darkness, he became disoriented and drifted off his usual route, ending up in the middle of a bog. He called the police station on his mobile phone, which brought out the Rovers search-and-rescue team and whatever officers Danny could spare. He was eventually located—by Danny himself and Tadhg Heaney—several kilometres deep in the woods and taken to Carbonear General, where Danny cursed him up one side and down the other.

"You stupid bastard," he'd railed. "This isn't England! You're lucky you aren't dead. Because that's what happens to people who go out in blizzards around here, Cillian. They die. They get lost and they freeze to death. How could you be so stupid?"

Ever since then, he'd taken careful note of the weather forecast and made sure to seek shelter well in advance of any foul weather. He hoped Jennice's husband would do the same.

Riley had already interviewed five of the people on his half of the list, learning nothing new or particularly exciting about Roland Evans. He was God-fearing, a regular churchgoer, didn't drink or smoke or fornicate, blah, blah, blah. When he checked in with Kevin, he discovered his luck was running in a similar direction, with no one offering any evidence of vice. Either Evans was a veritable paragon of virtue or the congregation members didn't know him as well as they thought.

Riley ate his sandwich in the car, listening to the news on the radio, which included updated weather bulletins about the blizzard. Currently it was sitting over Cape Breton, but would very soon be grinding its way east towards Newfoundland, with expected landfall about six that evening. With any luck, Riley would be safe at home by six, preferably with Kevin taking up his accustomed spot on the couch and a few bottles of Quidi Vidi Brewery's finest IPA between them.

He put the car into gear and headed towards Bay de Verde, a small fishing village at the northern tip of the peninsula. A man named Jack Prior attended Greg Jesso's church, and Riley wanted a word with him about Roland Evans. Given the little he'd discovered so far, he wasn't expecting much, but he owed it to the investigation to speak to the man. Prior lived in a house set off by itself, on a cliff overlooking the sea. Greg Jesso had indicated to Danny that the house was remarkable because it was painted a bright robin's-egg blue and had a large rusty anchor in front of it. Riley found it with very little trouble. He made his way to the front door with some difficulty, bent double against the wind and with nothing to hold on to. So strong were the gusts that twice he was nearly blown off his feet. He knocked a couple of times, and the door swung open to reveal a man about Riley's own age, with black hair and winged eyebrows that gave him a devilish aspect.

"I been waiting for ye," he said, standing aside to let Riley in. "Come into the warm. That wind is enough to blow the milk out of your tea, it is, so."

Riley had taken the precaution of calling ahead to let Prior know he was coming. "Thank you for seeing me," he said, stepping into the front porch. The house smelled of lemon soap and spruce logs, and a fire crackled in the wood-and-oil stove. "I won't take up too much of your time."

Prior offered him a seat at the kitchen table, and he took it, pulling out his notebook as he sat down. A large ginger tomcat roused from his sleep near the stove and stood up, stretching luxuriously before making his way over to Riley.

"You're not from here," Prior observed.

"No," Riley said, "I'm from England." He reached a hand down to the cat, who took this as an invitation to jump into his lap. A scratch or two under the chin and the cat settled down and began purring loudly, a grating noise like metal against metal. "You go to the same church as Roland Evans."

"Yes, that's right."

"Do you live here alone, Mr. Prior?"

"No, my brother Job lives here, but he's away for work right now, up to the Mainland."

"What does he do on the Mainland?" Riley asked.

"Works on the lake boats." Prior leaned over to look at what Riley was writing.

"And what do you do?"

"I'm on disability," Prior told him. "I broke my leg real bad when I was fishing for the Quinlans. Got caught up in the lines and went overboard."

Riley winced despite himself. "That must have been really painful."

"Just about hauled the leg off me. That was back in 2007. I been off work ever since."

"And you aren't married? No dependants?"

"No, just myself and Job, that's all."

"I'm wondering how well you know Roland Evans," Riley said. "What can you tell me about him? Is he close with anyone in the church?"

108

J.S. COOK

"He's close with the pastor's wife." Prior said this without even a smirk. "Ask anyone and they'll tell ye that."

"What do you mean by close?"

"He's doing it with her."

Riley was gobsmacked—not that Roland Evans had been shagging Mrs. Jesso, but that a member of Greg Jesso's congregation would announce it outright. "They were in a sexual relationship?"

"Oh yes. Been at it for ages now. Sure her husband's older than God." Prior got up, shuffled over to the stove, and lifted the damper to add another log to the fire. He came back to where Riley was and sat again, heavily favouring his left leg. "I daresay she's gone right off the head now, since he died."

Riley noted this down. "Can you think of anyone who might hate Roland? Someone who argued with him recently?"

Prior thought for a moment. "No, bhoy, I don't think. He was quiet, like. Kept to his self a lot."

"So there's no one you can think of who would have cause to harm Roland?"

"No." Silence reigned in the little house for a moment, save for the crackling and popping of the fire and the ticking of a clock. Then, "If anyone would have had it in for him, it'd be Pastor Jesso. I mean, she's his wife, right? But I don't see him doing anything like that."

"Are you aware that Roland was ill? He was suffering from muscular dystrophy."

"Oh yes. We used to lay hands on 'un, have special prayer for 'un, on Sunday nights after church."

"He had a girlfriend, a young woman named Gail Russell. We've heard from a reliable witness that Mr. Evans was very jealous over her, used to follow her around."

"That's the first I've heard of that," Prior replied. "Although mind you, I don't know everything about 'un. I only ever used to see 'un in church. I don't live in the Cove, so whatever he did outside of church, now, I wouldn't know."

The cat shifted on Riley's lap and began kneading his trouser leg. He reached down and smoothed the animal's soft fur. "Did Gail attend the same church?"

"No, she was Catholic. That's the queer thing about it. We don't usually mix with them."

Riley noted this down. "So were the other church members upset that Roland was dating a Catholic girl?"

"He wouldn't dating 'er, not as such." Prior scratched the back of his head. "I can't really say what they was doin'. He used to take her for rides in Heaney's truck. Sometimes on Saturday night I'd see the two of 'em up to the snack bar in Winterton."

"The snack bar."

"Yeah, this small restaurant up there. Fish and chips, that sort of stuff, and ye can go inside and play video games. I never went in there myself, but my niece likes going there." He shifted in his seat, easing his bad leg.

"Did you ever hear of Mr. Evans hurting Gail? Did you ever see them arguing?"

Prior thought for a moment, then shook his head. "No, bhoy, I can't say I did. That's not to say they didn't fight—just that I never seen 'em."

It seemed like Prior had no real knowledge of Evans's relationship— or lack thereof—with Gail Russell. Riley closed his notebook and put it in his pocket. "Mr. Prior, you've been very helpful. Thank you for this." He gestured at the cat. "I think he'd rather I stayed where I am."

Prior laughed. "Sammy loves the heat, he does, so. He's after taking a liking to ye." He came over and lifted the cat into his arms. "Come on, Sammy, bhoy. This nice man got to leave now."

Riley gave the animal a parting scratch under the chin. "He's beautiful. Thanks for letting me meet him."

The wind had risen even more, and he fought to keep his balance as he left Prior's house. He wrenched open the door of the patrol car and fell into the seat. So Roland Evans was having it off with Mrs. Jesso. That was interesting. But somehow not surprising, he thought, smiling. Even in small villages, people tended to obey their baser physical urges, and nobody was above a secret affair.

THE VISIT with the Jessos had jarred Danny's sensibilities, so he stopped at Strange Brew for a flat white on his way back to the station. Jennice was behind the counter, moving slowly and at the mercy of her enormously pregnant belly. He pitied her. It couldn't be easy, dragging all that extra weight around, along with swollen feet and hands, a bad back, and all the rest of it.

"How are you doing, my dear?"

She put a hand to the small of her back and winced. "If this one doesn't come out soon, I'm going in after her myself." She smiled in her usual bright fashion. "Flat white?"

"Please. If I knew how to make one, I'd come back there and get it." He watched, fascinated, as her hands worked the espresso machine deftly, packing coffee into the receptacle and tamping it down. She had just fitted the puck and locked the handle when she gasped, doubling over.

Danny came around the counter and caught her elbow. "Jennice? Are you okay?" He had no experience with pregnant women, but he doubted her sudden cry of pain was anything good.

"Best kind," she grunted through gritted teeth. "It's nothing. Just false contractions." She took a few deep breaths while he supported her, then straightened up. "I'm fine now."

"Are you sure? You don't look all that fine to me." He pulled out a chair for her. "Maybe you should sit down."

"Maybe you should stop fussing like Grandmother Grunt," she said. The sass was reassuring. Yes, she'd be all right now. "No customers this side of the counter, okay?" She pushed at him with her hand. "G'wan with ye."

"Only if you're sure." Danny went back around to the front. "I can call an ambulance if you like."

"I'm fine." She started the espresso machine, and anything else he might have said was lost to its loud metallic growl. She moved to steam the milk, then combined it and the fresh coffee before stirring in two spoons of sugar. "Most people take this unsweetened."

"I'm the very divil for sugar," Danny told her. He passed across the money for the coffee. "Listen, I'm going to check in with you later on, just to ease my own mind that you're okay. You got a way home after work?"

She scoffed. "I just lives over the road, Danny." She worried the ring in her bottom lip with the tip of her tongue, flicking it rapidly back and forth. "Are you all right?"

The question staggered him, rendering him temporarily speechless. "Yes. Why wouldn't I be?"

"He's been gone a long time. You must miss him." She glanced pointedly at the third finger of his left hand. "I remember when you were wearing his ring."

He picked up his coffee. "Thanks for this," he said tightly. "Keep the change." He turned and fled before she could say anything else.

THE MOOD at the station was subdued, like the weather, everyone hunched over their computers, working in silence. June glanced up from her desk as he passed by. "Bad weather coming, sir." She nodded at her screen. "I've been looking at the radar. This one's going to be a real big mess."

Danny leaned over to look at her monitor. A large multicoloured graphic of the approaching storm system took up most of the screen, with the deepest colours—lurid blues and purples—at the centre.

"That looks bad," he remarked. "Maybe contact Kevin and tell him to get back here as soon as possible." He didn't want Carbage stranded on the Heart's Content barrens when this thing came through, miles from home and without shelter. The barrens were true tundra, empty of all but the sparsest vegetation, home to roaming caribou and little else. He'd heard too many stories of people lost in its vastness for days on end, wandering and directionless.

"I'll call him right away, sir," June said.

"Better use the radio," he told her. "Mobile reception is pretty spotty in that area. Tell him to come back immediately. Tell him I said so. It's an order." He smiled to reassure her. "Kevin's not stupid. He knows when the weather's closing in."

He went into his office and laid down his coffee while he took off his parka. It hadn't yet started snowing, but the light level outside his window was more like early evening than afternoon. There was a tap on his door and Constable Sarah Avery was there, holding a laptop.

"Sir, I had a look at Gail Russell's social media, like you asked."

"Oh, good job, Avery." He beckoned her inside. "Let's see what you got."

She came round his side of the desk and opened the laptop. "That's the strange thing about it," she said, "there's nothing there."

"What do you mean? She doesn't have a Facebook account?" Even Danny had a Facebook account. It was useful for keeping in touch with former colleagues in other places, as well as Sandra.

"Oh, she got one," Avery said, "and as far as I can tell there used to be loads of stuff on it." She turned the laptop so he could see it. "That's what's h'odd." Her "round the bay" accent often added and dropped *h*'s at random. It was charming, really, although Riley often complained of not being able to understand a word she said. "'Tis all gone."

"What?" He looked where Avery's finger was pointing and saw immediately what she meant. Where various of Gail Russell's recent Facebook entries had been, there was simply empty space. In the section of the page designed to showcase a user's photos, all that remained were empty squares.

"The pictures and stuff was there," Avery told him, "but they're not displaying because someone deleted them h'off the server. They didn't bother deleting the entries—just erased everything in 'em."

"Why would somebody do that?" Danny's understanding of social media was limited, but he recognised the need to eradicate certain parts of one's past. There were no longer any photos of him and Tadhg together on his social media. "Did she break up with someone? A boyfriend? A girlfriend?"

"That's what I was thinking." Avery paged through to the profile section. "But not in this case. I think her Facebook was 'acked. You see here, where your username and picture usually are?" She indicated a space at the top of the page. "It doesn't say Gail Russell, and that's not a picture of her. Somebody took her picture down and put that there."

The photo was of a woman in late nineteenth- or early twentieth-century dress, complete with a small fancy hat with ribbons on it. She was gazing into the camera, unsmiling, holding two long-haired cats in her lap. Instead of the name Gail Russell, it read Vestal Virgin.

"Who is she?" Danny asked. "The woman in the picture."

"Don't you know?" Avery drew back. "Sir, that's Georgina Stirling, from Twillingate." She folded up the laptop and stepped away. "Marie Toulinguet. The opera singer."

CHAPTER ELEVEN

KAI MCNAMARA let himself into his flat, first checking to see that the small slip of paper he'd attached to the door frame with a dab of his own saliva was still there. It was. Satisfied that no one had entered in his absence, he pushed the door open and went in. He lived on the top floor of a newish building, a refurbished fire hall off O'Connell Lower, not far from Trinity College. The flat had cost an exorbitant amount, but McNamara was willing to pay to secure his own comfort. He wasn't twenty-five anymore, and his requirements in life included a flat with all the latest mod cons and a comfortable bed that didn't break his back. The work he did paid well, and even though he often employed a little subterfuge to get what he wanted, it was hardly what you'd call illegal. Well, not very illegal.

Tadhg Heaney was a smart man, but not so smart that he couldn't get seriously hurt, messing around with the people he was messing around with. McNamara admired him. It took serious balls to come all the way across the Atlantic on the trail of some fella who'd taken his money. But admiration wouldn't save him when Phelan's buddies came to play. It was on McNamara to make sure no harm came to him while he was in Ireland. McNamara had gotten him the job in Kenneally's Bar, had sourced the flat he now lived in, and made it his business to stay on Heaney's arse for every moment of the day and night. The building that housed Kenneally's belonged to McNamara, who had invested a family inheritance in real estate during the days of the Celtic tiger and had sense enough to get out before the property bubble burst once and for all. With what he'd made in the early 2000s he was able to purchase a handful of buildings slated for demolition and make them over into profitable dwellings for the up-and-coming—and those who wished they were. Having money made his work so much easier, enabled him to spread around a bit of cash when he needed to, and often coerced information out of those who would otherwise be reluctant to talk.

If that didn't work, he'd just beat the bejesus out of them.

He'd promised an old friend that he'd look after Tadhg Heaney as long as he was in Ireland, and McNamara took this promise seriously. The man in question was someone he trusted and to whom he owed a debt; more than that, he was someone McNamara genuinely liked, which was more than he could say for most people. The idea was that Tadhg Heaney was to be let alone, as long as he didn't get himself into any serious amount of trouble. It was McNamara's job to keep him safe, which wasn't the easiest thing to do since Heaney had a real talent for poking his nose in where he'd be better off keeping out of. It was all McNamara could do to keep him from bollixing up everything and getting himself seriously hurt.

He went to the sideboard in the dining room and poured himself two fingers of Jameson, carried it through to the sitting room, shrugged out of his heavy winter coat, and sank onto the sofa. It was just after nine in the evening and he was tired, but Heaney was coming here tonight to discuss how best to track Phelan down, and McNamara had a standing appointment to connect with Danny Quirke at nine thirty once a week, on Friday evenings. He stretched his long legs in front of him, propping his feet on the coffee table. The whiskey went down easy, smoothing off the rough edges, and he closed his eyes, sleep lapping at him. He'd had nothing much to eat all day, only a dried-up burger he'd bought from a Supermac's around noon, and he was hungry but much too tired to cook anything for himself. He took a mental inventory of what was in his fridge, but there was nothing there that appealed. Lately he'd been losing weight without really trying, and every few days it seemed he had to put another hole in his belt. He was always tired, but when he went to bed, he couldn't sleep, kept awake for hours with the pains in his body, as keen and insistent as a toothache. His appetite had deserted him as well, and he ate now out of necessity rather than enjoyment, forcing down food that tasted like ashes in his mouth. It wouldn't be long now. Not long at all.

It had all been so different once. Years ago, when the whole of Ireland was booming, flush with cash, and any man could make himself a fortune, he'd been with Nuala. Sure, she liked the fact that he was handsome, drove a fancy car, and always had money to splash out on whatever it was she wanted. And she liked the late nights out, dancing in a club or drinking at the Temple Bar, the evening's high spirits enhanced with an ounce or two of the best Peruvian blow that money could buy.

Aye, he'd always owned his vices. He and Nuala had enjoyed each other until the day he woke up after a horrendous night on the tiles, strung out on booze and cocaine, and decided enough was enough. When he told her there'd be no more of that, she was off like a shot. Upon parting from him, she'd found herself a tinker fancy man, a caravan-dwelling troglodyte who bred horses and sold heroin in places like Finglas. Not that McNamara had anything against the tinkers, far from it. His own mother had some tinker heritage, and indeed he'd grown up listening to her tales of the walking people. But Nuala's man, Jonjo, was a textbook psychopath, a genuine lowlife embroiled in selling drugs and women. He was the one who'd offed Stevie Power to keep him from blabbing about the business Phelan was involved in—as if everybody and his brother didn't already know. Jonjo and McNamara maintained an uneasy truce: McNamara wouldn't reveal Jonjo's whereabouts to the Gardaí as long as Jonjo treated Nuala properly. One mark on her, one step out of line, and McNamara would have his guts for garters. As long as their agreement was maintained, McNamara was willing to let Jonjo have a little bit of fun—even if that fun amounted to putting a gun to Tadhg Heaney's head and threatening to blow his brains out.

His mobile phone buzzed, and he fumbled around for it, realised it was in the back pocket of his jeans. He pulled it out and peered at the screen: Deiniol Quirke. He activated FaceTime and asked, "Danny, how's yerself?"

He wanted what he always wanted: a report on how Tadhg Heaney was doing, whether he was safe, if he was in danger. Was McNamara looking out for him, keeping him in his sights? Of course he was; that was what Danny Quirke was paying him for. The main thrust was that Tadhg Heaney not know that Danny had paid to vouchsafe his continued presence in Ireland without interference from those who might hurt him.

"You're still in love with him," McNamara said. He knew what that was like, the kind of love that held on despite all the odds being overwhelmingly against it. "He won't thank you for interfering."

"I'm counting on you to keep him from getting killed," Quirke said. "Kai, how are you?"

"I'm grand, Danny," he lied. "I'm grand, so I am."

"Ye don't look grand to me." That was the bastard FaceTime, showing him in the worst possible light. "You need to be seeing a doctor. Are you sleeping properly, and eating? When's the last time you had a decent meal?" This was Danny all over; he worried about everyone who came within range. He'd be better off worrying about himself.

"I'll be all right. Just need to get my head down for an hour or two."

"How is he?" Danny asked.

"He's still looking for Phelan. He's convinced once he finds him, Phelan's just going to bend and give his money back." McNamara laughed bitterly. "I know for a fact Phelan's got that money spent and then some. The best thing for him is to go home out of it."

"There's nothing for him here." Danny's face clouded. "He's lost everything he had. You know that. He's better off where he is."

"So I can take care of him? Is that it?" It was a facetious question. Danny was paying him to babysit Tadhg.

"Yes."

"Well—" McNamara forced himself upright. "—he's coming here in a little while to talk about finding Phelan. Is there anything you want me to tell him?"

"You know and I know Phelan hasn't got his money. He's on a hiding to nothing," Danny said.

"Yep."

"Kai, if you can just... keep him out of trouble. He's going to have to come home eventually. When he does, he'll be starting over from square one."

"That's a fuck of a position to be in," McNamara commented. "You think he's eager for that?"

"He's running, Kai. He can't face what's waiting for him back here. I'm content to let him run for a while, until he's tired of it." Quirke's face betrayed him. He was mad in love with Heaney, and having to be apart from him was tearing his guts out. McNamara'd had a few unrequited loves himself, the worst of course being the one love he would never talk about nor remember, even in the privacy of his own mind, the love that possessed him to a greater degree than Nuala ever had or could.

"I'll do my best," McNamara promised. "Danny, I'll do my best." He rang off, hoisted himself off the sofa, and went into the bathroom, shedding his clothes on the way until he was completely naked. He turned on the water in the shower, let it run for a while, then stepped in, immersing himself in the warm spray. It revived him, softening the sharp edges of the guilt until he was almost comfortable. He stepped out after twenty minutes and scrubbed himself dry with a rough towel, pulled on a clean pair of boxer shorts and a T-shirt. The door chime sounded, and he went to answer it.

"Sorry I'm late." Tadhg Heaney stood in the doorway, holding a bottle of Glenfiddich. "We'd a run on pints just before my shift ended."

"Come in," McNamara said. "I'm just out the shower. Give me a minute to get decent." He went to pull on jeans and a button-down shirt, ran a comb through his hair. When he re-emerged, Tadhg had poured a generous measure of Scotch into two glasses and was sitting on the couch, examining the flat.

"Not the sort of place I'd expect you to live," he commented.

McNamara felt that. "You figured I'd be living under a bridge?"

"Jesus, dial it back," Tadhg said. "No offence intended. I just didn't take you for the artsy, intellectual sort." He indicated the shelves full of books and the art prints on the walls. "Read a lot, do ye?"

"It passes the time." McNamara picked up his glass and took a sip. "I've been thinking about your situation lately." Tadhg's expression changed from open and interested to suspicious. "Done some asking around and even chased down a few leads myself."

"Oh?"

McNamara sank into an armchair just across from Tadhg. "This lad you're looking for, this Phelan. How much do you know about him?"

"I know he stole my money and ruined me."

"Besides that."

"He was friends with Stevie Power, before Stevie was killed."

McNamara tipped his glass to him and said sardonically, "And that should tell you everything you need to know."

"Is that a threat?"

"No, it's not a threat. It's nothing of the kind. But I wouldn't be much use if I didn't warn you. Stevie Power ended up dead, and I know who killed him."

"I'm starting to think there's a lot you know and a lot you don't tell." Tadhg laid aside his glass and stood up. "This is a waste of time." He started for the door.

"I know who killed Stevie," McNamara said again.

Tadhg stopped and turned around.

"Phelan killed him," McNamara said. "Now do you think tracking him down is a good idea?"

"He won't bother me," Tadhg replied, but McNamara could see he didn't really believe it. Over the years Kai McNamara had gotten rather good at reading people, and Tadhg Heaney was more transparent than most. He hadn't a clue what Phelan was really all about, and that was the scary part.

"He knows you're looking for him."

"Good." Heaney's expression tightened. "Then he knows I'm coming for my money."

"He doesn't have your money." Christ, he was infuriating! McNamara got up and went to where Tadhg was. "He spent it. All of it. And borrowed more, or stole it, from wherever he could get it." He poked Tadhg in the chest with his finger, hard. "You think because you've got a decent head for business that you're all over this. Well, boyo, I'm telling you that you're not. What you're going to get is not money. What you're going to get is dead."

Heaney gazed at him for a long moment, then broke into a spontaneous grin. "It's him that does it, isn't it? That Jonjo. I figured as much." He shrugged, and McNamara wanted to shake him till his head fell off. Bloody gormless eejit! "Maybe I don't care about the money anymore. Sure I know me money's all gone. I knew that as soon as he left the island. No, I'm after him now for what he did to me, and by the Jesus, I'll have him."

Right. So it was revenge, then. "Well, you know the old saying." McNamara stepped back a pace. "Dig two graves." He went to the sofa and sat again. The clock on the wall read 10:00 p.m., but it might as well be half-past midnight. "I'm tired of talking."

Tadhg nodded and went for the door.

"Go home, Tadhg." McNamara raised his glass. "Slàinte Mhath, you bloody fool."

KEVIN CARBAGE had made good time in tracking down and speaking to the members of Greg Jesso's church. Most of them lived in Victoria, a small town about five kilometres away from the larger Carbonear, and were amenable to being interviewed by a handsome young police sergeant—especially the ladies. One woman, a very fit grandmother in her fifties, invited Kevin to stay the night and even tried to prevent him from getting to the door. The last parishioner he spoke to was an overly earnest man in his early forties with a bushy black beard and thick glasses, wearing a heavy wooden cross on a string around his neck. He had nothing to say about Roland Evans, apart from a vague claim about "sin," which he declined to elaborate on.

By the time Kevin pulled onto Route 74 heading for Kildevil Cove, the light snow had thickened considerably and visibility was whatever the headlights of his patrol car could illuminate. He passed a Department of Highways snowplough going in the other direction and wondered if he should turn around and follow it. At least that way he could seek shelter in a Carbonear hotel for the night. There was already significant accumulation on the road, to the point where it was brushing the underside of the car and piling up underneath the wheels. He would soon be stranded.

He pulled off to the side of the road and took out his mobile phone but couldn't raise a signal. The patrol car's radio was operational—he knew this because his sister had called earlier and told him to come back—so he put in a quick call to the station to advise of his situation. Dougie Hughes answered the call.

"There's no way we can send anyone out. They're after closing the roads between here and the Heart's Content barrens." Kevin could hear the incipient panic in the young constable's voice. "The latest from the weather office is fifty centimetres or more before morning."

Christ. That wasn't good news. "Okay, thanks, Dougie. Tell Danny I'm heading to Carbonear behind the snowplough, see if I can put up somewhere for the night." June was probably having copper kittens by now, but it couldn't be helped. Anyway, it wasn't like he had never seen a snowstorm before. The car was outfitted with cold-weather necessities, and he was warmly dressed. He wasn't going to freeze to death or starve. If necessary, he'd hunker down somewhere and wait out the blizzard, then head back home when the roads were clear.

He caught up with the snowplough, which had turned down Swansea Road and then come out again. Instead of heading towards Carbonear, however, it exited onto Route 70 and was travelling towards Salmon Cove along the coast. The snow was likely to be even heavier that way, which meant that the odds of getting caught out unprotected were much greater. Kevin reluctantly turned around and got back onto Route 74, hoping the car could make it across the barrens and into Heart's Content. Even if the roads were fairly impassable, the patrol vehicle's big engine and its all-wheel-drive suspension would take him where lesser cars couldn't go.

He hoped.

It was slow going. In places the snow had piled into metre-high drifts in the road, and it was no longer possible to see any of the usual landmarks. He crested the rise of Glass Bottle Hill and descended slowly, the rear of the car fishtailing, then shuddering as the anti-lock braking system kicked in. Kevin was a good driver, with plenty of experience driving in inclement weather, but he was beginning to wonder if he shouldn't have pressed on to Carbonear. The tundra fell away for many kilometres in every direction, nothing moving except the wide bands of snow, which whirled and writhed like a living creature. His eyes burned from trying to see, and his death grip on the steering wheel sent painful spasms into his neck and shoulders. Just ahead, something stepped into the beam of his headlights, and he stood on the brakes, cursing aloud as the car shuddered to a stop, but there was nothing there. Whatever he'd seen was merely a trick of the light and the continually moving snow. He took a few deep breaths, waiting for his pulse to calm before moving ahead.

The kilometres crept by at an agonising pace, the landscape rising and falling in predictable rhythm despite the lack of visible landmarks. The patrol car's satnav had given up the ghost a while back, unable to maintain a stable connection with the satellite through the heavy cloud cover, and he was forced to navigate by sight. A quick glance at his watch told him it was half-past six, more than ninety minutes since he left Victoria, a trip that should have taken no more than twenty minutes in ideal conditions. He turned to look out the side window, could see nothing but drifting snow.

The radio crackled to life: "Missing person alert, mike." "Mike" meant the person was suffering from a mental illness or was otherwise under psychiatric care. "Area of Heart's Content barrens. Possible 10-60, victor. Please respond."

Someone with mental health issues was out in the blizzard, someone who might react with violence. Kevin picked up the radio handset and identified himself, indicated that he would respond, then radioed the Kildevil Cove station.

"278-A, this is 102." He waited, listening to dead air. "278-A, this is 102." Nothing. He huffed out a sigh, wondering now if he really had seen something in the headlights earlier. The radio crackled, and someone was speaking, but he must have entered a dead zone, because all he heard were occasional syllables. He assumed someone had radioed ambulance and fire service, which would be the usual thing to do, especially when a vulnerable person was missing in bad weather in an open area like this, where time was limited. The current temperature was -15C without factoring in the wind; to someone lost on the barrens, most likely wearing inadequate clothing, it would feel like -30. They had to be found quickly or they would die.

He reversed onto a small woods road and turned the patrol car back towards Victoria, squinting through the driving snow for anything that might indicate someone had passed this way. He picked up the radio again: "278-A, this is 102. 10-33. I need help." Nothing returned except static. Next to a disused gravel pit he slowed, peering into the woods. Had he actually seen something, or was it only an optical illusion, a trick of the meagre light? He rolled down the passenger side window, squinting through the snow, now falling like someone shaking out a bag full of feathers. There....

He pulled up and put the car into park. His first impression had been correct. Something was moving in and out of the trees, a humped shape, staggering and perhaps stumbling over the uneven ground. He pulled on a cap and gloves and got out of the car, leaving it running so the headlights could illuminate the way.

"Hello? Are you all right?" Standing very still, he listened, afraid to even breathe in case he might miss some subtle auditory cue. "I'm a police officer. I can help you."

Then he heard it, issuing from a clump of trees directly in front of him: a low moan, riding on the wind, a sound a wounded animal might make.

"Stay there. I'm coming to get you." He took three steps forward and plunged into an unseen hollow, snow settling around his hips. It was harder to move now, but he pressed on, wading through the drift. "It's all right. I'm going to help you."

Whoever it was had fallen and was lying in a shallow void beneath a large fir tree. He reached down, got an arm around them. Yes, definitely human. They were wrapped in a dark blanket, which they'd thrown over their head, probably to shield them from the snow.

"You're safe now." He shouted to be heard above the roaring of the wind. "Let's go back to my car." He hauled the person onto their feet and half carried, half dragged them through the drifts back to the shoulder of the road. He opened the passenger side door, and as he did so, the blanket fell away and he saw the frightened face of a young woman. "What's your name?"

"Ivy," she said. There was dried blood in the corners of her mouth. "Ivy Tobin."

Kevin fastened the seat belt around her and closed the door, then got in on the driver's side. He activated the car's interior light. "I'm Kevin," he said. "Ivy, how did you end up out here in a blizzard?" It was lucky he'd heeded his intuition and gone back to check. A few more minutes and she would have been beyond help.

"He come and got me." She stared out the windshield at the storm. "He said the doctor told him I could leave. He said I was better." Her gaze shifted to Kevin. "I'm not better. I won't ever be."

"Who came and got you?" he asked.

"Dunno his name. I didn't see his face."

"Is there someone I can call for you?" Kevin put the car into gear and pulled back onto the highway. The heavy vehicle groaned and slid, but the snow tires maintained their grip. "I'm going to take you to Carbonear General. Is that okay?"

"That's where I was to when he come and got me."

She was shivering violently by now, so he turned the heat up as high as it would go. There was almost zero visibility, and the powerful windshield wipers were fighting a losing battle with the snow. He wondered grimly if they'd even make it to Carbonear.

"You'll be warm in a minute." He extended a hand across the car to her, close but not touching. Sometimes agitated people didn't want to be touched, and he had no idea what this young woman had been through. "You'll be all right." He picked up the radio again. "278-A, this is 102."

The radio crackled and hissed, then Dougie Hughes's voice: "Acknowledge."

Kevin all but sighed with relief. "On my way."

CHAPTER TWELVE

THE IMPENDING weather Danny had been concerned about was now a full-on blizzard, with everything the meteorological office had predicted and then some. The view outside his office window was non-existent, and even when he squinted he could see nothing but an impenetrable wall of white, blown about by howling winds out of the northeast. Kevin Carbage had radioed to say he was at Carbonear General with a young woman he'd found wandering on the barrens and would shelter there until the weather cleared. Danny had stayed too late at the station to make it home and so elected to remain where he was. Cillian Riley, June Carbage, and Bobbi Lambert, as well as the two constables, had left early enough to beat the storm and were now safe in their own houses. That left just Danny and the blizzard. He didn't anticipate any criminal activity, but someone needed to man the phones and stay on top of things, just in case something arose that required police intervention—not that he'd be able to go anywhere. He'd need a snowplough to get through the drifts, and the last time he'd passed by the front door, it was covered in snow three-quarters of the way up. But he still had electricity, and in the event that the storm knocked out the power, the station could operate on its own generator, a feature Tadhg had insisted on adding when his subcontractors had wired the building.

The thought of Tadhg was painful, especially since they had parted on bad terms. In typical Tadhg fashion, he'd endured the betrayal and loss in silence, and it wasn't until Danny practically interrogated him that he'd opened up about the matter.

"Subcontractor ripped me off. Fella by the name of Phelan." They were sitting in Danny's rented house in Kildevil Cove, sipping whiskey after supper one evening, when Tadhg finally told him the truth. "Bastard cleaned me out." He wouldn't look Danny in the eye. "I should have seen it coming, but obviously I'm stupid now as well as broke."

"I'll get on to the RCMP," Danny said, "see if they can't—"

"No." Tadhg flicked a glance at him, then looked away. "I'd rather you didn't."

Danny stared at him. "You're not going to let this go, are ye?"

"I am."

Many times over the course of their friendship, Tadhg had done strange things, made decisions Danny couldn't agree with, but this had to be the worst. In order to satisfy his creditors, he'd had to sell all his assets, including the house on Eigus and even the island itself. When the dust settled, Tadhg was left with nothing except the clothes on his back. That was when he decided to go looking for Phelan. "I have to put an end to this," he'd said, "and anyway, I'm cleaned out. There's nothing left."

There's me, Danny wanted to say. *I'm still here.* But he knew it was futile. Tadhg's mind was made up, and Danny didn't even come into it. What he said instead was "How long will you be gone?"

"As long as it takes."

A little bit of detective work revealed that Tadhg was headed for Dublin. As soon as Danny knew this, he contacted Kai McNamara. He hadn't been able to find much on Phelan as far as a criminal record went, but that didn't necessarily mean anything. A quick call to the main Gardaí station in Dublin got him the information he needed and confirmed the worst of his fears. Phelan was involved in organised crime, a particularly vicious gang led, it was rumoured, by the infamous Christy Kinahan, the so-called "dapper don" of the Irish mob. Tadhg was wading into it like a lamb to the slaughter, with no idea of what awaited him on the other side of the Atlantic.

Danny already owed McNamara more than he could ever hope to repay, and this latest added to the debt. But he'd paid McNamara's expenses and was currently keeping him on retainer so he could have an eye to Tadhg and make sure the absolute worst didn't happen. Danny was counting on McNamara's considerable powers of persuasion to convince Tadhg that his quest was fruitless and he'd be better off home out of it.

He went into the break room to make himself a cup of coffee. It was just after midnight and the station lights had flickered a couple of times. The phone hadn't rung since eight that evening—June calling to make sure he was all right—and he desperately needed a break from the case files that lay open on his desk.

Danny took his coffee back to his office and brought up Wikipedia on the computer. The Marie Toulinguet detail wasn't mere happenstance; he was sure of it. What connection it had to the case he couldn't be sure, not yet, but someone wanted to make certain he was aware of it. According to the online encyclopaedia, Toulinguet was a stage name, adopted by Twillingate's Georgina Stirling, who was born in 1867. Stirling was a world-famous prima donna. She played in opera houses through Europe and the United States, but her career was cut short by throat problems. She died in 1935, and the cause of death was recorded as cancer. There was no obituary. He did a second search for any related news out of Twillingate and found nothing further on Georgina Stirling, but a news story from the previous year caught his attention: Historic Structure Destroyed by Fire Second Time.

> An historic house in Twillingate, and an important part of the town's heritage, was completely destroyed by fire over the weekend. The fire was first discovered at twelve midnight when flames were seen coming from Invercarie House, once owned by one of the town's oldest mercantile families. "This is only a small place," said Maureen Reardon, who owns the Devlin Inn directly across the harbour. "As soon as I heard the sirens, I ran to the window to look, but all I saw was flames." The article went on to say that the house had burned once before, in 1992, leaving nothing but the structure's main timbers remaining. A restoration specialist had been brought in from Nova Scotia to rebuild the house from the original blueprints. A subsequent investigation suggested arson, but this was never proven and no one had been charged.
>
> The house had been in the Stirling family for many years.

Danny started as a particularly violent gust of wind rattled the windows. The lights flickered, dimmed, then came back on again. His monitor froze, and he reached to restart his computer. The Stirling family house had burned. So what? Georgina Stirling had been dead since 1935, and it was highly unlikely she'd returned from the grave to burn the place down. He checked the Constabulary records for a copy of the investigation report on the 1992 fire and found it. The fire was deliberately set, using paper found on the premises and some kind of accelerant, most likely gasoline. It originated in what used to be the home's back porch, but which had in recent years been revamped into a conservatory. From there the flames had spread, destroying most of the structure. Danny knew there were any number of motives for arson, including vandalism, profit, and revenge, so which one applied here? Subsequent analysis of the scene found traces of blood and…

…cells normally found in amniotic fluid.

Mother of God.

Someone had given birth in that room back in 1992, and someone else had tried to cover it up.

People tried to hide, deny, or otherwise disavow pregnancy for various reasons: if the pregnancy occurred out of wedlock, if the parents were related, or if there was some perceived shame involved. That the child in this case had been born in the back porch of a house, rather than in hospital, was suggestive. Perhaps labour came unexpectedly, or the child was born before time. A stillbirth could also warrant a certain degree of concealment, the old adage that "what the eyes don't see, the heart doesn't feel." But concealment to the point of actually burning the structure where the birth had taken place?

On impulse he called Sandra. She picked up after four rings. "Danny. I hope you're sheltering from the storm."

"I'm at the station," he said. "Couldn't get away before the weather, so I'll stay put. Listen, now. I wants to ask ye something." He outlined the situation of the amniotic cells and the burned building. "Why would someone conceal a birth that way? I've been racking me brains and I can't think of nothing."

"If the baby wasn't wanted," Sandra replied. "Just pretend it never happened."

Like me? he felt like saying. The circumstances of his own birth were still muddy, despite a year-long quest to uncover the facts. His mother had been Welsh, hence the name "Deiniol." He had been born at the cottage hospital in Old Perlican. His father was unknown. Learning that he wasn't actually a Quirke, and that he and Sandra were not in fact brother and sister had thrown his entire life into disarray. The people he'd thought were his parents were long dead, and their parents as well. What information Sandra had was precious little, passed on to her by her mother, as well as a copy of Danny's birth certificate, which stated his real mother was a woman called Angharad Davies. He'd scoured the island's records for any trace of her, but there was very little. She had come from Aberystwyth to train as a nurse at St. Clare's, graduating in 1964 and taking a job at Old Perlican in 1965, two years before his birth. A request for information from the Wales Civil Registry had provided nothing. Before she took her own life, she'd made Danny's mother—the woman he thought of as his mother—promise to care for him and raise him, as he'd learned recently from Sandra. Whatever relatives she'd had back in Wales knew nothing of him, had probably not even known she was pregnant. She was an enigma, which made him a cipher as well, a man without origins or family, belonging to no one.

"You belong to me," Tadhg had said when Danny told him. "I'm your family." Which was a lovely thing to say but didn't change the fact he was a nameless bastard whose entire early life was nothing but a pack of lies.

"Infanticide?" he asked now. "Or a stillbirth?"

There was a pause as Sandra considered this. "It depends. A stillbirth would be buried in consecrated ground. In the case of infanticide, probably an unmarked grave somewhere. It's not something you'd be likely to advertise. In most cases, she'd have concealed the pregnancy."

Especially, Danny thought, if the child was the result of incest. He would never say this to her, not after what she'd suffered at the hands of their grandfather. "In that case I need to find out who was living in that house back in 1992."

"Why are you bothering about this, anyway?" she asked.

"It might have a connection to something I'm working on." He didn't feel like going into the whole mess about the tape recorder and Gail Russell's Facebook, or Roland Evans and the missing tooth. It sounded ridiculous inside his own head, and he'd no doubt Sandra would scoff at the very tenuous link between Georgina Stirling's burned house and the murder victims. "Probably nothing." He thanked her, told her to stay warm (a habitual joke between them and a ridiculous one, considering the temperatures in the Algarve), and rang off.

His neglected coffee had gone cold, the cream congealing on the top and making it undrinkable, so he went to the break room to dump it out and get another. The room was located on the long back wall of the building, facing a low hill and the narrow lane that ran in front of it. A line of windows, each longer than it was tall, were located at the top and overlooked the road and three or four houses. The first house, a traditional Irish cottage painted bright yellow, was Doug Thistle's house. Doug, a teacher at the elementary school, lived there with his sister Eileen. The dwelling next to it, a modern bungalow, housed Barry and Maureen Tulk and their three boys. The last house in, half hidden by a thick stand of spruce trees, had been empty for as long as Danny had been back in Kildevil Cove, yet it was showing a light in one of the windows. He distinctly remembered Tadhg telling him the house was up for sale but with little interest because it was in such disrepair. Maybe someone had taken shelter there during the storm? It wasn't inconceivable. Kildevil Cove had no homeless population, those who were unable to care for themselves either lived with relatives or had trained carers come in from the community, but someone who'd been caught out by the weather might have ducked in there to wait. He stood watching while his coffee percolated through the Keurig. Judging by the way the light wavered, it was either a candle or an oil lamp, not electricity. The play of shadows on the bit of wall he could see suggested someone was moving about in the room, probably unnerved by the wind. The coffee machine gurgled to a stop, and he removed his cup, took out the empty pod, and discarded it. A sudden gust threw snow against the windowpanes, momentarily shrouding the house from view. When he looked again, the light was gone.

His mobile phone vibrated in his back pocket. Thinking it was Sandra, he pulled it out. Another unknown number, this one different from before. The message comprised a .mov file, a video. He tapped to open it. It was a news report from ITV, one of the island's two main television networks, showing the historic Invercarie House in Twillingate as it burned to the ground.

He tapped out a reply message: *Do you want me to pay attention?*

A series of bubbles appeared. The sender was typing. *You're paying attention now.*

Danny took a sip of his coffee. *I am. What do you want?*

Some crimes are unforgivable.

He wished Dougie Hughes was nearby. Maybe he could trace the unknown number. No, it was probably a disposable, pay-as-you-go mobile phone, easily obtained anywhere for very little money. Dougie wouldn't be any use here, and besides he was safe at home with his wife and young daughter. Danny didn't feel like bothering him outside of hours.

What kind of crimes? he asked.

There was a pause while the bubbles wavered on the screen. He drank some coffee, realised he'd forgotten to put sugar in. The wind was rising, battering itself against the windows and making them rattle, and to his ears it sounded like the eldritch keening of the damned. Despite the coolness of the room, he was sweating.

Weakness is an obscenity.

The caller disconnected.

DANNY WAS just boiling the kettle to make breakfast when he heard the knock at his front door. It was the morning after the storm, and he'd stopped at home for a shower and a change of clothes before heading back into the station again. The ploughs had been mercifully early, and nearly all the roads in the Cove had been cleared. He switched the kettle off, thinking the visitor was probably Sandra, but when he opened the door he saw Sheila Fitzpatrick, huddled into a thick winter coat and shivering in the morning chill.

"Sheila, my God! Sure it's cold enough to kill ye. Come in, come in." He stood back to let her enter. She made a beeline for the woodstove, holding her hands over it to warm them. "Have ye had breakfast yet?" Danny asked. "Surely you'll have a cup of tea."

"I'd love one," she confessed. "The doctor told me to ease off on the caffeine, but I can't give up me tea."

"And a slice of toast," he said. "The cold out there this morning is enough to skin ye."

"Thanks," she replied. She unfastened her coat and sat down in the chair next to the stove. "Sorry to drop in on ye like this. I would have called, but I haven't got your number."

Danny poured a cup of tea for her. "Milk? Sugar?"

"Just milk is fine," she replied. He doctored the tea as requested and handed the cup over to her. She took a grateful sip. "My, that's some good. What kind of tea is it?"

"Barry's. It's an Irish tea. I lived in Ireland for a while."

"Our people are from Ireland, originally," she said, "mine and Roy's. My grandfather could still speak a bit of Irish, but he was one of the last. There's none around now that speak it. 'Tis too bad."

Danny put some slices of bread into the toaster, then shimmied the small kitchen table closer to where Sheila was. "Just as well to have our breakfast in the warm," he explained. "So how is everything? Yourself and Roy doing all right?" He'd barely spoken two words to the woman the day he and June visited their homestead, and he couldn't think why she'd shown up on his doorstep. "Nobody sick? We've been lucky so far this winter. I don't think anyone's had the flu, not yet anyway." He took butter and marmalade off the windowsill where it was keeping cool and laid it on the table.

"This used to be Harry Tuck's fish store one time," Sheila said, glancing around. "I knew they were at something with it, but I didn't think anyone was living here." Her expression said she thought it rather spartan for a man of his position in the community, but she was too polite to utter this thought aloud. She offered him an uneasy smile. "I suppose you're wondering why I'm here."

"I'm glad of the company, actually." The toaster spat out four slices of toast. He put two on a plate and passed it across to her. "Go ahead. There's butter on the table."

"I should have gone to the station." She dipped her knife into the butter and spread it across the bread in short, jerky motions. "I just can't stand people knowing me business, and ye knows yourself, it'd be talked all around the Cove."

"Of course." Danny collected his own toast and sat down across from her. "Is there something on your mind?"

"It's Roy," she blurted.

"What about him?" The short hairs on the back of his neck prickled, the way they always did when some important piece of information was being relayed to him. Funny how that happened, he thought, such an animalistic response. Humans really were clothed monkeys after all.

Roy was absent from the homestead a great deal of the time, she told him, and it was beginning to worry her. He rose early in the morning and went off on his snowmobile with enough provisions for the day, often not returning until very late at night. They had a cabin deep in the woods that Roy had built shortly after they moved to the Cove, and she supposed he was spending time in there, but for what reason, she didn't know.

"The two of you aren't from the Cove originally?" Danny asked.

"We lived in Twillingate for years," Sheila replied. "We're from Random Island—that's where Mam was born—but we're after moving around a lot. Me and Roy had jobs at the Toulinguet Tea Room. It's a tourist place, or it was. The house burned down a few years back. I used to do a bit of cooking and cleaning, and Roy looked after the animals they had. It was a kind of hobby farm, chickens and lambs and whatnot. The youngsters what used to come there loved it."

Had they left because of the fire? Or was there some other reason? Danny wondered how to put this question to her without offending. In the end, he just came out with it.

"Not exactly." She laid a hand on her pregnant belly and fell silent. Danny refilled her teacup and waited. "I shouldn't be telling you this." She sighed. "But I suppose there's no point in keeping anything back. I… did something… something I shouldn't have done, and people got up against us."

"What did you do?"

"There was a young girl used to live in the same house as the tea room. Part of it was a family home, and the rest was the tea room. She was there with her brother, I think he was, and this old man." She gazed at Danny. "Their grandfather? There was a woman there too. I don't know if that was the mother or not. They were a queer bunch, kept to themselves a lot, never mixed with no one."

"What did she want, this girl?"

"You're a man," Sheila said forcefully, her eyes boring into him, "so 'tis neither here nor there to you. She got pregnant, wouldn't say who it was, and between the jigs and the reels she come to see me. She wanted me to fix it."

"Fix it?" Too late, he understood what she meant. "Oh."

"There's plants. All kinds of things. My nan showed it to me, and her nan showed her. It's how the women made sure they wouldn't have too many youngsters, back in the old days. You couldn't even buy anything back then. Not...." She stopped to draw a slow breath. "Not condoms or nothing. So this girl wanted me to take the baby away."

Danny didn't feel like launching into a lecture about the illegal nature of at-home abortion, so he kept his mouth shut.

"She was too far gone for me to do anything for her," Sheila continued. "So I told her no. It wouldn't work. She'd end up poisoning herself. She got mad and spread it around that Roy was the one who got her pregnant, and we had to leave. But it wasn't Roy. It was...." She gulped some tea. "I always thought it was the old fella that lived in the house. He was a dirty old bastard. Roy never done nothing to her. I know Roy is a bit different. It's not his fault."

"What do you mean by different?" Danny asked. He wasn't about to divulge what Doris Coombs had told him, how Roy had driven her home from one of the parties and wouldn't let her out of his car.

"When Roy was a young fella, he went over the wharf on his bike and hit his head. He was under water for ten minutes or so. The doctor said he didn't get enough oxygen to his brain. He almost drowned. 'Twas only the cold water that saved him."

"Do you think Roy is going into the woods to be by himself?" It was a strategy that appealed to Danny as well. "Maybe he enjoys the solitude."

"No, it's not that. It's to do with the barn. He won't let me in there now. He feeds Lulu. Won't let me near her."

"Lulu?"

She smiled. "Our cow. Roy named her. She's a sweetheart, a Jersey. Gives the nicest milk. She's a pet, really."

"When were you last in the barn?"

"Before Christmas. So whatever he's at, it's got to do with the barn. I asked him about it, but he won't say what it is. Told me to mind my business." The hand on her belly moved in slow circles, as if seeking to soothe the child inside. He wondered who the father was. Her brother? Someone in the Cove? Incest in a place as small and remote as this would come as no surprise. Isolated people, thrown back on their own resources, tended to take advantage of certain situations. Maybe Roy had crept into his sister's bed some night.

"What's it like inside your head?" Tadhg asked him once. "You suspect everybody."

"Well, Sheila, I'm glad you told me. We'll certainly have a look around and see if there's anything going on." He pushed away his empty plate and stood up. "But until Roy does something actually illegal, there's not a lot I can do."

"But you'll look into it?" She rose from the table and pulled her coat back on.

"I'll look into it."

"Don't let on that I was here." Her hand came to rest on his forearm. "I don't want to make Roy feel bad. Please don't say nothing about me being here. He'll get mad. I don't want him to get mad."

Danny promised discretion, then saw her to the door. "The place that burned in Twillingate—that was Invercarie House, wasn't it?"

"Yes, that's the one." She looped her scarf around her neck and pulled up the hood of her coat. "Why?"

"Shame to lose an historic building like that."

"Is it?" Her mouth twisted in a sardonic smile. "You know, Inspector, if you want a good crop out of the berry grounds, ye got to burn the land. It clears away the old growth, and the next year, ye'll get a great crop of berries out of it. Myself and Roy, we're after burning the pasture up back of our place. We'll have some grand hay and silage come the summer."

"The cleansing power of fire," he remarked. "To clear away the crimes of the past?"

"Some sins are unforgivable." She stepped out into the cold of the morning and hobbled off down the road without a backwards glance.

WHEN DANNY arrived at the station, Bobbi Lambert was waiting for him outside his and Riley's office. "Look!" She waved a scrap of paper at him. "Finally got this unraveled. Took forever for the paper to dry."

"What is it?" Then it dawned on him. "The girl in the pond."

"Yeah, the girl in the pond." She followed him into his office and plopped down in a chair. "It's not what you think."

"What do I think?" Danny sat down behind his desk.

"You think it's a suicide note." Bobbi's grin was triumphant. "But it's not."

With a tap on his open door, June Carbage appeared, still dressed in her cold-weather gear, with snow melting off her boots and onto his carpet. "Morning, boss. Dr. Lampe is looking for you. I got a call from her this morning." She turned aside to sneeze, then reached into her pocket for a tissue, bringing out a doggy poo bag instead. "Whoops."

"How is Easter?" Danny asked. He missed Tadhg's little dog almost as much as he missed Tadhg and Lily. He'd trained himself not to think of them, but they crept into his thoughts a thousand times a day. The absence of them was a palpable ache that had settled into his bones and left the taste of ashes in his mouth.

"Best kind," June replied. She found the tissue she was looking for and wiped her runny nose. "She misses them, though. She doesn't understand why Tadhg won't—" She pressed her lips together. "As I said, Dr. Lampe is looking for you. She rang me this morning on my way to work when she couldn't get you. She's completed the autopsy on the girl we found in the pond."

"Excellent." Regan was coping admirably with the near-constant parade of corpses. "Why don't we get everyone together for an update?"

"I'll put on a pot of coffee," June said. "See you in a bit." The loud squeaking of her winter footwear accompanied her down the corridor.

"As I said, it's not a suicide note." Bobby laid the note on his desk, carefully sealed in a plastic evidence bag. "It's a mailing address."

"A mailing address."

"Here in the Cove."

He leaned over to look. "Does it give a name?"

"No, sadly. It's a post office box, the ones anyone can rent. But it's something."

"P.O. Box 27, Kildevil Cove," Danny read aloud. "I wonder who owns box 27?"

"Somebody who wants to receive mail on the sly," Bobbi replied. "Back in the nineties, my uncle ran this little fly-tying business out of his house. He didn't make a lot of money off it, but enough for a fly-fishing holiday in Labrador once or twice a year. Last thing he wanted was the busybodies around here knowing about it, so he took out a post office box. Best thing he ever did. People ordered his flies through the mail and paid him the same way, and nobody knew anything about it. He made up a little company name and put that as the address, instead of his own name."

"So somebody with a business they don't want anyone else to know about might run said business using a post office box instead of a street address. That's what you're saying."

Bobbi nodded. "That's what Uncle Frank did."

"This is excellent work, Bobbi. Thank you. I'll get someone to run down the identity of whoever owns box 27." As soon as Bobbi had gone, he rang Regan Lampe; the medical examiner picked up immediately.

"You're calling about the girl in the pond," she said. "No teeth missing."

"Oh." He immediately deflated.

"But I found something interesting when I ran a toxicology panel on her blood."

Danny waited, saying nothing.

"High levels of ketamine," Regan told him. "She was saturated with it. Far more than what you'd see in recreational use."

"So she wasn't a suicide?"

"Nope. Somebody made it look that way, but that girl didn't go into the pond under her own steam. I'm willing to bet she was drugged, and then the rocks were added to her pockets and her knapsack, possibly to weigh the body down. She was in perfect health, about twenty-three years old."

He suddenly remembered his conversation with the young boys outside Roland Evans's house—their assertion that a "ghost" had gone to visit Evans before his death.

"There's something really weird going on around here," he said. "Three deaths, all linked, except the timeline puts the girl in the pond as the first victim, according to the weather office."

"Maybe he only started taking their teeth after," Regan mused. "The first victim was him getting a taste for it."

"That makes sense," Danny replied, "but I'm not willing to jump to any unwarranted conclusions at this stage. Thanks for this, Regan. I really appreciate it."

"Of course you do," she said and rang off.

Five minutes later everyone had assembled in the briefing room, a low hum of conversation buzzing as he entered, with most people talking about the weather. Danny noticed a few weary-looking faces among the crew, which suggested they'd spent the earlier part of the morning shovelling out. Kevin Carbage was massaging his left elbow with his right hand, and Cillian Riley looked like he'd been run over.

"Kevin, good to see you made it back all right," Danny said. "The young woman you found?"

Kevin consulted his notebook. "Ivy Tobin, from Victoria. She's an in-patient at Carbonear General, the psychiatry unit. She was with a group who were shopping in Carbonear, and she wandered away."

"Not missing a tooth, is she?" Dougie Hughes.

"Constable," Danny warned. "Anything else, Sergeant?"

"She claimed when I spoke to her that someone had taken her away—a man. She couldn't see his face. I asked the attending physician about it, and he said she was prone to delusions." He shrugged. "I'm assuming that's what it was."

"*Was* she missing a tooth?" Danny asked.

Kevin turned to gaze at Cillian Riley before turning back to Danny. "As a matter of fact, she was. From what the emergency room doctor said, she'd done it herself."

"Which tooth was it?" Riley asked.

"One of her molars."

"Gentle Jesus," someone in the back of the room murmured. Danny was surprised to see Adrian Molloy. "Carry on," he said, waving a hand.

"So Dr. Lampe has completed the autopsy on the girl we found in the pond. She had high levels of ketamine in her blood at the time of death, which rules out suicide. Whoever put those rocks in her pockets and in her backpack did so deliberately, to make it appear she took her own life. Given the timeline of when the pond first froze, she could have been the first victim. Unlike the other two, she isn't missing any teeth."

"So you think he started with her," Molloy said, "and refined his technique as he went along."

"Exactly, sir," Danny replied. To the room at large he said, "Based on the presence of ketamine, we know these three murders are probably connected and were likely committed by the same person. He is someone who likes order and routine and who adheres to a very particular way of doing things. He has access to ketamine in an injectable form and uses it to anaesthetise his victims before he kills them."

"He doesn't want them to feel pain," Riley said. "Is that it? An angel of mercy?"

Thus kindly I scatter thy leaves o'er the bed.... "Yes," Danny said. "I think that's what he's doing. He chooses people he sees as damaged or vulnerable and kills them to ease their suffering. He's extremely dangerous because he's playing God, choosing who lives and who dies." He nodded at Kevin Carbage. "Any luck with the boat Gail Russell was in?"

"No, sir. I spoke to Uncle Mose Tuck about it. That type of dory, nobody uses it anymore, not since the fishery died. He didn't recognise it from the picture I showed him. He said it was probably an old one somebody had in storage."

"So no help there," Danny said. "June, you mentioned a few days ago you'd spoken to a man up the shore about the girl in the pond."

"Yes, sir." June flipped through her notes. "His niece was hitch-hiking, and he thought it might be her. I reconnected with him yesterday while I was at home, and he said she had turned up safe and sound. She went up to Whitbourne to visit her boyfriend and didn't tell anybody. We've broadcast a photograph of the girl from the pond, but nothing of any use came out of it, and nobody recognised the woman in the picture from the backpack."

"So it's not Lizzie Stride."

"No, sir. It's not."

He nodded his acknowledgement. "There was a piece of paper found in the backpack. Bobbi's people have been working on it, and it appears to be a mailing address. It's a post office box, number 27, here in Kildevil Cove. Constable Avery, I want you to find out who owns that box and speak to them. Try and find out why a murder victim would have a scrap of paper with their address on it. It may be that they're running some kind of business and the dead girl was a customer. I've also had a tip lately that Roy Fitzpatrick is up to something in the woods behind his property. Someone reported seeing him going into the area around Big Brook very early in the morning and returning late at night. Now, he might not be doing anything in particular, so don't assume it's illegal activity. Hughes, I'd like you to have a look, but you'll need to go in on snowmobile, especially after this last storm."

"Better pack a lunch, Dougie," Kevin said, smirking. "That's hard terrain in that way. You'll be a while."

"Kevin, the young woman, Ivy Tobin, that you picked up on the barrens. I'm assuming she's still a patient at Carbonear General."

"She is, sir."

"I'd like more information on what happened the night she ended up on the barrens. You said she was missing a tooth. I find it highly unlikely she pulled it out herself. I'm interested in hearing what she has to say about it. Feel like going back to see her?"

Kevin nodded. "Absolutely."

"Most psychiatric wards these days have open visiting hours, so anytime at all. Soon as possible, if you can. That missing tooth bothers me. There's more to her story than what you were told, and we need to find out what it is." He gestured to Molloy. "Was there anything you wanted to add, sir?"

"I came to talk to you," Molloy replied. "In private."

"That's it, everyone." Danny picked up his file folders. "Try and get as much information as you can, and I'll see you back here soon as." He waited while the others filed out, then approached Molloy. "I didn't expect to see you here, sir," he said. "It must be important."

Molloy rose to his feet, picking up his cap from the chair next to him. "It is." He glanced around, but they were alone in the room. "The man known as Martin Belshawe has been arrested in Dublin."

Danny's scalp prickled. Martin Belshawe had come to Kildevil Cove the year before, posing as a police officer. In reality he had been a major player in the human trafficking ring that Moira Fraser, Danny's former superior, was part of. His cover story had been so convincing that no one had suspected him, even for a moment, and by the time Danny realised Belshawe was a criminal, he was long gone. "In Ireland."

"He's being questioned by Interpol." Molloy drew himself up. "And he's named you as a co-conspirator."

"What?" The shock of it was like a bucket of ice water thrown over him. "Me?"

"I'm here to relieve you of duty, son. You're to go to Ireland for questioning as soon as possible."

CHAPTER THIRTEEN

THERE WAS never enough time with her these days. They'd find a safe place to meet, somewhere out of sight and hearing, but she could only stay for an hour, never more than that. Already the child was growing large inside her—his child—but everything would change when it was born. When *he* was born. They were certain it would be a boy. In the beginning she used to let him inside her, but now she was more reticent, afraid to undress because of the cold, or someone might see them. He practically had to beg now, plead with her, praying on his knees, and even then it was just a glimpse of her soft pink flesh. Last time she had put the warm nipple of her breast into his mouth, and he'd suckled from her. She was already full of milk. But too soon the invisible hourglass ran out and she was rising from the bed, fastening her clothes, telling him that it was late, she had to go, she had to hurry home.

"I knows what time it is," he said. "I always knows what time it is." With an entire wall of clocks, how could it be otherwise? He took great care to keep every one of them impeccably accurate, within a tenth of a second. If you accounted for your every waking moment, it was less likely that bad things would happen, and even if they did, no one could come back on you. You knew where you had been, and what you had been doing, for each stroke of the clock.

"Then let me go," she said. "He'll be wondering where I am. You know what he's like."

He stood in the doorway watching her leave, counting her footsteps. Twenty-three paces from the door to the road and then into her car. It was dangerous, coming here in the vehicle and leaving tracks behind. He told her this time and again, but she didn't listen, and she shouldn't have been walking on her bad foot.

"I wanted to see ye," she said. "I can't bear the things they're after doing to ye." She didn't understand that they couldn't harm him, not really. Like the substance of the universe, he was infinite, forever expanding, a benign force of absolute wisdom. "Don't say things like that." She didn't like it when he talked this way. "Ye sounds like something cracked." That was the worst thing she could have possibly said to him. It was what the old fella used to say.

"You're soft in the head you are, so." The old fella used to beat him with whatever he could lay his hands on, beat him around the eyes sometimes with the flat of his hand, and he bore it in silence. He clamped his lips closed and took it, because it was nothing to what the old fella did to Adeline.

Mam named her for the old song, "Sweet Adeline," so no one was surprised when she turned out to be a singer herself. She started lessons with Maisie Taylor when she was seven, and before too long she was singing solos at special masses, Easter, and Christmas. On Sunday afternoons some girls from her school would go around to the old folks' home and sing, and Father Murphy said she had a voice like tiny silver bells, so clear it was, and bright.

In the nighttime when it happened, she would wake him up and crawl in bed with him and the two of them would cry together. "He's at me again," she'd whisper. "Don't say nothing to Mam. Don't say nothing."

The things the old fella did shamed her; he used her when it suited him, took advantage of her. And him, he understood. He wasn't so young that he didn't comprehend what was going on. He heard her cries late at night, her sobbing, the sound of her silvery voice begging him to stop, stop, stop. He made promises to her of what he'd do once he was old enough, once he was big enough: "I'll kill the old fucker. I will, so. I'll chop his fucking head off with the axe. I'll keep fucking pieces of him for a souvenir."

When she had gone, he took his little box out from underneath the mattress and opened it carefully. There were four flowers in his collection now, four beautiful flowers, and they were all his to keep forever. He picked the most recent one out of the batch and held it cupped in the palm of his hand. It had three long, curving roots, and the surface was deeply etched with numerous bumps and dimples. It caught slightly on the rough edges of his skin as he drew a fingertip over it. He pressed it into the smooth skin of his cheek close to his mouth, savouring the touch of it, reveling in its completeness, this perfect ivory.

Adeline, one hot night in late August, had come to him in tears. "He hit me in the mouth." She laid the gem of it in his palm. "Here, you have it. You keep that for me. I'll make a bouquet for ye, I will."

He didn't want to take it, didn't care to own such a tiny piece of her, but she insisted. He kept it underneath the corner of his mattress, and sometimes at night when he couldn't sleep, he'd roll over and slip his hand down to touch it, roll its smooth perfection between his outstretched fingertips. Later there were others who gave themselves into his hands, and he loved them for it, came to think of what he did as a gift, an easing of their pain, a release. If only they would let him, he could make them so completely free, so free. If only.

IT WAS half-past three on Monday afternoon before Kevin was able to get in to see Ivy Tobin. Danny had been correct about the visiting hours, but Ivy was so over-scheduled with activities that she had hardly a moment to spare to answer any questions. He caught up with her by the main elevators on the psychiatric floor, just as she was coming from a Zumba class.

"Miss Tobin." He offered his hand. "Not sure if you remember me or not. Sergeant Kevin Carbage, RNC."

"You're the man who found me," she said. She was dressed in stretchy leggings and a long T-shirt, and her forehead was beaded with sweat. "Sorry," she apologised, "I'm in a ball of sweat here."

"That's all right. Sure, exercise is good for ye." He grinned. "I wonder if you might have time to answer a few questions. Is there somewhere we can go to talk?"

"There's the patient common room," she told him, "but it's pretty noisy in there this time of day. What about the cafeteria?"

"Sounds like a plan."

Kevin bought coffee for them both, and they found a table next to a sunny window. Ivy seemed to be cheerful, chatting to him about the weather and her family, who were originally from Crow Head, near Twillingate.

"I'm really grateful you found me when you did," she told him. "I was pretty scared out there in the snow by myself." She looked thoughtful as she sipped her coffee. "I would have froze to death if you never found me."

"I'm just glad you're all right now." Kevin wasn't comfortable with praise. Being thanked for something he'd done made him acutely embarrassed. "Do you remember how you ended up on the barrens?" He flipped open his notebook and took out a pen.

They had gone shopping, she said, with a nurse. They went to the mall and walked around for a while, and then went into a hamburger restaurant for supper. There were a lot of people in the restaurant, but nobody she knew personally. When she finished her meal, she went to the washroom. The others said they would wait for her outside, but when she emerged, she couldn't see them.

"It pissed me off because they said they'd wait. Nancy should know better." He gathered from the context that Nancy was the nurse who'd accompanied them on the trip.

"Did you catch up with them afterwards?"

"I couldn't find them, so I went out to the porch to use the pay phone. I was going to call someone to come and get me."

"I'm guessing that didn't happen," Kevin said.

She shook her head. "I decided to go look around the mall again, to see if I could find them." But she'd been unable to locate her friends. She was on her way back to the pay phone again when a man approached, wearing a heavy parka and a knitted cap, with a scarf pulled up around his face. It struck her as odd that he'd wear a scarf that way, especially indoors. He told her he knew Nancy, that he'd seen her buying lottery tickets at the kiosk down the other end of the mall, and he'd walk with her. Instead of going directly there, he ducked into a side corridor, claiming he needed to use the bathroom.

"He got sick or something and called out for help, so I went in. I couldn't find him, though. I looked under all the stalls, but I couldn't see his feet." She felt something hit her in the back of the neck, and she became very dizzy. "I was lying on the bathroom floor looking up at the ceiling… you know, those tiles with all the little holes in them… and then the holes got blurry. That's all I remember."

It sounded like she had been drugged. "Where was the man when this was going on?"

"I don't know. I could hear people walking back and forth outside the door, and announcements over the speakers, but nobody came in."

Most likely no one knew she was there, Kevin thought. "Do you remember anything else before you woke up on the barrens?"

"My face hurt," she murmured, one hand going to her cheek. "It was sore on one side, like someone hit me."

"Do you remember going to hospital?" Kevin had managed to make it to the emergency department that night and had stayed there with her until she'd been seen by the attending physician.

"Yes, I remember that." She raised her head and gazed at him. "What did he do to me?"

"He took out one of your teeth."

"What did he do with it?"

Kevin drew a slow breath. "We think he kept it, but we don't know why."

"Why would he want my tooth?"

"Again, I don't know." He wished there was more he could tell her without compromising the investigation, but that wasn't possible. "Ivy, you have been extremely helpful to me." He stood and tucked his notebook back into his pocket. "I'm going to leave my card with you. If you remember anything else about this man, give me a call."

"I do remember one thing," she said, after a moment.

Kevin paused in zipping up his parka. "Oh?"

"I pushed him off me. We were in his car, and he was taking me away somewhere. I pulled on his scarf and it came down." An expression of horror crept across her features. "He had no face. He had no face at all."

THE SLEEPING pill Danny had taken at Torbay Airport began to wear off as they were flying over Ireland. He sat up, momentarily embarrassed to find he'd been drooling on himself, and pressed the call button to ask for some water. "We'll be landing at Heathrow in just a few moments," the steward told him, "so you'll want to drink up." Danny did as he was told, flagging the man as he came back up the aisle to hand him the empty bottle. "Is London your final destination?" he asked. When Danny said he was going on to Dublin, the steward told him he'd have to hurry. "The Aer Lingus flight is leaving about ten minutes after we land, but I'll get the captain to radio ahead and have them hold the plane for you."

The flight across the Atlantic had been uneventful. He'd slipped one of the prescription tablets under his tongue, asked a passing steward for a blanket and pillow, and was asleep before the aircraft even reached cruising altitude. His dreams were queer and disjointed, for all that he slept deeply, and full of strange elements culled from his waking life: Sandra, his burned hand, the dead girl in the pond, images of Tadhg, both static and in motion. In one sequence, he was walking through the empty rooms of an abandoned house, where he discovered Tadhg looking out a window, but when he spoke to him, he was ignored, and Tadhg turned and walked straight through him, like a ghost. He tried to wake and couldn't, and the dream changed direction so that he was standing on the road outside his grandparents' old house in the middle of a snowstorm, more alone than he had ever been.

The Fasten Seatbelts sign came on, and the pilot announced they were beginning their descent into Heathrow. Despite the bottle of water he'd drunk, Danny felt dry-mouthed and apprehensive. Maybe he wouldn't go on to Dublin at all, he thought wildly. Maybe he'd get a flight to somewhere else—Iceland or Norway or the North Pole—and disappear, go to ground, hide himself so completely that no one would ever find him again. No, he wouldn't. *You're too fucking honest*, he thought wryly. *A cop to the marrow of your bones you are, so.*

He bypassed the luggage carousels, having only the one carry-on bag, and headed straight to customs and from there up a steep escalator already crowded with other travellers despite the early hour. The clerk at St. John's airport had already checked him through to Dublin, so he had merely to step through the security checkpoint and show his boarding pass. He scanned his phone for messages before take-off. He had a text from Sandra in response to his message that he was booked on a flight to Dublin. She said she was heading back to Portugal and enjoined him to stay safe. He hadn't been able to bring himself to tell her about the hearing; she obviously thought he had gone looking for Tadgh.

Other than that, there was a call from Cillian Riley, reassuring him that everything was well in hand. He'd had no worries about leaving the station in Riley's charge. Time and again he'd proven himself more than capable. He was an able investigator, and Danny was going to miss him when he left Kildevil Cove for law school. He'd briefed Riley on the direction the investigation needed to take and impressed on him that there still was no plausible suspect. Gail Russell's murder seemed to be entirely without reason, a series of events that might have been motivated by malice, lust, or any other emotion under the sun. Regan Lampe's post-mortem findings on both Roland Evans and the unnamed girl from the pond suggested all three murders were tied together.

"Sarah Avery is checking on who owns box 27," Danny reminded him as Riley dropped him at the airport. "Don't be surprised if they're renting it under a fake name. Get hold of the postmistress and find out what sorts of things are coming into that box. Don't let her put you off. Get a warrant if you have to, probable cause."

"I will," Riley promised.

"Hughes is going to follow Roy Fitzpatrick, see what he's up to in the woods all by himself. There's something weird going on there. Make sure you get a full report from Hughes, and make him write it up. He's a bit slack about stuff like that." By this time they were at the Departures gate, and Riley could go no farther. "We've had no luck finding anybody in the area with a boat missing, but try and send someone by that abandoned house at frequent intervals. I'm still not convinced it's always empty. Same with that house next to Barry and Maureen Tulk's. I saw a light in there the night of the blizzard. Did Jennice's husband, Dave, get home okay?"

"Danny." Riley put a hand in the middle of his chest, gently. "You told me all this. You even wrote it down. Yes, Dave got home okay." He smiled. "We'll manage. Just you come back safe from Ireland, all right?"

WHEN DANNY landed in Dublin just after dawn, it was raining, a cold rain driven by a chilly wind. It was January here as well as home. He was headed towards the main entrance and the taxi rank when he heard someone calling his name.

"Danny! Danny Quirke! Wait up, will ye?"

He turned and saw Kai McNamara, a bit older and more haggard than he'd been during their last FaceTime call. "When I called to tell you I was coming, I didn't mean you had to meet me," Danny said, reaching to shake his hand. "But I'm glad to see ye."

McNamara took his holdall and led him to the car park, where he unlocked a late model BMW and stowed Danny's case in the back. "I've reserved a hotel room for ye, right on Parnell Square. It's only a quick walk to the Pearse Street Station from there."

"Thanks, Kai." Danny buckled himself in. "It's odd to be back here."

"Sorry we couldn't have better weather for ye," McNamara said. "It's been a bit shite lately."

Both he and Danny were quiet during the drive. McNamara had the radio tuned to a local station that was giving out the morning news, but there was nothing worth commenting on. He hadn't told McNamara why he was back in Ireland, only intimating that the trip was to do with some personal business he wasn't at liberty to talk about, and McNamara didn't pry. Either he was being polite—not a personality trait he was known for—or he'd assumed Danny was there to fetch Tadhg home. The truth of it was Danny hadn't stopped thinking of Tadhg from the moment he first saw Ireland. The desire to see him, to touch him and bring him home, coiled and writhed inside him like a living thing.

"How…." It stuck in his throat and he had to start again. "How is he?"

"Your man Tadhg?" They were stopped at a red light, and McNamara turned to look at him. "I've been keeping him on a short leash, so. He's a knack for getting into trouble, that one."

A cold dread took form in the pit of Danny's stomach. "Is he in trouble?"

"No, nor is he going to be." The light changed and McNamara eased the car forward into the flow of traffic. "Not now, any rate."

"What do you mean?"

"After our last conversation, I went to your man's flat and had meself a wee look round," McNamara said. "Open up the glove box there and pass me out me cigs, will ye?"

Danny did as he was asked, handing across a packet of Marlboros. "Those things will kill ye."

"*Pfft*." McNamara pushed in the cigarette lighter, waited until it popped out. "Not much odds now," he said, between puffs.

"What do you mean?" The rain had slackened off, so Danny pushed the button to roll down the window on his side of the car. Cigarette smoke in close confines gave him a headache.

"That's a tale for another time." McNamara smirked and flicked cigarette ash out the open window. Despite the Irishman's good cheer, Danny sensed all was not well with him. McNamara had always been lean, but now he was practically gaunt, his clothes hanging on him like grave clouts, his skin an unhealthy shade of grey. He looked tired, but it was the fatigue of long illness rather than a lack of sleep, and Danny found it extremely worrying.

"By the way, I found something in your man's bottom drawer and took it off him. It's under your seat there if you're interested."

Danny gazed at him, but McNamara was intent on traffic. He reached under the seat and pulled out a cloth-wrapped bundle. "Jesus. Is this what I think it is?" He opened it to find a snub-nosed .38. "For Christ's sake."

"Yeah. I think he had notions. Going to do a bit of damage, he was." He flicked a glance at Danny. "I don't need to tell you he'd end up zippered into a plastic bag." A mirthless laugh. "Ye can thank me later."

"Have you seen him since?" Danny asked. "Does he know the gun's gone?"

"I had a nice little text message from him about an hour ago." McNamara laughed. "He says he's going to kneecap me next time he sees me, and if I know what I'm about I'd best bring it back to him." He drew on his cigarette and exhaled a long plume of smoke. "Like fuck I will."

Thanks to McNamara's regular intelligence, Danny was already well aware of Tadhg's plan to find Phelan, the man who'd stolen from him and forced him into bankruptcy. It was probably the stupidest idea Tadhg had ever had, and over the years, there had been a few humdingers—like the time when they were boys and Tadhg had collected all the old Remembrance Day poppies from the cenotaph and resold them as new, swearing up and down that yes, he absolutely was going to donate the money to the Legion. "Thanks, Kai." He rewrapped the gun and slid it back under the seat. "What will you do with it?"

"Throw it in the Liffey, most likely." McNamara shot him a look, eyebrows raised. "Isn't that what you did?"

"That was different," Danny said. "I'm not proud of it—any of it." Eamonn Nolan's death was on his hands, even though he hadn't actually pulled the trigger. He'd lived with it the past two and a half years and would likely live with it for the rest of his natural existence. "I had to. You know that."

"Oh, I'm not disagreeing with ye." McNamara pulled up in front of a neat white townhouse, the Hotel St. George, and put the car into park. "Here's your new digs. Can ye manage up the stairs by yourself?"

"Kiss me arse," Danny replied cheerfully. He reached for his wallet. "Let me give you something for your petrol."

"No, put your money away." McNamara nodded at the hotel's front door. "I booked ye a room on the top floor. I think the lift is broken." He grinned as Danny moved to exit the car. "Don't have a heart attack."

"Can I at least buy you dinner?" Danny opened the back door and retrieved his holdall.

"Sure. I'm not a cheap date, though. Let's say I pick you up at seven?" He flipped down the sun visor and brought out a card. "That's where he works. He's doing the early shift today. He'll be there at noon."

Danny took the card, albeit reluctantly. "I… didn't ask."

"Sure, you were thinking it." McNamara put the car into gear. "Seven o'clock. Wear something nice, eh?" He gave a salacious wink. "Show a bit o' leg." With that, he was gone. Danny stood for a moment, watching the BMW disappear towards O'Connell, and laughed. He looked at the card McNamara had given him: Kenneally's Bar, Thomas Street. Beer, Wine, and Cocktails.

Tadhg was as close as Thomas Street—almost close enough to touch.

CHAPTER FOURTEEN

IT WAS early Tuesday morning when Dougie Hughes parked his car by the side of the road about half a kilometre away from the Fitzpatrick residence and got out. He'd planned to go on Monday, get the situation with Roy Fitzpatrick nailed down as soon as possible, but the baby was teething and had developed a high fever to go along with it. He and Lisa were frantic, remembering stories of teething babies who'd started having fits, so he'd called in to work, then beat it across the barrens to Carbonear Hospital with the little one. Luckily a bit of liquid acetaminophen brought the fever down, and pretty soon the baby was her usual self.

It was a beautiful winter's day, with bright sunshine and a clear blue sky, the perfect kind of weather for a walk in the woods. He'd initially considered whether it might not be best to follow Roy Fitzpatrick on a snowmobile, but ruled it out because of the noise. An ATV was out of the question for the same reason. Instead, he'd gone into his garage and dusted off the snowshoes he'd used several years before when he was posted to Labrador. It took him a few strides before he got the hang of it, but soon he was tracking Roy Fitzpatrick with no trouble at all. He relaxed into it, enjoying the soft susurration of fresh powder beneath his feet and breathing deeply of the cold, fresh air.

Fitzpatrick had emerged from the house about five minutes after Dougie's arrival. Like Dougie, he was dressed in a heavy winter parka and snow boots, with a wool scarf wrapped around the lower half of his face and a knitted cap crammed down over his ears. He wasn't as fit or as young as Dougie, and the deep snow gave him some difficulty as he moved from the house to the garage. Dougie waited, shielded behind a stand of fir trees, until he heard the roar of a snowmobile starting up. It shot out of the garage with Fitzpatrick aboard, kneeling with one leg on the seat, and turned onto a narrow path leading into the forest. Dougie would have no problem following the tracks left by the machine's treads.

Fitzpatrick kept to a relatively slow speed, never taking the machine out of first gear and slowing around curves, feeding gas to the throttle a little at a time whenever he was forced to navigate a rise in the landscape. Dougie was careful to hang back, out of the other man's line of sight but close enough that he didn't lose Fitzpatrick. It took nearly an hour for Dougie to get where

Fitzpatrick was going, and by then he'd worked up enough of a sweat that he needed to unfasten his parka. They'd passed by Purchase Pond and the smaller Hoyles Pond, still on the same narrow woods road. The sun rose higher in the sky, and a slight breeze came with it, twirling the fresh snow into spindrift. Fitzpatrick stopped at the edge of Western Pond, pulling the snowmobile up to a small derelict structure seemingly cobbled together out of stray bits of lumber and salvaged driftwood. It looked for all the world like a tilt, the traditional house the island's early settlers had commonly erected for themselves. Dougie could make out a narrow door but no windows; a stovepipe projected upwards from the roof, breathing a thin plume of steam into the morning air. Fitzpatrick got off the snowmobile, removed a cloth bag that had been tied on behind it, and went into the structure.

Hughes crept nearer and peered inside. Fitzpatrick, his back to the door, was affixing a length of thin copper tubing to a shiny stainless-steel stockpot. The pot was huge and probably held about thirty litres, give or take. All at once Dougie understood why Fitzpatrick had been sneaking away into the woods, and perhaps also why he wouldn't allow Inspector Quirke and Sergeant Carbage into his barn.

He was making moonshine.

Dougie stepped inside and cleared his throat. "I'm assuming you have a licence for this."

Fitzpatrick startled violently and swore a long stream of colourful epithets. "How long have you been stood there?"

"Long enough," Dougie replied. He moved towards the still to examine it. The stock pot was set on top of a makeshift woodburning stove fashioned out of an empty oil drum. Currently the fire was blazing away nicely, and as Dougie watched, Fitzpatrick bent and shoved another thick birch log into the stove's mouth and shut the door. The copper line ran from the stock pot to a large plastic tub, elevated above ground on a small wooden table knocked together out of two-by-fours and a piece of plywood. "You drink that stuff and you'll blind yourself."

"Go 'way with ye," Fitzpatrick retorted. "Not my first batch of homebrew." He didn't seem contrite in the least, nor was he overly concerned that he'd been caught.

"You do realise," Dougie said, "that operating a distillery without the proper permits is illegal?"

"What are you gonna do about it?" Fitzpatrick asked sourly. "Arrest me?" When Dougie didn't reply, he continued, "I got a permit. It's at home.

I can even show it to ye." He raised an eyebrow and winked. "Or I can give ye a little present, something to keep ye warm on these cold nights, wha?"

"If I brought that home, Lisa would kill me." Dougie stood back as Fitzpatrick lifted the lid of the pot and, seizing a long stick, stirred the mash inside. The sour funk of it smelled like cat piss. "Are you sure that's just moonshine?"

"You want a little taste?" Fitzpatrick ladled something out of a second stock pot set to the rear of the stove and held it out to Dougie.

"Christ, no." He pushed it away. "God, that stinks."

"It might stink, but it'll get ye there." He leered. "I bet this'll get that pretty young wife of yours on the go. She'll be tearing the clothes off ye."

Fitzpatrick's insinuation, along with the disgusting leer, turned Dougie's stomach. "You are going to dismantle this immediately," he said. "If I come back tomorrow and it's still here, I will be issuing a fine. In case you don't know the law, that can range from five hundred to ten thousand dollars."

"Sure 'tis only a bit of home brew, bhoy!"

Dougie turned to go. "Get rid of it." There was so much junk piled up in the shed that there was hardly room for the still. He saw empty bottles and boxes, old lumber, and a large plastic drum of...

...industrial lye?

"G'wan, ye fucking nancy boy!" Fitzpatrick roared, but Dougie didn't bother to respond. In his years of policing, he'd heard all the insults, had been spat upon, had rocks and bottles thrown at him, and once he'd even been hit over the head with a shovel, a blow that laid him out cold on the ground. Arguing with people like Fitzpatrick was pointless and would gain him nothing.

Dougie took his time snowshoeing back to his car. He unbuckled his snowshoes, knocked the bulk of snow off them, and then drove back to the station. It was close to eleven by the time he arrived. He brought the snowshoes in and laid them next to the radiator in the front porch to dry.

Inspector Cillian Riley was in the break room when Dougie went in, standing by the Keurig and watching as it dribbled and gurgled to a stop. "You look all rosy-cheeked and bright-eyed this morning," he said.

"I went after Roy Fitzpatrick," Dougie told him. He took a clean mug from the pyramid of them on the counter and sorted through the various coffee pods. "You'll never guess what he's at."

Riley flipped open the top of the machine and took out the spent coffee pod, discarded it. "Probably not, so tell me."

"He's making home brew in the woods." As soon as he said it, the sheer ridiculousness of the situation struck him, and Dougie began to laugh. "He offered me some to take home to Lisa."

Riley rolled his eyes. "Mother of God. Did you take him up on it? You should have. I heard the stuff they make around here is something like a hundred fifty proof. You can set it on fire and it burns like the devil."

Dougie shook his head and inserted a coffee pod into the Keurig before closing the lid. "I'll stick with coffee," he said. "I like my stomach lining intact."

"Any road," Riley said, taking his coffee and heading out of the break room, "give him twenty-four hours to get rid of the still and then swing by to take a look. If it's not gone when you go back, you'll have to ticket him."

Dougie wondered if he shouldn't mention the other thing he saw while he was there, but he couldn't be sure if it was significant or just happenstance. He'd looked up home distilling on the internet when he'd reached his car, and the supplies were pretty basic: sugar, yeast, and some kind of grain, maybe barley or corn. He'd been trying to figure out what Fitzpatrick would possibly use lye for, but he couldn't.

"Okay, Constable?" Riley prompted. Hughes had been staring into space like an idiot.

"Yes, sir. Thank you, sir."

"Are you quite all right, Hughes?" The note of irritation in Riley's voice decided him.

"Quite all right, sir."

Riley nodded and left. The Keurig groaned, and a thin stream of fresh coffee decanted into Hughes's cup. Dougie waited until the apparatus had finished its cycle, then removed the coffee and dumped some cream and sugar into it. He opened the fridge and took out the half of a cake left over from somebody's birthday, rifled through the drawer until he found a sharp knife, and cut himself a large slice.

"Are you going to eat all that yourself?" Sarah Avery had come into the break room and was eyeing his piece of cake. "You'll be fat as a pig."

"Not likely," Dougie retorted. "I've snowshoed way in the country this morning and back again. Where have you been?"

"Post office." Sarah picked a clean mug off the pile and went to the Keurig, picking Dougie's empty coffee pod out and throwing it into the bin. "You'll never guess what I found in box 27."

"You're right. I'll never guess." Dougie grinned. He liked Sarah. She came from a tiny fishing village in Bonavista Bay, and she was smart, kind, and funny. She often came to their house for supper or babysat for him and Lisa when they wanted a night to themselves.

"Whoever owned it—or rented it—was running a business." She closed the lid on the coffee machine, grunted in displeasure when it refused to discharge hot liquid. "Jesus, Dougie, d'ye ever fill up the tank or what?" She disconnected the water tank from the side of the machine and carried it over to the sink to fill it with fresh water.

"What kind of business?" he asked, his interest piqued. "I thought Riley told you not to touch the contents of that box."

"When did he say that?"

Dougie raised an eyebrow at her.

"Go 'way." She scoffed. "Friggin' nosy hole. Inspector Riley told me anything that was in plain sight was free for the taking. Whoever owns that box hadn't bothered to empty it in donkey's ages. It was overflowing. Mrs. Driscoll was filling in for Pansy the day, and she had the works of it put aside. Told me to look through it if I wanted." She plucked her mobile phone out of her back pocket and thumbed through a series of photos until she found the one she wanted. "Look."

Dougie did. What he saw shocked him: a pile of letters some ten centimetres thick. "Who are they from?" he asked. "What do they want?"

"The company is called Charonyx," she said. "As near as I can tell, it's a portmanteau of the words Charon and Nyx. In Greek mythology, Charon was the ferryman who carried souls over the river Styx to the afterlife. He was the son of Nyx, otherwise known as Night."

"What does it do?"

The Keurig bubbled to a halt, and Sarah reached across to retrieve her coffee. "Every one of those letters is a request." Her smooth forehead knotted, and the corners of her mouth pulled violently downward. Dougie stepped forward and reached out his hand to her, but she backed away. "I'm fine." She pressed her eyes shut and drew a series of shaky breaths. "People contact this company and ask—Jesus, Dougie."

"Sarah?"

"They ask this person to help them die."

THE LAST time Danny had been in Ireland, he'd had blood on his hands. Eamonn Nolan's blood. Nolan was a local troublemaker who considered himself a hard man, a type Danny had run up against before. Between the jigs and the reels, Nolan had taken a young woman hostage at the Clontarf seawall and was threatening to kill her if Danny and the other Guards didn't back off. Ultimately, Nolan had shot himself, but Danny took full responsibility for the man's death. He wasn't a hostage negotiator, he should have waited until someone better qualified arrived on the scene, but he hadn't. He'd attempted to engage with Nolan by bringing in his common-law wife, but rather than soothing him, her presence had tipped him over the edge into suicide. There had been an official enquiry, and Danny was suspended from duty. It wasn't a period of his life that he relished reliving, but here he was again, back in Dublin awaiting a call on his mobile so he could go to speak to yet another board of enquiry about the human trafficking case that had gotten him demoted from inspector to constable.

It was utter shite. He'd nothing to do with it, hadn't been involved in the far-reaching circle of corruption that stretched from one side of the Atlantic to the other. But because Moira Fraser was his superior and because he'd mistakenly allowed Martin Belshawe to go on his merry way, he was suspect. It was only Adrian Molloy's intervention that allowed him to continue to work as a police officer—albeit in a greatly reduced capacity.

He'd showered and shaved after McNamara dropped him at the hotel and had eaten breakfast in a small café on Parnell Street, then wandered around for a while. The weather was cold and damp, not conducive to sightseeing, but he couldn't resist going by Kenneally's Bar on Thomas Street in the Liberties, where Tadhg worked. The bar was closed at present, but he took a look in the window. Kai had said Tadhg would be working at noon. Was he on the premises now, perhaps prepping food in the back or cutting up lemons and limes for drinks garnishes? He should knock on the door, see if anyone was there, and if so, they could tell him when Tadhg would arrive and he could come back. In his head it sounded so easy: he'd walk in and Tadhg would be there—

Here was where the fantasy broke down. He'd walk in, and Tadhg would be there, and what? They'd just pick up where they left off? Where they'd left off was with raised voices, fighting, slamming doors.

"You don't have to go. There's no point in you running off to Ireland."

"And what the hell am I supposed to do, Danny? Let that fucker get away with it?"

"You don't know what you're doing. These people could be *dangerous*."

"I'm going over there to get my money back. I refuse to let them run me out of business."

And that had been that. Three days later Tadhg was on a plane with Lily, and Danny was left behind. He'd waited in vain for a phone call, a text message. The wall of silence between them was seemingly impenetrable. Both he and Tadhg were equally stubborn and would rather die than be the first one to make contact. This personality trait had led to the months-long stalemate between them, neither man willing to budge. What Tadhg was doing was dangerous and foolhardy, but once he'd set himself upon a particular path, getting him to reconsider was like trying to coax the wind to change direction.

His mobile rang as he drew back from the pub window. "Deiniol Quirke."

"Constable Quirke, my name is Sergeant Guy Frederickson. I'm with the National Central Bureau, Interpol. I'm calling with regards to the enquiry." The voice was upper class, with an Anglo-Irish accent and a certain air of hauteur that put Danny off immediately. "You are required to present yourself at the An Garda Síochána headquarters at eleven this morning to answer charges."

Am I? Danny thought. *And you can go fuck yourself, so.* He didn't say this. "Oh?"

Under normal circumstances, anyone being investigated by Interpol would have a Red Notice issued, advising local area police they were wanted for questioning. In Danny's case, he would have been summarily arrested by the RCMP and brought to Ireland under guard. Because he was a police officer, he was allowed to travel on his own recognisance, which didn't mean he was free to do as he liked. He'd noticed two blank-faced men sitting a row behind him on the flight from St. John's, both of them dressed in expensive suits, their shoes shined to a mirror brightness. He was reasonably certain they were CSIS agents—Canadian Security Intelligence Service—and they were there to make sure he got to Dublin. He'd seen them again at the airport when he was getting off his flight, and lingering in front of the Hotel St. George, where he was staying.

"I'll be there," he replied. "Thank you." His throat tightened, like it was closing together.

"Very well," Frederickson said crisply. "Even though this is an enquiry and not a criminal trial, you are strongly advised to access legal counsel. For your own good." He rang off.

"Legal counsel," Danny murmured aloud. "How in the hell am I supposed to do that?" A man and a woman, passing by him hand in hand, turned to look.

DANNY WAS afraid. He didn't need anyone to tell him what he was feeling; he knew. He'd been terrified that the whole thing would be a monumental shit show, that he'd be hauled into the dock like you saw on those UK crime dramas he and Tadhg watched on Netflix, handcuffed and wearing an orange jumpsuit or one of those white Tyvek coveralls, the arresting officer's warnings echoing in his ears: *Anything you say can be taken down and used in evidence….* It wasn't like that at all. In fact, it was reassuringly normal, but he was still terrified.

The room was of a moderate size, painted a soft beige inside and hardly resembling a courtroom at all. That he'd been in here before was of no comfort to him. During his time with the Gardaí, he'd had cause to come in here, but never under these circumstances. His initial dismissal, after the death of Eamonn Nolan, had occasioned nothing more than uncomfortable words in his superior's office before he collected his things in a cardboard box and went on his way. This was different. He'd come here of his own accord and on his own recognisance—notwithstanding the two men who'd shadowed him every step since before he'd even set foot in Ireland—but he was under no illusions. He was the defendant in this trial. It was a trial, after all. He'd been unable to find legal counsel on such short notice, and so a solicitor had been procured out of a panel of those available on the morning of the enquiry. He was young, fresh-faced, with the wide blue eyes of a cartoon animal, and he looked barely old enough to shave. He met Danny in the corridor outside the room where the enquiry was to convene and introduced himself.

"Isaac Shapter. I'm to represent you, Constable Quirke." His handshake was firm, and he sounded confident, but not overly so. "I'm sorry you find yourself in these circumstances. Must have been a proper pain in the arse to come all the way over here for this." When he grinned, two dimples appeared in his cheeks.

Danny confirmed that yes, it was a pain in the arse, especially as it came on such short notice, and also because he'd no idea what the hell was going on or why he was being charged.

"They like to throw around words like 'charged,'" Shapter said. "Makes them feel all big and important. I had a wee glance at your file, and I think they're pissing into the wind myself."

A tiny spark of hope kindled deep inside him, but Danny quashed it. He wanted to be realistic about matters. If he ended up thrown into jail—

"You will not," Shapter said. Apparently Danny had spoken this last part out loud. "So put that out of your mind. They have no actual proof you were involved in any way, apart from Chief Inspector Fraser being your immediate superior. Belshawe's man is fishing."

Danny let out the breath he'd been holding. "Still and all, I don't like to fasten on to false hope."

"No false hope here." Shapter patted him on the back. "Come on, we'll go in."

He was seated now beside Danny in the first row. A small platform or dais, located at the front of the room, raised the presiding judge over the other attendees, and a small witness stand or prisoner's box stood to the side. He wondered whether Martin Belshawe would be seated there, brought into the room in shackles. *Give it up, Dan*, he thought. *Ye watches too many television programs ye do, so.* His burned hand was hurting, and he realised belatedly he should have redressed the wound before going out. He remembered being back at home in the Cove, able to dart in to see the doctor, get a bandage or a few stitches on the fly, before the various health authorities did away with that tradition. He should have redressed it. The last he'd looked, the edges of the wound were red and sore, the collapsed burn blister barely begun to heal. Surely to God it would be infected if he didn't see to it.

He had never felt more alone in his entire life. Even when Alison died, when he'd stood over her open grave and poured down a handful of earth to say his final farewell, others were there to offer comfort. When he'd stood on the Clontarf sea wall and watched, helpless, as Eamonn Nolan blew his own brains out, he was surrounded by Guards, his colleagues and his friends. When Tadhg had left him....

Martin Belshawe stepped into the room, accompanied by two Guards. He looked directly in front of him, nowhere else, and took his seat beside a woman Danny presumed was his solicitor, near the front of the room. He was wearing a dark grey suit and a navy shirt but no tie, unshackled and clean-shaven. Without his beard he looked years younger, his body held in a vulnerable posture, round-shouldered and defeated. After all this time, Moira Fraser had still not been located, and Danny wondered if Belshawe knew and wasn't telling. Maybe she'd been welcomed back into the fold of the organised trafficking ring, absorbed into their numbers as if she'd never left. Or maybe they did away with her, hid her body somewhere or disposed of it by other means. They might never know what became of her. Danny was betting Martin Belshawe knew.

"Stand up." Shapter tugged on his sleeve, and Danny stood. There was some business with the presiding figure at the front of the room, and then everybody sat down again. The air in the room was stuffy and close, making it hard to breathe. "There. Head between your knees."

Danny was gazing down at the room's grey carpet, and Shapter's hand was on his back. Had he fainted? He forced himself to draw in air and blow it out again. Someone was asking if Constable Quirke was well or did he need a doctor, and Shapter answered something while a young man in a Garda uniform passed across a cold bottle of water.

"Have yourself a drink of this," Shapter said, and Danny did.

"I'm all right." He sat up. "I'm fine."

Belshawe was looking at him, his dark eyes taking everything in, his face expressionless. His gaze flicked from Danny to Shapter and back again. He would take the stand first; then it would be Danny's turn. What would Belshawe tell them? Clearly he intended to implicate Danny. Had he found out something that had previously been overlooked? Like what? The only connection Danny had....

"The only connection my client has with this entire sordid mess is former Chief Inspector Moira Fraser," Shapter said, "who was his immediate superior during the time period in question."

Had they gotten here already? But Danny hadn't even been called to the stand. "Any evidence to the contrary is flimsy at best. If the court will permit, I have before me several documents attesting to Constable Quirke's exemplary character, both as a police officer and a private citizen."

In the few hours that Shapter had had to work on Danny's case, he'd managed to amass an enormous amount of evidence relating to the trafficking ring: statements from other officers who'd worked on the case, a timeline of the events up to and including Moira's flight from Newfoundland, as well as a detailed analysis of facts pertaining to RNC and RCMP involvement in the arrest of two main players, Felix Carter and Donovan Rowe.

"Rather than assisting in the trafficking of vulnerable women, Constable Quirke was instrumental in bringing down all existing members of the syndicate located in the Canadian province of Newfoundland and Labrador. Judge, I move for dismissal of the charges against Constable Quirke, as they are founded on incorrect information and exist entirely without proof."

Then it was Martin Belshawe's turn on the stand. He answered the questions put to him in a monotone, his replies brief. When asked what Deiniol Quirke's involvement was, he said, "None." The question was repeated for clarification. "None," Belshawe said again. He didn't raise his head to look at Danny.

Just like that, it was over.

"Let me buy you a pint," Danny said, outside the courtroom.

Shapter checked his watch. "Bit early," he said. He was right; it was just after noon. The whole proceedings, the event that decided his entire future as a police officer, had taken a little over an hour.

"Sorry." Danny was embarrassed. "I'm just so relieved." He caught hold of Shapter's hand and shook it. "Thank you," he said. "You can't know what you've done for me."

"It's all in a day's work, Constable—er, I mean Inspector—Quirke." Belshawe was coming out, walking between the same two Guards who'd seen him into the room. As he approached Danny he stumbled a little, bumping into him and knocking him off-kilter.

"Will you ever watch what you're at?" Shapter helped to right him, a hand on Danny's elbow. "Don't worry," he said. "Where he's going, he won't see the light of day for a long time."

"I owe you a great deal," Danny said. "One question: How did you manage to gather all that evidence? We only just met this morning."

Shapter picked up his case and grinned. "Like the police, we too have our little ways." He patted Danny's shoulder. "Have a good trip home."

"I will." He wondered if he oughtn't to go after Shapter, try to get more information out of him, find out what he'd meant, but Shapter had disappeared around a corner and the moment had already passed him by.

CHAPTER FIFTEEN

"I DON'T think I can keep coming back here," she said, after it was done and they were lying in each other's arms. The air in the room was cold, but he'd built a goodly fire in the stove to warm them, and they had lain together under a pile of blankets he'd brought from the old house. He hadn't bothered to keep anything else out of his meagre belongings; there was nothing much he wanted. But he knew the blankets would be useful, and so he'd packed them into a duffel bag, along with the few treasures remaining to him and Adeline's tooth.

"You said you wouldn't leave me." He lifted a hand and ran it through her hair—his bad hand, the one with the flesh all melted and warped, but she never bothered about that. It was one more thing he loved about her. She didn't care what he looked like. She'd never cared.

"He's after catching me sneaking out. He knows I'm at something."

"That's his trouble, then. He knows too much, or thinks he does." In a very little time it wouldn't matter anymore. She would have the child—his child—and they would go away together, somewhere he could live his life without the pointed stares and cruel curiosity of others. He'd build her a cottage in the woods, close to a little stream where they could get fresh water, and they'd grow vegetables in a garden patch outside the kitchen door. "We'll go away together, me and you."

But they would have to take the clocks. He'd promised Mam he'd wind them. He had to listen to what Mam had told him back then, even though she'd said bad things and even though she'd hurt him. Mam had been the only thing standing between him and the outside world, and it wasn't like they'd ever had anywhere to go. Him and Mam and Adeline; they were all he'd had and he was all they'd had. He'd done what had to be done, and he'd expected a reward. He'd taken the brunt of it, the horrific damage to his hand and face.

"It's your own fucking fault," he'd imagined Mam saying afterwards, as he lay in the hospital, alone and in pain. "What the Jesus were you waiting for? You stood there like a bloody fool watching it burn. Sure you haven't got brains enough to blow your nose."

There had been talk of him going down the States to a special hospital, and for a while he'd had a little bit of hope. But the special hospital was only for youngsters, and he was well of age by then, so they refused his doctor's application. None of the doctors in St. John's could do anything about his face, and there was no money to send him to Nova Scotia.

He'd have to live with it, he supposed, for all it was unfair. After all, he'd done it for Mam and Adeline. Someone had to stop the old fella. Someone had to make him stop doing the things he did to Adeline. But it was a high price to pay.

"I'm going home." She rose from the nest of blankets and stood naked before him, her pregnant belly enormous now, her breasts full and pink-nippled, her skin glowing. "He's after missing me by now. He thinks I went to bed early. He'll check. You don't know what he's like."

She was so very beautiful, the complete opposite of him, who had to hide away from common sight, like the monster he'd once read about, a mad genius living under the Paris Opera.

"We can make a special latex mask for him. It will hide the worst of the damage." The specialist said it would attach just underneath his eyes with a tiny dab of soluble glue. In time and with practice, affixing it would become second nature to him. He could grow his hair long, to cover the places where his ears had been, before the fire's immense and horrific heat had melted and erased them.

"Would you like it if I wore a mask?" He got up as well and pulled his clothes on, shivering a little in the frigid air. "They made one for me, years ago. I could wear it and I wouldn't look so bad." He despised the cringing sound of himself, begging her for something. "I could take you places, and the little one, if you wanted to go out."

"I should tell you." Fully dressed, she turned to face him now. In the firelight her face was pale, her expression stoic and composed. "I can't come here anymore. Not any of these places we've been." Her hands moved to cradle her belly. "I don't think it's healthy, and it's certainly not safe for the baby." She gestured at the mess around them, the empty tins and bottles, the discarded wrappers, brown paper bags stained with chip grease. The air smelled of rot and decay, the corners full of rodent droppings and dead bluebottle flies. "I'm afraid I might catch something."

He put his feet into his boots, bending to tie them up. She was standing in her stocking feet, and he brought her boots to her, knelt at her feet to help her into them. Her balance was bad, she couldn't manage on her own, and her club foot caused her to tilt over to one side, so she held on to him. "I'll find a better place," he promised.

"No." She shrugged into her parka and zipped it up. "When I leave I won't be coming back." He heard genuine regret mixed in with her words, but her eyes were dry, and she was more resolute than he had ever seen her. "I'm sorry. I've had enough now."

"I've got a mask," he said again. "It's here somewhere. I've got a mask, and I can wear it." He knew precisely where it was: in a shoebox under the bed, a yellow shoebox with his name marked on it.

"No. I'm done with all of this."

"But it's my baby," he said. "You're carrying my baby. You said…." The horror of what was happening stole over him slowly, seeping into his consciousness like a stain. "We would be together, the three of us. You said."

She caressed the bulge of her belly, both hands moving in small circles. She was looking at the rich roundness of herself, not at him, and smiling gently, a woman caught up in a happy daydream of her unborn child. "It's not your baby." Now she turned her gaze on him, and there was something cold and angry lurking in her eyes. "I know the precise moment this life entered my body, and it wasn't with you. This child is perfect, and you could not be further from perfection."

She was moving forward, and her hand was on the door when he caught up with her, the needle in his fist. When he touched her with it, she collapsed like a sack of old clothes, and he let her fall. He left the needle sticking in her neck, and then he went to find the sharpest knife he had. There was business to be done. That's what Mam always called it—business. He sang while he worked (*Thus kindly I'll scatter/thy leaves o'er the bed*), and when he was finished, the floor around her body was awash with blood.

CILLIAN RILEY was just finishing up his lunch when Bobbi Lambert found him in his office. Wordlessly she handed him her iPad. "What's this?" he asked.

"Carpet fibres."

"Oh?"

"From a 1977 Dodge Tradesman van." Her smile grew slowly. "Right?"

"Are you serious?" He scrolled through what was on the screen. The RCMP lab in White Hills had returned a hit on the carpet fibres Bobbi's team had found on Gail Russell's clothing.

"Bobbi, this is incredible." So Gail Russell hadn't been transported in the trunk of a car, but in the back of a van.

"Not my doing," she replied. "The Mounties found it. I'm just glad we had this small shred to go on."

"I'll tell Danny as soon as he gets back," Riley replied. "He'll be dead chuffed."

"He'll be what?" Bobbi reclaimed the iPad. "Is that some kind of Newcastle saying?"

"He'll be glad to hear it," Riley amended. "Now we just need to track down the van and we're in business." The best way to do that, of course, would be to release a media alert, but that might drive the van's owner into hiding. This case was notoriously complex, and they needed access to anything that could help them close the net. He decided on a discreet approach and sent Avery and Hughes out to look for the van. "Don't be shy. Search everywhere. If you see a closed garage, try and get the owner to let you in. We need to find this van, because we know it was used to transport Gail Russell. More than likely it's been modified with the Shore Taxi signage and emblem."

Avery headed out immediately to fetch her parka and winter boots, but Hughes lingered. "What is it?" Riley asked.

"I saw something in Roy Fitzpatrick's shed," Hughes said.

"Yes, an illegal distillery. You told me."

"No, sir. It was lye. A huge drum of industrial lye."

"Lye? What was he doing with that?"

"That's what I don't understand, sir." Hughes shook his head. "It's nothing to do with distilling home brew, so why does he have it?"

Riley tapped his pen against the desk blotter. "Check if it's there when you go back."

"Will do, sir."

"But wait until after you've finished looking for the van. That's more important right now. What Roy Fitzpatrick is doing with caustic soda might be anything or it might be nothing."

Cillian waited until Hughes had left, then did an internet search for industrial lye, finding several photos from people who'd had their faces and their lives destroyed by it. The pictures were especially unsettling, as in the case of an American woman who'd had lye thrown in her face by a vengeful ex-husband and who was now undergoing her second face transplant. *The man without a face.* Was there something to what Gail Russell had said to Danny as they loaded her into the ambulance? The young boys Danny and Hughes spoke to outside of Roland Evans's house claimed there was a "ghost" who came and went from that dwelling, always keeping to the shadows and never revealing himself. Maybe it wasn't merely youthful fancy or the whispered words of a dying woman. Perhaps there really was a ghost—not of smoke and shadow, but of real flesh and blood.

He pulled up Dougie's report and scanned it. The boys had definitely said there was a ghost whom they had seen going into the Evans house. The ghost had appeared the morning of Evans's death but hadn't been seen since. In the report, Dougie was dismissive of the boys' claims, but now Riley wondered if it deserved a closer look.

He caught up with Hughes before he left, found him in the front porch tying up his boots. "Do you remember the day Roland Evans was killed?"

"Sorry, sir." Hughes looked up. "Roland Evans?"

"Your report said the young boys that you and Danny spoke to mentioned a ghost in the area."

"Yes...." He returned to tying his laces.

"Do you think this might be Roland Evans's killer?" Riley leaned against the wall. "Or just boys making up stories." He remembered that Danny had searched the area where the boys claimed to have seen the ghost but found very little: a red button that could have come from anywhere and a silver coffee spoon with an obscure hallmark of a nightingale that they were still trying to trace.

"Hard to say, sir." Hughes plucked his parka off a peg by the door and slipped into it. "Gail Russell said the man that attacked her had no face. What if she was telling the truth? What if this fella was in an accident? He could be scarred, and the only time he can go out in public is in the dark or if he's covered up." He zipped his parka and pulled on a knitted watch cap.

Riley pondered whether or not to say what he was thinking. In the end, he went for it. "People have suffered horrific facial burns from lye."

"Exactly."

"Constable, when you're done looking for the van, how about swinging by Roy Fitzpatrick's still and taking another look."

"You got it." Hughes opened the door, letting in a gust of frosty air. "I'll let you know if I find anything."

Riley was halfway to his office when he heard Hughes yelling. He turned around and beat it back to the front door. Hughes was holding what looked like a bundle of rags and gesturing at it. "Constable, what's going on?"

"Look." Hughes held the bundle out to him. "She's still alive. My God, sir, she's alive." He stared down at the pile of rags. "I found her—she was in a snowbank. Someone left her in a snowbank. Christ, I don't—who'd do something like that?"

The bundle was a newborn baby girl.

A car pulled up in front of the station and a man got out, staggering so badly that Riley at first assumed he was drunk. He saw Hughes with the baby but only gazed at it blankly as he moved towards Riley. His mouth moved, no sound coming out, then, "She's gone."

It was Roy Fitzpatrick.

"Who?" Riley asked. He motioned to Hughes that he should take the baby inside.

"Sheila. She went out sometime last night." He watched Hughes going into the building. "She never come back. I checked her bed, but it wasn't slept in." His held his hands in front of him, fingers cupped but not quite touching, his shoulders rolled forward. "I don't know what's after happening."

"Come inside." Riley reached out and caught hold of his sleeve, pulled him into the front porch. "It's too cold to be standing about. You say Sheila is missing. Your sister Sheila."

"She wasn't in her bed. I looked." He gazed down at his hands as if wondering who they belonged to, and Riley realised the man was in shock. "Why wouldn't she be in bed? Where's she after going to?"

"Let's talk in my office." Riley guided him into the station and down the corridor. As he passed Marilyn's desk, he asked her to brew some strong tea. He pulled Fitzpatrick into the room and sat him in a chair. "I'll get you a cup of tea," Riley told him. "That will help you feel better."

"I don't want to feel better." Fitzpatrick gazed about him as if wondering how he'd come to be there. "I wants Sheila to come home."

"When did you last see or speak to your sister?" Riley brought up an empty incident report on his computer.

"Last night. I went to bed around eleven. I was going to stay up and watch the hockey, but they was losing so I figured what odds." He glanced at Riley. "Do you watch the hockey, yourself?"

"Now and then. It's all about football where I come from." He'd allowed Kevin to talk him into watching a few games of the previous year's Stanley Cup finals. Kevin was seriously into ice hockey, but Riley failed to see what all the fuss was about. "How did your sister seem when you spoke to her? Was she behaving normally?"

Fitzpatrick indicated she was perfectly normal. She had made a cup of warm milk with nutmeg and carried it up to bed with her about ten o'clock that evening, indicating that she would read for a while before going to sleep.

She was at a stage in her pregnancy where she was often tired, so she usually retired early.

"The child's father," Riley said, "had she been in communication with him?"

"I don't know." Fitzpatrick continued by saying he didn't even know who the father was. Sheila had been remarkably cagey about that, revealing absolutely nothing about her baby's paternity.

"Where do you think she might have gone? Was she in the habit of going for walks by herself?"

"She don't walk much. She got a club foot. Born that way, she was."

With a tap at the door, Marilyn appeared, bearing a laden tea tray, which she set down on the desk. "Here you are," she said. "Few biscuits there as well."

Riley thanked her and she was gone. "Your sister has a club foot." The revelation reminded him of something, but he couldn't think what. An image swam into his consciousness of a set of tire tracks in snow and a curiously misshapen footprint.

The abandoned house. Gail Russell. The strange footprint in the snow where someone had stepped out of a vehicle, quite possibly the vehicle that had carried Gail to her death. Sheila Fitzpatrick? Could she be involved somehow? Or was the footprint merely an aberration, the kind of mistake likely to happen if you stepped out of your car and your foot rolled over, if you were wearing boots that didn't quite fit, say, and—

He blinked himself back to the present moment and focused on what Fitzpatrick was saying.

"She drives everywhere she goes. Most times I haves to hang out the wash. She can't keep her balance too well." Fitzpatrick thanked him as Riley poured a cup of tea and handed it across to him. He watched as the man dumped four packets of sugar in, stirring vigorously before laying the spoon in the saucer.

"What time did you check her bed?"

"Well now, that's the thing, see. Usually she sleeps with me." Fitzpatrick sipped some tea. "In the winter anyhow. We've been doing that since we was small. Nowadays, she's after getting big, so she's more comfortable sleeping on her own. I went in this morning around half-past seven to see if she wanted her breakfast brought up. I knocked on the door but didn't hear nothing, so I went in."

Riley typed this information into the report. "And what did you find?"

"Her bed wasn't even slept in."

"Have you called her friends? Other family members? Does she attend church? Perhaps someone there knows where she is." He couldn't imagine that Sheila had a large circle of intimates. From what he knew of the brother and sister pair, they kept themselves to themselves, except for the parties they held once a month for the young people in the community.

A misshapen footprint in the snow…. He minimised the report window on his computer, then clicked on the folder containing the photographs taken at the derelict house, scanning through them one at a time. Graffiti, water stains on the walls, Fuck the Police, empty tin cans, tire tracks. Tire tracks and that one footprint.

"Mr. Fitzpatrick," Riley said, interrupting him. Fitzpatrick turned to look, eyes wide and blank. He's in shock, Riley thought. Definitely in shock. "Mr. Fitzpatrick, your sister has a club foot."

"Yes."

"Is it the right one or the left?" Riley's index finger hovered over the mouse, waiting to click the folder closed. Fitzpatrick's gaze was fastened to his face, his mouth slightly open. A door slammed somewhere else in the building, followed by the low stutter of a mobile phone ringing. Fitzpatrick shuffled his feet, the wet rubber of his boots squeaking.

"The right."

Jesus God. Riley exhaled abruptly, curling his index finger back into his palm. He reached to swivel the computer monitor away from Fitzpatrick. "Does…?" His voice rasped in his dry throat. He swallowed and tried again. "Is your sister dating anyone? She got any gentlemen friends?" More to the point, Riley thought, does she make a habit of hanging out with serial killers? Men who like to rip their victims' teeth out with pliers and take them home for souvenirs? He wondered what Fitzpatrick would say if he asked that question, the question he absolutely wasn't going to ask since he had no solid proof at this point, only the imprint of a boot shaped to accommodate a deformed foot, next to a tire track at a possible crime scene.

"She don't see no one." Fitzpatrick took a long draught of tea, wiping his mouth with the back of his hand. If he noticed Riley was acting strangely, he didn't see fit to mention it.

"Has she left the house before like this?" There was a commotion outside in the corridor; Riley heard Marilyn talking to Dougie Hughes about the baby, saying that a social worker had to be called. Their voices faded away after a moment, so he assumed they'd resolved the matter between them. Christ, he wished Danny were here. Danny had the ability to multitask in situations like this. No doubt he'd have already coordinated with Old

Perlican hospital about the baby's care and sent out a media alert for Sheila Fitzpatrick. Danny would know what to do about the misshapen footprint and the missing woman, and Danny would be able to tell immediately if she'd been consorting with a killer.

"No, never." He scratched his forehead with his thumb and index finger. "I don't know. I mean… maybe. These past few weeks she's been strange with me. She's been… not her normal self, you know? Not herself at all."

Riley wondered what he meant by that. How well did Fitzpatrick know his sister? Their relationship was odd, bordering on incestuous if not incestuous outright, two unmarried siblings living together in this day and age in a homestead off the grid, not caring what anyone thought or supposed about them. What did "normal" mean to people like them?

"All right." Riley filed the report with a couple of clicks of his computer mouse and closed out the window. "I'm going to put out an urgent alert for your sister, to see if we can't find her and bring her home." He glanced up at Fitzpatrick, who was gazing down into his cup. "Is there someone I can call for you? Someone who could stay with you tonight?"

"No." Fitzpatrick shook his head. "There's only ever been me and Sheila. That's all. Just the two of us." He clenched his hands and released them, stretching his fingers. "Can ye find her? That's all I wants. She got to come home. She can't be out beating the roads in her condition."

Of course. Sheila Fitzpatrick was heavily pregnant and due to give birth any time. Perhaps she had already given birth, and the baby Hughes had found wrapped in rags was hers. It was implausible, but that didn't mean it wasn't true.

"How did your sister feel about her pregnancy?" Riley asked.

"What do you mean?"

"Was she happy to be having a baby? Looking forward to the birth?"

Fitzpatrick blinked at him. "S'pose, bhoy. She never said nothing to me about it."

"And you have no idea who the baby's father is."

A disrespectful tone must have crept in, for Fitzpatrick stiffened, fists clenched. "My sister," he said icily, "is not a hoor."

"Of course not." Riley decided to leave it at that. "I have all the details I need for now. I'll put out an alert for your sister, but in my experience, these cases usually resolve themselves."

He sent Fitzpatrick home in a patrol car. A social worker from Harbour Grace had been dispatched to collect the baby and bring her to Carbonear General, and Riley requested they swab the child for a DNA sample.

"It's a long shot," he admitted to Marilyn, after the worker had come and gone, "but maybe we've got somebody's DNA on file that matches."

They had precious little to go on. Someone had left the child in a snowbank outside the police station, rather than coming into the station to hand her over, which meant he or she wasn't comfortable talking to anyone inside. They'd probably run into trouble with the RNC before, or they knew that abandoning a newborn baby in a snowbank was illegal. Either way, they'd fled before anybody got a look at them. The station's CCTV cameras detected only a shrouded figure in a dark snowmobile suit, their head and shoulders wrapped in a shawl or scarf. They laid the baby down by the front steps and fled. An examination of the footprints left behind revealed little; a glance through the database established the person had been wearing Sorel boots, which were so common as to make the identification meaningless. No joy there. The only hope of identifying the baby lay in her DNA, and Riley hoped the staff at Carbonear General Hospital would be diligent in collecting a sample.

There was nothing more to do except wait for the DNA sample, so Riley got kitted up in his warm parka and snow boots and went out to help search for the Dodge van that had carried Gail Russell to her final destination. Hughes and Avery had taken a side of the main road each and were busy knocking on doors, so Riley started at Secretary Road and worked his way towards Southwest Path.

The first house was a modest cottage, painted white with green shutters and a green door. Unlike Danny, Riley couldn't name everyone who currently lived in the Cove and knew only a fraction of the inhabitants, and the local phone book was little use, as it only listed the person's name and number, not their address. At his knock an elderly man came to the door, looked Riley up and down, and asked what he wanted.

"We're looking for a Dodge van," Riley said. "Do you have a garage or shed I could take a look at?" But the man didn't drive and had never owned a vehicle. He told Riley that his son Cyril took him wherever he needed to go.

The next house was empty, located behind the police station, and the place where Danny had seen a light the night of the blizzard. A little farther along the same lane, he came to a split-level bungalow with a variety of children's toys in the front yard. When he knocked at the door, a harassed-looking young woman appeared with a crying toddler on her hip. No, they didn't have a van either. Two more houses on and Riley was having no luck at all, so he stopped into Strange Brew to get a coffee to warm his fingers. He was surprised to see a young man behind the counter instead of Jennice and inquired where she was.

"She's in the hospital," the young man replied. His name tag identified him as Fergus.

"Is she all right?" Riley asked, alarmed.

"Best kind," Fergus said. "And the baby's doing well too. A little girl."

He chatted to Riley while making his coffee. Jennice had gone into labour during the blizzard, and for a while it looked like she might end up giving birth in her bedroom. With the storm at its height and no ambulance able to get through, her husband, Dave, fired up the snowmobile and took her down to Old Perlican, where the baby was born.

"Let me get this straight," Riley said, "he drove her to hospital on a snowmobile in a blizzard?"

Fergus laughed. "You don't know my sister. She said either he drove her or she was going herself." He laid a flat white on the counter. "There you are. That'll keep the cold out."

"Please give her my best," Riley said. He liked Jennice—everyone in the Cove did—and he was glad she and her baby were safe and well. He'd drop by later in the week with some flowers for her.

Invigorated by the hot flat white, Riley returned to knocking on doors, but no one on Secretary Road had ever owned a Dodge van. He crossed the main highway and turned onto Belgium Road, past the old schoolhouse, now turned into a youth recreation centre, and the remnants of an abandoned playground. The first house on the right past the school yielded a little information. A teenaged boy living there told Riley that Dosh, the dispatcher at Shore Taxi, bought an old Dodge van from his uncle, who had sold it when he moved to Ontario the year before.

"Mint condition too, buddy. Finest kind. I wanted 'er, but the fucker wouldn't give 'er to me. Said she was worth money."

"Did you or your uncle see him when you made the sale?" Riley asked.

"No. He left the money at the post office, and my uncle drove the van out to the point by Heaney's and left it for 'un. He must have come in the night, because next morning the van was gone."

"So neither one of you saw him at any time." Who was he, the bloody Phantom of the Opera?

"No, sir. Nobody round here sees 'un. He's like a ghost, sure."

Riley thanked him, grateful for the scrap of intel but knowing it didn't help unless he could track this Dosh person down. When Danny initially spoke to the owner of Shore Taxi, after Gail Russell's death, the man professed not to know where Dosh lived. He was apparently unreachable because he had no phone or internet, and no one knew where his lodgings were. It seemed like everyone in the Cove had heard of Dosh or spoken to him when calling for a cab, but no one had ever seen him.

Riley made a stop at the Shore Taxi stand and spoke to the owner, who was brusque and uncooperative.

"I already spoke to that other one," he said, "that Quirke fella. I told him the same thing I'm telling you. I've never seen Dosh. He comes to work and leaves when I'm not here."

"So who mans the phones after you've left and before he shows up?" Riley asked.

"I puts the answering machine on."

Christ. It was a wonder he had any business at all. "I assume Dosh has a key."

"He do, and I do, and that's that." He pushed past Riley, who was standing in the door, and busied himself for some time washing out a single teacup in the small sink by the window. "I don't know what else you wants me to say."

"How is he paid?"

"I leaves an envelope with money for 'un. He comes and gets it."

So Dosh was paid in cash, rather than a cheque or by electronic transfer, both of which would have been traceable. He really was doing his utmost to remain under the radar. "When does he come?" Riley asked.

The man was silent, scrubbing the teacup.

"Well?" Riley demanded.

"He'll come the night." He turned around and laid the cup on a paper towel. "After supper is when I leaves his pay out for 'un."

"What time?"

"Oh, he's always right on time." The man coughed, then leaned over the sink and spat something green and sticky into the bowl. "Eight o'clock on the dot."

"I'll be back then." Riley laid his card on the desk. "If I find out you've tipped him off, I'll arrest you. So keep your gob shut, yeah?"

He canvassed all the other houses on Belgium Road, but there were no further reports of a Dodge van. He called Hughes and told him and Avery to return to the police station, that he was going to put together a search party to look for Sheila Fitzpatrick.

"Did you find the van, sir?" Avery asked.

"More or less," Riley told her. The winds had picked up since dinnertime, and he shivered. He needed another flat white to warm him through. "I know who owns it, but finding him might be difficult. We'll talk when I get back."

He rang Roy Fitzpatrick, but the call went directly to voicemail. Probably out looking for his sister, Riley thought. He remembered the drum of lye Hughes had discovered in Fitzpatrick's shed and couldn't think what possible use he could have for it. Fitzpatrick was a homesteader, a man who farmed his own food and hunted. Certainly, lye was used to make soap, but given the traditional division of labour in the Fitzpatrick household, that would be Sheila's purview, not his. And why was he storing it in the same shed where he made whiskey? Why wouldn't he keep it at home? It didn't make any sense, but then, very little about this case made sense. Maybe, Riley reasoned, they'd been going about this the wrong way, looking in the wrong direction.

Danny had already established that Roy Fitzpatrick was an odd bird, a "queer hand" who went his own way and didn't seem to care much what others thought of him. All this time, Riley and the others had assumed—perhaps incorrectly—that Gail Russell and Roland Evans and the girl in the pond had been murdered by some nameless, faceless entity, never by someone like Roy Fitzpatrick. If Fitzpatrick was their killer, then maybe those three weren't his only victims. Perhaps there had been others, and those particular three were left out in the open as a message—a reminder that he could kill anyone he wished, in any manner and at any time. He could display them or not. He could dispose of anyone.

A human body could quite easily be disposed of, if it were dissolved in lye.

CHAPTER SIXTEEN

SARAH AVERY and Dougie Hughes left off their search for the Dodge van on Inspector Riley's orders and were now back at the station, writing up the obligatory reports Riley insisted on, even when they'd done very little and found nothing at all. Sarah had spent a good hour trying to find the appropriate words to describe, in official language, that they'd knocked on doors, but her vocabulary kept veering towards the profane. Around three o'clock she stood up from her desk, stretched, and asked Hughes if he wanted another coffee. He didn't, so she fetched one for herself, then settled in with the pile of letters she'd found in box 27.

Whoever rented the box had taken out the lease in a false name—Darryn Bambrick. She'd searched the local phone directory for it and the police database and had even googled it, but her searches turned up nothing. As she'd told Hughes earlier, the letters were requests from various people who wrote to Charonyx asking for assisted suicide. The letters were as numerous as they were sad. A man in Bishop's Falls who'd suffered for many years from uncontrollable diabetes asked for help to end his life because he'd already lost both legs above the knee and couldn't face another round of amputations. A woman in Clarenville, dying of motor neurone disease, wrote asking for someone to smother her in her sleep. A military veteran with PTSD who had done three tours in Iraq and who had just lost his service dog to old age, asked to be shot at point-blank range and his ashes buried beside his beloved canine companion. Reading them made Sarah want to cry, and she felt powerfully ashamed of herself for all the times she'd complained about something as trivial as a sore back or a slight head cold.

Her mobile rang, and she answered it absentmindedly. It was Danny, calling from Ireland. "Constable, how are you doing with box 27?"

"It's a suicide service, sir. Whoever owns the box hasn't bothered to check it for some time. It was overflowing. I was able to collect a fair number of letters to take with me. Some of them are pretty sad. Basically they are asking for help killing themselves or asking someone to kill them. It seems whoever rents the box was running it as a business."

"And you've no idea who it is."

"Sorry, sir. It was rented under a fake name, which makes sense, I suppose. If I were to link it with our girl from the pond, I'd say she contacted them, wanting help, and they obliged."

"So it was murder," Danny said. "At her request, but still."

The scrap of paper Bobbi had found in the retrieved backpack the girl was wearing had the mailing address of box 27, but so far, Sarah told Danny, she hadn't found a matching letter in the pile she'd taken from the post office. "And the photo of the girl we broadcast hasn't returned any matches. Ditto with the picture of the woman we found in the backpack." She hated to sound so discouraging. "Sorry, sir."

"Not your fault, Avery. Thanks for the update."

She wanted to ask when he was coming back, but didn't. Inspector Riley was every bit as competent as Danny, and she didn't want to cast aspersions on his management style. He was doing everything he could to solve the murders of Gail Russell and Roland Evans, as well as the nameless girl from the pond. Besides, whispers around the station indicated that Inspector Quirke was in Ireland to bring his partner home—that Mr. Heaney had gotten into some kind of serious trouble and needed police intervention. She wasn't about to enquire into something so private and personal.

Inspector Riley approached as she was finishing up her report. "Feel up to going out again?" he asked.

Avery knew it wasn't a question, not really. "Of course, sir."

"Sheila Fitzpatrick is missing. We need to find her before dark." He didn't need to say that a pregnant woman on her own at night, in freezing temperatures, was in serious danger. "I'm just about to call the RCMP detachment in Harbour Grace, see if the Mounties can lend us a handful of constables, but I'd like you and Dougie to get started. Why don't—" He was interrupted by his mobile phone. "Riley." He listened for a moment, thanked whoever was on the other end, then rang off. "That was Dr. Lampe."

"It sounds serious," Avery said.

"The baby that was left on our doorstep wasn't born in the usual way," he told her.

Avery arched her eyebrows. "Oh? I don't follow, sir."

"There are abrasions on her forehead and lower belly, and Dr. Lampe indicated the umbilical cord wasn't cut with a scalpel. Her preliminary investigation suggests it was done with—" He paused, looking uncomfortable. "—a kitchen knife."

The implications of this struck Avery all at once, and she gasped aloud. "Someone actually did that?"

"Yes. The baby was cut from the womb perimortem or post-mortem."

"So the mother is probably dead." She stood up and reached for her parka.

"Very probably."

"Do you think it's Sheila Fitzpatrick?" Avery asked.

Riley nodded. "It's a distinct possibility."

THE RESOLUTION of the Martin Belshawe case felt like something of an anticlimax for Danny, and he stood on the pavement for some time, watching the traffic pass by and wondering what he ought to do next. It was just past noon, but he wasn't hungry, his stomach and his appetite still operating on Newfoundland time. When he looked about him and realised he was standing in front of a newsagent's, he went inside and bought a copy of both the *Irish Independent* and the *Irish Times*. Both papers carried stories about how the Gardaí were cracking down on organised crime, specifically that related to drugs and human trafficking. He wondered what that would mean for Donny Phelan, and whether Tadhg would get to him before the police did. McNamara had indicated that Phelan was gone deep underground after the death of his henchman Stevie Power, so finding him would be difficult, if not downright impossible.

There was a Costa Coffee on the corner (there was, seemingly, one on every corner), and he went inside, purchased a cup of tea and a bun, and seated himself at a small table near the window. The interior of the coffee shop was teeming with people, some of them obviously barristers, given the preponderance of court dress, while others were clerks and secretaries. Since he'd come in, a long line had formed at the counter, and the babble of conversation escalated into a full-on din. Most of these people appeared to know each other, probably worked in the same offices and often had lunch together. They talked and laughed with ease, comfortable in one another's company, assured of their own belonging. It made Danny feel lonelier than ever.

He took out the card McNamara had given him, with the address and opening times of Kenneally's Bar. He'd stood in front of it early this morning, before the hearing, but maybe Tadhg was there now. Perhaps if he went there and knocked at the door, someone would let him in. It was hours yet before he was due to meet McNamara for dinner, and he needed to find some way to fill those hours or else he'd be off his head with boredom. But the newspaper stories about Phelan intrigued him, and he wondered about the status of the

Gardaí investigation. He could ask McNamara but doubted whether he had any drag in that direction.

Obviously Tadhg would be tracking Phelan as well, hell-bent on collecting what Phelan owed or, barring that, enacting some sort of revenge. Tadhg was well out of his depth, Danny reflected, and that's what made the entire situation so bloody dangerous. Tadhg had no idea what these people were capable of, and his naiveté could very well get him seriously hurt or even killed.

"If anything ever happens to me… I want you to take care of Lily. Promise me." They had been lying in bed together early one morning when Tadhg had said this to him.

"Don't be so bloody foolish. Nothing's going to happen to ye."

But Tadhg would not be dissuaded, had made him promise, hand on heart, that if anything happened to him that he, Danny, would adopt Lily and look after her as if she were his own. He'd had no trouble making that promise, because he loved her and already considered her half his anyway. In that moment, he'd have promised Tadhg anything.

And what had they done? They'd pissed it all away, the two of them.

He lingered in the coffee shop as long as possible, leaving only when a young woman wiping down tables started shooting poisonous looks in his direction. Danny left a tip next to his empty cup and stepped out onto the street, wondering what to do with himself. Tadhg should be at Kenneally's by now, but maybe Tadhg wouldn't want to see him, would put him out the door the moment he set eyes on him, the memory of their last bitter argument still ringing in his ears. Danny had come to Ireland to answer charges in the Interpol investigation into Martin Belshawe. Now that was over, so he was free to return home…

But Tadhg was here, in Dublin. Close enough to talk to. Close enough to touch. Maybe Danny could get Tadhg to himself long enough to… to what? Say he was sorry?

He briefly considered hailing a cab but decided to walk to Thomas Street instead. After the morning's enquiry, he could use the fresh air. There were a few people about on the streets now, many of them workers popping out for coffee or to meet business acquaintances, some chatting on mobile phones while they walked or waited at a zebra crossing. He walked quickly, enjoying the brisk exercise and for once not having to deal with the pain in his knees. The weather was much warmer than what he'd left behind in Newfoundland, and the sun was shining, which put him in a good mood.

When he reached Kenneally's, the interior lights were on, so he tried the door. It opened and he went in. A young woman in dark Gothic clothing stood wiping down the bar, at which two old men were seated, one on either end.

"Good day," Danny said, when she looked up. "I'm told Tadhg Heaney works here."

She looked him over sceptically, chewing hard on a wad of bubblegum. "And who might you be?" Her accent was Manchester. Not local, then.

"Danny Quirke. I'm his partner."

"Is that right?" The girl moved to the spirit optics, her back to him.

"Is he here?"

"Well, normally he would be." She turned around again and began plucking clean glasses out of a dishwasher below his eye line. "But he won't be. Not today."

"Is it his day off?"

She smirked. "You might say that. He's gone. Quit. Buggered off. Didn't even work out his notice. Just up and left."

"What?"

"You heard me." She sucked her chewing gum back into her mouth before blowing it full of air and snapping it with a noise like a dozen guns going off.

"He just left today?"

She rolled her heavily kohled eyes. "He was supposed to work today, and he didn't bother showing up. So yeah, you could say he left today."

"Did he say he was quitting?"

"No. He didn't say anything. He just *didn't show up*."

"Do you have any idea where he might be?" Danny asked. He felt like he was playing Twenty Questions with her.

"Nope. You can try his flat." She tore off a piece of paper towel and scribbled an address on it, slid it across the bar to him. "This is where he lives. If you catch up with him, tell him the boss wants to talk to him about doing a runner and leaving the rest of us in the shit."

The address she'd given him was within walking distance of the pub, so he set off again on foot. The flat Tadhg was renting was above a shop, up three flights, and the door was closed when he got there. He pressed the buzzer, his heart hammering more with anticipation than exertion. If Tadhg was at home, he would see him. For the first time since their acrimonious parting, he'd see the man he loved more than life itself. Maybe he'd forget all the horrible things they'd said to each other and just take Tadhg into his arms.

Maybe his anger would overwhelm him and he'd punch Tadhg in the face. In that moment he honestly couldn't have said.

He rang the buzzer a second time, and again there was no answer, so he knocked. Someone down the hall was playing their stereo: Fleetwood Mac, the *Rumours* album, "Second Hand News." He knocked again, then pressed his ear against the door. Nothing. On impulse he tried the knob, and it turned. The door opened into an empty room.

"Tadhg?"

The air in the flat was musty, as if it hadn't been inhabited for a while. There was a thin layer of dust on various flat surfaces, such as the coffee table and the appliances in the kitchen. He opened the refrigerator and looked inside, but it was empty except for a small bottle of milk and a half loaf of bread dappled with blue-green mould. The cupboards were similarly bare. Nothing about this was reassuring.

He went through to the bedroom, which was a scene of utter chaos. The bed had been torn apart, the mattress wrenched off the springs and slashed open in several places. The floor was awash in feathers shed by two gutted pillows, their cases torn open and the contents disgorged. Every drawer of the bureau had been pulled out and dumped on the floor and the laundry hamper upended, clothing strewn around the room. A wall-mounted mirror had been smashed in its frame, the discarded fragments crunching beneath his feet. He bent low to look at them, saw traces of blood.

Jesus. Tadhg.

In the adjoining bathroom he found similar damage, the door of the medicine cabinet wrenched off so it hung by one hinge. Boxes of over-the-counter pain relievers had been dropped into the sink, along with an electric beard trimmer and its charging stand. Shampoo had been opened and poured into the bathtub, and the toilet was clogged with tissue. A robbery? What did Tadhg have that was worth stealing? He'd left the island with little more than Lily and the clothes on his back. Whoever had come here hadn't been looking for money or other valuables but something very specific—something they knew Tadhg had and they wanted.

The blood on the mirror. The pattern of breakage suggested a single point of impact, like a fist or a face. He'd seen the kind of damage such an assault could do, wondered what else they'd done to Tadhg. Was he still alive and being held captive somewhere? Or had they done away with him already? If he had something these people wanted, they could conceivably hold on to him and torture him. Danny pressed his eyes shut, willing away the intrusive images that flooded his mind. Never jump to conclusions, he told himself. Never give in to despair. At times like these he often imagined his wife, Alison, dead these five years, regarding him with her usual sardonic smile and making some wry pronouncement that inevitably set him right.

Don't stand there like an arsehole. Go look for him!

He pulled out his mobile and dialled Kai McNamara's number, counting the rings impatiently. He hung up after twelve. Without McNamara, he had no idea where to even begin looking for Tadhg. A second walk-through of the flat provided little in the way of clues, so he dug deeper, opening kitchen drawers and rifling through them, finding nothing much except a pitifully small collection of cutlery and leftover condiment packets from various takeaway places. In the cupboard under the sink, he found a rubbish bin, upended it on the floor, and started picking through the contents. Tadhg had been here recently; he was sure of it. There were fresh orange peels in the bin that had barely begun to wilt, and a crumpled-up copy of the previous day's *Independent*.

On impulse he unfolded the newspaper and looked through it. A Garda motorcyclist had been injured in a collision but was expected to make a full recovery; a woman had been arrested for stealing someone's dog; a giant bonfire had collapsed in Portadown. In the Business section, he saw articles about shortages due to Brexit, a lack of capable lorry drivers, and a predicted rise in inflation that would surprise consumers. It wasn't until he got to the commercial properties for rent that he struck on something: Tadhg had circled an advert about industrial units for lease in Glasnevin, on Botanic Road. Had he planned to establish a new business here in Ireland? But he'd need permits for that, permission from any number of government agencies, and that could take months. But obviously he was interested in renting premises. Something was written on the side in Tadhg's dreadful handwriting: *Phelan.*

A number was appended to the advert. Danny called it.

"Laxminh Properties," a woman's voice answered. Danny gave her the property services register number and waited while she looked it up. "Yes, sir, that property is currently empty, but we are entertaining offers to lease. Shall I put you in touch with an agent? I'm sure—" But Danny had already hung up.

He tried Kai McNamara's number again, and again there was no answer. It wasn't like McNamara to be out of touch like this, and especially inconvenient now when Danny needed him. He couldn't go barging into the building all by himself—that would likely get him arrested for breaking and entering—and he wasn't on such good terms with the Gardaí that he'd even consider calling and asking for their help. Unless….

Danny had been seconded to the Gardaí two years previous, and had become friendly with a young Garda sergeant named Toby McConnell. McConnell, along with his superior, Inspector Róisín Reardon, ran an organised-crime task force involved in detecting suspected illegal activity introduced into the country from outside of Ireland. He was smart, tough, thorough, and very good at what he did. During Danny's time with the Gardaí, he'd grown to appreciate McConnell's approach, which saw him arrest and charge several high-profile gang leaders while protecting their victims. Danny hated to presume on that acquaintance, and maybe McConnell wasn't even at the Pearse Street Station now. Their paths hadn't crossed in ages, and McConnell might not even remember him. Still, it was worth a try.

He rang the Pearse Street Station and was put through immediately to McConnell's extension, but got his voicemail. He left a message identifying himself and asking McConnell to call back, all the while knowing the sergeant was most likely busy with other matters and wouldn't have time for a man he'd once worked with two years before.

It was a lot to ask.

He scraped up the spilled rubbish and put it back in the bin before washing his hands at the kitchen sink. Then he went downstairs and hailed a cab to take him to Botanic Road in Glasnevin.

CONSTABLES AVERY and Hughes had made a complete circuit of Kildevil Cove's empty fishing stages and abandoned garages. There was no sign of Sheila Fitzpatrick's body. "We've been beating the roads for donkey's ages," Hughes commented. He lifted his flashlight and shone it at the front window of Llewellyn Thomas's shop, which had long since closed for the day. "There's nothing here." He turned in a slow circle, making a sweep with the light. "It's mental. It's like the woman just disappeared."

Avery shook her head. "No, she's got to be around here somewhere."

"Unless her killer hid the body."

"No." Avery trained her own flashlight on the snow-covered road underneath her feet. "There'd be blood, a fair bit of it, if he tried to move her. We'd have seen it by now." They had been in and out of every uninhabited structure in the Cove. "There's something we're missing. I feel it."

Hughes nodded. He wasn't one to dismiss female intuition. "What do you want to do?"

"That old house up behind the station. It's been empty for ages. You remember Inspector Quirke mentioned someone being in there the night we had the big storm?"

"Yeah. We had a poke around, though," Hughes replied, "and there was nothing there."

"Let's take a look," Avery said, "just in case."

"Come on, then, we goes." Hughes flicked his flashlight off and pocketed it. They backtracked the way they'd come, heading southeast on Secretary Road, past Llewellyn's shop and down a narrow lane that ran along the shore. "A shortcut?" he asked, after several minutes of shuffling along behind Avery, up to his knees in snow.

"We'll come up on the back of the house this way," she replied. "If there's anybody still in there, they won't see us."

They cut across a narrow strip of snow-covered meadow and came up onto a dirt road that ran behind the police station. Avery put a finger to her lips and tilted her head in the direction of a small white bungalow, its windows smashed out and the rear entrance covered with particleboard.

Hughes recognised the smell the moment he stepped inside. He turned to look at Avery, knew at once she'd smelled it too. She shook her head. They moved forward, passing from the front entrance directly into the living room, empty except for an ancient sofa, its springs broken and sticking up through the upholstery, and a wooden chair. The carpet had originally been beige, but time and mould had done their work. If there was any trace evidence left here, it wasn't visible to the naked eye. The kitchen was similarly empty and showed the ravages of neglect; a saucepan full of fuzzy mould sat atop the stove, next to a discarded wooden spoon. They moved towards the hallway, where the bedrooms were, and the smell was so much stronger here that Hughes expected to see dark droplets suspended in the air.

"She's here." Avery's voice shattered the unearthly silence. "Christ, what a mess."

Sheila Fitzpatrick lay on her back amidst a pile of dirty blankets and discarded clothing, nude from the waist down. Her legs were spread, exposing her nakedness, but that wasn't what drew Hughes's gaze. Her belly had been sliced open from hip to hip, exposing the viscera beneath. He turned his eyes away, wanting to preserve something of the poor woman's dignity. "Mother of God," he whispered and crossed himself. "What kind of—"

Sarah was on her radio, calling the station. Hughes heard her speaking through a kind of dissociative haze. "...one female decedent, approximately thirty-five years old...."

CHAPTER SEVENTEEN

CILLIAN RILEY had been sitting in an unmarked car at the far end of the Shore Taxi parking lot since 7:00 p.m. It was now five minutes to eight, and so far there was no sign of Dosh. Maybe he knew they were looking for him and had gone to ground.

His mobile phone rang. "Inspector Cillian Riley. How can I help you, sir?"

"Are you the man in charge?" The voice was that of a mainlander, probably from Ontario, if Riley had to guess. He sounded a bit put out.

"I am."

"I'd think in a place like this that an old man's personal belongings would be safe no matter what, but I find that's not the case."

"I'm afraid you've lost me."

"I've been living on the mainland with my family for a number of years, but we've always come back to the old home place for holidays and in the summer. I just arrived last night and what do I find?"

He was certainly talking in circles, Riley thought. "Well?"

"My father died in June of last year. We've kept his house pretty much the same as it was when he was alive. Until now, nothing was ever touched."

Lord God, Riley thought, *will you get to the point?* "I see."

"No, you don't. This property has been tampered with."

Do tell.

"An antique dory that my father built with his own hands is missing. It was stored in a shed on the property, and the lock has been broken."

A dory. Stolen. "Your father's dory was stolen." He activated the Record Call function on his phone. "Tell me everything you know."

Who had access to the property? Riley asked. Nobody, the man replied. The house was situated far back from the road, and many people didn't even know it was there. Had anyone been looking after the house while they were away, keeping an eye on the plumbing and making sure no one had broken in? Yes, his cousin Peter Elliot. Was this cousin trustworthy?

"He's a bit weird," the man said. "That branch of the family lived in Twillingate for years. Peter is my Aunt Mag's son."

"Mag?"

"Her name was Margaret. Margaret Elliot."

"So do you think this Peter could have taken the boat?"

"It's possible. He's the only one who would even know it was there." He huffed, clearly exasperated with Riley's line of questioning. "That boat has great sentimental value to my family, and I want it back."

"Do you have a telephone number for Peter?" Riley asked. "Perhaps a work number?"

"I know he works at some taxi place as a dispatcher, but he's hard to get hold of."

Riley's hand clenched spasmodically around the phone. "Would that be Shore Taxi?"

"Yes." He cleared his throat. "He, ah, suffered serious facial burns some years ago in a house fire, and it's left him rather unfortunately scarred. He doesn't go out much."

Riley thought back to the conversation he'd had previously with the taxi stand owner: "I've never seen Dosh. He comes to work and leaves when I'm not here." And Gail Russell's last words to Danny: "The man without a face."

"I'll follow it up, sir, and get back to you as soon as possible." He noted the man's name—Jonas Elliot—and thanked him for the information.

A pair of headlights appeared at the top of the car park, dipping down as the vehicle's driver took the turn off the main road. A white 1977 Dodge Tradesman van, emblazoned with Shore Taxi's distinctive red stripe and seagull logo.

Dosh was here.

Riley slid down in the seat until his eyes were level with the dashboard. The interior of the car was dark, and he was wearing black clothing, so hopefully he couldn't be seen. He brought up the video recording app on his phone and pointed the lens at the approaching vehicle. The fake taxicab drew up close to the building and stopped, but the driver didn't turn off the motor or get out.

"What the hell are you up to?" Riley murmured. He could see little of the man except the hood of his parka, pulled close around his face. As he watched, the man, Peter Elliot, slid across the seat to the passenger side and bent low. Opening the glove box, probably. But why? What was he looking for? A knife or a gun? Riley himself carried no weapon, but he was reasonably confident he could disarm Elliot in a fight if it came to that.

Elliot straightened up and slid back across to the driver's seat. He sat there for several minutes, the engine running. Then slowly, reluctantly, he opened the door and put one foot on the ground.

Riley's heart thumped in his chest. *Come on, you bastard. Get out in the open.*

The foot withdrew back into the vehicle. The door slammed shut.

Fuck.

The van reversed and then drove off, Elliot hunched over the wheel. Riley exhaled. He waited until he saw the headlights moving along the main road, then started his own car and followed. Why had Elliot changed his mind at the last moment? Had the sight of Riley's car tipped him off that something was wrong? Or had someone warned him? Apart from the other officers at the station, no one besides the cab company owner knew of Riley's interest in Dosh. Yet if Dosh had been warned, he'd have stayed away completely. He hadn't done that. He'd driven up to the building the way he normally would to collect his pay packet, but at the last moment he'd changed his mind. Had some animal instinct alerted him?

Riley kept a fair distance behind, driving slowly and without lights. It wouldn't do to spook Elliot. He wanted the man out in the open, not leading a chase down narrow, snow-filled rural laneways unfamiliar to someone from away. If he were lucky, Elliot would stick to the main roads to get where he was going.

They passed out of the Cove and into a wilderness area, uninhabited except for foxes, snowshoe hare, and caribou. The roads, seldom traversed, were imperfectly ploughed, and in some places the drifts were a couple of feet high. Several times Riley's car slipped, fishtailing, and he was forced to spin the steering wheel savagely, steering into the skid. He hated driving in snow. The taillights of Elliot's van kept appearing and disappearing in the various dips and valleys, and Riley panicked once or twice, thinking he'd lost him. Elliot kept to a steady speed, the vintage van grinding through the heavy snow easily. He signalled left at New Melbourne, turning onto a side road that led down to the beach, and Riley followed, ploughing through deep drifts and twice getting stuck before managing to free the car. At the road's terminus, Elliot paused, then turned right, following a narrow secondary road that ran parallel to the beach.

Riley had already radioed the station to advise them he was in pursuit of Elliot and to pass on the information about the stolen dory. He'd asked Avery to find a street address he could use to track Elliot back to his home, but she hadn't come up with anything—and Elliot showed no signs of stopping or turning off anywhere. Since leaving the car park, he'd been leading Riley on a merry chase. "Where are you going?" Riley muttered. "Got to stop driving sometime, don't you?"

Elliot's Dodge van sped up, and Riley followed, pressing his foot down on the accelerator. Something had changed; it was as if Elliot knew he was being followed and was determined to get away. "Must have seen me. Bastard." He contemplated putting on the lights and siren but decided against it. No point now.

Elliot turned onto a side road—Barrett's Lane, if Riley remembered correctly—and sped up until his taillights were tiny spots in the darkness. Riley stomped on the gas pedal, and the patrol car shot forward, tires spinning as they fought to gain purchase on an icy patch. He eased off, but by now he could no longer see Elliot's van ahead of him, and the road was so slippery that he could only advance with the car geared down to neutral. A glance at the car's satnav showed a relatively straight stretch of highway until he hit Brownsdale, so he gunned the motor, closing the distance between Elliot and himself. The landscape outside flashed by at a blinding rate of speed, white snow and dark trees, and the poorly lit road twisted and turned unexpectedly. Then a dark shape, moving quicker than he would have ever thought possible, burst out of the forest on the right-hand side of the road. Riley caught a glimpse of the animal's massive shoulders and its head, crowned with an enormous set of antlers, as he stood on the brakes, willing—praying—that the car would stop in time.

The moose plunged into the trees on the opposite side of the highway and was gone. The patrol car's engine groaned and squealed, the anti-lock brakes shaking the vehicle's front end as the system fought to decelerate, and Riley saw that he was at the bottom of a hill, sliding sidelong into a concrete bridge abutment much too fast. He lifted his hands from the wheel and smacked face first into the airbag as it deployed, the impact rocking him back as the seat belt locked hard across his chest. With a shriek of tearing metal, the car rolled slowly onto its side and came to rest in the centre of the highway. The last thing he heard was a squeal of static from his radio.

THE TAXI driver let Danny out on the opposite side to the address he wanted, so he had to sprint across four narrow lanes of traffic. At this hour of the day, cars and buses were already plying Botanic Road, and no one was in much of a mood to stop for the silly bugger gesturing on the side of the road. He managed to find a gap between two taxis and a giant lorry and reached his destination feeling as though he'd narrowly escaped death.

The building was made of grey concrete brick, set behind a steel fence. The main entrance had a fancifully decorated portico that suggested high notions unlikely to be met anytime soon and small windows separated into individual panes, probably in an attempt to give it the look of Georgian architecture. The attempt failed resoundingly. There were no vehicles in the car park, which meant little on the face of it. Anyone wanting to access the building could have come by bus or taxi or even on foot, and more than likely there were other entrances round the back that weren't readily visible from the street. He tried the front door, but—not surprisingly—it was locked. He patted his pockets and pretended to be fumbling for a key, then went around to the side. A small service entrance crouched malevolently between an industrial-sized rubbish bin and a stack of wooden pallets. This was unlocked and opened into a narrow corridor lined with metal shelving, all of it empty.

He followed the corridor to where a door stood open at the end, and went through it. A second corridor stretched away to the left, with numerous doors opening off it. Too bad he didn't have some kind of primal instinct that would let him know when Tadhg was near. He'd already tried Tadhg's mobile, but either he'd changed the number or he wasn't picking up. There was no point, and Danny didn't have the time to methodically go through every single room on every single floor in the bloody place. If Tadhg were here, then Danny needed to find him, and quickly. He stood very still and listened, mentally cataloguing the things he heard: the ticking of the radiators, the wind rattling a windowpane, vehicles passing by on the street outside. He disregarded the swishing of his blood in his ears and the small tremor of his pulse, and slowed his breathing until it was completely silent.

Are you here? Show me where.

Still early in the day, and if Tadhg had been tracking Phelan's daily habits, keeping him close and within sight, he'd have stopped just long enough to determine if Phelan was here. If he wasn't, Tadhg would be elsewhere. This kind of surveillance and tracking was exhausting… and usually the province of experienced police detectives.

A slight tinkling sound betrayed itself to him, and he automatically pivoted in its direction. A floor above, to the right of where he stood, something small had fallen onto a hard floor, something that would never have fallen in an otherwise empty building. He glanced around, saw a fire door with a set of stairs emblazoned on it, and started upwards. The sound had come from the northwest corner of the building, but the stairs ended on the diagonally opposite side of another long corridor. He moved in that direction and found himself in an empty meeting room that obviously hadn't been used in donkey's ages. A long wooden table had been pushed back against the opposite wall, and several chairs were stacked on top of it, dusty from disuse. A row of windows ran along the northwest wall, and he saw at once what had made the noise: an abandoned wind chime hanging from an air vent in the ceiling above. Obviously it had been stirred by an errant draught, probably from a leaky windowpane.

He sighed. Tadhg wasn't here, and neither was Phelan. Danny turned to go, then froze at the sound of footsteps on tile. He'd been wrong. Someone was here after all. He hoped to God it wasn't Phelan or one of his buddies, seeing as how he was alone and weaponless. If he was quiet and quick, maybe he could slip out the door and down the stairs before—

"Danny. Figured I'd find you here."

Jesus. He let out a breath. "Toby. Christ, you scared me half to death. How'd you know where I was?"

The young Garda grinned. "I've been keeping track of you on your mobile. I got your voice message. What's your Mr. Heaney doing tangled up with the likes of Donny Phelan?"

"That story would take too long to tell." He caught hold of McConnell's outstretched hand and shook it. "Thanks for finding me. Look, I know this is probably outside your purview, but—"

"Anything you need help with," McConnell replied, "and I'm your man." He lifted his left arm and glanced at his wristwatch. "Well, until six o'clock. I'm on the night shift." He tilted his head towards the door. "Let's see if we can't track your man down, then, eh?"

McConnell had come in an unmarked car, a grey Kia sedan. He unlocked the passenger side door for Danny. "We've been keeping Phelan in our sights," he said as he got in and started the vehicle. "Doing everything we can to keep eyes on the bugger, short of implanting him with a tracking chip."

Danny blinked in surprise. "You can do that? Legally, I mean?" He'd heard the Gardaí had recently been granted new, wide-ranging surveillance powers, but implants were something else altogether. "How the hell did you get government permission for that sort of thing?" McConnell was laughing, and too late Danny realised the young Irishman was codding him. "You're still an arsehole, you young bugger."

"Had you going, though, didn't I?" McConnell stopped for a red light. "Phelan is like a country bus," he said. "He has his particular route and he never deviates from it. Whether it's from habit or choice, I couldn't tell you, but we've had an undercover officer in with his organisation now for the past eighteen months. The regular reports are that Phelan has his home, his favourite newsagent's, a betting shop where he puts money on the horses, and a pub. One, two, three, four. Like a waltz." The light changed and McConnell drove on.

"Does he go to mass?" Danny asked.

McConnell lifted his free hand and waggled it back and forth. "Yes and no. That's the one area where he's unpredictable. Goes to St. Kevin's on Harrington Street, sometimes to confession before mass on Sunday, but he's not a regular."

"You've got someone following him into the confessional?"

McConnell gave him a sour look. "Don't be so bloody foolish. Of course we do."

"Now I know you're full of shite," Danny said.

"Oh no." McConnell turned left onto a narrow side street lined on either side with tall oaks and maples. In summer it would be wonderfully green and shady, but now the trees were bare, their naked limbs extended towards the winter sky like dying Famine victims. "Father Cathal O'Brien was a Garda before he got the call."

"The call?"

"Before he became aware that he had a vocation to enter the priesthood."

"Oh."

"He's reluctant, of course, to break the seal of the confessional. You know yourself what's said in there is between you and God. But...." McConnell took a right turn at the end of the street, and they were suddenly on another busy road. "If it's something that's important to our ongoing investigation, he'll pass it on, although, mind you, it pains him to do so."

"So he's keeping track of Phelan?"

"As are we all." Another red light. McConnell turned in his seat to look directly at Danny. "You have got to get your man away from Phelan. Out of the country as soon as possible. I cannot stress this strongly enough. I'll be honest with you—he's not only endangering himself, he's putting our investigation at risk, and I can't be having that sort of thing."

"I know," Danny replied with a sigh. "He's cut off all contact with me. I've been calling and messaging him. He won't answer. He knows how dangerous it is, what he's doing, but it's like talking to the wall."

The light turned green and they were off again. "Danny, I won't lie to you. If it comes to it, I'll arrest and charge him. It's no skin off my arse."

Danny nodded. "Understood."

They pulled up in front of a hairstyling salon, which was apparently out of business, seeing as how the windows and door were shuttered. McConnell turned off the car and pocketed the key.

"Phelan's been in here since late last night," he said. "We haven't been able to figure out why. He came here, parked around back, and went inside, and nobody has seen him since."

"A beauty parlour?" Danny asked.

"That's what it says," McConnell replied. He reached into the car's glove box and brought out an expandable police baton. "Better safe than sorry," he said with a grin. "Come on. Let's see what this bugger's up to."

The front door was concealed behind a heavy metal shutter, the kind that pulled down from above; it was locked at the bottom with a heavy padlock. McConnell hammered on it, shouting that whoever was inside had best come down, but there was no response. There was a second door to the left, presumably leading to a self-contained flat above, but when Danny tried it, that was locked as well. McConnell knocked again, and pressed hard on the door buzzer, but if Phelan was inside, he wasn't answering.

"Maybe he's gone to ground in there," Danny said. "Biding his time and hoping we'll go away."

"Not a chance. He's most likely on his mobile, ringing up a few of his buddies to come and save him." McConnell moved to the door on the left, flicked open what looked like a Swiss army knife and inserted one of the implements into the lock. "Anybody asks, you didn't see me do this." He grinned at Danny, who shrugged.

"Needs must," Danny said, "when the devil drives."

They went up a narrow flight of stairs together, McConnell leading. At the top was another wooden door, fitted with a pane of frosted glass. It stood slightly ajar, as if someone had only recently passed through and forgot to close it behind them. McConnell laid a finger against his lips and then gestured that Danny should come closer. He pointed at four small oval marks on the glass.

Bloody fingerprints.

McConnell pushed on the door with the point of his elbow. It opened into a long, narrow room that widened towards the back. The only light in the room leaked through gaps in the newspaper-covered windows, illuminating a series of disembodied heads, all sitting on a long shelf, facing inwards. At first Danny thought they might be dolls' heads and this room was the site of some strange ritual, but then he realised they were hairdressers' practice mannequins. Apparently at one time this had been a beauty school.

The mannequins were not alone; they were accompanied by two men. One sat slumped in a wooden chair against the wall, with what remained of his head lolling on his chest. The wall behind him was splattered with blood, shards of bone, and a pinkish-grey material Danny recognised as brain matter. He was without a doubt very, very dead.

The other man was Tadhg Heaney. He too was sitting in a chair, staring blank-faced at the dead man, his hands covered in blood.

CHAPTER EIGHTEEN

CILLIAN RILEY opened his eyes to a sea of whiteness, dimly lit and with a backing soundtrack of electronic beeps and whistles. He tried to turn his head, but steel fingers of the purest agony gripped his neck, and he cried out.

"Shh. Stay still." A warm hand came across his chest, the palm cupping his cheek, and Kevin Carbage was there, dressed in civilian clothes. "You've got whiplash, my love."

"What happened? Last thing I remember was…." His mind was a blank space with no pictures in it. He glanced at Kevin in alarm. "Why can't I remember?"

"You broke your leg, and the doctor had to operate. The anaesthetist gave you midazolam. It wipes out your short-term memory." He caught hold of Riley's hand and squeezed it reassuringly. "You're in Carbonear General Hospital. You hit a concrete bridge in Brownsdale and flipped your car. The seat belt broke two of your ribs, and you've got a steel rod in your thigh bone, along with six titanium pins." Kevin smiled, but Riley could see the traces of recent tears on his face. "You're like the bionic man."

"How did I get here?" He recalled a set of red taillights vanishing into the winter night and his own hands on the steering wheel. "A bridge."

"A bridge." Kevin stroked his cheek. "You scared me half to death. We got the call at the station, and Dougie Hughes and I came out right away. The ambulance was already there."

"How?" Someone called an ambulance?

"A local man was passing by—at least, that's what he said—and called it in. You're lucky he did. You were pretty banged up." He touched Riley's lower lip with the ball of his thumb, then leaned in to offer a gentle kiss. "But you're all right now."

Riley knew he wasn't "all right." Far from it. Leave it to Kevin to try to shield him from the unpleasant truth. A fractured femur was serious and took at least three to six months to heal completely. Fuck, he'd be out of commission, unable to do anything other than desk work. Christ.

"You don't know that. Six months is the outside estimate," Kevin said. "It might not take you that long." Obviously Riley had spoken aloud without realising it.

Something else occurred to him. "Who called the ambulance? Did you get a name?"

"Sarah Avery took the call." Kevin frowned. "I don't think he gave a name. Just said that he was passing and saw you there."

"Trace the call," Riley said. "I'm willing to bet it was him, Peter Elliot. He probably came back to see—" He moved very slightly, and a savage bolt of pain seared along his broken leg. "Fuck!" Kevin reached for the call button and pressed it. "Oh God, that hurts." He clenched his fists and squeezed his eyes shut as hot tears slid down his cheeks. "Oh Christ, oh sweet Christ." He clung to Kevin's hand and panted like an animal.

The door opened, and a male nurse came in, took a quick look at Riley's IV, and said, "I'm Ryan. How bad is the pain—on a scale of one to ten?"

"Eleven," Riley gasped.

"I see they forgot to mention the PCA pump," Ryan said dryly.

"PCA pump?" Kevin asked.

Ryan picked up something that looked like a TV remote from on top of one of the monitors. "Patient Controlled Analgesic. This white paddle with the green button will deliver a dose of pain relief into your IV." He tapped the button. There was a small click, and within a moment or two, Riley's death grip on Kevin's hand eased. He drew a slow breath, then another, and his features relaxed.

"Thank you," Kevin said, "so much."

"Don't hesitate to call me if you need me." Ryan squeezed Kevin's shoulder and left the room.

"Kev...." Riley was swiftly slipping into unconsciousness. "Track that call. Find out who made it... think it was... him." He tried to squeeze Kevin's hand, but the world was warm and soft, and he was so sleepy. He was so sleepy now.

SARAH AVERY was still there when Kevin arrived back at the station. Marilyn had long since gone off shift, which meant Jack Mansfield was at the desk. Jack was an old-timer, a veteran of the RNC who was close to retirement age. He'd grown tired of the hectic pace of life in St. John's and applied for transfer to Kildevil Cove. He was a steady personality who tended to take things in his stride. Kevin liked him because if Jack was on the desk, it meant anything that came through the door during the night shift would be handled long before it caused any unnecessary amount of trouble.

Avery was scrolling through the portion of Roy Fitzpatrick's file that had been appended to their database, a cup of tea at her elbow. She glanced up as Kevin appeared. "How is he?"

"Bad break in his right femur. They had to put a steel rod in." Kevin grimaced. "He'll be feeling that for a while." He leaned to look at the screen. "Roy Fitzpatrick?"

"I thought…." She huffed out a sigh and waved a hand in the air. "I don't know what I thought."

"Sheila Fitzpatrick."

"You didn't see her, Sergeant. She was hacked open like…."

"I know." He didn't have the heart to tell her that this was probably the least of what she could expect to see if she stayed with the Constabulary. "Why don't you go home, get some rest?"

"I'd rather be here." She tried to smile, but her lips were trembling. "My boyfriend, Sam, is on the rig for the next three weeks, so I'm alone in the house. Too much time to think." She stretched her arms out in front of her, fingers interlaced. "I'll take anything you've got for me to do."

"Are you sure you don't want to go home?" Kevin checked his watch. "It's almost eleven o'clock."

"I'm not tired."

He rolled his eyes. "Fine. But if I come in here and find you asleep at that desk, I'm making you clock off."

"No falling asleep at the desk," she promised. "What have you got?"

"This is more Dougie's area, but I wonder if you could trace the phone call to 911 when Inspector Riley was injured. He was in pursuit of a Peter Elliot when he went off the road. We think this Peter Elliot may be the faceless man Gail Russell spoke of. There's a lot of evidence pointing in that direction."

"I'd be happy to," she replied. "If that bastard ran Inspector Riley off the road—"

"We don't know that he did any such thing," Kevin interjected quickly. "Nor are we certain this Peter Elliot killed Gail Russell and Roland Evans, so don't jump to any conclusions. Just get on to the emergency services and track down where that call came from."

"Okay," she said quietly, chastened.

"We're all worried about him," Kevin said. "Me most of all. But he's in good hands, and he'll get excellent care at Carbonear General."

"I'll get busy tracing that call for you."

"Thank you," he replied. "And drink your tea before it gets cold."

He went back to the office Riley shared with Danny and sat down behind Riley's desk, running through a mental list of what else needed to be done in relation to the accident. The car was a complete write-off and had been towed to a salvage yard in Harbour Grace, while the remaining debris had been cleared off the highway. The bridge itself didn't appear to be damaged, but the town council had erected Caution signs, and an engineer was coming in the morning to inspect the structure for cracks and instability. Kevin would contact the ambulance service to take a statement from the paramedics who'd attended to Riley at the scene. They were known for being thorough and very observant, and if anything appeared amiss, they would tell him about it. Bobbi Lambert had sent two forensics techs out to the scene as soon as it was called in; there were numerous photos of tire tracks that Kevin had already examined, all of which showed without question that Riley's car was the only one on the road at the time. If the man who called it in had attended the scene, he hadn't done so in a vehicle, nor had he arrived on foot, since no extraneous prints had been observed in the area. Forensics did detect the tracks of a very large moose, a detail which would probably put that part of the situation to rest. From the preliminary forensics analysis, Riley had most likely swerved to avoid the animal and run into the bridge.

There still remained the question of the man who had called it in. From what Kevin could tell, he hadn't actually approached the scene, so he'd either witnessed the accident from a nearby house, or…

…he'd known in advance it was going to happen.

The thought made Kevin uncomfortable, and it made him angry. Riley had been tailing Peter Elliot at the time of the crash, on a road that was poorly lit and ran mostly through uninhabited areas of the peninsula. Elliot was from this area and knew the roads, whereas Riley didn't. Most likely he'd accelerated to draw Riley off, and Riley had smashed into a bridge he couldn't see at the bottom of a hill he was unfamiliar with while swerving to avoid a moose. Bastard.

At a tap on the door, he looked up to see Sarah Avery. "Found it," she said. She passed him a sticky note on which she'd written a phone number. "The 911 dispatcher said the call came in from that number. Bad news is, it's a burner phone, one of those disposable pay-as-you-go jobbies."

"Actually it's good news," Kevin said, reaching to take the scrap of paper from her. "Nobody uses burner phones around here unless they're doing something they shouldn't. Guaranteed this is Peter Elliot. The real bad news is, we can't use the phone to trace him, but now we're reasonably certain he's the one who called it in." They had already had a look around the property that Elliot was caretaking for his cousin, but there was no sign he'd been there recently, except to steal the dory. Wherever Elliot was holed up, it was well hidden. "Good work, Constable. Now maybe you should go home."

She stifled a yawn. "What about Roy Fitzpatrick?"

"What about him?"

"I was looking through his record."

"Yes, but there's nothing much there," Kevin said. "Most of the convictions are juvenile offences. Truth be told, that should have been expunged."

Sarah straightened her back. "Lucky for us it hasn't been."

Her tone piqued his curiosity. "What do you mean?"

"When Roy Fitzpatrick was seventeen, he was charged with a serious assault on a young woman in the community and sentenced to six months in the youth detention centre in Whitbourne."

"I remember it vaguely," Kevin said. "Roy and Sheila's crowd were younger than June and me. I was at university then, but I heard about it."

"He served his time and was released back into the community," Avery said. "The young woman wasn't so lucky."

"Oh?"

"Doris Coombs was sixteen years old. She was attending a party with some friends," Avery told him. "Fitzpatrick enticed her outside with the promise of liquor. He gave her something to drink, all right." Danny had said something about Doris Coombs having throat problems, something to do with her vocal cords. She couldn't speak above a whisper. "Drain cleaner," Avery said. "Mixed with homebrew. The two had been dating, and apparently he was angry that she wouldn't agree to have sex with him."

"Jesus," Kevin murmured.

"We need to arrest Roy Fitzpatrick," she continued. "If he did that to Doris Coombs, he's capable of anything. Maybe he's the one who hacked his sister open and stole the baby."

"Just wait a minute—"

"No, Kevin!" She blinked. "I mean, Sergeant Carbage. Sorry."

"If Roy Fitzpatrick deliberately burned Doris's throat with drain cleaner, why would she agree to go to their parties?" Kevin asked, choosing to ignore her angry outburst. "Why would she put herself within any kind of proximity to the man? She wasn't forced to go. She attended of her own free will." He cast back through his memories, but nothing immediately came to mind. The Fitzpatricks were not only younger than him and June, they were Catholic, which meant neither Kevin nor his sister ever socialised with them.

"I was told Doris and Sheila were best friends," Avery said. "They've been best friends for years. I'm thinking she's been going to that house to see Sheila, not him."

"Okay. We'll bring him in and see what he has to say for himself." Kevin reached for the phone and called his sister at home. "June? I think we need to arrest Roy Fitzpatrick."

DANNY STOOD back as Toby McConnell and a second Garda led a handcuffed Tadhg down the stairs. Tadhg gazed at him bleakly.

"Don't say anything," Danny warned him quietly. "I will find a solicitor and meet you at Pearse Street Station."

"I didn't do this, Danny," Tadhg whispered. "You know I didn't do this." He ducked his head and got into the back seat of the patrol car. The Garda officer got into the front and drove off. Danny watched until the vehicle was out of sight, then turned to Toby McConnell.

"There's no way he killed Phelan," Danny told him. "You don't know him—"

"I know he was found in the room where Donny Phelan got his brains blown out," McConnell replied, anger flashing in his dark eyes. "He was the only other person there, in fact."

"Phelan was shot," Danny said. "Did you find a gun? Did you?"

McConnell drew back, affronted. "We will. SOCO are on their way from Pearse Street."

Forcing himself to breathe, Danny said slowly, "Scene of crime officers won't find a gun."

"They will," McConnell insisted, standing his ground. Danny recognised the posture from years before when they'd served together: feet planted, head jutting forward, chest up. It meant that McConnell had made up his mind. Danny knew how stubborn the young Garda sergeant could be. It would take overwhelming evidence to the contrary to change his opinion, but in this case he was dead wrong. Tadhg was a lot of things, but he wasn't a murderer.

"No, Toby. Tadhg didn't kill anybody. One of Phelan's cronies did this, and you can bet he took the gun with him when he went."

McConnell moved towards the car he and Danny had arrived in. "I can give you a lift back to your hotel."

"Not a chance," Danny said. "I'm going to Pearse Street." He ducked under the blue-and-white crime scene tape and opened the passenger side door.

"You're not helping him," McConnell said tartly as he started the car. "In fact, your interference is going to make things a lot worse."

"You need to interview Phelan's closest associates immediately," Danny said, ignoring McConnell's previous remark. "Someone had a score to settle with him. They knew he was going there to meet Tadhg, and they brought the gun with them, shot him, and pissed off out of it. Someone in that organisation knows who did this."

McConnell's eyes narrowed. "Don't you dare tell me how to do my job," he snapped.

"I'm not," Danny retorted. "I'm trying to keep you from making a career-ending mistake by charging the wrong man and letting the right one go."

TADHG HAD already been processed and taken to a cell when Danny arrived at Pearse Street with McConnell. His request to see Tadhg was immediately denied, which was as he'd expected, and he was directed to a waiting area with chairs and a water cooler. "I am his next of kin," Danny protested, but the young female Garda behind the desk wasn't having it.

"I don't care if you're the Holy Ghost," she said, "you're not seeing the prisoner." When he tried to argue, she turned her back on him and pretended some busyness at the filing cabinet. Danny took a seat near a window and called McNamara on his mobile. This time, finally, Kai answered.

"Kai McNamara."

"Kai, it's Danny. I'm at Pearse Street Station. Tadhg's been arrested for Phelan's murder."

There was a long silence. "Oh," McNamara said finally, "well, that's unexpected." Danny heard the succinct click of a cigarette lighter, then the sound of McNamara inhaling. "Do you want me to come where you are?"

Danny paused. Perhaps he'd been taking unfair advantage of McNamara's good nature during his time in Dublin. After all, the man had all but stated outright that he was unwell. Maybe it would be better to leave him alone, stop pestering him.

"You do want me to come down?" McNamara prompted.

"I'm being a pain in the arse, I know," Danny said.

"No, no, it's not like I've got anything else to do. I'll be there." McNamara rang off.

Danny tried to sit and wait until McNamara's arrival but couldn't. He made the best use of his time by ringing round to various solicitors' offices, but no one was willing to take on Tadhg's case at short notice. In desperation and uncaring of the exorbitant roaming charge, he called Adrian Molloy. The chief inspector picked up on the first ring. "Danny? Is it yourself?"

"It is, sir."

"I see that whole business has been resolved with Martin Belshawe. Didn't expect that."

"Nor I, sir. But that's not why I'm calling." Danny outlined the situation with Tadhg and told Molloy how he needed decent legal representation as soon as possible. "There's no way he'd shoot Phelan at point-blank range. I'm trying to get that through their heads here, but nobody wants to listen to me."

"If he's charged with Phelan's murder, he'll have to apply for Criminal Legal Aid, and then the judge will decide whether he qualifies or not. It's a drawn-out process, and he'll be remanded in custody while he's waiting," Molloy said. "What about the man who represented you? Were you satisfied with him?"

"Very much so," Danny replied, surprised that Molloy knew about Isaac Shapter. "You're talking about Shapter, right? I'd assumed he was legal aid."

Molloy chuckled. "Oh no. Mind you, he's done his service in that area. The lad is way past that now."

Confused, Danny asked, "Sir, how do you know Isaac Shapter?"

"He's my son."

This revelation so shocked Danny that he was rendered temporarily speechless. "Your son?"

"It's a long story. Danny, look. I'm going to call Isaac and see if he can't make room in his schedule to help Mr. Heaney."

"Thank you so much, sir." It was like he could finally breathe. "I can't tell you how much I appreciate this—for Tadhg and for myself."

He closed out the call and went to sit by the window again, next to an elderly woman with a shopping bag on wheels and one of those plastic rain bonnets his grandmother used to wear.

"'Tis pure shockin'," she said to no one in particular. "What they get away with." She nodded, as if in confirmation of some inner dialogue only she could hear. "Yes, so you are, so you are."

Danny picked up a copy of the *Irish Independent* and had a look through it while he waited for McNamara. The female Garda at the desk went on a break and was replaced by an older man with deep pouches under his eyes, like a sad dog. He murmured to himself and sang snatches of song while rearranging a pile of file folders. Now and then he'd call a name, and someone would stand up and shuffle their way to the desk. Two boys in hooded sweatshirts came in through the front door and stood next to a poster urging men to Use Your Brains, Not Your Fists and whispered to each other. One sniggered loudly and executed a trio of dance steps on the tiled floor. A radiator on the opposite wall clicked and muttered; traffic went by on the road outside. A man in a green winter parka folded his long body down into the seat next to Danny—Kai McNamara.

"How long have you been here?" he asked.

"Too long," Danny said with a sigh. "Not long enough. They won't let me see him."

"That's the usual way of things." McNamara reached into his pocket and brought out a pack of cigarettes, then remembered where he was and cursed quietly under his breath.

"I was trying to get hold of you." Danny was suddenly very glad of McNamara's company. "You had me worried. Where were you?"

"Oh, I was out getting a tattoo."

"A tattoo."

"Yeah." McNamara unbuttoned his denim shirt, baring his chest to the breastbone. The hair had been shaved from the area, and a small round dot with three lines coming off it had been tattooed there in blue ink. With a sinking feeling, Danny recognised immediately what it was.

"You have lung cancer."

McNamara gave him a lopsided grin. "So it would seem."

"Jesus, Kai, I'm sorry." The tattoo was intended to target the focused radiation therapy McNamara would receive. "How long have you known?"

"Six months, give or take." He shrugged. "Everybody's got to go sometime. I start chemo next week. That'll be fun. Anyway, what's the situation?"

Danny explained about Phelan's murder and Tadhg. "They're going to charge him unless they find compelling evidence to the contrary."

"More than likely Phelan pissed somebody off and they decided to get their own back," McNamara said. "Let me look into it, see what I can find. Might be that somebody knows something. I'll put the word out." He stood up. "You okay here by yourself?"

"Yes." Danny got to his feet and held out his hand. "Thanks, Kai. I really appreciate it." He held on to the other man's hand a bit longer than was strictly necessary. "Please take care of yourself, will you?" All the long months while Kai had been watching Tadhg and safeguarding his life, he'd been seriously ill, and he hadn't said a word about it. Danny felt like two cents. All this time he'd been harping at McNamara to not let Tadhg out of his sight, to basically babysit him, and the Irishman was himself at death's door. "I wish you'd told me," he said.

"Not your circus," McNamara said with a grin. "Not your monkeys." He gave Danny's shoulder a brief squeeze and was gone. Danny couldn't shake the unpleasant thought that he would never see McNamara alive again.

CHAPTER NINETEEN

"HE WAS alive," Tadhg said, "for a little while after he was shot. I tried to help him. There wasn't much I could do." He glanced down at his hands, cuffed to a metal ring on the table. "I didn't kill him. I swear on my daughter's life."

Toby McConnell drew a slow breath and sat back in his chair. He nodded. "So you allege that you couldn't possibly have killed Donald Phelan, since you were not in possession of a firearm."

"That's right." The whole business felt surreal, as if he'd temporarily stepped into someone else's life—or their nightmare. He very much wanted Danny in the room, but McConnell's superiors wouldn't allow it. "I do not have a gun. I didn't then, and I don't now. I've never owned a gun." He wisely didn't mention the .38 he'd acquired upon his arrival in Ireland, the same gun that McNamara had confiscated.

"You claim you were with Phelan when a third man entered the building where the two of you were meeting, tied Phelan up, and shot him in the head." McConnell opened a file folder and laid a series of photographs out on the table. They showed—up close and in nauseating detail—the damage done to Donny Phelan's skull.

"There is no 'claim' involved in it," Isaac Shapter said. "My client is telling the truth."

"I don't need to look at pictures," Tadhg spat. "I was in the fucking room."

"SOCO collected trace evidence from the room in which Donny Phelan was killed. Your DNA was detected, as was Phelan's, but no other DNA was found."

Shapter laughed. "I find that very hard to believe," he said, "especially since that room was a known meeting place and safe house for members of a criminal organisation, of which Donald Phelan was a part."

"Sorry," McConnell said, "I should have said no other *significant* DNA. Now, tell me again, Mr. Heaney, how this supposed third man entered the room where you were meeting with Phelan and managed to tie him up and shoot him in the head without leaving anything of himself behind."

He's asking the same questions over and over, Tadhg thought, *trying to trip me up.* He remembered a conversation he'd had with Danny, about the ethics of police interrogation techniques.

We hardly go at suspects with the thumbscrews, Danny had scoffed. *The objective is to get them to tell the truth.*

Is it? Tadhg had countered. *Or is it to get a conviction, no matter what?*

"My client has already advised Garda McConnell that Phelan's killer was dressed in coveralls and a balaclava and was wearing gloves. Clearly, he'd taken measures to protect against leaving trace evidence at the scene," Shapter said. "If there are no more questions, my client would like to go home."

"Your client's not going anywhere," McConnell said. Every time he spoke, Tadhg liked him less. He was an arrogant young bugger with high notions. Probably trying for a promotion. "We are not done here. Tell me again, Mr. Heaney. Where were you when the alleged killer entered the building?"

"I'd gone to the toilet, down the hall. I was washing my hands when I heard someone coming up the stairs. Then I heard the gunshot."

McConnell took out a piece of paper, on which was a rough sketch Tadhg had made earlier, showing the location of everyone in the room. "So you entered by the same door."

"There's only the one door."

"And what did this man in the coveralls do when you appeared?" McConnell asked.

"He fucked off."

A muscle twitched in McConnell's cheek. "And you allege he then left the building."

"He did leave the building."

"CCTV footage obtained from across the street clearly shows a male figure, dressed as my client has described, leaving the building by the side entrance and escaping down an alley," Shapter put in.

"I know that," McConnell said.

"Just refreshing your memory."

"Mr. Heaney, why were you in Ireland in the first place?" McConnell collected the crime scene photos, returning them to the file folder.

"I was looking for Phelan." Mother of God, how many more times was he going to ask? Tadhg had already told him in detail how he came to be in Ireland and what he was doing there. "He embezzled money from my company and drove my business into bankruptcy."

"So you came over here for a little... payback? Isn't that what they call it in America?"

"I'm not an American," Tadhg reminded him. "Newfoundland is an island off the coast of Canada. Until 1949 it was a sovereign nation."

"Sorry." McConnell smirked.

"And no," Tadhg continued, "I did not come here looking for payback. I came here to get my money."

"So you had no intention of exacting revenge on Phelan for driving you into bankruptcy?"

"No."

"That's very magnanimous of you."

"Garda McConnell, the sarcasm does you no justice," Shapter interjected, "and it is out of place here."

McConnell reached to pause the recording. "Interview suspended." He gathered his materials and got up. "Someone will come to take you back to your cell."

"Wait!" Shapter stood up. "You can't stick him in a cell and leave him there to rot. You have to charge him or let him go, and given the overwhelming lack of evidence—"

"I can keep him for twelve hours," McConnell said. He pulled the door open.

"He's been here for four hours," Shapter replied, checking his watch, "without food or drink."

The Garda rolled his eyes, exasperated. "I'll see that he gets a cup of tea and a biscuit." The door swung shut behind him.

Two officers came to fetch Tadhg, unhooking his cuffs from the desk and refastening them behind his back. Shapter promised to expedite his release, but Tadhg wasn't sure how much the young solicitor could actually do. "Tell Danny...." Christ, this was hard. "Tell him I'm sorry. Tell him I want to see him." His throat closed together. "Tell him I love him."

"I will see to it that you are freed as soon as possible," Shapter said. He squeezed Tadhg's shoulder. "I promise."

KEVIN AND June went to the Fitzpatricks' homestead together, but the house and outbuildings were all empty, with no sign of Roy Fitzpatrick anywhere.

"Where the hell is he?" Kevin asked, exasperated. "Did you check anywhere else?"

"Of course I did," June snapped. "Nobody's seen him. The only place he goes is over to the Legion, drinking, and it's closed."

"We'll have to put an alert out for him," Kevin said. "I don't like the idea of him out roaming all over God's creation."

They walked back to where they'd left the patrol car parked beside the road. June got in on the driver's side. "Do you really think he did that to his own sister?" she asked as Kevin slid in and buckled his seat belt. "I mean, the assault on Doris Coombs was years ago, and even if she thinks he's a bit weird—"

"He's more than a *bit* weird."

"That doesn't prove he killed his sister." She turned the key and started up the car, put it into gear, and pulled out onto the main road. At this hour, there was no one around, most other inhabitants of the Cove having long since gone to bed. The night was clear and very cold, with a full moon overhead. "Remember when we used to go sliding on nights like this," June remarked. "When we were youngsters, me and you. I used to love being out after dark."

"We went out after dark to get away from Dad," Kevin said sourly.

"Kevin...." June turned to gaze at him. "About Dad."

"What about him?" He pried his notebook out of his inside pocket and flipped it open, jotted a reminder to himself about the alert needed for Roy Fitzpatrick.

"You said you were going to look for him." She paused, her eyes on the road ahead. "After Ford died. You said you were going to look for Dad."

"Means, motive, opportunity," Kevin replied.

"You lost me."

"You asked me if Roy Fitzpatrick was capable of doing that to his sister." He turned to look at her, the dash lights illuminating her face from below. "He had the means. He certainly had the motive, and he fucking well had the opportunity."

"Means and opportunity, yes, but motive?"

"Yes, I found him," Kevin said, after a moment or two.

"And?"

"He's dead."

Something about the way he said the word "dead" chilled her. Even though she and Kevin were siblings and twins, they were no longer as close as they had once been. Ford's death by suicide had done something to Kevin. He'd never really dealt with it but had instead allowed it to make him bitter, hard inside. She was afraid he had walled off that part of himself and would never again allow anyone to get as close to him as Ford had done. He was in a relationship with Cillian Riley, but the Englishman was headed for law school eventually, and maybe Kevin wouldn't go with him. Maybe Riley would go and Kevin would stay behind, not waiting for him but not moving ahead with life either. It made her sad to think of her brother forever alone. That their father was dead made no odds to her either way. The man had been a violent and abusive bastard who'd murdered his own daughter, June and Kevin's disabled younger sister. How had he died? Had it been natural causes, like a heart attack or a stroke, or had Kevin found him and done what he'd vowed for years to do?

Did she really want to know?

"What motive?" she asked now. "I don't understand."

"Doesn't it strike you as odd that neither of them ever married?"

"Uh, no, not really."

"The day you and Danny went to see the Fitzpatricks, that morning after Gail Russell was murdered, you met up with Roy first, right?"

"Yes." She remembered it quite clearly. Roy had been shovelling snow outside the house when she and Danny arrived.

"Danny doesn't know them, so he'd have no idea Roy was Sheila's brother."

"What does that have to do with anything?" June asked. She slowed down to allow a tabby cat to cross the road in front of them. It moved slowly and deliberately, as if it had nowhere in particular it needed to go.

"Did Danny refer to Sheila as Roy's wife?"

The cat had safely reached the other side of the road. "Yes." She frowned. "Yes, he did. He said he wanted to talk to Roy and his wife."

"And I bet Roy didn't correct him."

The car dipped and swayed a little as June navigated a frozen pothole. "He didn't."

"He let Danny think that Sheila was his wife." Kevin shook his head. "How many other brother and sister pairs do you know of who are still living together as adults in the same household?"

"Oh, go 'way, Kevin! You're making something out of nothing," June said.

"Am I? Think about it. They practically live in the woods." He ticked each item off on his fingers. "They only ever socialise at their own house, never go out anywhere else. She keeps house for them both, does the cooking and cleaning. He does the rest of it, chopping wood and such. They have their own little self-contained world of two, and then suddenly out of the blue, Sheila is pregnant. Who's the father?"

The idea turned her stomach. "Kevin, now you're going too far."

"No, I'm not."

"So Roy is the father of Sheila's baby." Her gorge rose at the thought of it, Sheila and Roy living in the same house, having sex with each other, making a baby, for Christ's sake. "Let's say for a moment your ridiculous theory is correct. Why on earth would he kill his own baby?"

Kevin shrugged. "I'm just telling you what everybody else in the Cove has been saying for years."

June turned off the main highway and onto Secretary Road. "I think you're reaching for something that isn't there." She pulled into the station parking lot and turned off the car. "I'm going to walk home," she said, reminding him he'd pulled her out of bed for this. "It's a nice night."

"Are you sure that's safe?" Kevin asked. He caught the keys as she tossed them to him.

"I'll be careful to watch out for Roy Fitzpatrick," she quipped.

THERE WAS nowhere else to go now. Not now, when she was lying on a cold mortuary slab, drained entirely of life. He shouldn't have done that, but she shouldn't have tried to leave him. People were always leaving him, and it was wrong. It made him angry when they left, and he didn't want to take their lives away, but once they'd transgressed beyond the point of redemption, there was no other choice. Dying flowers couldn't be allowed to languish, pining, on their stems. Once their precious scent was gone, they had to be laid ever so gently to rest. It's what he had done for Adeline.

The old fella came for Adeline at night and took her into his room, where he smothered her screams while he used her body. It was wrong, what the old fella did, and even their mother raged at him, her own father, but he wouldn't stop. Adeline was a beautiful blossom, he said, and it was his right to pluck her as he pleased. It was his duty to make her sing, and sing she did, night after night, while he lay in his bed, his pillow wrapped about his ears to block it out, that awful sound. It wouldn't do for the missus to hear, but her and the mister slept upstairs, way over on the other side of the old Toulinguet mansion, away from such degradation. What her servants did in their own time was no affair of hers, as long as they performed the duties they were being paid for. It was their mother's job to clean and Adeline's to help her, and he went about the place shining shoes and laying the fires in each of the guest rooms during the high season, when people came from all around to stay.

"This is your heritage as well," their mother said. "She was your ancestor, Marie Toulinguet, and don't you ever forget it."

But the house no longer belonged to them. Once the fishery failed, there was no money to pay for the necessary repairs to maintain the huge old Queen Anne revival mansion in the style to which it was accustomed, so they put it on the market. It sold for a decent price, considering. "The Nightingale of the North lived here," Mam would say to visitors as they arrived. "If you listen carefully, you may hear her singing in an upstairs room."

But it wasn't her, not really, but only him, with his clear boy's soprano, singing sentimental old songs down in the laundry room, where there was a ventilation pipe that led up, up, up through the house and into certain rooms.

"Sing 'The Last Rose of Summer,'" Mam would say, or, "Sing 'The Fields of Athenry.' Sure sing the 'Ave Maria' for 'em," and he would. It never seemed to matter to anyone staying at the elegant bed and breakfast that the ghost of the famous Marie Toulinguet, who had so perfectly mastered singing bel canto, never sang any opera. No one ever complained.

Then one day his voice broke, in the middle of "Down by the Salley Gardens," came out as a godawful croak, like something monstrous being born. His mother, working in the kitchen, heard it and came thundering down the stairs.

"What in the name of Almighty God was that? What?" She beat him about the head with her fist until he saw stars. "If ever I hears you make that noise again, so help me God I'll kill ye. I will."

But there was nothing much she or anybody else could do about it. He was growing up, and nature always made a way for itself. After that, he was never able to sing a note without his beautiful boy's soprano cracking straight down the middle and that awful croak resounding through the house. Visitors to the house asked why the Nightingale didn't sing anymore, and his mother made some vague reference to a visiting priest who had blessed the house, thus driving her away, but no one really believed this. The tourist trade began to drop off as travellers went to spend their money in the larger centres like Corner Brook or St. John's, and then word came from the missus herself that the house would now be closed up for part of the year. Him and Mam and the old fella and Adeline would have to shift for themselves, and Roy, who took care of the grounds, and Sheila, who helped Mam in the kitchen, they'd all have to go on somewhere else. It wasn't bloody good enough, Mam said, us working here like slaves, and now you're turfing us out with nowhere else to go.

Couldn't be helped, the missus countered, and anyway, there's loads of work in St. John's. Why couldn't they go there and work? Except Adeline had been feeling poorly for months now, and eventually it dawned on him and everybody else that Adeline wasn't just sick, she was going to have a baby.

The old fella's baby.

She came creeping into the room one night while he was reading a comic book before going to sleep. "I don't feel well."

"Go away and leave me bide. I'm reading."

"Peter, I'm sick." And her with blood and water all down the front of her nightdress, the hem of it soaked and dripping. "I'm sick. You got to help me."

He had stared at her, knowing at once what was wrong but not understanding what she was asking him for. This was women's business, nothing that he, as a male, would ever be a part of under normal circumstances. It had to do with blood and bodies, the arcane mysteries into which he would never be initiated. "Go away from me. I wants nothing to do with that. Ask the missus or Mam."

But their mother had gone to bed, and it was more than either of their lives was worth to disturb her. She hovered in the door of his bedroom, sobbing and clutching her swollen belly until he shouted at her, "Do something about it yourself, will ye?"

It was morning when he found her down in the back porch, lying on the floor next to what had come out of her. She'd staggered into the kitchen and taken a long knife out of the butcher block and stabbed the infant again and again, then dragged the blade across her wrists until her blood flowed out like water.

It was over. The whole long nightmare had finally come to an end. Now was the time to purge the evil, and that could only be done with fire. He found a can of gasoline in the potting shed, intended for the lawnmower, brought it back to the house and spread it over the floor, splashed it on the walls and over Adeline's dead body. Then he dropped a match.

It ignited with a deafening noise like the roaring of the sea, redoubled a thousand times. Flames licked along the floor and up the walls as the fire mounted the ceiling. He turned to leave and found his exit blocked by flames, and then a sudden burst of intense heat as a violent flashover ignited the smoke. The fire was everywhere—in his eyes and mouth, burning inside his clothes and melting his skin like wax. The last thing he heard was the sound of his own voice, screaming.

When next he woke, he was in hospital, his entire head swathed in thick bandages. He'd suffered third-degree burns to 75 percent of his body. Mam and the old fella were both dead. Adeline was dead. Sheila and Roy Fitzpatrick had fled in the night for parts unknown. The Toulinguet ancestral home had burned to the ground.

A kindly nurse put a ticking clock next to his bed so the sound would give him some aspect of normalcy to cling to. He couldn't see, and for a long time doctors feared the fire had permanently blinded him, but eventually the light came back, and he was able to read a little and watch TV. There were many surgeries over the next few years, each intended to undo the damage wrought by the fire, and doctors managed to restore most of the function in his hands, but there was nothing they could do about his face.

His terrible face.

He could no longer live in society, couldn't go about in daylight where people would see him. His face made little children shriek in terror while their mothers made the sign of the cross or the horns behind their back, to ward away the evil thing before it could consume them. He was seventeen when he arrived in Kildevil Cove one cold October night and took refuge in a house belonging to a distant cousin. At first he hid himself away, but eventually the need to earn a living drove him out into the world, and he worked at various odd jobs that could be done under the cover of darkness: chopping wood and mending nets, building rustic furniture that he then sold for not much money. He acquired a computer, learned how to use the internet, and did all his banking and shopping online, even took a correspondence course by email that taught him how to program and manipulate communications systems, to interrupt the flow of digital traffic coming along a particular network and redirect to his benefit. This particular skill set came in handy when he understood how he was meant to purify the world, and when he heard the owner of Shore Taxi needed someone to work at night, he was all set.

It was child's play to reroute the evening calls for cabs that came into the office, and he could act as both driver and dispatcher. He bought the Dodge van for a song, had it repainted in the company colours, and waited for the right phone call to set him on his predetermined path of righteousness.

She was his ultimate last rose of summer. That was her name, really, and how he liked to call her. Sheila Rose Fitzpatrick, his precious flower that would bear fruit he would eventually pluck when the time was right. They met up again when he was doing some work for Roy. He believed it to be fate reuniting him with the Fitzpatricks.

He did odds and ends for Roy, like chopping wood and getting in the hay. He gave Roy a hand with the homebrew too, and Roy let him have the best of each batch for himself. She saw him working in the cold and called him in, made him some tea and toast, bade him sit down to the table and eat like a human being. She didn't faint the first time she saw his face, nor did she scream in terror, but merely gazed at him, her eyes playing over the warped and twisted flesh that looked like nothing so much as melted wax.

"I'm grotesque," he told her, the first time she asked to see him as he truly was. He hid his face with scarves and such, so as not to frighten her. "I don't have a face, not really. It was burned in the fire."

"Let me see it." So he did. "You are not grotesque," she said, "you are unique."

The rest came later. One afternoon she was alone in the house, and she brought him in to drink a cup of tea. She rose from the table and took him by the hand, led him into her bedroom where she stripped him naked, guiding him into her. The physical act of coitus, which other people took so much for granted, was a revelation. Her only stipulation? That they not tell her brother.

"You don't know Roy," she told him. "He's shocking jealous."

He confided in her how the need rose in him from time to time, and how he was nearly powerless to resist it. The desire for destruction and its necessity led him to the weakest among them, so killing them was a mercy and a release. He'd considered making Sheila one of his flowers when first he'd met her, when he saw her club foot, the bodily aberration she'd been born with. She was flawed, and flaws needed to be erased. But Sheila endeared herself to him, promising to help him, and on the night of their belated New Year's Eve party, she kept Gail Russell waiting at their house until he could collect her in his taxi... until he could come for her and put her out of her misery. Sheila did that for him, because she loved him.

They became inseparable, meeting wherever he happened to be: abandoned houses, fishing stages, and once in the back of his taxi. She too had known rejection, she told him, because of her club foot and her unusually close relationship with her brother. All these years he'd known her as Sheila who helped Mam in the kitchen, Sheila who worked at the Toulinguet manor, Sheila whose brother cut wood and got the hay in, but he'd never come closer than arm's length to her. How strange that they should meet again in Kildevil Cove, which he'd never even heard of or known about until he'd landed there himself. When she became pregnant, he was astonished and then frightened, but ultimately glad. Of course the child wouldn't be disfigured as he was. His ugliness was due to the fire. That wouldn't happen to their child, their boy. He was certain it would be a boy.

It wasn't. That was the first suggestion that something in his plan had gone awry. He'd assumed if he did as was dictated and purged the world of weakness, took away those who really were better off dead, then he would gain the very desires of his heart. But the child was a girl, a weakling, and when he cut it from her womb, he saw the ugliness of it, purple and screaming and covered in blood and slime. Another girl to be a victim in the world. Another imperfect rose. He dropped her in the snow and left her there to die. *Thus kindly I scatter thy leaves o'er the bed....*

Eventually they'd come for him. It was only a matter of time, and time was something he respected. Night and morning it was time for his injections, and he did them, pinching up the soft skin of his belly and inserting the needle. Night and morning he wound the clocks and set them all to ticking in perfect unison, the seconds and minutes dropping away like the petals of a dying flower, so beautiful.

He had been walking for a long time, but with no real idea where he was. He stood now on a low hill overlooking a space of pastureland, the whole of it illuminated by the glow of the moon. The lights of the town were far away and dim now, sparkling like a net of far-flung diamonds, and he only had to keep walking. It was so far to walk, and his legs were tired, but he would keep on. He would keep on now.

He would keep on till the end.

CHAPTER TWENTY

DANNY KNOCKED on the door of Kai McNamara's flat and waited. It was just after seven in the evening, and McNamara had sent word that he had uncovered some information that might be useful. At first Danny hesitated to disturb him. McNamara was a very sick man, and maybe it would be better if he rested.

"Don't be a fecking eejit," McNamara said when Danny called him. "And stop acting like I'm already in the ground." Chastened, Danny had apologised, and stopped by an off-licence on the way over to pick up a bottle of decent Irish whiskey. He found McNamara dressed in a warm sweater and a parka, waiting at the door.

"Are we going somewhere?" Danny asked. He handed over the whiskey.

"We are," McNamara replied. "Oh, thanks. This is a good one. Must have set you back."

"Never mind that. Are you sure you should be going out?"

McNamara raised an eyebrow. "Keep on," he said sourly, "and I might have to kick your arse."

"All right." Danny raised his hands in surrender. "Not another word." He followed McNamara out into the cold. The skies over Dublin were clear, but a chill had descended on the city, thanks to an arctic air mass that was keeping most people indoors. The pavements were slippery underfoot, and several times Danny nearly went arse-over-teakettle. "Couldn't we have taken a taxi?" he asked.

"It's just around the corner, sure." McNamara pointed ahead of them, but Danny could see nothing except the dark bulk of a church.

"We're going to mass?"

"In a manner of speaking." They reached the front steps, and McNamara moved to pull open the door. He paused and turned to Danny. "It's best if you let me do the talking. These fellas can be a bit unreasonable."

"Kai, if you—"

"Sh." McNamara put a finger to his lips. "Quiet now."

They stepped into the vestibule, which was warm and hushed and smelled like beeswax. To the right was a small marble font full of holy water; McNamara dipped an index finger in and made the sign of the cross on himself. Danny, who had long since lost his childhood faith, didn't bother.

He followed McNamara into the nave, which was empty save for a single man kneeling in one of the front pews.

"Jonjo," McNamara called. "You got company." The man didn't rise but stayed where he was, head bent. Praying, supposedly. There was a strange smell in the air, Danny realised, overlying the beeswax smell of the candles. Something earthy, like freshly turned soil after a rain shower. "Jonjo, don't make out like you can't hear me."

They were maybe a metre away from the kneeling man when the smell hit Danny full force. His gorge rose, his mouth filling with saliva, and he turned aside, fumbling for his handkerchief.

"Jonjo," McNamara said again, then, "Jesus Christ."

The kneeling man had no legs. What Danny had initially taken for a kneeling posture was simply his torso sitting on the severed stumps, where each leg had been crudely hacked off at the thigh. The amputations had been done while he was still alive, given the enormous pool of blood that spread out around him. He had soiled himself and emptied his bladder, and where his eyes had been there were now only empty sockets, dark and bloody and horrible.

"Come on," McNamara said, tugging at Danny's coat sleeve. "We've got to get the hell out of here." He dragged Danny back through the church and out onto the street. "Somebody knew we were coming here to meet with Jonjo Driscoll. This wasn't an accident. Whoever killed him is probably the same person who killed Donny Phelan. These people don't fuck around."

"What the hell do we do now?" Danny asked. He sounded a little hysterical, even to himself. This kind of situation was so far out of his purview that it might as well be in outer space.

"We get gone," McNamara said. "As quick as possible, and that means getting your man Tadhg out of the Pearse Street Station lockup. If I were you, I'd be on a fucking plane tonight back to that rocky island of yours." He started walking quickly towards his flat, Danny following. McNamara might be deathly ill, but he was taller than Danny, with longer legs, and Danny was having trouble keeping up.

"That's not going to happen," Danny said. "I'm not leaving without Tadhg." If for no other reason than to tear him a new arsehole. But even his anger wouldn't allow him to leave an innocent man to face prison.

McNamara whirled around. "Goddammit, they aren't going to just let him go. The Gardaí need to make an arrest in Phelan's death, or else the whole fucking network thinks the police are nothing but a bunch of eejits. What do you think is going to happen then? Whoever killed Phelan—Jesus, whoever killed Jonjo Driscoll—can do whatever the hell they want." He turned around and started walking.

"Kai, I am not leaving without him."

"Then you had bloody well better find something to tell Garda McConnell that'll get your man off the hook." He glanced around him. "Now come on. You can't stand out here in the fucking street."

They arrived back at McNamara's flat, and Danny went to put the kettle on. "Don't even say it," he warned. "Yes, it is my answer for everything."

"You're as bad as me fucking grandmother," McNamara retorted. "Make it a strong one." He pulled out his mobile phone and started scrolling. "There's no point trying to get hold of anyone in Phelan's mob. They've gone to ground."

"Who are you calling, then?" Danny shrugged out of his coat and dropped it over the back of McNamara's sofa.

"Keep your friends close," McNamara quoted, "and your enemies closer." He shrugged and tapped the screen of his mobile. "You'd better pray that this works or we are so far beyond fucked it's not even funny."

THEY DRANK tea and waited in McNamara's flat for a call back. Around eleven, Danny ordered a pizza, and they ate together at McNamara's kitchen table.

"You really love him, don't you?" McNamara asked.

"I...." Danny's gut clenched. "Yes," he said, finally. "I love him. God knows why."

"I was in love once," McNamara said conversationally. He reached across for a third slice of pizza. "Believe it or not."

"Why wouldn't I believe it?" The idea that McNamara—crusty, devil-may-care McNamara, with his flinty disposition and his various idiosyncrasies—had never been in love hadn't crossed his mind. He firmly believed there really was someone for everyone. That probably made him ridiculously sentimental, especially to someone like Kai McNamara.

"Twice, actually," McNamara said, with the lopsided grin that meant he was about to reveal something deeply personal about himself. "One more than the other."

"Now this I have to hear," Danny said. They had since graduated from drinking tea to the whiskey Danny had brought, and he reached out to refill both their glasses. "You, in love."

"Now don't be like that." McNamara finished the rest of his pizza in two bites and took a big swallow of the whiskey. "This woman I knew. Nuala was her name. Cracking lass she was. Real party girl." He reached for his pack of Marlboros and lit one up, pretending to ignore Danny's frown. "She was originally Jonjo's woman, and after she kicked me to the curb, she went back to him." Laughing, he detailed the long, strange trip their relationship had been, the drinking and drugs, the frenzied sex in public places. Nuala had a liking for every vice there was and then some, and the fact that she knew Jonjo meant she had a direct line. Whenever a shipment came in, she liked to be there at the docks, waiting to sample the merchandise, and Jonjo—who didn't know she was screwing McNamara—let her have whatever she wanted. For a long time it went on like that, with her playing both ends against the middle, until McNamara had enough of her profligate lifestyle and called a halt.

"And she went back to Jonjo?" Danny prompted, sensing there was more to the story.

McNamara laughed, choking on his cigarette, then waving away Danny's offer of assistance. He took another gulp of whiskey to recover, then said, "He married her."

"Really."

"I shit you not."

"Where is she now?"

"I assume she's still married to Jonjo. Well, she's his widow now." McNamara started to say something else, but it turned into a coughing fit that grew progressively more violent. Danny reached across and snatched the cigarette out of his hand, crushed it out in a nearby ashtray. He got up and poured a glass of water from the tap, set it in front of McNamara.

"Take a few sips." He rubbed McNamara's back, knowing the dreadful spasm was part of the Irishman's illness and there was little he could do about it. McNamara was trying to breathe in awful, whooping inhalations, his body shaking. Danny crouched beside him and wrapped his arms around him, holding him tightly. "Breathe, Kai. Slow and gentle, that's it."

"I'm all right," McNamara whispered. His face was wet with the effort of trying to breathe. "Inhaler—drawer on the right."

Danny fetched the inhaler and passed it across to him. McNamara shook it and took a deep draught of it, then another. He dropped his head between his shoulder blades and shuddered as the powerful drug took effect. Danny smoothed his back with the palm of his hand, moving in gentle circles. After a few moments, McNamara straightened up, nodded, and tried to smile.

"Thanks," he whispered.

Danny hugged him. "Drink your water," he said. He was just about to ask McNamara to continue his story when Kai's mobile rang. The Irishman was all focused attention, his fit forgotten.

"McNamara." He listened in silence, then nodded at Danny. "Oh, it's you. Long time, yeah. So you've heard. News travels fast, or were you in on it?"

Danny leaned closer, trying to catch some of the conversation. The voice on the other end was a woman's, and she was obviously taking serious exception to what McNamara had just said.

"Stop trying to bullshit me. You forget, I know you. Where?" He covered the phone with one hand and told Danny, "She wants us to meet with her."

"Where?"

McNamara held up a finger. "No, no. I'm not into that cloak-and-dagger shite. ... Sure, if you can find one that's open. When? ... You're cutting it a bit fine. That's well past my bedtime. ... Okay, we'll be there." He ended the call. "This may be our little glimmer of hope."

"Oh?" Danny collected the dirty mugs and the empty pizza box from the table and carried them through to the kitchen.

"We're to meet her at midnight."

"Meet who?" Danny asked.

McNamara smirked. "Nuala. Seems true love never does run smooth. From what I gathered, Jonjo was a proper arsehole, and she's glad to be clear of him."

"How did she know?"

"Don't be asking. Nuala's like a spider sitting in the middle of a great big web and feeling the vibrations on all the strands."

Danny ran some water in the sink and put their used mugs and plates in, seized the nearly empty bottle of Fairy liquid and squirted some into the stream of hot water. "So where are we meeting her?"

"Are you my fucking housemaid now?" McNamara gestured at the sink. "Go away from that, for the love of God. I can do me own washing up." He moved towards the door and took his coat off the hook. "We'd better get a move on. She's not the type that likes to wait."

Danny's pulse quickened, and he shrugged into his own coat. "Are you sure this is okay?" he asked.

"No." McNamara tilted his head and winked. "But what's life without risk?"

TADHG HAD tried in vain to find a comfortable sleeping position on the thin slab of foam in his cell. He had been served supper around six: a scrawny overcooked leg from a chicken that had probably died of old age and two small potatoes boiled to an unappealing mush. He thought longingly of the wonderful meals he'd eaten in the past: roast Sunday dinner, pan-fried cod with new potatoes and scruncheons, fish and chips from any one of the numerous chip shops lining the far eastern end of Freshwater Road in St. John's. A hotdog eaten from a cart late one night after coming off a riotous pub crawl on George Street. Mussels cooked in a billy can on the beach. Toast dripping with butter. Lily's vegetarian lasagna.

Christ, he'd really fucked it up good and proper. It wasn't bad enough that he'd lost everything, but he'd managed to drag Danny into it as well. He was well on track to set things right himself. That had been the plan in the beginning, to get hold of Phelan and get the money off him, go back home and reclaim everything he'd lost. Except now Phelan was dead, and according to Jonjo Driscoll, the money had vanished, never to be recovered. Tadhg was the prime suspect for Phelan's murder, and unless someone could come up with overwhelming evidence to the contrary, he would stand trial and most likely be convicted of a murder he'd had nothing to do with.

The door of his cell rattled and then swung open. Garda Toby McConnell was there, looking tired and haggard, his shirtsleeves rolled up to his elbows. "I can't keep you too much longer," he said. He leaned against the door frame. "But I can't actually let you go either. I think we're both kind of fucked, me and you."

Tadhg slid over on the pallet, gestured at the empty space. "Sit down before ye falls down."

McConnell came over and slumped down beside him. He dropped his head and rubbed his palms over his face. "Did you kill Phelan?"

"I'm supposed to have my lawyer present," Tadhg said acidly, "before you ask me anything like that. And what in the name of Jesus are you at this hour of the night?"

"Listen now." McConnell turned to face him. "Jonjo Driscoll is dead. They found him just now."

"Jonjo?" Tadhg well remembered the lunatic who'd put a gun to his head. "How?"

"No suspects yet, but it's almost certainly gang related. They chopped his fucking legs off and gouged out his eyes." McConnell grimaced.

"Why?"

"Payback for something, probably."

Tadhg thought about this for a moment. "Maybe it was his job to protect Phelan and he fucked it up."

"Well, it's all gone to shit now." McConnell sounded about a thousand years old. "Anyway, unless I charge you, I have to let you go, and unfortunately the Director of Public Prosecutions doesn't think we have enough evidence. You were found in the room with Phelan and you had his blood on your hands, but he was shot at close range, and when we tested your clothes for gunshot residue, we didn't find anything." He grimaced. "Perhaps I'll still have a job after this. Who knows?" He stood to go.

Tadhg felt a pang of pity for the young sergeant. Maybe he was a bit arrogant and trying too hard for a conviction, but he could hardly blame him. During his short time in Ireland, Tadhg had heard horror stories about the toll organised crime was taking on the country. Certainly McConnell had been a bit ham-fisted in the way he'd handled Tadhg, but it was done with the best of intentions.

"Have you spoken to Danny yet?" he asked. "He might have some insight, and I find he's always a good man in a crisis."

McConnell's expression hardened, and Tadhg realised he'd made a grievous error. "I don't need anyone showing me how to do my job," he snarled. "Believe it or not, I am capable."

"I didn't mean—"

"You should try to get some sleep," McConnell said. He went to the door and banged on it. A guard appeared to let him out. "I'm still of two minds whether I should charge you or not."

"I want to talk to my solicitor!" Tadhg got up and went to the door, but McConnell was already moving swiftly down the corridor. "Hey! I have the right to legal counsel!"

"I'll let you use the phone in the morning, sure," McConnell called back over his shoulder. The door at the end of the corridor opened and shut and Tadhg was alone.

He went back and lay down on the slab of foam, one arm tucked behind his head. A thin stream of light from a nearby street lamp came through the narrow window above, illuminating the small room. It wasn't quite enough to read by, if he'd had anything to read, but the silvery light was a comfort.

It seemed to him that young Garda McConnell was desperate for a conviction, and he wondered why. True enough that organised crime gangs had the entire republic overrun, and maybe that lay at the back of it. Tadhg knew the Gardaí had put the fear of God into men like Joey O'Leary—head of an international human trafficking syndicate that stretched from Istanbul to God knows where—and Tam Roche, himself an importer of both high-quality blow from the Americas and the deadly *krokodil* from Russia. Men like Roche and O'Leary had swiftly gone to ground as soon as the Gardaí started cracking down; a flurry of high-profile arrests that saw some powerful players sentenced to life in Portlaoise had seriously kneecapped several organisations. Nobody was in a rush to fill positions left vacant by arrest, knowing the Gardaí were waiting to swoop in and put the boots to it.

If McConnell was able to make an arrest, make it public, he'd show those most concerned that the immediate threat from the Garda Síochána was, if not entirely removed, at least lessened for a time. That would benefit him in a couple of ways: first, he'd arrested someone for the heinous crime of murder, and second, those most likely to be nicked by the Guards might relax a little, knowing the heat was off. They'd begin to creep out in the open, make themselves a bit more known, and then McConnell's squad could finally nab a couple of the most serious offenders. If they could pluck certain men off the top of the pyramid, the whole works of it would be destabilised. It made perfect sense, and suddenly Tadhg knew what he had to do.

He rolled off the bunk and called for the guard at the end of the hall. "I need to speak to Garda McConnell," he said. "The sooner, the better."

DANNY WASN'T thrilled about being in a church so soon after seeing what was done to Jonjo Driscoll, but Nuala insisted. They found her sitting in a front pew and gazing at the altar, a well-kept woman in her mid-forties, smartly dressed in designer clothes and looking every inch the wealthy widow.

She rose when she saw them and extended a leather-gloved hand towards Danny. "Nuala Reardon." Her voice was a husky Bette Davis drawl that sounded like too many cigarettes and too much whiskey. "Kai has told me absolutely nothing about you, but that's how he likes to play things." She approached McNamara and offered her cheek to be kissed. "There's a good boy." In the dim lighting of the sanctuary, she was beautiful, but Danny suspected that anyone seeing her in the cold light of dawn would be able to make out the myriad small lines running from the corners of her cat-green eyes. "So dear Jonjo's gone and got himself killed." She made a small moue, her full lower lip pushed forward. "I always knew it would end badly. Ah, well." Her sudden smile was startlingly white. "Que sera sera, as the old song says. Now, what can I do for you gentlemen?"

She listened without comment while McNamara told her, now and then turning to gaze at Danny with wide-eyed insouciance, a smile curling the edges of her mouth. Then she lifted a dark red curl out of her face and said, "So you want me to whore myself." She tutted. "And here I thought you both were gentlemen." She sank onto the pew and pulled her gloves off. Her snow-white hands were long-fingered, elegant, with bright red claws on the ends. Yes, Danny thought, she was indeed a very dangerous animal. He could absolutely understand what Kai saw in her. "If I do this, what's in it for me?"

"I could pay you," Kai said.

Her eyes flashed angrily. "Don't be vulgar."

"Nuala, immunity from prosecution isn't mine to give. I'm not a cop."

She turned to Danny. "What about you? Could you be persuaded to show a girl a good time?" And when he didn't immediately reply, "No, never mind. You look far too moral for me. I'd never be able to get off with you looking at me all sad and concerned, wondering how you could possibly save the fallen woman." She stroked one long red talon over his forearm. "Pity. You're as fit as fuck."

A door at the front of the church opened and a young priest came in. He'd obviously been out in the weather because the shoulders of his coat were wet and his dark hair was dripping at the ends. "We're about to close for the evening," he said. "So I'm to ask you to finish up your prayers elsewhere."

McNamara nodded. "We're just going, Father." He fumbled in his trouser pocket, looking for change to put in the poor box.

"All right," Nuala said, bouncing to her feet. "I'll do it. For old times' sake." Her expression hardened. "But you'll see to it that I disappear soon after and that I'm not bothered again." Her winged eyebrows arched, and Danny again caught a glimpse of the predator inside her. "I've got my eye on a seaside cottage in Dorset. You'll make that happen, won't you, Kai?"

McNamara exchanged a glance with Danny. "Of course I will. You'll be free to go where you please; that's the agreement. As long as you testify."

She drew back. "I don't know about that. What if they clap me in irons and drag me away? Have you given any thought to how vulnerable I'd be in prison?"

Danny stifled a laugh. She was about as vulnerable as a buzz saw. Incarcerated, she'd probably start her own gang and be running the place inside a fortnight.

The young priest was going around extinguishing the lights, so they all three moved towards the door, Kai pausing to drop a handful of small change into the poor box. It had begun to rain while they were inside, a cold, spiteful rain with ice in it. Danny pulled up the collar of his coat and wished he'd thought to bring a hat. Nuala pulled a cashmere scarf over her hair and tied it under her chin.

"Gentlemen. Until tomorrow morning."

"Nine a.m.," McNamara said, "Pearse Street Station."

"Oh, I'll be there," she replied. She leaned up on tiptoe to kiss his cheek. "You don't look at all well, my dear."

"That's because I'm dying." He pulled out his cigarettes and lit one. "Nine. Ask for Garda Sergeant McConnell."

"Will do." She turned on her heel and walked away, leaving behind a cloud of expensive scent.

"She's really something," Danny observed.

"She's something all right." McNamara consulted his watch. "Just enough time to drop in on Garda McConnell before the clock strikes and I turn back into a pumpkin."

"I'll walk with you."

They went along in silence, each man lost in his own thoughts. After a while Danny said, "You told me you were in love twice."

McNamara squinted at him through smoke. "I was."

"So who's the other one?"

McNamara sagged visibly, and Danny wished he hadn't asked. "That's a long, sad story," McNamara said quietly. He took a final drag on his cigarette and tossed it into the gutter, where it died in a shower of sparks. "In the old days there was a proper term for it—*anam cara*."

"Soul friend," Danny translated.

"Yes. Well, this person was—is—my soul friend, my *anam cara*." They were passing through an older neighbourhood near the core of the city, where grand Victorian buildings rose above the smooth face of the Liffey. "Love it was, in every sense of the equation, but me, stupid eejit, didn't realise until it was too late."

They came to an intersection and waited at the zebra crossing for the light to change. "Where are they now?" Danny shoved his hands deep into his pockets against the bone-deep chill and shivered. Something about this area of Dublin gave him the willies, or maybe it was merely his overactive imagination.

McNamara gestured at a large red-brick edifice on the other side of the street. "In there. Long-term care facility."

Danny didn't follow and said so.

"Persistent vegetative state, they call it." His mouth twisted, and he turned away to hide his distress. "Coma. A very deep and very profound coma, as it happens."

"Christ."

"Oh, he's no help." The walk sign appeared, and they started across the street. "Believe me, I've tried. Wore the beads out between me fingers saying the Rosary. Published novenas in the paper. 'Never known to fail,' they always say. Between you and me, I think there's a cottage industry for someone if they'd a mind to it: making up no-fail novenas for use when even St. Jude couldn't be fucked to lend a hand." He drew a ragged breath that turned into a savage fit of coughing that bent him double.

"Let's get you home," Danny said.

"No. I need to see Garda McConnell. He and I are overdue for a little talk, and I want to get it out of the way." He straightened and wiped his mouth on his handkerchief, hands shaking. "You go on, and I'll meet you at Pearse Street tomorrow morning."

He didn't look as if he'd survive until the next morning, but Danny said nothing. He squeezed McNamara's arm. "I'll see you then."

CHAPTER TWENTY-ONE

JUNE CARBAGE came in early the next morning, eager to get started on the task of finding Roy Fitzpatrick. Kevin had stopped off on his way home the previous night and started the ball rolling, drafting an alert and emailing it to all the media outlets across the island and into Labrador. The newspapers and radio stations would pass on the message, and a renewed appeal would be broadcast that night on the six o'clock news.

She stopped at Marilyn's desk to chat for a moment, before going to the break room to put the kettle on. "Milk in yours?" she called.

"Perfect," Marilyn replied. June heard the main desk phone ring, and then Marilyn answered. She was still talking with whoever it was when June returned with a mug of hot tea for her. She hung up, shaking her head. "You'd think they'd find something better to do," she remarked.

"What is it?" June asked.

"Dave Critch, up in New Perlican. He had his boat hauled up on the slipway for the winter with a tarp over it. It was there yesterday, around four o'clock, but he went by this morning to check on it, and it was gone."

"His boat is gone." It couldn't possibly be coincidence, and anyway, June didn't believe in things like that. "Stolen."

"Looks like." Marilyn applied herself to her cup of tea. "Oooh, that's good on a cold morning."

"Is Kevin in yet?"

"I haven't seen him."

"Okay." June went back to her desk and pulled up Kevin's number. Had he gone home the night before, or was he visiting Riley in hospital? She couldn't remember. He'd stopped at the station to write up the media alert, and then—

"Hello? June?"

"How come you're not here?" she asked.

"It's my day off," he snapped. "Thanks for waking me up, by the way."

"Dave Critch's boat is missing." With her free hand she grabbed a notepad and started scribbling down the details as Marilyn had given them to her. "Sometime between yesterday afternoon and this morning."

"What?" He sounded wide awake now.

"Are you thinking what I'm thinking?"

"Probably." She could hear him rustling around on the other end. "Give me twenty minutes."

She wondered who the victim would be this time.

While she waited, her mobile phone rang. It was Kevin, calling from his car. "You'll never guess what."

"Try me."

"The volunteer fire department were called out early this morning. Reports of a vehicle on fire on the beach near Offer Island. I went down to have a look. I'm not entirely certain because the fucking thing is just about burned to the axles, but it might be a Dodge van. I'll ask Bobbi's crowd to see if they can get the VIN. That's the only way we'll know for sure."

"See if it's got Coldmax tires," she said. "One of them will have a screwhead embedded in the rubber."

The pieces were all falling into place now. The stolen boat, the burned van. It was impossible to stay ahead of this man, who seemed to be running rings around them. If Danny was here, it might be different, but with him in Ireland and Riley firmly out of commission, she and Kevin were the senior officers here. She picked up the phone to call Adrian Molloy, told him about the boat and the van.

"I'm leaving now," he said. "It'll take me a couple hours to get to you, depending on the driving conditions on the highway. Carry on, Sergeant, as best you can until I get there."

ONCE BOBBI Lambert's forensics team had been dispatched to the beach to try to find something to identify the burned-out van, June joined Kevin in the police cruiser. He looked like he'd had a hard night, and June wondered if her brother had slept at all.

"Have there been any sightings of the boat?" she asked, getting in and fastening her seat belt. She'd dropped into Strange Brew, just over the road from the police station, and fetched a couple of coffees for them.

"Not so far," Kevin replied, taking the cardboard container from her. "Thanks," he said. "I need this. I was at the hospital last night until the nurses chased me out."

"How is he?"

"In pain, still." Kevin's forehead creased. "I'm worried about him."

"That's inevitable," June teased, "seeing as you're mad in love with the man."

"No, I'm not."

She wanted to retort, *Yes you are*, the way she did when they were young and she was pestering him but held her tongue. "What about the Coast Guard? Mightn't they have an eye?"

"They've placed the whole Avalon on watch," Kevin said. "So if anything floats by, they'll see it." They were passing out of Kildevil Cove now, moving north towards the tip of the peninsula, and June watched out the window, scanning the sea with a pair of binoculars while Kevin drove.

"I wonder if this one will show up in the harbour, like Gail Russell did." She moved the binoculars in a slow line from right to left, but there was nothing much to see except the ragged fall and swell of the ocean. "Molloy's on his way out from town."

"What's he going to do?" Kevin asked. "Look." He slowed the car and pointed out the windshield. "Is that something out there?"

June handed him the binoculars and waited. After a moment he lowered them and passed them back across to her. "Nothing?"

"Ice," he said. "Probably the leading edge of a pack on its way down from Greenland."

They drove as far as Brownsdale but saw nothing.

"Head south," June suggested. "Up the shore towards New Perlican." She pulled up a chart of the local tidal streams on her mobile phone, checking to see which way a boat launched from New Perlican would drift. "We should see something along there. According to this, the wave direction is northwest...." She trailed off. "Impossible to pinpoint when the boat was launched. Could have been anytime after four until now."

"Look." As they came around the curve of Buckler's Hill into Kildevil Cove, Kevin spotted something. "You said the tidal stream was northwest."

Just inside the harbour mouth, a small open boat drifted, rudderless and without independent means of propulsion. It rose and fell, each wave lifting it up onto the moving crest of water before dropping it back into a trough. The lone figure inside had been placed on its back, arms folded across its midsection, the body lying in repose like a saint in a holy picture. Kevin pulled the patrol car up on the beach, and he and June got out.

"Is it a man or a woman?" June asked. She lifted the binoculars and peered through them at the tiny craft.

"I can't tell." He squinted into the glare. "Sun's in my eyes."

"We're going to need a recovery team."

"Call Gus Durdle," Kevin said, referencing a local fisherman. "We haven't got time to wait for the Coast Guard to come out from St. John's."

They waited on the beach until Gus arrived in a pickup truck, towing an inflatable Zodiac on a trailer. He and his two grown sons made quick work of the drifting boat, getting a rope around it and hauling it into shore, where June and Kevin dragged it up onto the shingle beach.

"It's not a woman," Kevin said, leaning down to examine the figure in the boat. "Not this time."

"He's well wrapped up," June commented. "Wait, no...." She fell silent, confused about what she was seeing. "Is that a bed sheet?"

He'd wound it round his naked body like a shroud so it covered everything, even his face.

"Lazarus, come forth," Kevin quoted. He pulled on a pair of nitrile gloves and reached in to take the covering down from the man's head, revealing the face. Only it wasn't a face at all.

"Oh my God," June said. She moved back, one hand over her mouth. "Oh my God, the poor thing."

The head was completely bald and covered with mottled skin obviously grafted from multiple source donors of different ethnic origins. He had no eyebrows, no lashes, and the eyes, wide open to the winter sky, were a pale, watery grey, sunk far into the head. Where a nose would be there were only two holes, and the mouth was little more than a gash.

"The man with no face," Kevin said. He turned away, shaking his head.

"Do you think it's him?" June asked.

"Yeah."

They both looked up at the sound of an approaching vehicle. Bobbi Lambert got out, accompanied by two forensics technicians. "What's on the go?" she asked. She caught sight of the man in the boat and stopped short. "Oh," she said. Slipping on a pair of gloves, she ventured closer. "Burn victim. Early childhood by the look of it. Dear God, to go through life with a face like that." She palpated the head, moving it back and forth on his neck, then pressed her fingers into the jaw. "Hard to tell how far advanced rigour is, considering the cold, but he's definitely dead." Glancing up at June, she asked, "Is this our killer?"

June nodded. "I think so, yes."

"Let's get him transported to Carbonear General," Bobbi said. "Regan will be able to give a more accurate time of death."

They waited while the hearse arrived, and only when the man in the boat had been loaded in and the doors closed behind him did June allow herself a sigh of relief.

CHAPTER TWENTY-TWO

BY EIGHT the next morning, it was already too late. Tadhg had been formally arrested and charged with the murder of Donny Phelan. His trial date was set for April. He appeared before a judge with Isaac Shapter and Toby McConnell in attendance, gave his name, answered "Not guilty" when asked for a plea, and was then led away. McConnell made an announcement on the steps of Pearse Street Station that they had arrested the man responsible for the death of "one of the country's most wanted." Someone in the crowd shouted, "Give that fecker a medal!" But no one was laughing, not really. Danny had arrived at the courtroom as soon as he'd heard but was sent away; when he approached McConnell later that day, he was told that Tadhg had been formally charged and there was nothing anyone could do.

"But we provided you with a witness," he raged, "you son of a bitch! Are you telling me her evidence is useless?"

McConnell merely regarded him blandly from behind his desk, twirling a pencil between his fingertips. "It's out of my hands" was all he would say. "The matter has been set over for trial."

Kai McNamara was waiting outside the Pearse Street Station. "Well?" he asked. His face gave away that he already knew the answer.

"Useless," Danny told him. "Fucking useless. He's been arrested and charged. They're going to prosecute an innocent man, just because he happened to be in the same fucking room as Phelan when that stupid fucker got his head blown off." He appealed to McNamara to help him, do something, talk to somebody, but the Irishman had already done everything within his power, and anyway, he was ill, he was dying.

"Get back on the plane," McNamara said, wrapping an arm around his shoulder and steering him away. "Go home. It's the best place for you to be now."

"He'll die in prison," Danny said. All at once the horror of it reared up before him, dark and terrible. He was going to lose Tadhg for good, and despite every stupid thing Tadhg had done to put himself in this position, Danny didn't know if he could bear it. Tadhg would go to prison, and he would die in there, and there was nothing, absolutely nothing, anyone could do about that.

He'd have to tell Lily, and he couldn't imagine how she'd react to the news that her father was gone for the rest of his natural life. Sandra would be disgusted with him, accuse him of not trying harder to save Tadhg, who would likely never see the light of day again. Ireland took murder seriously, even the murder of a scumbag like Donny Phelan, and Tadhg had crossed the ocean looking for him, wanting to get his own back on the man who'd destroyed his business and sent him into bankruptcy. It would weigh against him at his trial.

"What am I going to do?" he asked, but that was a question with no answer.

In the end, he went home with McNamara and they sat around drinking strong whiskey until Danny staggered into McNamara's guest bedroom and fell unconscious. He was faintly aware of McNamara covering him with a blanket and of some whispered words of comfort softly spoken in a language he didn't understand before the black dark rose up and devoured him.

It was full daylight when next he became aware of the outside world. He'd slept soundly, no doubt helped along by McNamara's whiskey, strong and fiery and little better than raw poteen. He sat up slowly, waiting for the headache to slam into him, but he felt all right—calm and dry-eyed and resigned. McNamara knocked on the door, entering with a breakfast tray on which rested an envelope.

"I took the liberty of booking your ticket myself," he said. "Made you some eggs, and there's toast. I'm out of jam or marmalade."

"Why don't I have a hangover?" Danny asked.

"Oh, those last few drinks were little more than water," McNamara said. "And I poured another glass or two into ye before ye went to sleep. A hangover's nothing but dehydration."

Danny took the ticket out of the envelope and looked at it. The flight left late that afternoon. He might as well go home; there was nothing for him here. There was nothing for him back in Kildevil Cove either, truth be told, but he had to go somewhere. It didn't matter where he went. Without Tadhg, his life was meaningless and empty.

His mobile rang as he was packing his case later that morning. It was June. "Sir, we have him. The faceless man, Peter Elliot. He was working as a dispatcher for Shore Taxi."

"So it was him after all." At least some good had come out of all this, he reasoned. Now Gail Russell's parents could have some sense of closure at seeing that bastard behind bars.

"He won't be going to prison," June corrected. Danny wasn't aware he'd spoken the last part aloud. "We found him floating in an open boat in the harbour. He's dead." According to Regan Lampe, Peter Elliot was a diabetic who had self-administered an overdose of insulin shortly after climbing into the boat and setting it adrift.

"Why did Gail Russell say he had no face?"

"He's a burn victim, sir. According to Dr. Lampe, he was likely caught in a house fire when he was a young child. We suspect it may be an old house in Twillingate that burned down back in the 1990s. I've got Dougie Hughes following up leads."

"Good work, June. Look, I'm coming home now. I'm on the two-thirty flight out of Heathrow, so I should be seeing you soon. Thanks for holding down the fort."

There was a long pause on the other end; then she said, "I'm glad you got everything sorted out, sir. It'll be good to have you home."

KAI MCNAMARA handed Danny his suitcase at the Departures gate in Dublin airport. "Safe travels, Danny." The Irishman smiled, but it didn't reach his eyes. "I'm sad to see ye go. Imagine that."

Danny surged forward and hugged him impulsively, holding on for longer than was appropriate. McNamara was very ill, and Danny knew the survival rates for lung cancer were pretty grim. "Promise me you'll come and visit. I've been to your island. Now you've got to come to mine."

"'Course I will." McNamara made to say something more, but then the boarding call for Danny's flight was announced and they were out of time.

"Take care of yourself," Danny whispered. He reached out and cupped McNamara's stubbled cheek, not caring who saw or what they thought. "Thank you… for everything. Kai, I wish—"

"Go on, now." McNamara grinned. "You've got to be on that flight." He gave a little wave of his hand, and Danny turned to go, hurrying towards the check-in counter. Just before he stepped onto the jetway, he turned back, hoping to catch a final glimpse of McNamara, but he was gone.

Then there was the airplane, and loading his holdall into the overhead compartment, and finally falling into his seat. Home. He was going home. He closed his eyes and rested his head back, wondering if he'd be able to sleep after they left Heathrow. The journey across the Atlantic was notoriously dull, with nothing to see but ocean. Maybe they'd show a decent film, and he'd have that at least to help him while away the lengthy voyage.

"Is this seat taken?"

He opened his eyes. A man in a long overcoat, accompanied by a teenaged girl, was standing in the aisle. Danny couldn't see the man's face for the felt fedora he wore, and the girl was swathed in so many colourful scarves she looked like a mummy. "This is 21 A and B, right?"

"Yes," Danny said grudgingly. This was all he wanted, seatmates. No doubt the girl would spend the entire trip listening to some ridiculous techno-pop through headphones, while the man would want to talk. People always wanted to talk to Danny. "You have one of those faces," Alison had often said. He lifted his coat from the middle seat and stowed it under the chair in front of him, then turned his gaze firmly towards the window. Almost immediately the girl and the man began talking to each other.

"...don't think he realises anything... wonder what's out the window...."

"Must be interesting... here, I'll take my hat off."

"What can we do to make him look?"

"You poke him with your elbow. See if that helps."

A sudden stabbing pain in his ribs and Danny turned, ready to lash out. But instead of a stranger, he saw...

Lily.

And Tadhg.

"How?" he managed to say, shocked nearly wordless.

"Scapegoat," Tadhg said. "Now that I'm supposedly going to be serving a life term in Portlaoise, the bad people will come crawling out of the woodwork. At least, that's the theory."

"I don't understand."

"I did a deal with Garda Sergeant McConnell. Your pal McNamara's lady friend gave him lots of useful information, enough to pull in a few hard cases and put them behind bars. He did arrest me, but the charges were quietly dropped behind the scenes." Tadhg smirked. "I saved the day. Almost single-handedly."

Danny drew a few deep breaths to compose himself, then gave Lily a hug and asked if she'd mind exchanging seats with her dad. When Tadhg was settled next to him, he said, "You got lucky. Toby McConnell is a good man. Otherwise you'd be rotting in Portlaoise about now." He wasn't ready to forgive Tadhg, not yet, and maybe not ever, and while it was good to see him alive and well and on his way back to Newfoundland, it didn't undo any of the emotional damage Tadhg had inflicted.

"Lucky?" Tadhg asked, laughing. "I think I handled myself pretty well, all told."

The blood froze in Danny's veins, and he turned in his seat to gaze at Tadhg. He seemed unscathed by his experiences, untouched by seeing a man's head blown apart in front of him. He was proud of himself, gleeful.

"Pretty well?" He forced himself to whisper. "You think—" It stuck in his throat and he swallowed hard. "You handled yourself... pretty fucking well?" His fists clenched so hard that the muscles in his forearms ached. "Are you mental?"

"Danny," Lily said, sounding a warning, but he wasn't listening. The ice in his veins turned to lava, all the anger and fear and pain threatening to erupt and burn down the world.

"You should be dead," he spat. "Lying on a fucking slab in the police mortuary. You did not 'handle' yourself well." Who was this person? Who was this arrogant bastard? "D'ye think you're—" He struggled to find an appropriate metaphor. "—James Bond? Is that what you think? That you just swept into Dublin and fought off the Irish mob single-handedly?"

"Well, I was only saying—"

"Don't." His face grew hot, suffused with blood. "Just fucking don't."

Tadhg fell silent for a moment, then, "Well, excuse me." His tone was bitter, nasty. "Maybe I'll get them to turn the plane around and send me back. Or they can just drop me in the sea, parachute or no." He nudged Lily with his elbow. "Think anyone would throw me a life ring?"

"This is not funny!" Danny shouted, rising from his seat. He miscalculated the distance between his head and the overhead storage bin, ramming his skull into the hard plastic and jolting the discs in his neck. "Not everything in life is a fucking joke, Tadhg. Jesus Christ. You could have been killed. You could have gotten other people killed. D'ye not understand how much Toby McConnell put on the line for you?" He cocked his arm, fist clenched. "For fifty cents I'd push your fucking face in."

Tadhg drew back, clearly shocked by this professed promise of violence. He stared at Danny for several long moments, an interval finally broken by the steward, who came hurrying down the aisle towards them.

"Sit down," he said, glancing from Danny to Tadhg and back again. "Or I will call the Guards and have you escorted off this aircraft." He was a big young man, close to two metres tall and built like the proverbial brick shithouse; his expression said he would brook no argument from either of them. "Sit down," he repeated, laying a huge hand on Tadhg's shoulder.

"I want to change my seat," Danny said.

"The flight is full. You'll stay where you are." He lingered beside their row for a moment while Lily sobbed quietly into her hands. Danny was suddenly very ashamed of himself.

"I'm sorry," he told the man. "It won't happen again."

"Good. Now in a wee bit the drinks cart will be coming around. I suggest you both have a nice cup of tea and behave yourselves."

"Lily." Danny reached across to her, but she pulled away from him. The gesture broke his heart. "Lily, I'm sorry, I—"

"Leave her alone." Tadhg's voice was quiet, in deference to the dozens of fellow travellers who were still staring at them both. "She's no longer your concern."

"What?"

"When we're back in Newfoundland, Lily and I will make our own way home, and you can do as ye like."

"What do you mean?" His gut tightened. This was it, then. "Are we over with?"

"The fuck do you think?" Tadhg crossed his arms on his chest and gazed ahead of him, ignoring Danny.

The flight to London Heathrow was relatively short, and soon they were disembarking, Lily and Tadhg first, pushing ahead of him and down the aisle without even a backwards glance. Danny hefted his case and followed, keeping them in his line of sight. At the Departures counter, he watched while Tadhg tried, unsuccessfully, to book himself and Lily on a different flight, then moved to the extreme opposite end of the waiting area from Danny, sitting with his back to him. It was so childish—and so completely characteristic of Tadhg—that it should have been funny. He realised, with devastating clarity, that he'd seriously fucked up, and what ought to be a joyful reunion was instead a bitter ending. The events of recent days had taken their toll on him, and he felt like he'd been dragged backwards through a knothole. More than anything, he wanted to put his head down and cry like a child at the bloody horrible unfairness of it all.

He tried to watch the TV in the Departures area, but nothing that he saw made any impression. The weather forecast predicted a mild day with rain coming towards evening. Where would he be this evening? In Kildevil Cove, alone in his empty house? The Met Éireann announcer seemed unnaturally cheerful, with her bright red lipstick and orange-tinted tan. Her teeth were big and white, as square as windowpanes, and he resented her happy façade more than he could bear. Who the hell was happy to be giving out the weather?

He closed his eyes, resting his forehead in the palm of his right hand, just wanting the misery of it to be over. There was nothing left now but to get on the flight and go across the sea to home and try to work, despite the cold and empty chasm in his heart.

"Don't cry." The hand on his shoulder was as light as thistledown. Lily slipped into the seat next to his. "Dad's being an arse."

"I'm not crying," he protested, pointlessly.

"Come over and sit with us," she said. She caught hold of his free hand and squeezed it.

"Your father won't want that." He wiped his face on his sleeve. "I'm leaking like a basket, sure."

"Do you know why Dad went to Ireland in the first place?" She snuggled close, her head on his shoulder.

"To get away from me?" It was a feeble attempt at humour, and they both knew it. "He went after the man who stole his money."

"Nope."

This was news. He turned to look at her. "What?"

"He was ashamed, Danny." Lily raised her head. "He felt like a failure."

A failure? Tadhg? "What happened wasn't his fault." Tadhg had to know that.

"He blames himself. It's been a nightmare for him. He felt like he let you down. All that bragging he's doing? He doesn't mean it. He's trying to cover up how ashamed he is." Lily picked at a stray thread in Danny's sleeve. "When Grandpa Heaney was alive—"

"Don't mention that bastard to me," Danny said. Tadhg's father had treated him horribly when he was a boy. The regular beatings were bad enough, but what damaged him beyond repair was the emotional abuse. As far as the elder Heaney was concerned, Tadhg was less than worthless.

"Let's all sit together." Lily stood up, tugging him with her. "Come on."

He hefted his bag and followed her across the carpeted space to where Tadhg was, sinking into the seat beside him. Tadhg feigned interest in the TV, but Danny knew he was acutely aware of everything around him. He studied him for several long moments, his gaze playing over the sweep of Tadhg's nose, the curve of his lips, his strong chin. He knew every centimetre of that face intimately, and the man inside it even more so.

"Can I do something for you?" Tadhg didn't take his gaze from the TV.

Danny's insides shuddered. "Yes."

"Such as?"

He wet his dry lips with the tip of his tongue. "If I talk to ye, will ye listen to what I've got to say?"

Tadhg still wouldn't turn around and face him. "So talk."

"Ye scare the shite out of me, you do, so." His agitation was so great that his jaw was trembling like someone in the grip of a fever. "Ye get yourself in trouble, and then you take the most dangerous way out. Ye took my heart so many years ago, Tadhg, and I'm fair terrified of what ye'll do with it, of how you can quite possibly destroy me. I know, I'm talking soft, I am, so. But I can't help it, not with you."

Now that he'd started talking, he seemed unable to stop, and everything he had thought and felt over the past several months overflowed. He told Tadhg how worried he had been, and how devastated when Tadhg had taken Lily and gone to Ireland without him, and how he wished Tadhg had asked for his help instead of assuming that Danny was angry with him for losing his business, his reputation, and the island he'd called home.

When he finally fell silent, he was utterly spent, empty of all coherent language. He waited for Tadhg to say something.

"Air Canada flight 2479 to St. John's, Newfoundland, is now boarding." The announcement came over the PA, and the other travellers stood up, gathering their belongings. "Passengers seated in rows 55 to 44 may now board through Gate 27."

Danny looked at Lily, then back at Tadhg, still silent. The people around them began moving towards the jetway, and if there had been a moment when everything would fall back into place, it was gone. It was all gone. He took his bag and boarded the aircraft with the rest.

DANNY FOUND himself seated in an otherwise empty row, with Tadhg and Lily a few rows ahead. He attempted to sleep but couldn't relax enough to make that happen, and every time he closed his eyes, all he saw was a parade of unpleasant images: Tadhg being led away in handcuffs by the Garda; Phelan sitting in a chair with half his head blown away; Jonjo's violated corpse. He drank a cup of tepid tea that tasted like someone's dirty socks had been swirled about in it, and ate half a dry biscuit. There was nothing to see out the window except the tops of the clouds. The drinks cart went by about halfway into the flight, and he asked for and was given Glenfiddich, neat, a rather generous portion. He was lost in his thoughts and wondering whether it was politic to ask for another when someone slipped into the seat next to him.

Tadhg.

"I've been following our flight path on the little screen." He gestured at the seat back in front of him with its tiny TV monitor. "We'll be able to see the island soon."

"Won't be long now," Danny replied. He flipped the tray table down and put his empty glass on it.

"Getting all oiled up?" Tadhg nodded at Danny's tray. "I've had a couple myself." His eyes were red, his nose and cheeks blotchy, but not from drink.

He knew Tadhg, knew him better than anyone. Tadhg's pale complexion flushed readily when he was in the grip of strong emotion. "Danny...." He coughed, tried again. "Look, what I said—"

"I know." It was painful to look at him, so Danny pretended to be gazing out the window at the passing clouds. "The whole thing got on top of us, both of us."

"I didn't mean for it to go so far."

"You never do." Danny slid the window blind down. "You never mean for anything to happen, Tadhg. But it always does." He turned to look at Tadhg. "Things get out of your control, and you never understand how or why."

"I had to go to Ireland. I couldn't just let Phelan—"

Danny interrupted him. "Lily told me the real reason." No matter how successful Tadhg became in life, the shadow of his upbringing still hung over him like a noxious miasma. His father had taught Tadhg to hate himself, to be ashamed of himself, and the lesson had stuck. "Tadhg, none of it was your fault. You were taken advantage of. You couldn't have known."

"Really?" He offered Danny a lopsided grin. "Or maybe I'm just stupid."

"No. You're not." He reached across the space between them and caught hold of Tadhg's hand. "I love you. I will always love you. It's going to be all right." For some reason he believed this. Maybe he was the stupid one. "Move in with me. The house I was renting in the Cove hasn't been taken. We can get it back, and you and me and Lily can live there together."

"Yeah?" Tadhg attempted a laugh, but it was edged with tears. "So you're all right with Lily's mess? With the dog hair everywhere and putting up with me? It's hardly ideal."

"Life isn't ideal, Tadhg." He cupped Tadhg's cheek in his palm and leaned towards him. "That's just the way it is. I love you. I love Lily. The dog is adorable."

Tadhg drew a shaky breath. "We're almost home now."

"Yes," Danny said. "We're almost home."

EPILOGUE

DANNY HAD been back at work a mere three days when an elderly man walked into the police station. He apologised for taking up their time and said he'd come on the bus all the way from Millertown. "I saw it on the news about that girl, and I had to come and tell yez."

When he'd been ushered into Danny's office and given a cup of tea, Danny asked him what he meant. "My name is Bertram Tupper. That young one ye found in the pond up a ways in the woods. That's my granddaughter, Mary Rose."

"Your granddaughter."

"The picture you put out on the news, the girl in front of the Christmas tree. Well, that was my daughter Teresita. She died a few years back, when Mary Rose was only young." He shook his head sadly. "'Twas a bad thing. She used to always get right down in her mind and cry a lot, and then one day she done away with herself."

"I'm so sorry for your loss," Danny said automatically. "Is there anything we can do?"

"I'd like to have Mary Rose sent home for her burial," he said. He fumbled in the pocket of his parka and brought out an envelope full of banknotes. "I'll pay for her to come home, however they does it. I can pay."

An invisible fist squeezed Danny round the heart. He reached out and touched the old man's hand. "I will see to it that your Mary Rose comes home to you."

"That's all I wanted to know." The old man proffered the envelope, but Danny refused.

"No charge," he said. "It's how we do things around here."

He saw the old man to the door and was headed back to his office to call Green's Funeral Home when Sarah Avery intercepted him. "Sir, I was going by the dry cleaners on my way in, and I picked up your coat."

"Oh, thank you," Danny said, touched by her kindness. "How much do I owe you?"

"Five dollars is fine," she said. She accepted the bill from him and thanked him. "Oh, I almost forgot. They found some stuff in the pockets of your coat and asked me to give it to you." She handed him a clear plastic bag containing several Irish coins, a wrapped throat lozenge, and a folded piece of paper. He took it to his desk and opened it, wondering if he'd written a reminder to himself and then stuck it in his pocket.

The handwriting wasn't his, and it wasn't a reminder. In thick black ink someone had written the word *Soon* and underlined it twice. His gut instinct told him it wasn't a joke. Where had it come from? How had it come to be in his coat pocket in the first place? Had someone slipped it in without his knowledge? It wasn't the sort of thing Kai McNamara would do, and neither Tadhg nor Lily had any reason to leave him cryptic notes. So who else had he been close enough to who could have dropped this note into his pocket? McNamara's ex-girlfriend, Nuala? She'd already indicated he wasn't her type, and she wouldn't give him the time of day. McConnell would have simply told him outright if he'd had anything to say, so that left....

No.

The day he'd gone to court to testify against Martin Belshawe, they'd run into one another briefly in the doorway. Martin Belshawe, who for a few brief seconds was close enough to Danny to slip a note into his pocket before they took him away.

He smoothed it out on his desk and looked at it again. Soon. Was it a threat or a promise? What did he mean by "soon"?

Was Martin Belshawe safely locked away, or was he loose?

If he was loose, he'd come for Danny, sure as shooting.

It was only a matter of time.

Keep Reading for an Exclusive Excerpt from
Dark Vows
Book 5 of the Kildevil Cove Murder Mysteries
by J.S. Cook

PROLOGUE

Early September, Newfoundland
Monday

THE ROAD in front of his house was empty, a bare space of crumbling, pitted asphalt dotted with deep holes, some still holding water from the previous night's rain. A lone seagull circled above, calling endlessly, its white wings outstretched to catch an upwards-tending thermal that would eventually bear it out to sea. The boy on the bike circled too, sketching a series of concentric rings on the wet pavement, vague shapes that expanded outwards as he moved farther away.

Maman had told him to stay nearby. She was going out, but he was a big boy now, big enough to see to himself while she dashed to the shop to purchase milk. Maman had made him promise to stay in front of the door and not go riding off down the harbour or over to the Point, where the land fell suddenly away and all that was beneath was the roaring maw of the North Atlantic. "*Cette terre maudite*," she often said. This cursed land. This cursed land seemed to be the sum and total of her woes. She hated it, hated that they'd had to come here, despised Papa and his inability to stay rooted in one place. Maman feared and hated the sea and believed it would one day eat them up if they weren't careful. "*Cette terre nous dévorera.*" This place will devour us.

There was no one else about; all his friends had gone to school, but that morning Maman had felt his forehead and said he wasn't well enough to attend and had better stay in bed. Staying in bed was boring because his bedroom had only a tiny window set high up in the wall, too high to see anything interesting. Around nine he said he was feeling better, and could he go outside to ride his bike a little in the fresh air? *D'accord*, but only if he stayed where she could see him from the window. That goddamned window. He tried the word aloud: "Goddamn." He liked the shape of it in English, the way his tongue curled around the first part, holding it until the second half exploded like a bomb. "God*damn*."

He expanded the outward radius of his latest circle, pushing past the Apostolic parsonage and towards the abandoned school. A glance back over his shoulder told him Maman was nowhere in sight, so he pedalled a little farther, his small legs pumping hard, driving the bike forwards. At the intersection where the main highway met Secretary Road, he stopped, looking up and down both ways like he'd been taught, but there was nothing to impede his progress, and he took this as a lucky sign. It was safe. Nothing bad was going to happen. Just for luck, he crossed himself and started across the road. All he saw was the road in front of him, the abandoned schoolhouse, and the tantalising ditches on either side, full of interesting bits of rubbish. The white pickup truck, its windows tinted dark, drew close to him, its driver peering unnoticed at the small boy on the bike.

The truck pulled to a stop just as the child's house exploded behind him in a roar of flame.

CHAPTER ONE

Monday

INSPECTOR DEINIOL Quirke—Danny to his friends and intimates—was waiting in an examination room for the arrival of his doctor, who was probably bringing news he didn't particularly want to hear. For the past two or three years, he'd endured ever-increasing pain in his knees, coupled with a loss of flexibility, and it had gotten to the point where he could no longer ignore the toll it was taking. It was his husband, Tadhg, who'd forced him to make the appointment, after growing tired of hearing Danny complain about the agony in his joints.

"Go and see the doctor," Tadhg insisted. "Get some X-rays taken. It's not normal, Dan, the way you're always in pain." They'd been married less than six months, and Tadhg had slipped far too easily into the role of nagging spouse.

A rustle outside the door of the examination room announced Dr. Roman St. Croix was there.

"Danny! Good to see you. You're looking well." St. Croix was about thirty years old but looked much younger and was tall, thin, and with the dark eyes and olive skin that suggested a Mediterranean ancestry. Danny had been seeing him for the past five years, ever since his own doctor had retired and moved back to Hong Kong. "Wish I could say the same about your X-rays." He sat down at the desk and touched a key to bring the computer out of hibernation, then another to retrieve the images from the digital bank where they'd been stored. "I'm afraid the news is not good."

"Oh?" Danny's gut tightened in anticipation. St. Croix wasn't one to beat around the bush. If he said something was bad, it was definitely that and possibly more.

"Take a look at this." The doctor pointed to the image displayed on the screen. "This is your left knee. Now normally there would be a significant space between the two ends of the bone, right here."

Danny leaned forward to gaze at the monochrome images on the screen. "Okay."

"But the space between your bones has all but vanished, and the X-ray picked up several osteophytes—bone spurs—growing where there should be healthy cartilage." He sat back and drew a deep breath. "You have advanced osteoarthritis in both knees, with subsequent breakdown of the cartilage. This would explain the pain you've been feeling, especially at the back of the knee. The loss of cartilage means the tendons back there are working overtime to take the load that the knee cartilage would normally handle."

Danny knew enough about arthritis to know it wasn't fatal, but neither was it a cause for celebration. "So what should I do?" Surely there was some prescription St. Croix could give him. He wasn't expected to live like this. Was he?

"You are going to need both knees replaced. I would recommend sooner rather than later. The degree of deterioration is significant, and I don't want to wait to get this remedied."

Knee replacement? That was major surgery, wasn't it, with a long recovery time, months off his feet, and even when he was able to stand unassisted, he'd be using a walker or crutches. "How long will that take?"

St. Croix peered at him over the tops of his glasses. Danny had long suspected the doctor didn't actually need spectacles but simply wore them to give himself a certain air of gravitas. He was ridiculously young. "Depending on what we find when we go in there, as well as other factors—lifestyle, how well you respond to physical therapy—it might be up to six months."

Danny felt like a bridge had fallen on top of him. "Six *months*?"

"For each knee."

"I don't have a year. I can't just…." He laughed even though there was nothing funny. "Good God! I can't take a year off work. That's mental. You can't expect me to…." He fell silent, aghast at what St. Croix was proposing.

"Danny, this is serious. If you don't take care of this problem, eventually you are going to lose function in both knees. When that happens, you're looking at joint fusion surgery. Your knees will never move again."

"If you're trying to scare me," Danny said dryly, "it's working." He scrubbed a hand over his face and drew a deep breath. The examination room air was dry and smelled like antiseptic soap. "Is there anything we can do in the meantime, until I'm able to have the surgery? You wouldn't do both knees at once, would you?"

"It depends on the surgeon," St. Croix replied, "but no, they're usually done one at a time. Until you have the surgery, there's not much I can offer you except NSAIDs and physiotherapy."

"I can't take NSAIDs. They tear up my stomach."

St. Croix sat back in his chair and tapped his pen on the edge of the desk. It was a beautiful September day outside, with the sun shining and a light breeze from the northeast. For once the weather was nice; there were no gale-force winds or lashing rain. Danny had made plans for a picnic lunch with Tadhg near Single's Bridge, a local swimming spot. Now he wasn't in the mood for anything of the sort. "There is one other alternative."

"Oh?"

"We can inject your knees with hyaluronic acid, otherwise known as viscosupplementation. This can potentially give you up to six months' relief." St. Croix obviously saw Danny's hopeful expression and quickly countered with "But it's not a cure, and you will eventually require joint replacement."

"I'll have that viscose stuff," Danny said, getting to his feet. "Can you make the appointment?"

"No need," St. Croix replied. "I can do it in the office. We don't currently have any on hand, so I'll have to order it in. It will take a week or so." He wrote something on a prescription pad and tore off the sheet, handing it across to Danny. "That's for Tylenol-Codeine #3. The pharmacist will have to give it to you from behind the counter. Use it only when you absolutely need it. I don't need to tell you it's habit-forming."

Danny had thanked him and was on his way out the door when his mobile phone rang. It was Cillian Riley. "Bad situation," Riley told him. "We've got a house explosion and fire. No word on casualties, but the fire department's currently on site." Riley's warm Newcastle accent did nothing to mask the concern he obviously felt.

"Witnesses?"

"None that we know of, although a fair-sized crowd has gathered. The usual gawkers and rubberneckers."

"Thanks, Cillian." Danny had reached the parking lot by now. "I'll be there as soon as I can." He unlocked his car and slid in, grimacing as his painful knees protested. The car was lower than the battered antique Land Rover he'd been driving the previous year, and getting in and out of the driver's seat was proving to be quite the feat. He remembered the old Rover with a wistful fondness, wishing he'd never sent it to the scrapyard. But it represented a dark and difficult time in his life, when his entanglement with the criminal Martin Belshawe had almost ended his career. All that was over now. The new Royal Newfoundland Constabulary head, Adrian Molloy, had reinstated him, and Danny and Tadhg had married in Inverness on Danny's birthday in April. Things were finally looking up.

Inspector Cillian Riley, still limping from a badly broken leg the previous winter, was waiting when Danny arrived at the scene of the explosion. In deference to the warm weather, he was wearing a short-sleeved shirt and pressed chinos, but the beard he'd taken such pains to grow was nowhere in sight. Riley looked odd without it.

"Young couple living there with their lad," he told Danny. "Nobody at home as far as the fire department can tell." He glanced back at the smouldering heap of embers that had once been a house. "Bloody good thing too. Gerard Caron, his wife, Amalie, and the boy's name is Joseph."

"Caron," Danny remarked. "French?"

"Just moved here from Quebec a few months ago," Riley replied. "The husband got a job with Newfoundland Power as an electric linesman." According to the neighbours, the marriage was not a happy one, and the couple could often be heard fighting, shouting at each other in French, sometimes late into the night. The boy, six-year-old Joseph, went to the local elementary school just up the shore in Winterton and was sometimes seen playing with some of the boys from the Cove.

"So where is the boy? Wouldn't he be at school today?" Danny asked.

"I called the school," Riley replied. "According to the secretary his mother signed him off sick today. Some of the neighbours said they saw him riding his bike in front of the house around nine this morning. He hasn't been seen since."

"All right." Danny glanced around at the assembled crowd, noting the presence of a few familiar faces, the usual curtain twitchers and rubberneckers he'd expect to see. "What about the mother—Amalie, is it?—what's she do? Is she at work?"

"I've heard conflicting reports. One woman said she works in a shop in Carbonear, while someone else said she doesn't work outside the home." There was a sudden shout from the assembled spectators as the outside wall of the house collapsed in a shower of sparks. Two firefighters immediately ran forward with a hose to douse any remaining hot spots while Constables Sarah Avery and Dougie Hughes struggled to hold back the crowd.

"Hughes, Avery!" Riley shouted to them. "Get those people out of there." He turned back to Danny as the constables began working to disperse the crowd. "Apparently the Carons don't really mix with anyone else in the Cove. Keep themselves to themselves."

"Language barrier?"

"No. From what I've been told, they speak better English than you and me." This was the case with most Quebecois Danny knew: they spoke both official languages fluently and were able to switch between them with enviable ease. He'd taken French classes all throughout school, but his own mastery of the language was barely adequate.

"Do you want to go back to the station and start a database search?" Danny asked. "Get off that bad leg. Put out an Amber Alert for the missing boy."

Riley nodded gratefully. "Thanks. It's been aching like a bastard all day." He'd shattered the leg in several places the previous winter, the result of a high-speed chase on slippery roads and an untimely encounter with a moose. Surgery had pieced the bone back together, but he would never be the same.

"If the Carons are originally from Quebec, we should probably contact the Sûreté. Oh, by the way, how's the application for law school going?"

The Englishman smiled. "Suspended," he said, "indefinitely." He pocketed his notebook and Danny knew not to pry any farther. Perhaps Riley's law school aspirations had succumbed to the demands of his injured leg. Or maybe his relationship with Sergeant Kevin Carbage had matured to the point of mutual contentment and he was reluctant to leave.

"Sorry to hear it," Danny replied automatically. He wasn't, not really. Riley was an extremely capable cop, and over the two years he'd been posted to Kildevil Cove, he'd become a close friend. Danny would have been sorry to see him go. The Cove's small RNC detachment didn't really need two inspectors—Chief Inspector Adrian Molloy had promoted Riley the previous year—but as long as he was useful, Danny saw no reason for him to leave.

Riley shrugged. "I think I'm better off as a copper," he said. "See you back at the station."

Danny moved closer to the site once Riley left and the constables had dispersed the crowd of onlookers. He wondered if it was merely luck that nobody had been at home when the explosion occurred, or if the arsonist had planned it that way. It wasn't unknown for someone to destroy their own property in the hope of recouping greater value from the insurance money. In a larger city, he could see how this would be the case, but Kildevil Cove was tiny, and most houses were not worth much more than the cost of the land.

"Found something you might be interested in." Danny looked up as Alan English, the volunteer fire chief, approached. He was holding something in his hand, a length of scorched wire with a metal apparatus attached to one end. "This wasn't any ordinary fire. The house was rigged to explode."

"Really?"

"This was attached to the doorbell. Whoever rigged it knew what they were doing. It might look simple, but something like this requires advanced electrical knowledge." He pointed to the metal apparatus. "Ringing the doorbell would trigger it, but this sort of thing could be activated remotely, using a mobile phone."

"So this fire wasn't an accident," Danny said. "This was deliberate."

"Yep."

The idea of someone rigging a house to explode and then simply walking away appalled him. "Nasty." He fished around in his pocket until he found a plastic evidence bag. He dropped the device in and sealed it. "Thanks, Alan. Will you let me know if you find anything else?"

"Absolutely. We won't be able to have a good look until we're sure the hot spots are all out. We'll keep the site secured until you can get the forensics people in."

Danny thanked him again, then got back into his car for the short drive to the police station. The Kildevil Cove RNC detachment was located in a former Loyal Orange Lodge building across from the Pentecostal Church. It housed the Criminal Investigation Division, of which Danny was the head. The CID was responsible for investigating any serious crimes that might occur. There was a time when crime in Kildevil Cove was confined to fisheries violations: taking too many cod during the recreational fishery or selling undersized lobster. With the arrival of hard drugs like methamphetamine and fentanyl, however, crimes like murder and human trafficking were on the increase, and the influence of organised crime syndicates reached into even the smallest coastal fishing villages around the island.

He had just pulled onto the road when a small red car screeched to a halt in front of him, missing his vehicle's front fender by mere centimetres. The driver's side door flew open, and a man in his mid-thirties tumbled out, nearly falling in his haste. He stared, wide-eyed, at the remains of the fire, then started forward, a look of horror etched on his features.

At the cordon he was stopped by Dougie Hughes. "Sir, you have to stay back."

"*Où sont-ils?*" he shouted. "Where are they?"

J.S. COOK grew up surrounded by the wild North Atlantic Ocean, in a small fishing village on the coast of Newfoundland. An avid lover of both the sea and the outdoors, she was powerfully seduced by the lure of this rugged, untamed landscape. This love of her island heritage and its deeply Irish culture led her to create The Kildevil Cove Murder Mysteries series, police procedurals that feature career detective Deiniol Quirke and his partner, millionaire property developer Tadhg Heaney.

Her interest in police procedurals was recently reignited by an opportunity to work with a police profiler from the Los Angeles County Sheriff's Department, editing two forensic field manuals to be used by LA County law enforcement and as part of the curriculum at the California Institute of Criminal Investigation. She maintains an avid interest in forensics and often designs and conducts her own forensic experiments, including a body farm in her backyard.

Reviewers have called her past work "…strong, solid detective fiction… with a depth and complexity of plot and characters…."

When she isn't writing, J.S. Cook teaches communications and creative writing at the College of the North Atlantic.

ON AN ISLAND, NOTHING STAYS SECRET FOREVER....

DARK WATER

A KILDEVIL COVE MURDER MYSTERY

J.S. COOK

A Kildevil Cove Murder Mystery

They say trouble comes in threes. Detective Danny Quirke is already mourning his wife and mired in an internal investigation that will likely spell the end of his career. Now he must return to the Newfoundland fishing village of his youth to bury his abusive grandfather. At least his three are up. Right?

Then the bones of local boy Llewellyn Single, drowned thirty years before, wash up on the beach, and secrets Danny thought were buried forever rise violently to the surface. Only two people know what really happened: Danny Quirke and his former best friend, millionaire Tadhg Heaney.

Danny and Tadhg have been bitter enemies for years. But when Danny is accused of Llewellyn's murder, he needs Tadhg's help exposing the truth—before those who believe he is responsible get their revenge.

After all, on an island, nothing stays secret forever….

www.dsppublications.com

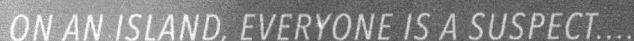

ON AN ISLAND, EVERYONE IS A SUSPECT....

DARK MIRE

A KILDEVIL COVE MURDER MYSTERY

J.S. COOK

A Kildevil Cover Murder Mystery

You never know what trouble will rise from the bog.

When the body of an unidentified woman is found in a Newfoundland bog, Inspector Danny Quirke must scramble his team of investigators to find her killer. But what initially seems like a straightforward case soon becomes mired in a tangled web of lies and deliberate obfuscation.

With the strange mutilation of the body—one eye gouged out completely—evidence seems to lead to a fringe religious group with bizarre beliefs. But while the pathologist indicates mushroom poisoning as the cause of death, Danny thinks circumstances point to something more sinister—especially when he begins to receive anonymous messages with links to horrific pictures of damaged human eyes.

Three more bodies join the first, with seemingly nothing to link them but a little girl in a yellow party dress who flits in and out of the mystery like a creature from the old legends. Then an old friend from his childhood reappears, and Danny is forced to confront uncomfortable truths about his own nearest and dearest.

On an island, everyone is a suspect…

www.dsppublications.com

ON AN ISLAND, THERE'S NO ESCAPING THE TIDE....

DARK TIDE

A KILDEVIL COVE MURDER MYSTERY

J.S. COOK

A Kildevil Cove Murder Mystery

They say it never rains but it pours. Royal Newfoundland Constabulary Inspector Danny Quirke would have to agree.

First someone murders a vulnerable Kildevil Cove man and dumps him in an abandoned well. Then the body of a sex-trafficking victim washes up on a nearby beach. Danny has to get to the bottom of both deaths, but with few leads and little support from his superiors, he's spinning his wheels in a mud pit of a case. Vital resources go missing, witnesses disappear, and suspects proliferate.

Each step toward the truth brings him two steps back. Help comes in the form of Scottish investigator Martin Belshawe, but he may not be who he says he is, and someone in the highest echelons of the Newfoundland Constabulary is lying to Danny. Even Danny's lover, Tadhg Heaney, whom he looks to for emotional support, seems to know more than he should about the shady characters who keep popping up in the investigation.

With time running out, Danny must decide who, if anyone, he can trust—before the sex traffickers claim their next victims. But on an island, there's no escaping the tide.

www.dsppublications.com

For more
great fiction
from

DSP PUBLICATIONS

visit us online.

WWW.DSPPUBLICATIONS.COM

www.ingramcontent.com/pod-product-compliance
Lightning Source LLC
Chambersburg PA
CBHW051148030726
47504CB00004B/1092